PRAISE FOR MARIA V. SNYDER

"Oh. My. Stars! I just raced through Maria V. Snyder's *Navigating the Stars* and *Chasing the Shadows*, and I'm blown away! ...The plot is fantastic, the pacing spectacular, the intricacies, the snark, the banter...oh my! Go, go, go. You'll love this!" Amanda Bouchet, *USA Today* bestselling author on The Sentinels of the Galaxy series.

"Smart, witty, and full of heart, *Navigating the Stars* had me hooked from the very first page!" Lynette Noni, bestselling author of *Whisper*

"This is one of those rare books that will keep readers dreaming long after they've read it." Publishers Weekly, starred review on *Poison Study*

"Snyder deftly weaves information about glassblowing into her tale of magic and murder." Library Journal on *Storm Glass*

"Filled with Snyder's trademark sarcastic humor, fast-paced action, and creepy villainy, *Touch of Power* is a spellbinding fantasy adventure." USA TODAY

"A wonderful, thoughtful book full of vivid characters and a place—Inside—that is by turns alien, and breathtakingly familiar." Rachael Caine, etc.... on *Inside Out*

Also by Maria V. Snyder

Discover more titles by Maria V. Snyder at
mariavsnyder.com

DEFENDING

THE

GALAXY

MARIA V. SNYDER

Defending the Galaxy / Maria V. Snyder—1st edition
Cover design by Josh Durham of Design by Committee
Interior art by Hillary Bardin
Published by Maria V. Snyder

Print ISBN 978-1-946381-00-2
Digital ISBN 978-1-946381-03-3

To all my Soulfinders! You bring joy into my life.

2522:247

The term "mind-blown" is one of those expressions that doesn't really mean anything. People say it all the time, but it's just an exaggeration. No heads actually explode because a person is confronted with a new concept or an unbelievable revelation. Brain matter and blood doesn't splash on the walls.

Yet, as I sit cross-legged on my bed and scrunch my blanket in tight fists, I'm scrambling for coherent thought. And I fear, if I let go, I will blow apart and be scattered throughout the Milky Way Galaxy.

What revelation, you ask, has reduced me to this state? The Q-net, also known as the Quantum Net, a technological advancement that has allowed us to travel well beyond our solar system, has told me that it is an alien consciousness.

The Q-net said it wasn't invented but *discovered* by our Earth scientists in 2066, and used to perform the ultra-complex calculations needed to build special engines that can cross vast interstellar distances.

And. Yes, there's an *and*. Bear with me please. With these five simple words, the Q-net has blown my mind: *I AM THE MILKY WAY*.

It claims to encompass the Milky Way Galaxy, meaning all the matter, dark matter, and energy contained within its boundaries has a consciousness, or soul if you prefer.

This…being…has been tasked with protecting us humans from the Hostile Life Forms (HoLFs), which look like shadow-blobs, that we inadvertently allowed back into our dimension. 'We' being Jarren, the murdering looter, and his nefarious collaborators. To think, Jarren and I were once good friends. He and his looters have been destroying a number of the Terracotta Warriors that were discovered on exoplanets throughout the Galaxy—long story. However, the short version is, that by breaking the Warriors, Jarren inadvertently made the Q-net's task to keep us safe almost impossible.

Since the Q-net can no longer protect us without our help, it has chosen me—yes, me, Ara Yinhexi Lawrence, Junior Security Officer on Planet Yulin, age seventeen Actual years old—to be its…voice, I guess.

Why me, you ask? Good question. It seems my activities and actions in the Q-net have drawn its attention. I'm good at worming through the gaps in the security programs, getting into places I shouldn't. Of course now I wonder about all the data clusters and files that humans have placed in the Q-net. The Department of Explored Space (DES) has pretty much moved in and set up house in the Q-net. And the star roads, the deepest, most complex layer of the Q-net, are what we use to navigate through the Galaxy and crinkle space.

So now you know why I'm grappling with all this brand-new information, and bandying about the term "mind-blown", because I think I've a pretty good example going on inside my head. Right now.

The standard response is "I'm going insane" and the conversation with the Q-net was all a delusion or figment of my imagination. That's a fair point and I can't prove otherwise. Although, my imagination just isn't on *that* level of creative. And, from the various things the Q-net has done, it being sentient explains a lot. Like removing my image from the security feed so Jarren wouldn't learn I survived his attempt to murder me. Also I've encountered other questionable strangeness—shadow-blobs and Warrior hearts, and they turned out to be very real. So that's a hard no on being crazy.

What's next? There's the possibility I'm mistaken. That I'm anthropomorphizing the Q-net, like I did with the Terracotta Warriors when I was younger. Perhaps I've reached an overly helpful Q-cluster that provides data quicker than any others. And the fact I can entangle with the Q-net without entanglers, or without being close to a terminal, is just a glitch and not a gift from a sentient Q-net. I'm more than willing to go with that explanation.

A light tap on my door sends me three meters into the air. A startled cry escapes my lips, which the tapper translates to "come in."

Niall pokes his head inside. "Dinner's ready."

I stare at him as if I've never seen him before. His black hair is a little longer than regulation—but not enough to warrant a comment from his father who is the Chief of Security—and is still wet from his shower and slicked back. Piercing blue-green eyes and sharp features, he's handsome and all mine. Normally pale due to eighteen years spent living on space ships, he's currently almost ghost white. It's because he's recovering from almost dying from blood loss and brain trauma, which the Q-net claims to have healed because *I* asked.

"Mouse?" Alarmed, he steps into my room, grabbing for a weapon that's not there because he's wearing jeans and a T-shirt and not his security uniform. "What's wrong?" Niall scans the small space as if searching for intruders. "HoLFs?"

Wow. I must look terrified. Shaking my head, I say, "No. I…"

"You?"

"I was in the Q-net." Which is true.

"Something scare you?" He sits on the bed next to me.

I breathe in the scent of his shampoo—sage grass—and scooch closer. He wraps an arm around my shoulder and pulls me to him.

Melting against him, I relax for the first time since the Q-net's big confession. "I was trying to find information on the sensors and brain damage to see if there's a reason why you can't entangle with the Q-net." Again, all true.

"From your expression, I gather the prognosis is dire," he teases. "Please, don't worry about it. If I can never entangle with the Q-net again, I'll be perfectly happy. I'd rather have a heartbeat."

I can't argue with that.

He squeezes me a little tighter. "Are you sure it doesn't have to do with your encounter with Jarren?"

Unable to stop, I shudder. The murdering looter and his minions attacked our base after tying to destroy it with a missile. A *missile!* Jarren had then taken me hostage and attached an explosive device to my back. An *explosive* device! The four gouges in my skin, now healing ignite with pain at the memory. He told everyone he'd disarm the device once he was safely away, but I knew better. So to keep him from setting it off and killing me and everyone near me I ended up clinging for my life to the landing gear of his shuttle.

Niall loops his other arm around me, hugging me. "You're safe now."

Best boyfriend ever. "I know." My team rescued me and Jarren is currently locked in detention. "It's just...a lot has happened."

"No kidding."

And I can't deal with the Q-net right now, so I push it to the back of my mind to be ruminated on later. Much later. Yes, it's denial. No surprise, I'm the queen of denial after all. Besides, I need more information about the Q-net before I can make an intelligent decision.

"I'm sure my dad will let you have a few days off." Niall puts a finger on my lips, stopping my protest. "It so happens, that I also have a few days off to heal. And I'm thinking the best way to recover is to take you on another proper date. What do you think?"

"I think it's an excellent idea." I smile up at him and am rewarded with a sweet kiss.

"Dinner's getting cold," Radcliff says from the threshold.

We jump apart as Tace Radcliff, Niall's dad, gives us a pointed look. Not only is he our boss, but also our self-appointed chaperone. Since I'm not eighteen A-years old, I've been living in his unit. I guess I could return to my parents' housing unit since everyone in the base knows I'm alive, but it would be too far from my job and Niall. Did I tell you I'm going to be eighteen in sixty-seven days?

I. Can't. Wait.

Niall and I follow Radcliff to the kitchen. My parents are already there. One of the best things about this living situation are the family meals. Before we were all too busy—my parents, the archeological Experts on the Terracotta Warriors, are in charge of the research base on Planet Yulin. But with the looter base located on the other side of the planet, they're more focused on survival than on research at the moment. We all are.

The lovely scent of roasted beef causes my stomach to roar. It's Niall's favorite and I wonder if Radcliff cooked it on purpose. The man may be a gigantic pain in the butt, but he sure can cook, making amazing dishes with the limited and artificial quality of the ingredients. It's not like we can get fresh supplies. We are fifty thousand light years from Earth and a supply ship is not due for another three A-years.

My parents, Ming and Spencer Daniels—yes, they have a different last name than me due to the fact I had to change mine to play dead, and well...Ara suits me better—eye me with their parental X-ray vision turned to maximum. No doubt assessing how freaked I am about Jarren. I tuck into my meal and ignore them. See? My appetite hasn't been affected.

"What's the status with the scientists?" Radcliff asks my dad.

"I'm working on a schedule to get all the base's personnel trained with pulse guns and to learn the basics of guard duty," Dad says, between mouthfuls.

"We've run out of beds for the prisoners," Mom says. "If our base had been fully staffed, we wouldn't have any. Of course they're not happy with sleeping on the hard ground." Mom shrugs. "I find that I don't care."

Not when they invaded our base with the intention to kill us all. "How many prisoners do we have now?" I ask.

"Sixty-seven plus Jarren," Radcliff says.

"And they're all in Pit 1?"

"They have access to all four pits. Except no one wants to go into Pit 2." Radcliff's smile is cold.

No surprise. The shadow-blob rift is in Pit 2, and while we have defenses to keep the HoLFs out, that's ground zero if they return. Unlikely, but they could develop some type of armor to block the radio waves we used to destroy them. They're intelligent. Another shudder rips through me.

"And we're going to put them to work," Mom says, stabbing a fork in the air. "We're requiring them to help reconstruct the Warriors *they* destroyed, starting with Pit 1."

Nice. "Jarren, too?"

"No. Jarren will remain in detention until he answers our questions," Radcliff says. Then he turns to me.

Oh no.

"Too soon," Mom says, giving Radcliff one of her warning glares.

However, Radcliff is immune. In fact, I don't think the man is afraid of anything. But then I remember Radcliff when Niall was unconscious and his prognosis wasn't good. I guess no one is *that* fearless.

"We don't have the luxury of time," Radcliff says to my mom. "They're on the other side of our planet and can attack us at any time. They have shuttles and soldiers and missiles. There's no need for them to even leave their base to kill us."

"And we have sixty-eight of their people," Mom counters.

"It didn't seem to matter when they sent the missile before. When we had sixteen of them."

Good point. But my mother doesn't give up and I've had seventeen years of reading her body language to know she isn't about to back down.

"What do you need me to do?" I ask Radcliff, stopping the battle to come.

Radcliff faces me. "Our escape hatch through the Q-net blockade around our planet has been compromised. We need to reestablish another secure connection with DES. Even though we have Jarren, the blockade is still up."

I remember that there is a redirect worm on our tunnel, sending all our messages straight to the looters instead of DES. Before that, we were able to contact DES long enough for them to help us design the null wave emitters, which proved invaluable against the HoLFs. "I can work on it right after dinner."

"Dorey is off duty," Radcliff says. "He tried to breach it all day."

Without me? His partner? I'd be hurt, but I'm sure my mother insisted Radcliff give me some time off. "Is Officer Morgan on duty?"

"Yes."

"Then she can help me and talk with DES."

Radcliff raises an eyebrow. "You're *that* confident? Jarren wasn't working alone when he put up the blockades. You said so yourself, telling me there had to be other wormers involved."

"And there are, but they might be struggling to regroup now that Jarren's gone." And before he or my mother can counter that, I add, "It won't hurt to try."

"Unless they decide that you're too big a threat," Niall says. "And send a missile to stop you."

Argh. He's right. "Then I won't let them know what I'm doing."

"Too risky," Radcliff says. "You can go in with Officer Dorey tomorrow morning."

I consider arguing. There is no reason to wait; we've already wasted so much time. Then I realize everyone's staring at me. "All right, I won't worm into the Q-net and try to contact DES tonight. I'll wait for Beau."

A general sense of relief rings the table. Niall, though, gives me a contemplative half-squint. The conversation returns to the many items on the To-Do list for the base. Eventually, my parents leave and Radcliff retreats to his room, giving Niall and I some semblance of privacy.

We sit on the couch in the living room. Niall automatically tucks me under his arm. I pull my legs up and snuggle against him.

"You agreed too easily. What are you up to?" he asks.

"Nothing. You made a good point."

"Uh huh. I'm the sensible one, remember?"

"Doesn't mean I can't be sensible, too."

"Oh, I'm sure you can. You just *choose* not to."

"Ha ha." I need to change the subject. "Are you upset because I'm not getting time off for our proper date?"

"It would be rather selfish of me if that was the case. We're still not safe." He leans forward. "However, if you don't overexert yourself tomorrow and have a horrible headache, then after dinner, we'll have a modified proper date."

"Like an improper date?" I grin lustily.

He groans. "You're killing me, Mouse."

And then I remember that he'd flatlined when in surgery and that sours my teasing mood. I think about what he said about overexerting myself. "That was pretty smart."

"What?" He gives me an innocent look that I don't fall for.

"How you gave me an incentive not to use all my energy finding a way to contact DES. Not that I'm complaining."

"I think people should be rewarded for reaching their goals. You did promise not to exhaust yourself again."

"I did."

He peers at me. "Now I'm worried that you found some clever loophole."

"Not a loophole, but…"

"But?"

"Sometimes I go flying with the Q-net when I'm asleep. Sometimes, I can do things while flying, like when I contacted Chief Vasily and fixed the worms in the satellite. What if I create another escape hatch while I'm sleeping?"

Niall is quiet for a few heartbeats. "That's why you promised not to worm. I thought you were hedging."

I huff. "Hedging. I guess that's accurate. My interactions with the Q-net are not... Actually I've no idea what they are since no one's ever had this..." I press my hands to my head, tangling my fingers in my hair. "Connection. It's scary."

Niall grasps my wrists, and gently pulls my hands down, holding them. "I can only imagine what you're going through, but your connection has given us a chance to survive this. Without you, we'd have been killed way back when the shadow-blobs first appeared." He squeezes my hands. "Maybe it's the opposite of what happened to me."

"What do you mean?"

"My sensors were fried when I lost all that blood and now I can't connect to the Q-net. Perhaps yours were amplified by your injuries." He frowns—no doubt remembering all the times I've been injured or knocked unconscious. "It fits the timing of when your abilities improved."

That made more sense than a sentient Q-net. It would also mean I imagined the conversation with the Q-net, but I'm willing to accept that. I experienced a traumatic abduction that I'm still recovering from. Yet... "What if it's not a result of my injuries, but the Q-net did something *to* me?" Once I say it aloud, it sounds ridiculous.

Niall tries to hide his smile. "I know you have a unique way of looking at things, but that's just ridiculous."

"You're right." I relax against him.

"Besides, no one can say you didn't keep your promise if you were asleep when it happened."

And I keep my promises. Unless it's to a murdering looter, then there's no guilt when I break it. Not wanting to think of

Jarren, I say, "True. In fact, I promise to kiss you until you're breathless."

A spark of delight flares in Niall's eyes. "Now that's a great promise."

Once I claim his lips, he doesn't say anything more as I'm true to my word.

After Niall returns to his unit, I lie in bed, thinking about our conversation. He's right that all my new abilities arrived after a trauma. Yes, I'm better at worming, but I'm also able to use the Q-net without tangs or a terminal. My link to it is never severed. It's always in the back of my mind. I just need to turn my full attention to the Q-net and I'm there. It gives me an advantage, which we desperately need.

The other unique thing that happens to me, and no one else, is that I can fly with the Q-net. So far, it's only happened while I was asleep or unconscious. If Niall's right, and my improved skills with the Q-net are due to my injuries, then I shouldn't be able to fly with it while awake. Right? That would be another improvement and I haven't been injured. Well, not lately.

In order to test the theory, I decide to try to fly while awake. I close my eyes and imagine lifting my arms up. *Let's fly.*

A strange floating sensation rushes through me. It's as if my consciousness has been yanked from my physical body and I'm suddenly untethered. Then the entire Milky Way Galaxy spreads out before me. My fear soon turns to joy as I fly, looping and twirling and spinning and dipping and soaring. There are no barriers. No limitations. No need for permission. No need to worm. There's nothing to prevent me from going anywhere. It's a feeling like no other.

A feeling I can access at any time. Does that mean Niall's theory of my injuries enhancing my worming abilities is wrong? Or perhaps it means my enhanced abilities include unlimited flying.

IT MEANS YOU ASKED. I COMPLIED.

And Niall's theory of my injuries causing my amplified abilities?

I CHOSE YOU. NO OTHER REASON.

And you're the Milky Way Galaxy and also the Q-net?

I AM.

And you have the ability to connect with a human being?

OBVIOUSLY.

Along with the ability to be sarcastic. Lovely. So now I'm convinced, but will anyone else believe it? *Is this a secret?*

YOUR CHOICE.

Why is it my choice? Do you want others to know or not?

YOU WILL KNOW IF IT BECOMES NECESSARY.

Great, just great. I consider. No one is going to believe me. Well, maybe eventually. They've believed me before. But would they accept yet another wild theory from me? Or have I reached my limit? At this point I've no idea. So I decide to trust the Q-net and wait until it becomes necessary. After all, nothing's going to change. Right?

2522:248

I report to Beau's office at oh-eight-hundred. My partner is blowing on a steaming mug of coffee. His short brown hair is freshly spiked. The blond dyed tips give him the appearance of a hedgehog, which is his nickname. His sharp gaze snags on the extra-large cup of coffee in my hands.

"Rough night?" he asks in a neutral tone.

Beau was part of the team that rescued me from Jarren. No doubt he's worried that my recent adventures are causing me to lose sleep. I'm not only the youngest officer in security, but I have the least experience.

"Yeah," I say. It's the truth. Nightmares have been haunting my sleep.

Beau grunts. "I told Radcliff it was too soon."

"So did my mother." We share a smile. "This is too important." I sit next to him.

His office has dual Q-net terminals, which allows us to entangle with the Q-net together and work in tandem. With my new...skills, I don't need to be here, but everyone's really uneasy about them, especially Beau. I can't imagine what he'll do if I confide in him about the Q-net. Actually, I can. He'll be majorly freaked out and never want to worm with me again.

"What happened to our escape tunnel to DES?" I ask. We managed to get through the looters' blockade and create a hidden link to DES before Jarren discovered it and installed a redirect worm, so our messages went to him instead of DES.

"They collapsed it. And I can't find another way out." A scowl creases his handsome face and there's no sign of the cocky confidence he usually wears.

"Let's start there."

He sets his coffee down and inserts his entanglers in his ears. The small round devices link with the sensors implanted into his brain and allow him to access the Q-net through the terminal. There are screens as well, but they're not really needed, unless another person who is not in the Q-net is watching. The connection in our brains allows us to see, unless we're worming, and then it's more like feeling your way through the layers of the Q-net, finding gaps. The best wormers can wriggle through without creating ripples that will alert the security programs to an unauthorized person.

In this case, Jarren and his evil minions created a blockade around Yulin, stopping all messages from reaching DES. They set up a vast web of alarms so one wrong tug and they'll know we're searching for a way out. Not that they don't expect us to try. The best-case scenario is that we get through to DES without them knowing. Hard to do since they also have their claws in DES, which isn't as secure as it should be considering they guard the gateway to the star roads.

"Ready?" I ask.

"Tangs?" Beau glances at me expectantly.

I shake my head. "They make me too heavy." Sounds strange, but it's true. I no longer need tangs at all, but when I use them, I'm grounded. Not that I'm going to fly when I'm with Beau, but without my tangs, I'll be able to slip through the gaps easier.

He presses his lips together, but turns his attention to entangling. I close my eyes. We enter the Q-net. I follow Beau as we worm to the ruined escape tunnel. It's been flattened as if stitched closed by security programs. Jarren's fingerprints are all over it. He must have cut us off from DES before invading the base.

I wonder who is monitoring the security now. We know he wasn't working alone. If we trip an alarm, who would respond?

What's wrong? Beau asks.

Nothing, just thinking.

Should I be worried?

Probably.

Not funny.

Did you set off any alarms when you were trying to find a way to reach DES after Jarren's attack? I ask.

No. Why?

Should we make our attempts to breach the blockade obvious and see who comes to investigate?

Would we be able to tell who it is from this side?

Maybe. If I were flying, I'd have a better chance of learning their identity, but I hesitate to suggest it.

We should discuss it with Radcliff first, Beau says.

All right. I turn my attention to the problem at hand. Last time I used Jarren's hole to escape the blockade. Theoretically it could still be there. Then I remember that Jarren was on Yulin. His base is located on the opposite side of the planet. He needed to be able to send messages to his associates throughout the Galaxy. There has to be an access point through the blockade for his people still left on the base to use.

Too risky, Beau says after I explain. *We'll be too close. And remember we tried to find information about that base before? We couldn't get near them.*

You're right. But that was before the Q-net revealed itself to me. Yes, I'm finding lots of things I can now do, but can't because I'm a chicken. I suspect I will have to fess up sooner rather than later.

That was too easy. What are you thinking now? Beau asks.

Instead of confiding in Beau, I refocus on our current challenge. The logical thing to do would be to find a different location for our new escape tunnel. But what if we used the same one? Or, even better, what if we create three more of them. They wouldn't expect either move. I tell Beau my ideas.

Four tunnels? You can do that? His wary tone is mixed with disbelief.

We won't know until we try. I concentrate on the intricate weave of the complex program that created the blockade. There's another almost-invisible thread through it as well. I wish I could highlight each one with a color to really see—

What the hell! Beau cries out in surprise as a green line snakes through the program followed by a thin purple one.

And I have to admit to being *very* concerned about the Q-net reading my mind. Yes, I know it's *in* my mind all the time, but I wasn't thinking *at* it at that time. *Green is for the main program and purple is the hidden one,* I explain. *There has to be a way through.*

Where? It's a tangled mess.

It's just like worming, Beau. Look for the gaps. Another idea occurs to me. *Our tunnel doesn't have to be straight. It could be serpentine and still work.*

We labor to insert a long, thin, and flexible tube that's going to be our tunnel between the green and purple lines. I make it orange so it stands out. It's a hard and grueling and delicate task and I'm reminded of people who defuse bombs—one wrong move and boom!

Hours later, we're rewarded with an escape tunnel through the barricade.

I didn't think that was going to work, Beau says. *Then he groans. And you want to make three more of them?*

Yes I do.

And just like that three more orange tubes snake through the barricade in different places. There's a very long moment of silence. And it becomes very clear to me that it's necessary to divulge my latest discovery.

Beau asks, *Ara, is there something you want to tell me?*

You're not going to believe me.

Let's just say after what I've just seen, I'm more inclined to believe you.

Not now, I say. *We need to create a secure connection to DES first. One that the looters can't access.*

He huffs. *You mean you need to.*

Not this again. It's times like these where I wish the alien Q-net picked Beau to be its voice. I'd like to think I'd be happy for him and not bristling with jealousy. I stifle a sigh. Even with my limited interactions with the alien Q-net—I need a shorter and better name for it—I suspect that it won't do anything that I can't do myself. Meaning that I have to prove I can break through the barricade once and Q will do the rest if I ask.

CORRECT.

I startle with a small cry. *Stop doing that!*

Stop doing what? Did we trigger an alarm?

Beau can't hear Q. I'm not sure if that's a good or bad thing.

No. Once we've established a secure connection, the Q-net can repeat the action if we need to create a second one.

It can? In that case, we had a secure connection to DES before the last attack.

We did! See? I need you. I direct a query toward Q. *Can you reach DES security, please? The officer who liaised with Radcliff before?* I envision a link to DES that is unbreakable...or rather, unwormable. Our orange escape tunnel pulses. And a dozen messages pour out. All from DES, with increasing priority levels. Guess they've been trying to contact us since Jarren cut us off nine days ago.

Stars, Beau says.

Do you want to send her a reply or should we wait for Radcliff? I ask, hoping to get him back on track.

We need to talk to Radcliff. Now. Beau disentangles.

Since I'm not flying, I need to extricate my mind from the Q-net. By the time I'm done, Beau is already out the door.

Radcliff is working at his desk. He glances up as soon as Beau bursts into his office. "What's wrong?"

Beau jabs a finger at the chair in front of Radcliff's desk. "Sit," he orders me.

The dangerous expression on his face stops my sarcastic comment. Instead, I perch on the edge and Radcliff stiffens. No doubt bracing for the bad news. This isn't going to be pretty.

"What's going on, Dorey?" he asks.

"That's what I'd like to know." He glares at me. "Care to explain what the hell you were doing in the Q-net?"

I've never seen him so angry. If I say no, would he grab my shoulders and try to shake it from me? Both men are staring at me. How do I explain? "Working with you, creating escape tunnels and a secure connection to DES."

"Not that. When you requested the Q-net to make more tunnels and it obeyed." Beau's lips move, but his teeth remained clamped.

"At ease, Dorey," Radcliff orders, picking up on the man's fury. "Tell me what's going on."

Beau rounds on him. "She's interacting with the Q-net as if it's…" His hands go up as if he's trying to pull the right word from the air.

"Sentient," I say. Might as well.

Both men turn their attention on me.

"It is. Sentient. The Q-net is an alien consciousness that encompasses the Milky Way Galaxy. Humans did not invent it, they discovered it. The Q-net has allowed us to use it in order to advance our tech enough to travel throughout the Galaxy. It's directive is to protect us from the HoLFs, but since Jarren allowed the HoLFs to enter our dimension, the Q-net now needs

Radcliff looks at his screen. But he's clearly distracted.

I connect with Q. *Can you prove your existence to Officer Radcliff?* I ask.

NO.

Not the answer I expected. *Why not?*

I CHOSE YOU.

I understand that, but you chose a person who has no authority to do anything! I need him to believe me.

I CHOSE YOU.

In other words, make them believe you. Wonderful. Yes, I'm being sarcastic.

"What are you doing?" Radcliff asks me.

"Trying to get Q to back me up. But it'd rather not."

Beau and Radcliff exchange one of those how-do-we-humor-the-crazy-person glances.

"Guess you need to either trust me or not." I stand. "Just remember what happened in the Q-net, Beau. You know I never could have done all that so fast. And for your information, Officer Radcliff, Q healed Niall. Without its help, he'd still be in a coma. That's why his sensors are fried." With that, I head for the door that connects Radcliff and Beau's offices. There's really nothing else left for me to say about Q.

"Where are you going?" Radcliff asks.

"Back to work."

"Doing what?"

I turn. "Now that we can communicate with DES again, we need to ensure that no one can worm into our messages. Otherwise our escape tunnels will be shut down." Another idea occurs to me. "And we should dig out the looters from DES's organization. Jarren said they're in deep."

"We? As in you and the Q-net?"

"No. *We* as in Beau and me. Unless you'd rather stand there all day?" I ask Beau. When he hesitates, I shake my head and leave.

I sit at Beau's dual Q-net terminals. The temptation to fly with the Q-net is strong, but, while that way is easier, I don't get the same…touch. Instead, I return to the escape tunnel and consider how to protect our outgoing messages. It's tricky, but I weave a web inside the tunnel. As messages travel through, they will be coated with strands of security programming so they will have an extra layer of protection. And now Q can coat all the rest. *Right, Q?*

CORRECT.

May I call you Q? Do you have another name?

CALL ME Q.

Beau arrives in the Q-net. I brace for him to yell at me, or humor me, which would be worse.

There you are, he says in an even tone.

I decide to pretend I haven't just flipped his world upside down. Without missing a beat, I ask, *What's next?*

I thought we should clean up the worm holes in DES. You said that Jarren's organization was in deep.

That might tip them off. How about we take a look and see how bad it is and where they are concentrated?

All right.

We escape through one of the tunnels and worm to DES's central cluster. DES is spread throughout the Q-net and I imagine their connections are like roots, spreading out and digging deep. They guard and control the star roads, which are vital for us to travel the vast distances across the Galaxy. Once I thought Jarren and his thugs had gained access to the star roads, and were using them to travel to the different Warrior planets, but now I have a different theory. If they're using the Warrior portals in the pits, there's no need for them to worm into the star roads. I believe that each Warrior pit guards a portal to another Warrior planet and this is why, when Jarren and his looters attacked us, they only stole certain key Warriors.

A chill rips through my body. Being able to travel to the different planets without invoking the time dilation is a huge deal. It's basically instant travel. And being the person or organization to control that ability would be enormous. Big enough to kill for.

Beau and I search for worm holes, but it doesn't take us long to realize that Jarren and his super wormers are skilled enough to not leave holes or cause any ripples. Yet that doesn't sit right with me. There has to be at least some fingerprints. Unless they found a way to access DES legitimately—a scary thought. Once a person has the proper clearance, then they can use those established clusters.

A sudden worry occurs to me. *Beau, has Radcliff considered that there may be someone in DES working with the looters?*

It's always a possibility. They do security background checks and have safeguards on the information, but you know nothing is ever completely secure.

True. And this place is too clean. After searching for a long while, I finally find an unauthorized breach. *Q, can you highlight it and find the rest, please?*

Beau curses as splotches of red light up DES's network. *Can you warn me when you're going to do that?*

Sorry.

A huff. *What does it mean?*

They're all the places where a wormer has gained illegal access to DES.

There's a million of them! He pauses. *Are they over the course of the Q-net's lifetime?*

Please show the age of each one, I ask the Q-net "aloud" so Beau can hear.

The red shifts into various shades from a super bright red to a pale pink. A guide flashes—the most recent are the eye-aching red color.

Can the Q-net fix those gaps in security? Beau asks.

YES.

Did you hear that? I ask Beau, hoping maybe now Q will allow him to hear it.

Hear what?

Great. *You know that's not helping, right Q?* But I say to Beau, *Yes, the Q-net can fix those because we fixed dozens of them before.*

Then why didn't it do it before? If it's...aware... then why not protect DES?

CANNOT INTERFERE.

Huh? But you're interfering now?

NO. YOU ARE.

Because I'm asking?

YES.

But what about hiding me from Jarren? When you removed

my image from the camera feeds?

YOU ASKED FOR PROTECTION.

Talk about a loophole.

Ara? Beau asks. *I can only hear one side of your conversation.*

The Q-net won't interfere on its own, I say, and then I explain that I need to ask Q.

Then ask it to plug those holes!

I do.

IT WILL TAKE TIME.

Okay. *Q is going to be busy for a while,* I say to Beau. *What do you want to do in the meantime?*

I think we can follow these neon-red lines back to the looters and figure out where they're hiding, but not today. For today, maybe we can discover who in DES might be communicating with them.

That's a great idea. Q, please keep the lines in place even after you fix the holes.

WILL DO.

Before we can sort through the red lines, Radcliff's voice sounds behind us. "Conference room. Now," he orders.

From the icy tone of his voice, I know the meeting isn't going to go well for me.

Not at all.

2522:248

Beau and I disentangle. This time Beau waits for me. He pauses with his hand on the doorknob. "How much do you want to bet your parents will be there?"

"I'd bet my entire life savings that they *will* be there. The million-credit question is, will there be an ambush?"

"What kind of an ambush?"

"Dr. Edwards and his medical staff. Radcliff probably asked them to bring a confinement jumpsuit for my own protection."

"I think you're being overly dramatic," Beau says.

I wait.

He gives me a slanted grin. "They're not going to wrestle you into a suit. Edwards is probably packing a hypodermic full of La-La juice."

"La-La juice?"

"Yeah, stuff to make you go to La-La land."

"La-La land?"

"You know…" He twirls his hand in the air. "A floaty place where everything is calm and peaceful and magic is real."

"And you said I was being dramatic. This isn't helping my nerves."

Beau opens the door. "Relax, it won't be that bad."

Not for him. But he's being nice. I squint at him in suspicion. "I thought you were mad at me."

"I was, but I've had time to think about it."

"And?"

"And if I want you to trust me and be able to tell me anything, then I shouldn't jump down your throat when you do. Besides, truth or not, we accomplished three days of work in one afternoon and I can't deny that."

We head toward the conference room. To avoid thinking about my upcoming doom, I ask him, "La-La Land? Where do you find these words anyway?"

He mock-bristles. "I'm more than a pretty face."

"You've been in the colloquialisms cluster again, haven't you?"

His handsome face brightens. "There are so many forgotten words and phrases that just need an advocate to get them back into our vernacular."

"Like skedaddle?"

"Exactly! I heard a tech use skedaddle the other day. I almost whooped with joy."

I pause at the doors, trying to guess the mood of the room from the murmur of voices.

Beau's hand touches my shoulder. "It'll be fine. How many crazy theories have you presented us with so far?" He doesn't wait for an answer. Instead, he counts on his fingers. "Invisible aliens, Warrior ghosts, alternate dimensions, Warrior hearts, portals in the pits, and now a sentient Q-net. We haven't locked you up yet."

Yet is the key word. "Still not helping. But since you're so confident, you can go first and Edwards can stab you with his hypodermic."

"Fine."

He enters. When he isn't attacked, I follow him. All the usual suspects are there: my parents, Radcliff and Morgan. Much to my relief, Dr. Edwards doesn't tackle me, and he's alone. Bonus. Niall's attendance is a surprise. He's wearing civilian clothes and gives me a questioning look. I shake my head sadly. *Sorry,* I mouth to him. Because he's bound to be upset at me, too. I settle next to Beau. From his earlier comments, he might be my only advocate.

"Lawrence, please explain to everyone what you told me earlier," Radcliff orders.

The please is a nice touch. I draw in a breath and release it, considering how to put the best spin on it. But there's really no way to say this without sounding insane. "The Q-net is sentient."

Morgan is the only one who doesn't react. Everyone else's reaction are almost comical; I mark when confusion turns into astonishment and then into worry followed by alarm. I half expect Dr. Edwards to pat the pockets of his lab coat for a syringe full of La-La juice. It doesn't take long for my mother to demand clarification.

I oblige, repeating everything I told Beau and Radcliff earlier. I end with, "I know it's impossible to believe, but so were the HoLFs, and the Warrior ghosts, and the Warrior hearts." I don't add the others because they haven't been proven. Yet. "And all those things ended up being true." I glance at Beau, now understanding why he pointed these out to me earlier. Thanks, partner.

He gives me an and-you-thought-I-was-being-a-jerk look before he says, "I don't know if I believe the Q-net is an alien consciousness that encompasses the entire Milky Way Galaxy, but I do know that Ara's ability and ease with working in the Q-net has leaped many orders of magnitude since Jarren invaded. She thinks it and the Q-net does it. That fast. It's another weapon in our arsenal. Whether or not she's right, I don't see any harm in continuing with our work in the Q-net."

Radcliff grunts. "Say Ara's right and the Q-net is sentient. It does what she says, so what happens if she gets mad and it decides to lash out at whoever she's upset with?"

"It doesn't work like that," I say. "Its directive is to protect us."

"And how do we know it's not lying?" he counters.

"Why would it lie? If the Q-net wanted to harm us, don't you think it would have done it by now? And if it decides to in the future, we can't do anything to stop it. It's integrated into all our lives." Another thought propels me to my feet. "And before you accuse me of using this special link with the Q-net to my advantage, let me remind you of all the times that I've risked my life for this team and the base. I should have *earned* your trust by now, and if I—"

"That's enough, Lawrence," Morgan says. "Sit down. Officer Radcliff's just playing devil's advocate."

Oh. I sit on the edge of my seat.

"From her glower," Morgan says mildly, "I'd say if the Q-net was going to lash out at anyone for making her upset, it would have been you, Radcliff. Any ill effects?"

"You made your point," he says. "Take us through it again, Lawrence. Why did it choose you?"

I suppress a sigh, but realize that this time he's paying attention versus reacting to the news. "I gained its notice when I protected the Warrior hearts from the looters. The Q-net reached out to me because it could no longer protect us from the HoLFs. Today I learned that the Q-net can't directly interfere on its own, but if I request something, like information or help to reveal a hidden program, it will assist."

"And you asked it to heal Niall?" Radcliff asks.

"Not quite. I didn't know about its sentience then. I was trying to figure out how to help him. That's when the Q-net showed me Niall's brain—or what looked like a graph of his neutral pathways. I asked Q to send the diagram to Dr. Edwards, but instead there was an impressive light show and then nothing. I never considered that Q healed him until yesterday when it told me."

"But you didn't prove to the Q-net that you could heal him."

Huh. "No, I don't think I did." Perhaps another loophole?

"Think?"

I bit back a growl of frustration. "I was very emotional at the time so I've no idea of my exact words."

Radcliff glances at Dr. Edwards. "What are your thoughts?"

Startled, Edwards asks, "About what?"

"About Niall's recovery. Could it be due to the Q-net?"

The poor man blinks at Radcliff as if he just asked him to flap his arms and fly. "I…Niall's…" Edwards snaps his mouth shut. He visibly pulls it together. "With the amount of blood loss Niall experienced, his brain was affected, but the amount and degree of the damage is unknown. His electrical brain activity was below normal but not by much. However, the longer he remained unconscious, the more I worried that the damage was extensive. Brains do regenerate, but not that fast. It takes years for a full recovery. I tested Niall after he woke and, cognitively, he's fine with no outward signs of any damage. It's possible that the coma was due to other issues. It's so difficult to tell the direct cause when dealing with brain trauma."

"What about his sensors? Do they normally stop working after a trauma?" Radcliff asks.

"Those sensors don't malfunction. Ever. The problem is always with the brain. Some people can't handle the interface." Edwards looks at Niall. "I suspect the reason he can't use the sensors is because there is some brain damage. I hope with time, he'll heal and be able to use them again."

"In other words, there is no way to prove the Q-net healed him?"

Out of all the stuff I said about the Q-net, Radcliff really seems determined to disprove this one.

"I can pull up his brain-wave chart during the time Ara said she requested help. That might show unusual activity. It might take me some time to find it."

Radcliff gestures to the terminal. Edwards inserts his tangs and sits in front of the screen. The desire to ask the Q-net to give the information to the doctor pulses. It would do it in a fraction of the time. I decide not to scare the good doctor.

"Are you in the Q-net now?" Mom asks me.

How to explain without upsetting her? "Not exactly."

"That's not an answer."

"I'm not in the Q-net right now. However, I just need to…reach out, and I can fly with Q." I hold up a hand, stopping the questions. "Flying is different than worming or just using the Q-net. It's like the structure is gone. There's no clusters or barriers or restrictions. I can go anywhere. But when I need to unravel a program or work with data, I have to entangle, and that requires more effort."

"Is the Q-net reading your mind all the time?" My mother sounds horrified.

"No. When I'm entangled, it does pick up on my intentions, but, when I'm not, it's more like Q is in another room and if I want to communicate, I have to raise my voice and call out to it. Otherwise Q doesn't invade my privacy." Or, at least, I don't think so, but I'm smart enough not to mention that. Is it strange that it doesn't freak me out to think the Q-net is privy to my deepest thoughts and emotions? Probably.

"At least it has the same goals as us," Dad says. "We need to keep the HoLFs out of our dimension."

"We don't know if—"

"I've been reading through Lan's file," Dad says, interrupting Mom. "I know there's no evidence that there are multiple dimensions, but her translations indicate that the aliens who left the Warriors behind believed that the HoLFs are from another one."

"Q confirmed that the Warriors, when they're intact and

have hearts, are protecting us from the HoLFs," I say.

My dad focuses on me. "Did it say what the HoLFs are or where they come from exactly?"

It almost sounds as if my father believes me. A bit of hope warms my insides. "When I asked about the nature of the HoLFs, Q sent me Lan's research."

"Can you request more information?"

"I can, but so far Q can only supply what's already been discovered by us. It doesn't have its own…files, but will pull information together for me into a file."

"Ara, what day and time was the light show?" Edwards asks. A graph is on the screen above the terminal. Various colored lines zigzag across the graph.

I think back. "Day two-forty-three." Struggling to recall the time, I remember it'd been dark and quiet. "I think it was after midnight."

OH-TWO-SIXTEEN.

I jump in my seat and almost slip off the edge. "Oh-two-sixteen."

Radcliff turns to me. "That's rather precise."

"Here it is," Edwards says, saving me from replying. He hums to himself as he studies the graph.

We all wait in silence. Niall is watching Edwards with a slightly pained expression. I've been avoiding his gaze since the big revelation, and I suspect I'll have to apologize later for not telling him about Q. Although, in my defense, I still wasn't certain about Q when we last spoke.

"There was definitely a great deal of activity starting at that time. See this?" Edwards points a finger at the graph where the lines aren't as jagged. "This is a standard pattern for a sleeping brain, but at oh-two-sixteen, something happened." The new spot has as many zigs and zags as if it was a seismograph recording of an earthquake. "Lots of activity for two minutes before the lines smooth. Except they don't quite go back to a deep sleep. In fact, his readings improved steadily until he woke." Edwards swivels around to face us. "It was so subtle, I didn't notice at the time." He peers at me. "Ara, did you talk to Niall at this time?"

"I talked to him before I fell asleep." I don't mention that I also bawled like a baby. "Then I had a nightmare where Jarren told me Niall was in a vegetative state, and that's why I was in the Q-net frantically trying to find a fix for him."

"Hmmm." Edwards turns back to the screen. The lines and graph flow backward then stop before he has it scroll forward. He points to a yellow line that's more spiky than the rest. "You can see where Ara talked to him for about four hours. Even unconscious, patients recognize voices, which is why we tell family members to talk or read to them."

I glance at Niall. He meets my gaze and there's a softness in his expression. Maybe I'm not in as much trouble with him as I'd thought.

"While this is very interesting, is there any evidence that the Q-net was responsible for those crazy squiggles from oh-two-sixteen to oh-two-eighteen?" Morgan asks.

Edwards slowly rotates back. "No. Sorry, Ara."

Then we just wasted a bunch of time. "Does it matter if there's proof?" I ask everyone. "You don't have to believe me. It's not like the Q-net will attack and kill people like the HoLFs.

Q has been nothing but super helpful. Officer Dorey and I are able to get much more done. Nothing is going to change. Well…not for us right now. Maybe in the future. Unless, once we stop the HoLFs, Q goes back to being…silent."

"That's true," Mom says. "But we're concerned about you and why you're so convinced. Could the voice you're hearing be from another super wormer?"

Wow. That didn't occur to me. Huh. I consider her question and am shocked by the answer. "It's possible. But the person's skills would have to be tremendous. Like beyond genius level. I'm getting a response to my requests in a fraction of a second."

"And you weren't verbalizing them until I grumped at you," Beau says.

"But why would they help me if they're another wormer that was working with Jarren?" I ask.

"To gain your trust in order to learn what we're doing and planning," Radcliff says.

He has a point. Yet. "That level of skill would be frankly terrifying," I say.

"More than the Q-net being sentient?" Radcliff asks.

"Yes." The truth. "Sure I was freaked when Q started communicating with me, but now, it makes perfect sense. It explains why I don't need tangs or a terminal. I was able to send messages when I was clinging to Jarren's shuttle high in the air and well away from the base." I shudder at the memory, rubbing my arms. "There's no other explanation about why I can do that. Not even a mutant super wormer could do that to me. I still believe Q is sentient."

No one comments. Edwards exchanges a glance with my

parents. Uh oh. Here we go.

"As I said, we're concerned," Mom says. "Dr. Edwards would like to do another brain scan. And we would also like you to undergo a mental health evaluation."

A double whammy. I wilt in my chair. "I thought we didn't have a psychologist on base."

"Dr. Bharathi has experience," Edwards says.

"Fine," I say. Refusing would just cause more problems.

"You're to stay out of the Q-net until the results come back," Radcliff orders.

Triple whammy. "I won't reach out to it, but if I'm worried about something and fall asleep, I can't promise I won't connect."

Dr. Edwards clears his throat. "You'll be given sleeping pills to help you sleep."

They want to drug me? Quadruple whammy. I scan my parents' faces and then Edwards, Radcliff, and Morgan. They decided this before I arrived. They never intended to believe me. It was an ambush just like I feared. An ache pulses in my chest and I can't even glance at Niall. What if he's nodding in agreement? What if he's looking at me in pity?

I stand. "I just need to finish the task I was working on with Officer Dorey right before this amb…meeting." It's somewhat true. We were interrupted.

Beau jumps up beside me. "Yeah, we need to complete it, otherwise we'll risk our escape tunnels being discovered."

"How long?" Radcliff asks with his suspicious squint firmly in place.

"Two hours," I say.

"All right. Two hours and then you're to report to the infirmary."

"Yes, sir." I leave the conference room with Beau at my heels. The impact of Radcliff's orders reminds me of when he told me I was his for ninety days. I'd thought I was heading for detention, instead I ended up on probation. This time betrayal throbs in my heart instead of fear. Well, I'm scared, too. What if I'm never allowed to talk to Q again? Yes, I know they can't stop me, but I'd no longer be part of the security team. I wouldn't be involved in stopping the shadow-blobs.

When we're far enough away, I say, "Thanks for covering for me, Beau. I owe you one."

He huffs. "They're overreacting. What do you want to do before…you know?"

"I wanted to start searching DES to find who might be communicating with the looters. Since there's over two million employees, it's going to take a long time without Q's help. So if we do a couple then Q can do the rest."

We reach his office and entangle with the Q-net. I take the lead and find one of those breaches into DES, tracking it to an employee's cluster. A queasiness swirls in my stomach as this is borderline eavesdropping.

Beau senses my reluctance. *If they're helping the looters, then they've no right to privacy.*

But what if they're innocent?

Considering the consequences of the looters gaining information from DES, do you think they will mind if they are?

I know I wouldn't mind, but not everyone feels the same way. At least it's not their personal cluster. *How can you tell if they're innocent or not?*

Security has a program that scans messages and flags certain phrases. We also have another one that looks for unusual correspondence between people who normally don't have any interactions. Although I don't know how to use them in this situation. We use it for those under investigation.

Please show me where they are.

We withdraw from the suspect's cluster and Beau takes me to a security cluster. I weave the threads of the programs together and loop it to those breaches. It's delicate work and Beau helps with connecting it in to DES. The resulting program will scan a person's correspondence, and if there is suspicious activity, their name will be listed in a file in my special cluster. But once we prove the looter-detector program works, Q will then be able to scan the rest of the employees. Well, when Q is finished with closing all those breaches.

CORRECT.

We test our hybrid program and it concludes that the person we are currently investigating is not communicating with any illegal entities. Then we test a few more until a name appears in the suspected-looter-colluder file. A sense of accomplishment fills me. I savor it as I expect that feeling will be rather elusive during my mental health evaluation.

Beau must sense my mood. *I'll be honest. I don't know if I believe you about the Q-net. But, from what I've seen, it's either true or you're a genius level wormer. And I'll do everything I can to back you up.*

Thanks.

That's what partners do. Is there anything else?

Our two hours are almost up.

No, but can I have a couple minutes alone? Not that I'm ever alone in the Q-net.

Sure. Beau disentangles.

I inform Q that I'll be unable to interact with it for a few days. *Can you help Beau while I'm gone?* I ask.

I CHOSE YOU.

Well everyone thinks I'm nuts so I can't do anything to help stop the HoLFs. You chose poorly.

I CHOSE YOU.

It's like I'm arguing with a toddler instead of an alien intelligence. I do my own equivalent of disentangling. Standing, I head for the door.

"Do you want me to go with you?" Beau asks.

"Thanks, but I can find the infirmary on my own. I've certainly been there enough times." I give him a mock salute and leave.

Radcliff and Morgan are in his office. They're sitting close together, discussing…something. I ignore them.

But when I reach the doorway, Radcliff calls, "Make sure you take an overnight bag with you, Ara."

I give him a tight nod and bolt before the tears welling up my throat can flood my vision. Halfway to my unit, I finally gain control of my emotions. Then I chastise myself for being so wimpy. I've faced shadow-blobs for stars' sake, I can handle a psych eval. Except, that's not what I'm upset about. I guess deep down I really thought everyone would believe me.

My mother is waiting for me in my room.

I so don't want to have this conversation right now. She was acting reasonable during the ambush, which just led me into a false sense of security. Underneath her calm exterior she must have been freaking out. Or the fact that she knew I was going to be ambushed helped her to keep her composure.

"I brought you a backpack," she says, holding a blue pack trimmed with orange.

"Thank you." I take it and unzip the main compartment. Then I grab my pajamas, and my regular clothes, which include two pairs of jeans and a few T-shirts—all hand-me-downs donated from similarly-sized women in the base.

"I've been meaning to give that to you since you lost yours," she says.

My backpack was actually stolen by Jarren, but I suspect she is avoiding the J-word. I shove everything in except one pair of jeans and a shirt. Then I tuck the picture of King Toad and Queen Mouse that Niall drew for me into a side pocket. My sole personal possession. I leave the room with the extra clothes.

"Where are you going?" Mom asks, trailing after me.

"Washroom." I duck inside and close the door before she can join me. Changing into the civilian clothes, I grab my toiletries.

Mom is waiting for me right outside. And like a puppy she follows me back. Is she feeling guilty or ensuring I don't run away? I toss my uniform onto the bed and try hard not to think that I'll never wear it again. The sudden knot in my throat tells me I'm unsuccessful. Then I add the rest of my stuff, zip the pack closed, and sling it over my shoulder.

"Ara, I—"

"I get it, Mom." I step past her and head for the unit's

entrance.

"I just want—"

"What's best for me. I know. And I agreed, so there's nothing more to say."

I'm just about to escape when she asks, "Do you want me to come with you?"

Glancing over my shoulder, I say, "No." It's a harsh no, but I don't feel too bad. She had to know I'd be upset.

I thank the universe that no one is in the hallways as I cut through the area of the base that's just for security. I avoid going by the training room because the door is always open and I don't want Elese to see me. One perk is that I won't have to explain my absence to the rest of the team. Radcliff can do the honors. But there goes my reputation as a sane person. I'd just earned their respect when they all touched a Warrior heart and could finally see the HoLFs and Warrior ghosts. One of my favorite moments was when they all apologized for doubting me.

And just when I think I've avoided everyone, I spot Niall waiting for me by the double doors. I so don't want to talk to him either. Yes, I'm a chicken and don't want to learn my boyfriend doesn't believe me either. That would destroy my control.

"Aren't you supposed to be resting?" I ask, then realize he's wearing his uniform.

"I'm on light duty," Niall says shrugging. "I was bored."

We stand there awkwardly for a few moments. When he keeps staring at me with pity, I go for humor. "Looks like I'm getting those couple days off after all. A vacation for one in a rubber room. Lucky me."

Niall doesn't laugh. "Mouse—"

"Don't say it."

He cocks his head. "Say what?"

"What's written on your face." I gesture. "The stress has gotten to you, Mouse. It's for the best."

"Does the Q-net allow you to read minds now?"

That surprises a laugh from me. "Yes. Q is a divine being that has granted me great powers. That's genius, Toad. I can add megalomania to my list of mental disorders."

"Are you done?" Now he's angry.

I sigh. "Yes."

"Did you ever think that I might believe you?" he asks.

Oh no. "You said it was ridiculous."

"When you were *speculating* that the Q-net did something to you. You didn't tell me about your conversation with the Q-net. You never said you thought it might be sentient. I didn't have all the facts."

"Since you thought the speculation was ridiculous, it doesn't take a genius to figure out that you'd think the rest was crazy."

"How can you assume that? Haven't I supported you from the beginning? Who showed you that video from the pits when everyone thought the HoLFs were just a concussion-induced delusion?"

"I..."

He waits.

"I'm sorry."

"That's it? You're sorry?" His tone is icy.

Wow, I've really pissed him off. "It was a knee-jerk reaction. A part of me thought everyone would believe me in that meeting. When they didn't...I felt betrayed and immediately went on the defensive. If I'd stopped and thought about it, I'd've realized you would be on my side. Except, I didn't. I jumped straight into wallowing in self-pity."

The tension in his shoulders eased. "And when you do something, you're all in."

"Hey!" I try to act insulted, but can't maintain it for long. "So, yes, I'm sorry for not thinking you might believe me." I pause. "Does this mean you believe me?"

"I believe in you."

That's an interesting response. "What does that mean?"

"Obviously something happened. Your skills with the Q-net have gone off the charts. There's a reason for it. You say it's because the Q-net is sentient and chose you. That could be the reason, or there might be another explanation. I don't know." He holds up his hand to stop my reply. "What I *don't* believe is the reason is because you're mentally unstable or stressed or suffering from PTSD. I know you're competent and capable. I believe in you."

I just about melt. "I can live with that." And it's close to what Beau said.

He smiles. "Good. Now I can give you your present."

My mood lifts. "A kiss?"

"I'm in uniform."

We both glance at the camera.

He digs into one of the many pockets of his black tactical pants and brings out two candy bars. I laugh as he hands them to me. He remembered when we'd been on the Interstellar Class space ship and I'd told him if I was sent to the brig he had to smuggle in candy for me.

I hide them in my backpack. "Thanks."

"I only brought two because I've full confidence that you won't be there more than two days."

"I hope I don't disappoint you. See you later." I give him a half wave.

"I'm going with you."

"You don't need to. I know the way."

"Uh...I've been assigned to escort you there." He has the decency to look embarrassed.

My mood turns dark and scary. "I hate your father right now."

"At least he didn't assign someone else."

True. That would have been torture. "Still hate him."

"Been there. Do you want me to channel some of my childhood anger and join you in a mutual Radcliff hate fest?"

"Would you?"

"Of course."

Best boyfriend ever. We spend the trip to the infirmary reminiscing about all the times Radcliff caused each of us to hate him with the power of the burning sun. It's fun until we stand outside the doors. All my good humor drains and I'm left with an uneasy, slightly nauseous skittering in my stomach.

"I'd rather go fight shadow-blobs," I say.

Niall gives me a quick hug. "You'll be fine."

We go inside and a nurse spots me. He hustles over with a portable in his hand. "We've been expecting you, Miss Lawrence. This way, please." He glances at Niall. "No visitors are allowed until Dr. Bharathi gives permission."

The news of no visitors is actually a relief. Except for Niall and maybe Beau, I've no desire to see or talk with anyone. "Later, Toad," I say.

"Two days, Mouse," he says and leaves.

I follow the nurse to a part of the infirmary I haven't been in before. It's past ICU and all the small bays for recovering patients. We go through a sturdy pair of double doors, down a carpeted hallway, and into a room that's bigger than the ones I've stayed in when I was healing from my multiple injuries. A soothing blue plush carpet covers the floor. The bed is normal—no rails or machines. There's a bureau, desk, and a chair. No terminal or screen, but there's a washroom.

The nurse hands me the portable. "Dr. Bharathi asks that you complete the questionnaire. Once you're finished, she'll be in to see you." He leaves.

The door clicks shut and I wait for the snap of a lock. It doesn't sound, but I test it anyway. It swings open and I peek out. The corridor is empty. No guards. Perhaps this won't be like detention. I retreat inside and inspect the door. There's no way to lock it on this side. Setting my backpack down on the bed—there's no way I'm unpacking—I examine the room and find the hidden camera in the side wall. No surprise, but it's still unsettling. Is someone going to watch me sleep? I check the washroom next and am relieved when I don't find a camera. I also don't find a lock on that door either. Okay then.

I sit on the bed and bring up the questionnaire, reading through it first. There's a series of personal questions about my thoughts and dreams. Things like do I have nightmares, and, if yes, how often? Followed by a space to write in details of any recurring nightmares. Then there's the queries about my mental health. Things like do I experience times of overwhelming anxiety? I have to laugh over the series of hypothetical scenarios with four choices—if you're feeling overwhelmed do you do A—confide in a friend, B—tell your legal guardian, C—keep it to yourself, or D—ignore it.

It doesn't take me long to figure out what they're seeking. Depending on how I answer the questions and the choices I make, I can either come across as perfectly harmless or seriously disturbed. Should I lie and let them think everything is all sunshine and roses in my world? Or do I have fun and allow them to think I'm stark raving mad? I'm tempted to be a brat. After all, I agreed to be here, but I never promised to cooperate.

In the end, I decide to answer the questions honestly. Mental health issues are serious and I shouldn't be treating this like a joke. These evaluations actually help people and I'm being an insensitive jerk. I concentrate on the form.

Do you have nightmares? Yes.

How frequent are they? Every night.

Please describe a typical nightmare. They're all about Jarren. Every night he comes into my room carrying an explosive device. I'm lying in my bed and he places it on my chest. It's heavy and so cold it burns my skin. He tells me to stay still and not to cry out. The slightest movement will detonate it. Terrified, I lie frozen in place, sipping the air so I don't jostle the device and set it off.

What I don't add is that's when Q arrives and rescues me. We fly to the edges of the Galaxy and, by the time I return, Jarren and his device are gone and I'm at peace.

2522:248

About an hour after I finish the questionnaire, there's a light knock at my door. That knock is a promising sign. I call out a "come in." Dr. Bharathi enters. She'd patched me up after a skirmish with the shadow-blobs when Dr. Edwards was busy saving Niall's life. I'm guessing she's in her late thirties. Her long brown hair is pulled back into a French braid. She has big brown eyes, light brown skin, and is wearing a lab coat over a pink blouse and black dress pants.

"Hello Ara, how are you doing?"

That's a loaded question. "Do you want pleasant small talk or the truth?"

She doesn't miss a beat. "I'll take the truth every time."

"In that case, I'm very unhappy, and I want this over as fast as possible. So what do I need to do to get back to work?"

"Keep up the frank honesty and we'll get along just fine."

That's easy to do. Let's hope I don't give her nightmares. "Great. What's next?"

"Are you always this impatient?"

Am I? "Only when we're wasting time."

"All right then, let's go to my office for a chat."

I follow her down the hallway, through a small medical lab, and into her office. Instead of sitting behind the pristine desk, she gestures to a couple of armchairs that are next to each other—not quite facing, but angled so you don't have to crane your neck to talk. I plop into the one on the right. Bharathi snags a portable from her desk and sits in the other chair with a graceful elegance. Straightening, I cross my ankles. Who are you calling self-conscious?

"I've read through your responses." She scrolls through them on her portable. "The nightmares are concerning and might be an indication of PTSD, but since your abduction was so recent, they're also normal for what you've been through." Bharathi sets the portable down on her lap and meets my gaze. "Let's talk about the Q-net. When's the first time it spoke to you?"

I suppress a groan. "I was following Jarren through the Q-net when I lost him. And I was just like, 'Where did he go?' not expecting an answer. But Q answered. It said, 'here,' and showed me where he'd been hiding." On the opposite side of Yulin! Talk about scary.

"And were you entangled at this time?"

"No. I was asleep and flying through the Q-net." And then she asks me to explain. "After I fell asleep while entangled in the Q-net, I started dreaming of being in the Q-net at night. It only happened when I was worried about something. I thought they were just dreams until I found out that what I did while asleep actually happened. I left a dream message for Chief Vasily that he received."

"Why didn't you tell someone about this right away?"

Seriously? "Uh, I was in the Q-net without tangs and without a terminal nearby." I point to the two of us. "I didn't want *this* to happen. Besides, I got a killer migraine and convinced myself it was all a dream."

"And the next time it happened?"

"Much harder to deny. And then when I accessed the Q-net via a portable while I was in the middle of the desert, I knew I had to fess up." Plus Niall made me promise.

"Did you think the Q-net was sentient then?"

"No. Just super helpful."

"What about when Niall woke up from his coma?"

"I thought the missile exploding above the base did it. It was so loud and everything shook so hard. It wasn't until Q told me it healed Niall that I knew what really happened."

"The Q-net told you it is sentient?"

I think back to our conversation. "I was trying to find information on the sensors in our heads and to see if anyone else could access the Q-net without tangs and a terminal. I thought, 'I can't be that special,' and Q replied." I detail the exchange as best as I can remember.

She absorbs the information before asking, "Did the Q-net ever say it was sentient?"

Huh. "No. It claimed to be the Milky Way Galaxy and didn't correct me when I said it was an alien consciousness. Also Q used 'I'."

Bharathi jumps on that. "You said?"

How to explain? "There were...pictures and thoughts spoken that weren't mine." Wow, that sounded super crazy. I hurry to cover it up. "Look, I never ever in a million years would have thought the Q-net was anything but pure science and technology, invented by humans. But those visions were all from Q."

"And this conversation happened a couple days after you were rescued from Jarren?"

"Yes."

A pause. "I can understand how having the Q-net be so...attuned to your thoughts would be comforting during a stressful situation. Could you have created this all-powerful persona as a way to not feel so alone when you were clinging to the shuttle with your life literally in your hands?"

It's a valid question. At the time I was terrified and desperate. And I did call out for the Q-net to help me when Jarren was about to shoot at Niall, Rance, and Zaim. It shut off the power. Could that have actually been me? Or maybe one of the security team knocked it out! I never considered that.

"I'm willing to go with your theory, Dr. Bharathi. Except this all-powerful persona didn't reveal itself to me until two days later. Why wait? It's not comforting me now." Quite the opposite.

"The idea of a savior germinated in your subconscious during the incident. Once you had time to recover, your consciousness had a conversation with the Q-net to legitimize what happened. Your own abilities scare you so you invented a sentient Q-net."

Huh. The woman does make sense. Unease rolls through me. Was I having conversations with myself? "I am freaked over this..." I spin a finger around the side of my head. "Ability to connect with Q with a thought. And perhaps you're right, it's my way of coping." I lean forward. "But how do you explain my new abilities?"

She consults her portable before saying, "This all started after you were shot with an energy wave gun and almost died. The concussion you experienced must have been more severe than we realized and the damage didn't show up on any of our scans. The ensuing stress and trauma has exacerbated your condition. It may seem like a super power to you Ara, but it is a misfiring of the brain's synapses."

Another valid point. I dig my fingernails into the fabric of the chair to keep from screaming. "Say you're right. I'm willing to accept the Q-net might not be sentient. So what's the problem? Why can't I continue using my screwed-up brain to help? We've murdering looters living on our planet. They have missiles and shuttles and who knows what else—oh, wait, I can probably *find out* with enough time to worm through their security. Thing is, we're wasting time with this evaluation."

"The problem is you might damage your brain beyond repair. You could go into a coma and never wake up."

I jump to my feet. "I'm willing to risk it."

"But it's not your decision."

"Oh come on! My eighteenth birthday is in sixty-six days. We could all be dead by then!"

"Still not your decision."

Which means none of the adults are going to break the rules. Flopping back into the chair, I mutter every single curse word I know—and I've learned quite a number of new ones from the other security officers. When I've regained my control, I ask, "So what's the cure, Doc?"

She smiles. "If that is the cause, then it's letting your brain heal by not interacting with the Q-net."

I don't like where this is heading. "How long?"

"As long as it takes."

And I make the mistake of remembering what Dr. Edwards said earlier about it taking years for full recovery. I sink lower in my chair.

"You've taken on such a huge burden, Ara," Bharathi says. "The fate of the base and all the lives inside it are not on *your* shoulders. We have a security team."

Which I'm a part of. While I don't want to sound egotistical, I was a vital part of that team. Was—how can one word hurt so much?

No. I *am*. I tap into my inner guardian lion. "You said *if* that is the cause. What if it isn't?"

"Then there will be other treatment options. The first step is to rule out all other causes. Tomorrow we're going to do a full physical and mental evaluation. In the meantime you must be hungry."

Now that she mentions it, my stomach rumbles its displeasure over being ignored for so long. "I am." Although eating alone in my cell—pardon me, my room—holds no appeal. I can't believe I'm admitting to missing Radcliff, then I remember I hate him and alter my statement. I miss his *cooking*. It's Radcliff's only redeeming quality. Well…there was his plan for Operation Looter Attack—a work of genius. Bah. I can't even hold a grudge.

Bharathi stands. "Come along, then."

our help to protect us." I take a shaky breath. They're staring at me as if I'm speaking a foreign language. "For various reasons, the Q-net has chosen me. That's why I can connect to it without tangs or a terminal."

They continue to stare at me. And I experience what it must be like to be Medusa—the mythical goddess who turned people to stone. I rake my fingers through my long black hair. No snakes, just frizz.

The silence becomes awkward. "I warned you that you wouldn't believe me," I say to Beau.

"Why…When…How…" Radcliff tries.

Wow. I've rattled the Chief of Security. Go me. "It just revealed itself to me yesterday. I couldn't decide if anyone would believe me or not. Hell, I'm still in shock. But working with Beau made me realize I can't keep this to myself."

Beau glances at Radcliff. "I told you it was too soon for her—"

"Oh, for stars' sake! It's not PTSD. Unless you have it, too?" I ask Beau. "You saw what happened." I gesture to Radcliff's terminal.

"I did," Beau says, but his pained expression say he's not happy admitting it.

"What happened?" Radcliff asks.

"Once we pierced the blockade, it created another three escape tunnels. We have to prove that we can do something first, then it will copy the action," I say. "Since we already created a secure channel to DES, I just had to ask Q to do another one, which it did in a fraction of the time. There are messages from DES security for you."

Curious, I follow her to the medical lab. A number of techs, nurses, and Dr. Edwards are gathered in small groups, talking.

Edwards spots me. "Are you all settled in?"

Seriously? "Like a bug in a rug." No, I've no idea where that simile comes from. It's one of Beau's archaic expressions.

He gives me a quizzical look. "Um…glad to hear it."

"Everyone's here, let's go," Bharathi says.

"Go where?" I ask as everyone moves to the exit.

"The cafeteria." She smiles and I decide she has a soothing smile. "You've been cooped up in security for so long I thought you might like a change of scenery."

I could grow to like this woman. After all, it's not her fault I'm here. It's my parents' and Radcliff's and, if I'm being honest, yeah, I know denial is usually my go-to, it's also my fault. I should have kept my mouth shut on the entire the Q-net is sentient thing.

The cafeteria is about half full. It's a little early for dinner. The scent of cabbage is an unfortunately familiar aroma. As we join the line, I scan the tables, searching for anyone I recognize. Officer Rance is eating with his family. His two sons are miniaturized versions of their dad—too cute. But there's something not quite right.

It hits me as I grab a tray from the stack. There's no buzz. No bursts of laughter. Conversation is muted and expressions are strained. There's no smiles from the workers standing behind the counter handing out plates. Also they're only giving out a single slice of mystery meat and a scoop of mashed potatoes. Odd.

When it's my turn, Bharathi says, "She's a security officer," to the lady filling plates.

The woman looks up and meets my gaze. She grins at me. "Thank you, lass, for saving us."

Suddenly uncomfortable, it's an effort to return her smile. "Uh…you're welcome."

Adding another slice and two scoops of potatoes to the plate, she hands it to me. And it clicks. Everyone's been getting half portions because we're now sharing our food with sixty-eight prisoners. With Interstellar Class space ships only coming once every two to four A-years, food supplies on a research base are carefully calculated to last until the next delivery.

I give the plate back. "I don't need all this. I'm not—"

She waves it away. "Sure you do. Extra rations for the security team. Or else how are you going to keep up your strength? Off you go, lass."

Except now my appetite is ruined. I'd no idea what's been going on in the base. Bharathi's right, I've been spending too much time in security.

Joining the medical personnel, I claim there is no way I can eat everything—I can't—and share my extra portions with a few grateful nurses. Even Dr. Edwards takes half a scoop of potatoes.

An image of the doctor passing out during surgery because he's malnourished flashes in my mind.

He sees my slightly horrified expression. "Not to worry, Miss Lawrence. Everyone is getting their daily requirement of calories." He pats his stomach. "And some of us can stand to lose a few kilograms."

The nurse who escorted me earlier leans in and says in a conspiratorial whisper, "We're still having ice cream night once a week. We're not sharing *that* with the prisoners."

I smile my thanks and find I have an appetite after all. In fact, I'm one of the first to finish. Leaning back in my chair, I scan the room. More people have arrived, but the buzz is still missing. A few spot me and come over to express their thanks. The desire to turn invisible pumps through my veins. Why are they thanking me? They're still in danger. As Niall said, we may have won the battle, but the war is still ongoing. If the looters launch another missile, we can't stop it. Jarren destroyed the satellite with our defensive weapons.

Bharathi must sense my discomfort because she offers to escort me back. When I don't say a word, she asks me what's wrong. "I thought you'd enjoy getting out."

"I did. It's just…"

"Truth, remember?"

"It's just seeing what's at stake. Rance's two sons, the scientists and techs, the sweet lady serving the mystery meat, you, Dr. Edwards, and the nurses."

She stops. "It's not up to you to keep us safe."

"I know. It's up to Officer Radcliff and my parents. But they rely on a team of people. They need me. I'm not bragging, Dr. Bharathi. If I hadn't helped them, Operation Looter Attack would never have worked." And that's what really hurt. I'm talking deep level pain. That the four of us didn't have a discussion before they ambushed me.

"That's a great deal of pressure, Ara. You're young. You should be attending soch-time and not worrying about saving everyone's life."

Horrified, I ask, "You're not going to make me go to soch-time, are you?"

She laughs. It's a light sound that's almost a giggle. "No."

Whew.

Then she sobers. "Do you understand the point I'm making?"

"Yes. And I agree, it's a ton of pressure. But guess what?" I don't wait for an answer. "I didn't fall apart. I fought HoLFs, and escaped from Jarren. I didn't crack under the pressure."

"Are you sure about that?"

I open my mouth, but her comments from earlier replay in my mind—that a sentient Q-net is a survival mechanism that I created to help me get through the trauma. "I guess that's what I'm here to find out."

She grabs a portable from her office before we go to my room. Once there, she says, "I hope everything is comfortable."

It's a polite comment and doesn't require a response, but she said she wanted honesty. "Actually, it's not very comfortable."

"Oh?"

"Is the camera necessary?"

Her polite demeanor drops. "You're not supposed to access the Q-net while you're here."

"I didn't."

"Then how did you find it?" she demands.

"I inspected the room. I'm training to be a *security* officer. If I didn't find it, my instructor would have made me run a hundred laps."

Her stiff posture relaxes. "It's for your own safety."

"Do you think I'm suicidal?"

"No."

"Do you think someone will come in and attack me?"

"Of course not!"

I wait.

"I'll check about turning it off."

"Thank you."

Bharathi hands me the portable. "There's a series of tests that you'll recognize. I need you to go through and answer them."

I glance at the screen. It's the program to measure the effects of a concussion. Everyone on the base is required to take the test before they have a concussion, then if you have one (or they suspect you might have one), you take it again and the program compares your replies. I've done it a million times since I was shot by the looters. Once your pre- and post-concussion responses match, you're technically healed.

"Someone will be back later to pick it up. Good night, Ara." She leaves.

I try not to think about Niall and how we snuggle on the couch after dinner every night. Instead, I go into the washroom to change into my pajamas—might as well be comfortable—and freshen up. Then I place my backpack in a certain location that may or may not be blocking the camera. Before hopping on the bed, I take out Niall's picture and set it on the night table. Miss you, King Toad.

Then I go through the series of questions and play the games that test my reflexes. I'd rather be playing *Mutant Zombies on Planet Nine* with Niall. I hope we all live long enough so he can take me on another proper date. I might just let Niall win the game this time. Just kidding! He's going down. Hard.

A nurse arrives when I finally finish the test an hour later.

Guess they're worried about leaving a portable with me for too long. Which is just silly. She hands me a small white cup with two brown pills and a glass of water.

I raise an eyebrow at her, inviting her to explain.

"Your sleeping pills."

How could I forget? Anger simmers in my guts and I set them on the table. "I'll take them later."

"No. I need to watch you take them now."

Watch me? That's just inviting me to figure out a way *not* to swallow them.

She gives me an annoyed huff. "I've been doing this long enough that I can tell if you don't swallow."

A challenge! But then I relent. It would only cause more trouble and my goal is to get out of here as fast as possible. I down the two pills and hand her back the empty cup and glass. She uncovers the camera by moving my backpack, then turns out the lights before she leaves. A night light shines like I'm two years old and afraid of the dark. Sheesh. I wiggle under the covers and try not to think about Q.

It hovers nearby. If I focus on Q, it will help me worm into my tests results. I resist the temptation and also don't cover the camera again. I've never had sleeping pills and might have an adverse reaction.

I don't even know I'm asleep until I wake up. Wow. No nightmares. No midnight visits to the washroom. No flying with the Q-net. Nothing.

The overhead lights are on and there's another nurse in my room—I should probably learn their names—and he's talking to me, but it takes me a moment to comprehend.

"…busy day. You should wait until later to shower. Breakfast will be here soon. Did you sleep well?"

I'm smart enough to keep my first response—I slept like the dead—to myself. Instead, I croak out a yes. Satisfied, he nods and hustles out.

When I finish eating and drinking, the cobwebs in my mind are gone. It's kind of amazing how energized and refreshed I am. No, the coffee hasn't kicked in yet. That had to be my first solid night's sleep in… Obviously the pills didn't improve my math skills. At least since before the looters attacked the first time.

When Dr. Bharathi said I was going to have a full physical and mental evaluation, she wasn't exaggerating. The medical technicians measure everything. I run on a treadmill with sensors plastered all over my body, including places I'm not gonna name. I enjoy the running, though. I miss the physical activity. They take samples of all the fluids in my body. Yes, they even collect the mucus in my nostrils and my stomach acid. I hope I never have to experience having a thin tube go up my nose, down my throat, and into my stomach again. It's not painful, just really really weird, and hours later I still have a tickle at the back of my throat.

An alphabet of scans commences next. Various machines hum and buzz and clang around my prone body. Then I have another heart-to-heart with Dr. Bharathi and we talk about everything except the Q-net. Kind of fun until the subject turns to Jarren, then not so much.

"It's okay if you still consider him a friend," she says. "To you it's only been two-hundred and fifty or so days since you and Jarren were good friends. Since you were sad to leave him behind. To him, it's been over twenty-two Actual years since he last saw you. He's changed quite a bit."

Yeah, into a murdering looter. "There are times when I admire his skills with the Q-net, but Jarren is not my friend. He is the enemy."

"He has spared your life a number of times."

I open my mouth to correct her. He killed me once and had every intention of doing it again until I tricked him.

"He could have killed you in the pits that first time you encountered him. And he's had plenty of opportunities since. Yet he didn't. Why do you think he spared you?"

I mull over her question. "The first time because we were friends and he didn't consider me a threat. The second, when I was a threat, he claimed I'd figure out the mystery of the Terracotta Warriors, but he wasn't ready to kill me. Instead, he offered me a chance to join forces." Tempting for a nanosecond. "The third time, he wanted information about how we stopped the HoLFs." He was right about one thing. I am a threat. I'm close to figuring out the Warriors. I just need time to uncover all the details and prove my various theories. Too bad I'm stuck here.

"But each time he was thwarted, Dr. Bharathi, he didn't hesitate to kill me. I hold no warm and fuzzy feelings for him." Phantom pain pricks my back. Although I know the explosive device is gone, there's still a weight between my shoulder blades.

"Do you regret not killing Jarren when you had the chance?"

Shocked, I stare at her. What kind of question is that? "I never considered killing him!" I tap my chest. "I'm one of the good guys. We don't kill people unless there is no other option."

And I just about quoted Jarren. Is that a symptom of mental unbalance? No, it's just accurate.

We talk some more until I start yawning. It's been a long day and we only stopped for two short breaks so I could eat. Bharathi hands me another portable to take back to my room.

"Just one more cognitive test before bed."

"Oh joy."

She laughs and shoos me from her office. "I'm sure you can find your way."

I appreciate the trust as I return to my room. Yes, I know there are cameras in the hallway, but it's still nice. Before doing the test, I take a shower, washing away the sticky residue of the sensors and dried sweat. Donning my pajamas, I hop into bed and cue up my homework while munching on one of my candy bars. Mmmm…fake chocolate.

While I'm answering the various questions, I can't help thinking of Niall, wondering what he's doing. Is he back on regular duty or still taking it easy? I imagine him sitting on his couch drawing a picture in one of his sketchbooks. The desire to join him throbs in my chest. Will we ever get another proper date? All the emotions I've been suppressing since this first started well up my throat. I hunch over the portable as unstoppable tears leak from my eyes.

The portable's screen turns black for a second then a photo of Niall appears. He's standing in the middle of the hallway that runs through the housing units for the officers. Wearing a black T-shirt—my favorite one and he knows it—and jeans, he holds two pieces of paper toward the camera. One says, *Miss you, Mouse*, with a heart. The other is a drawing of me. I'm wearing my jumpsuit while holding a null wave emitter. There's an army of Warriors behind me with fierce expressions. He's titled the picture *Queen of the Shadows*. His expression has a little bit of a snark in it. As if he knows I'll be watching even though I'm not allowed. I laugh as more tears fall. The Q-net has given me this gift and I save the photo to my cluster. Then I wipe my eyes and return to the test more determined than ever to prove to everyone that I'm not imagining things. Thanks, Toad.

The nurse arrives after I finish and I take my sleeping pills without complaint. Another night of nothing and I'm woken by Keath-the-nurse-who-has-Ara-babysitting-duty-until-dinner. He informs me that I have another session with Dr. Bharathi after I finish breakfast.

This morning's heart-to-heart focuses on the looter attack and why I didn't run away when I had the chance. I explain about wanting to cover the hatch to the factory and save the Warrior hearts, but this time, I'm honest.

"I felt compelled to protect them. In here." I tap my chest. "After I'd touched that heart, I had a...connection to the Warriors. I just didn't know it at the time. Huh."

"Huh?"

"Of those who have touched a heart, I wonder if they feel that connection as well. Have you asked anyone else?"

She clears her throat and smooths the sleeves of her lab coat.

I'll take that as a no. But I wonder if everyone would be more open to the idea of testing out a Warrior portal if they had that bond as well.

There's a light knock at the door. Bharathi is quick with the come in.

Keath pokes his head into the room. "Is Ara ready for lunch?"

"Yes, we're done. For now."

That "for now" sounds ominous. After a trip to the cafeteria with Keath, I'm back with Dr. Bharathi and her endless questions. More tests in the evening are followed by the oblivion that is sleep. The fourth day is more of the same and a heavy sensation weighs on my shoulders. Niall predicted I'd be back in two days. I'm letting him down. Before leaving Bharathi at the end of the day, I ask her if I have to stay here much longer.

"It depends on the test results." She holds up a finger. "I'm waiting on a few more. Once I have them, then we'll have a conference."

Day five isn't a good one for either of us. Here's an example of one of our exchanges:

Me (impatient and grumpy): You asked me that question three times already and the answer has been the same *All. Three. Times*. Why don't you go through your recordings if you want to hear the answer again?

Her (shocked and suspicious): How do you know I've been recording our sessions?

Me (frustrated and annoyed): I'm not an idiot. And I'm a security officer.

Her (exasperated and condescending): You're a *junior* officer in *training*, Ara, you're not—

Me (angry and accusing): I'm not what? A part of the team? Not responsible for the safety of the base?

Her (sighing): Perhaps we should take a break.

Yeah, I'm not proud of day five. And I suspect Dr. Bharathi isn't either. Day six is better because I'm told early in the morning that the results of all my tests have been collected and reviewed and we're going to have a conference at thirteen hundred hours to discuss the next step. Finally, progress!

With my stomach threatening to turn inside out, I arrive at Bharathi's office a few minutes early. Anxious to get this over and done with, I practically run into her office. Then I stop dead. My parents are there.

2522:253

Another ambush. Or so it feels. If I hadn't been so preoccupied with getting the results, I would have realized that my parents would be invited to the conference. They're sitting in two chairs facing Bharathi's desk. There's another one set up next to them. My mom and dad hop to their feet with exclamations of love and support. I'm soon squished in a parent sandwich. Except I'm not in the reciprocating mood. Quite the opposite. And when my arms refuse to wrap around them, they step away awkwardly and resume their seats.

Bharathi's keen gaze notes all this, but I don't care. Wary of this entire encounter, I move my chair, increasing the distance between me and my parents and angle it slightly so I can face all three adults. We are not in this together. No. It's me against them. And that's exactly what my body language says. Bharathi can write a medical paper on it and get famous.

The Doc clears her throat and begins, detailing all the tests she ran. My parents are attentive, but keep sneaking glances at me. I keep my expression neutral. When Bharathi finally reveals the results of all those tests, all I hear is normal. Normal. Normal. Normal. Normal.

"She does have elevated levels of adrenaline, cortisol, and norepinephrine. All three are stress hormones, but that's to be expected considering what she has been through," Bharathi says.

Then back to another string of normals. Music to my ears.

"Her brain activity is different than both before and after the concussion. Since she's been scanned a few times after the attack, we have a record of the changes. Each time the neural activity was somewhat altered until this most recent one, which is very different."

"Is that bad?" Mom asks.

"They're all normal, but people don't usually change that drastically or that quickly."

I jump in. "But they do change?"

"Yes, during major life events, and as a person learns new skills."

"Dr. Bharathi, I think both those qualifiers can be applied to me."

"Which is why I'm not that concerned."

Whew. I relax back in my seat.

The doctor continues, "Another interesting result is her cognitive scores. They've actually improved quite a bit since before her concussion. I tested her twice and the results were the same. Her analytical thinking scores were by far her strongest. They are well above average for her age group and are another skill that has improved."

Go me.

Bharathi finishes her report then places her elbows on her desk, laying her arms on top of each other. She leans forward and I brace for the big announcement. Something like, I'm sorry, but Ara has a brain tumor. Or, I'm sorry, she's totally and completely nuts.

"According to all the tests, Ara is completely healthy, both physically and mentally," Bharathi says.

I resist the temptation to jump up and yell, Told You! And I don't whoop with joy and kiss the doctor either. Because there's that whole body-language thing, and no one appears as happy as I do. They're tense and bewildered and frowning.

"But what about her belief that the Q-net is sentient?" Mom asks.

"It is not causing her any stress. Her quality of life isn't affected by it. It is most likely a coping mechanism. Considering what she's been through, it's...a bit odd, yes, but not concerning."

The unspoken *not yet* hangs in the air so I say, "And I'm happy never to mention it again."

My parents aren't appeased. "What about the change in her neural activity?" Dad asks. "Could that be a sign of undiagnosed brain trauma?"

"Or perhaps that her interactions in the Q-net have damaged her wiring?" Mom adds.

Oh for stars' sake, did they not listen to the woman? "Dr. Bharathi, can't you match the changes in my brain activity to what was going on in my life?" Because I know that every time my skills with the Q-net improved something major was going on.

She purses her lips. "There's no evidence that her wiring was damaged."

Great. I stand up. "Can I go back to work now?"

"No," Mom says, also getting to her feet. But it's not as impressive as she's nine centimeters shorter than me.

"Why not?"

"There's something going on and, until we figure it out, you will stay out of the Q-net." She turns to Bharathi, probably hoping for an ally. "You said time will heal brain trauma, right?"

Frustration pulls all my muscles into one giant knot. "There's no proof of any brain trauma. No evidence. You're a *scientist*, for stars' sake." And then it hits me. She's also a mother. A mother who saw her daughter in the hands of Jarren, who'd shot her. Saw her with an explosive device attached to her back. Thinking about it, it had to have been pretty horrific to watch. Perhaps Mom is suffering from PTSD. "You can't ground me because you're terrified."

She crosses her arms. "Technically I can."

Point to her. "Let me restate, you can't risk everyone's lives in this base because you're terrified of losing me."

"We have Tace and his team, and Jarren is in our custody. We'll figure it out," she says. "Besides the rest of the looters are not going to blow us up when we have sixty-eight of their people."

I don't remind her that they sent a missile to do exactly that when we had sixteen of their people. "I wish I had your optimism, Mom, but I've seen what they can do and they're quite clever. I'm sure they'll find a way to attack us again and avoid killing their people."

"No. I'm your legal guardian, and I'm in charge of this base."

Which means she can ground me and tell Radcliff I'm no longer allowed to be on the security team. No doubt he'll take her side. He's done it before—the rat bastard. Time for some negotiations. "Mom, you can't keep me from accessing the Q-net unless you drug me all day and all night. I'd prefer to avoid that," I hurry to add. "How about a compromise? If you allow me to keep training with Elese and working with the security team, I'll promise not to entangle with the Q-net."

"No. I don't want you in security. You're coming back to our unit."

And now who's the crazy lady? I meet my father's gaze. Do something! But he gives me the helpless you-know-how-stubborn-your-mother-is shrug. Infuriating. Because I do know. She has decided that I'll be safer with her, where she can keep a close eye on me, thinking that she's protecting me.

In the end, I trail them back to my prison. Mom is holding a bottle of sleeping pills—good luck getting me to take them—and my dad is carrying my backpack like I'm two years old. They chat about...I've no idea. I'm not listening. Instead, I'm trying to decide what I should do. Do I be a model daughter and wait them out for a few days? Or do I completely ignore them and go help Beau right away? I promised to stay out of the Q-net during the medical evaluation and I did. I've been declared heathy by a medical professional. As far as I'm concerned, I'm under no obligation to continue with that promise.

We reach my old bedroom and Mom opens the door. "See? It's just as you left it."

I peer inside. Not quite. The terminal and screen are

missing. My mother is in serious denial. At least I still have my own washroom—the only thing I missed while living with Radcliff.

"Why don't you rest up before dinner? Tomorrow is going to be a busy day."

That's unexpected. "Oh?"

"Yes, you've lots of schoolwork to catch up on. You can use my portable. I copied all your assignments to it. You'll also work in my office in the morning."

I blink at her. Is she serious?

"And you'll be going to soch-time. I've already informed the facilitator to expect you."

Oh. My. Stars. I don't know whether to cry or laugh. I opt for staring at her in stunned silence.

Which she ignores. "You're forbidden to go in the Q-net. And tonight I'm making your favorite dish." She hurries off to cook dinner.

See here's the thing. My mother is used to her daughter, Lyra Daniels, being a good girl. Other than minor infractions like worming in the Q-net, sneaking out of the base, and having some hooch with the chemists, Lyra was pretty mild and she earned high grades. Same as her brother Phoenix. Nice kids, no real problems. My parents are expecting Ara Lawrence to be the same way. Well, they're in for a big surprise. Because Ara isn't like Lyra. And if they're going to treat Ara like a teenage delinquent, well, then that's what they're going to get. This might actually be fun.

I toss my backpack on the armchair. This room is bigger than my room at Radcliff's. There's more furniture, a bigger desk, and a huge closet that seems even more cavernous without anything in it. It's weird. Like I'm in another person's bedroom. Someone who has moved out or is attending university and I'm just visiting.

There's no decorations on the walls. I miss Niall's mother's paintings. Thinking of Niall, I check under the bed for dust bunny assassins. I also scan the room for hidden cameras without looking like that's what I'm doing.

No dust bunnies, but I spot one camera. I try really hard not to hate on my mom. She's worried about me and trying to do what she thinks is best. And I'm hoping that this crazy person she's turned into will eventually go away and my sensible, loving mother will return. In the meantime, I'm going to fix a few things.

I test out the softness of the bed. The sheets and my favorite blanket smell clean and fresh. It's been an exhausting day, so I lie down, rolling on my side so the camera's at my back. Then I connect to Q. I'm welcomed back. Not with words, but a general atmosphere of happiness. And no, I'm not sharing that with anyone. I've learned my lesson. My own emotions are mixed between a sense of rightness and guilt.

Tapping into the camera's feed, I check what part of my room it's recording—the bed and desk. At least it doesn't have an infrared sensor. I let it record me faking sleep. My first task is checking for any messages for me. There's three from Niall. One for each day I stayed past his guess that I'd be there only two days.

2522:251: Hey Mouse. I was wrong. I figured you'd be done by now, but you're either not cooperating or getting the full work up. Knowing you, I'd say they're doing a complete and thorough evaluation. Good. Then you'll have proof of your competency, and I'm willing to wait a couple extra days so you don't have to go through this again. But not too many days, Mouse. I miss you like crazy. Also dinners are excruciating. All my dad and your parents discuss is the base's security. No one mentions you. It's like there's this giant black hole in the middle of the kitchen that everyone edges around and ignores. Weird. I've asked if I can come visit you and the immediate answer of no was curt and dismissive as if I just asked to strangle a puppy. <rolls eyes> I don't know if you'll get this or not. I'm using a portable and it's not going through the Q-net so it wouldn't break your promise to read it. They have to let you access your personal messages… right? I did send you another message, but if you're being good, you won't see that one. You're curious now, aren't you? <smirk> Stay the course, you can see the message when you're back with us. Don't forget, you're Ara Yinhexi Mouse Lawrence, Refuses to Be Ignored. Love, Toad.

I laugh over the additional middle name and wonder if it would make a cool acronym. AYML. Uh, no. Then I wonder if I fess up to seeing the other message, if I'd get into trouble. I decide I don't care. Not anymore. What will they do? Put me in detention? At least I wouldn't have to go to soch-time.

2522:252: Hey, Mouse. I can't believe how much your absence is being felt and not just by me, but the rest of the security team as well. Elese is snapping at everyone. Morgan is gruffer than usual—I know, hard to believe. Beau is grumpy and tired—I think he's putting in extra hours in the Q-net. Even my dad. I catch him glancing at your room as if expecting you to come out and join us for dinner. And I keep thinking I'll see you in the hallway or in the training room or at Dad's only to be disappointed when you're not. At least I've been cleared for regular duty. I'm assigned to guard detention. I think my dad's afraid I'll freak out if I go back to the archeology lab since I almost died there. I believe I'll be fine, but I can't go until I touch a Warrior heart and I'm waiting for the one you promised me. You literally and figuratively have my heart, Mouse! Love, Toad.

Ha! I must admit to being happy that everyone is cranky. Perhaps Radcliff will talk some sense into my parents. I've warring emotions about Niall's heart. I took a Warrior heart for him from the factory, but then we received a warning of Jarren's attack so I'd set it down in the archeology lab and just haven't gone back there to retrieve it yet. He shouldn't wait for mine. If the HoLFs return, he'll need to see them to fight them. Although, I'm touched by his loyalty and his sentiment. Love you, too Toad.

2522:253: Wow, I didn't expect it to take this long! I hope you're okay, Mouse. Your parents won't tell me anything. Your Mom practically ripped my head off when I asked when you're coming back. I've a bad feeling about this. But no matter what happens, you're still mine. Okay, that sounded very possessive and maybe a little creepy, it's not. It's supposed to reassure you. I remember that you were worried that I'd break up with you because of your super Q-net power. Don't worry. I'm not going anywhere. If I have to sneak into the infirmary to see you, then I will. In the meantime, here's an update about the security team. Dad tried to interrogate Jarren again and got nowhere again. Beau's been working hard, trying to break through the security around the looters' base.

If I don't hear from you soon, I'm going to arm myself with a couple candy bars and attempt a break-in. I might have to bribe a nurse or two with the sweets, but I'm sure you'd rather see me than eat chocolate. Right? Mouse? Hello? Hmmm. You do have a serious sugar addiction. <searching frantically for more candy just in case> Love, Toad.

No surprise Jarren won't talk to "Officer Tight Pants." He hates the DES and won't give them anything. Niall's messages have soothed my soul and I compose one for him so he doesn't storm the infirmary.

2522:253: Hi Toad! I'm free! Well, not quite. I'm currently grounded and in my old room in my parents' unit. Go ahead, laugh. This is despite my clean bill of health from the very sweet Dr. Bharathi. She thinks my belief that the Q-net is sentient is a coping mechanism because of all the stress and trauma with Jarren, the murdering looter. I'm quite content with that diagnosis and plan to say no more on the matter. However, my parents are freaked out big time and have decided I need to stay out of the Q-net so my brain can heal. As you can tell, I didn't promise to stay out. They believe they still have the power to prevent me. It would have worked with Lyra. But Ara Yinhexi Mouse Lawrence refuses to play nice. Funny, that if it was an order from your father, I'd listen. Don't tell him that! And you'll get a bigger laugh out of this—I'm to report to soch-time tomorrow! Yes, my parents have gone insane.

Thanks for the messages, they were sweet and what I needed right now. And I did see your other... communication. Don't jump to conclusions. I was missing you and thinking about you when a photo of you popped up on the portable's screen. It was a shot taken from the camera feeds. It was from my unconsciousness—I didn't seek it or connect to the Q-net so I kept my word. I even offered to stay out of the Q-net if my parents allowed me to continue training and working with security. That was a big fat no. So here I am. If I'm still stuck here when I turn eighteen in sixty-one days, my status officially changes from grounded to kidnapped. You have my permission to grab Beau and Elese and come rescue me! I hope I'll be able to have visitors, but normally being grounded means no outside contact expect for soch-time. Yes, this isn't my first time. I miss you like crazy, too, Toad. I love you more than sugar, Your Mouse.

Satisfied with my message, I send it to Niall's portable since he can't access the Q-net because of his injury. Then I worm deeper into the Q-net, searching for Beau. And find him gently poking at the defenses around the looters' base.

You'll never get in that way, I say, popping up beside him.

Ahhh! What the hell? Ara you scared the bejabbers out of me. There's a pause. *What are you doing here? Are you allowed? Does Radcliff know?*

I came to help you. No. No.

Another significant pause. *You gave your word.* Disappointment weighs down his words.

I did and I kept it, enduring five days of no Q-net while I cooperated fully with the entire medical staff. Then my mother turned insane and decided to ground me despite Dr. Bharathi's diagnosis of, and I quote, "According to all the tests, Ara is completely healthy, both physically and mentally." It's something I'm never going to forget. I can send you all the test results if you want.

No. Don't. I trust you.

That's nice. I wish more people would. However, I did not give my word to my mother that I would stay out of the Q-net. You can decide if you want my help. Or if you want to inform Officer Radcliff. Or if you want me to go away.

And if I pick go away?

Then I'll find a way into the looter base without you. But it'll be boring without my partner.

And if I inform Radcliff?

I'll be sad and in trouble. I give him a mental equivalent of a shrug. And then I'll find a way into the base without you. Again, boring.

If I let you help, this isn't going to end well, he says.

Probably. But what's getting into trouble compared to figuring out what they have at that base? I'm willing to risk it. Are you?

Hell yes. Welcome back, partner.

We work for a couple hours, but the security around the looter base is super tight and I might have to fly with the Q-net in order to get inside.

Try again later? Beau asks.

Yes. It'll have to be late so my parents don't interrupt me. Does twenty-three hundred work?

Yup. See you then.

Dinner is an awkward affair. My parents try to engage me in conversation and explain their reasons for their decision. I respond with one-word answers. Afterwards, I bolt for my room. I plan to spend as much time in here as possible. Unpacking my bag takes all of three seconds. Niall's drawing goes next to my bed and I send him a quick message, asking if he'll lend me some of his other drawings so I can use them to decorate my room. He hasn't read my first one yet, but that's because he's on duty until twenty-one hundred.

I rummage in my desk drawer and find a deck of cards. Perfect. Sitting at my desk, I angle my body so the camera only sees the side of my face. I shuffle the cards and play solitaire. It's something I can do while touching base with Q. I can't go in too deep just in case Mom or Dad tries for another heart-to-heart. Good luck. Plus playing cards will appease my parents if they check the camera feed.

Accessing Q is just a matter of thinking about it. I check on security and catch up on what's been going on regarding the prisoners. They're not happy being forced to reconstruct the Warriors that they'd smashed into thousands of pieces. Too bad. Not sad.

Then I dip into the astrophysicists' notes regarding the shadow-blobs and that rift that is still in Pit 2. Seems Drs. Zhang and Carson are building another sensor to send through the rift. I wonder how they're going to collect the data. Can you communicate between dimensions? Would be interesting to find out.

A light tap on my door interrupts me. No way to avoid it, I grunt a "come in." My father pokes his head through the gap. The sweet smell of cookies melts some of my resolve to be surly and monosyllabic. Careful to avoid my cards—I'm just about to lose again—he sets the plate on my desk, but remains mostly outside.

"May I come in?" he asks.

"It's your unit. You can do whatever you want."

Dad presses his hand to his heart, miming shock. "Two full sentences."

I grunt. Stupid sugar addiction.

"Truce?" he asks.

The cookies are chocolate chip—my favorite—and they're

still warm. "Temporary."

"I'll take what I can get." He enters fully and peers at my game. "You want to play Sevens?"

I shrug before I remember the truce. "Okay." We pull the desk out and he grabs another chair so we can sit opposite each other.

Dad shuffles and deals the cards. I watch his deft fingers closely—the man likes to cheat. I concentrate on my hand, searching for the seven of clubs. We share the cookies as we play for a while in companionable silence. It's not horrible.

After ten minutes, he says, "Watching you fly away, clinging to that shuttle with an explosive on your back, and knowing I'd probably never see you again was the absolute worst thing I've had to endure in my life."

It wasn't a picnic for me either. But I clamp down on my sarcasm when I glance at him. Tears shine in his eyes. Oh no. Parental tears are lethal to snarky teenagers.

"The only thing keeping us from freaking out was your message. You were so brave and calm. Tace said you did the right thing by jumping on that shuttle, but it didn't feel that way at the time. I just wanted to do something to protect you. Tace promised to bring you back, but the wait was excruciating—the longest seven hours of our lives."

I sense where this is going.

"So you'll have to forgive us if we're rather clingy right now," he says. "We can't help it. Just give us some time."

"I understand being overprotective. It's your parental right. However, you've gone too far this time. Did Officer Radcliff tell you what he found when they landed at Jarren's base to rescue me?"

My dad gives me an I-know-what-you're-doing look, but he plays along and answers. "Jarren unconscious and you hiding in the trees."

"That's right. I still needed my team, but I rescued myself. The device was off. Jarren was drooling on the ground." I wait for that to sink in. "I proved I can handle myself. I'm capable of protecting myself. And yet, you, Mom, and Radcliff—"

"Tace disagreed with us."

Huh. Nice to know. "You and Mom didn't bother having a discussion with *me* regarding the Q-net. What does that tell me? I get that it's hard to believe that the Q-net is sentient, and perhaps it is a coping mechanism. However, it's not that you don't believe me that hurts, but the fact you don't trust me. That's what it tells me. You don't have faith in me."

"We..."

"I'm willing to give you some time. You and Mom can pretend we're a happy family for a few days or a few weeks. But as soon as the base is in danger, I'm going to help my team." And with that comment our temporary truce is over.

At twenty-two hundred, my mother enters my room without knocking. I'm changed into my pajamas, and am now trying to build a house of cards. Seems the task of adding on a second story is equally as frustrating as my parents. Mom holds a glass of water.

"Here." She sets the glass down and hands me two brown

pills. "Take these."

I drop them onto the desk. "No."

She gapes at me. "It's not a request."

"No." I meet her gaze. She doesn't scare me anymore. Not compared to shadow-blobs and murdering looters.

She's not quite sure how to handle this. Fun. I'm fascinated by her struggle to keep her cool.

After a huff, she says, "If you take your pills at night, I will allow Niall to come visit you."

Ouch, that's underhanded. As much as I'd love to see Niall, I'm not negotiating. "No deal. You had your chance for a compromise." Niall will be disappointed, but I know he'll support me.

Not expecting that answer, Mom jerks back. "If you don't take your pills I'll—"

"Ground me?"

She ignores that. "I'll send you to help in the kitchens washing dishes."

I call her bluff. "All right. It's better than being here."

Fury flashes in her eyes and I suck in a breath. Have I've gone too far? Mom grabs the pills and leaves. But I don't celebrate the win. My mother is smart and I'm sure there will be consequences. And sure enough, a few minutes later the lock on my bedroom door engages. Ah, yet another alteration to my old room. The door now only locks on the outside. I'm torn between outrage and amusement. And decide on humor. It's a petty revenge on my mom's part. Besides I'm not planning to sneak out...well, not tonight. After Jarren's invasion was thwarted, my parents changed the master code for the base. It'll only take me a few seconds to find it.

A couple minutes before twenty-three hundred, I get ready for bed. Then I slip under the covers and turn off the light. Beau's waiting for me in the Q-net.

Any trouble? he asks.

Some family drama. What do you think my odds are of being granted emancipation by DES?

He grunts. *That bad?*

Not really.

Good. Because by the time you get a response to your request, you'll be well past your eighteenth birthday. Hang in there, partner.

We worm to the looters' base and probe their defenses. I ask the Q-net to highlight the threads of the security programs.

Beau doesn't react to my request, but when the various colors snake through them, he says, *Stars. It's like a kaleidoscope. How are we going to make sense of that tangled mess?*

I suspect that's the point.

Uh, could you...ask...the Q-net...if there are any holes?

I can't keep the grin off my face as I make his request. Three bright circles of yellow glow. We move closer to get a better look. Could it be that easy? No. The circles are gaps in their security that have been heavily patched. We pick at the edges, hoping to peel the patches off.

Any chance the Q-net could just...make a tunnel? Beau asks.

CAN NOT.

No, I say because only I can hear Q. *We have to do it first, remember?*

But this thing is impenetrable.

Nothing's impenetrable. You taught me that, I say. *They have to be accessing the Q-net somewhere.*

After two more frustrating hours, we stop for the night.

Tomorrow? Beau asks.

I have schoolwork to catch up on in the morning and soch-time in the afternoon—don't laugh.

He chuckles. *Too late.*

I'm glad someone's amused. Are you going to be in the Q-net?

Yeah. All day.

I'll join you if I can.

And if you can't?

Then we'll have to meet at twenty-three hundred again.

A sigh. *Time's not on our side.*

Tell my parents.

Radcliff's tried. They're not listening to reason.

No surprise. We disconnect and, while I'm tempted to fly with Q, I'm also tired. I do the sensible thing and go to sleep. Mr. Sensible would be proud. I fall asleep thinking of Niall.

My mother wakes me at oh-so-early. More revenge for my defiance. After breakfast, I follow her into her office. Mom gestures me to her work table. She cleared a space and now there's a portable and a large screen on it.

"They're connected," Mom says. "So I can see that you're working on your assignments."

I'm impressed that she thought ahead and also angry over

the sheer waste of time. Sitting down, I cue up the first assignment. Her desk is right behind me so she has a good view of the screen. It's been a lifetime since I've done any school work. The microbiology worksheet is written in a foreign language. Well, foreign to me. I don't speak microbiology anymore. But Q does. I ask it to fill out the answers like it's me, but at a fifty percent slower pace since it's been a while. Q can go back into my school records and determine the exact timing. Answers start appearing on the screen. In my mind's eye, I go into the Q-net and search for Beau. But he's not entangled yet so I check my messages and there's a new one from Niall.

2522:254: Mouse! Getting your message made my day! And, yes, I laughed. Soch-time! Those poor kids have no idea what they're in for. I'm flattered you want to hang my pictures and I'll gather a few favorites for you. Hopefully, your parents will let me visit. I don't think I can last another sixty days without seeing you. Don't worry, we'll bust you out if we need to. It might be sooner rather than later. My dad's on edge and losing patience by the second. Beau hasn't gotten any info on the looters yet. We need someone to look at it from a different direction.

I stop reading. It hits me like an energy wave pulse. From a different direction. Why didn't I think of it sooner? With excitement pumping through me, I quickly finish reading Niall's message and send him a fast reply. Then I search for Beau again. He's entangled and I don't waste time on pleasantries.

I know how they're connecting to the Q-net, I say.

Don't keep me in suspense.
Through the Warrior portals!

2522:254

Beau doesn't reply so I keep talking. *The looters stole all those Warriors—the important ones with the alien symbols. They must have them set up so they can travel from planet to planet. Maybe the looters are using the portals for more than just travel. Maybe they're sending messages through them as well. It would make the messages impossible for us the trace back to the looters' physical locations.*

Also remember when I chased that worm who was targeting DES's high security areas? I lost it, but Chief Hoshi tracked it to Xinji—where there's no one. I don't add 'alive.' *With this portal communication, they could access the Q-net from a different planet and throw us off.*

You do realize that those portals haven't been proven to exist. Another long pause. *Is this something the Q-net told you?*

No. I came up with it on my own. Well, Niall helped.

Niall?

He said we needed to look at the problem from a different direction.

That certainly is different.

I'm not sure if his comment is a compliment or not, so I continue. *It would be easy to prove. We can open the portal in Pit 21 and see if I can access Q through it.*

In what universe? No one and, I mean NO ONE, is going to allow us to go to Pit 21 and wake the Warriors.

Then we should go without them.

There is so much wrong with that sentence, I'm not even going to reply. And I'm going to pretend you never said it. Think of something else, Ara.

You're no fun.

That level of trouble is not fun. Trust me.

"…Ara?" My mom's voice penetrates my concentration.

Oops gotta go. Later. I disconnect.

"Are you listening to me?" Mom asks.

I turn around. "Yes."

"Lunch is ready. How far did you get?"

I gesture to the screen.

She leans closer and peers at it. "Further than I expected." She aims her X-ray vision on me.

I wait. If she accuses me of using Q to help, she will be admitting that the Q-net is indeed responding to me as if it understands. Theoretically, I could have written an actual program to have the Q-net answer the questions, but that would have taken all morning.

Instead of accusing me of cheating, she says, "Better hurry, you don't want to be late for soch-time."

Swallowing my snarky reply, I go into the kitchen. Mom made me a couple thin sandwiches. Seems the rationing is affecting everyone. After lunch she insists on walking me to the socialization area. Every research base and colony has one or more, if there are enough children under the age of eighteen. Since all our education is through the Q-net, we are required by law to spend two hours together 'socializing', which we kids refer to as soch-time.

The area is colorful and soft. It's geared toward the younger kids, who often spend most of their day here while their parents are working, but there is a game room that the teens claim as their own for the two hours. When we enter, the babysitter…oops, the *facilitator*, brings me a portable. I have to sign the waiver that I understand all the rules of soch-time. At least I'm listed as Ara Lawrence.

My mother promises to return in two hours like I'm a four-year-old upset about my mommy leaving me with strangers. I shake my head at the ridiculousness of this entire endeavor.

The facilitator peers at me. "This is a rather…unusual situation, but we'll make the best of it." She straightens. "There's no one your age, but perhaps the girls in the game room will include you."

Not likely, they're four years younger than me. "I'm not really interested. Maybe I can help you, Miss—"

"Norris. Thank you for the offer, but this time is set aside for you to socialize. The kids have been…unsettled since we had to evacuate. So try not to stir them up."

I scan the room. Everyone is staring at me. Lovely. Not that there are that many kids—about twelve, plus the four in the game room. We're the first crew for this base so the population is small. There'll be more kids when the next Interstellar ship arrives with more personnel. If it does.

Yanking my mind from those dire thoughts, I find a comfy chair and wonder if Miss Norris has been told to ensure I don't connect with Q. Doubtful my parents would want to scare her with my freaky super powers. Instead, I watch the other kids. They've resumed their activities, but the kids in one particular group are stealing glances at me and elbowing each other. I recognize Rance's two sons and a few others. If I had to guess, I'd say they were all between the ages of eight to twelve A-years old.

I try to calculate how long it's been since I attended sochtime.

EIGHTY-THREE DAYS.

I flinch at the sudden words. I don't think I'll ever get used to that. But then I consider the number of days. That's it? I don't doubt Q, but that's not enough days for everything that has happened. Talk about a time dilation.

"Are you the girl who died?" a young boy asks me.

His friends hover behind him as if they dared him to talk to me. I expect smirks and giggles, but they're all quite concerned.

"Yes," I say. I'm not going to lie to them.

"Told you, Yong," a boy in the back row says.

"Shut up, Miguel," a girl snaps.

"Stuff it, Val," Miguel counters.

"But..." Poor Yong looks confused.

"But I was revived by the base's doctor." I grin. "I'm all better now." No need to scare them.

"Then why did they tell us you were dead?" another boy demands.

These kids are smart. "To keep the bad guys away."

"That didn't work," Miguel says.

Thank you, Mr. Obvious.

"Are the bad guys coming back?" Val asks.

"Are we gonna have to hide in the pits again?" Yong asks. His forehead is creased in concern.

"Nobody will tell us nothin'!" Miguel huffs.

"Are we gonna die?" another girl asks in a small voice.

Stars, hasn't anyone explained anything to these kids? I scan their expressions. Unsettled is putting it mildly. They're terrified.

Sensing the mood of her charges, Miss Norris hustles over. "This is not an appropriate discussion for soch-time, children. You need to talk to your parents about this." She shoos them to go back to their toys, but they remain in place. Defiance shines in all their gazes. Wow. A soch-time rebellion.

The woman appeals to me. Well, she widens her eyes at me in the standard plea for help. Body language is worth learning, people.

"I got this," I say with confidence.

Two of the younger kids start fighting over a toy and, after a moment of hesitation, she leaves to facilitate.

I gesture the kids around me closer. Leaning forward, I lower my voice. "Here's what you need to know. We've got the best security team in the universe right here." I jab my finger at the floor for emphasis. "That team is gonna do everything they can to protect us. However, if they tell us to go hide, then that's what we're going to do as fast as we can. You know why?"

"So we don't die?" the shy girl asks.

"That's the goal. To keep you all safe and to keep you from getting in the way. Hopefully, the bad guys won't come back. I'm not gonna lie, there is a small chance they will, so you need to be ready to move as fast as possible when the alarm sounds. Just by being in that pit, you're helping the security team."

There's a moment of silence as they all absorb the information. Did I just terrify them, making it worse?

"What else can we do?" Miguel asks.

"Yeah, we want to help," Yong says, and the others agree.

Huh. Their fear has turned into determination. "Do you want to learn some self-defense?" I ask.

The response is immediate and unanimous. Yes, they do.

"Okay, first a warning. Do *not* go seeking bad guys when the order to evacuate sounds. Do you understand?"

Nods. I wait.

"Yes."

"Good. It's called self-*defense* for a very good reason. Anyone know what that reason is?"

"To defend yourself?" the shy girl asks.

"Right. If someone attacks you, then you can defend yourself. But you don't go seeking a fight. Ever. Understand?"

"Yes!"

"And if you start a fight, you're out of the Soch-time Defenders Club." I hook a thumb over my shoulder. What? Every club needs a name.

The kids clear a large space and everyone teams up. My partner is the shy girl. I ask her name.

"Kuma," she says. Then adds, "It means bear."

"That's a great name."

She ducks her head.

"I'm going to help you release your inner bear, Kuma." Then I growl with my fingers bent like claws.

Surprised, Kuma looks up and I grin at her, showing my teeth. She laughs.

I spend the rest of soch-time teaching them how to break wrist and arm holds. Their laughter is loud enough that the girls from the game room come out to investigate. It doesn't take them long to join in.

Miss Norris pulls me aside at the end of soch-time. "I don't know if I approve of what you're doing with the kids. But…the atmosphere has changed and it's a life skill, right?"

"Indeed it is." I grin at her until I spot my mother waiting in the doorway for me. My good mood poofs just like a shadow-blob in the light.

Mom asks me all the stupid mom questions—did I have fun? What did I do?—I ignore them. Then she says I can spend the rest of the afternoon doing school work. Fine by me. I'll check on Beau.

We round the last corner to my parents' unit and my smile returns. Full force. Niall is standing in the hallway right next to the door to the unit. He's not in uniform. Bonus!

Mom marches up to him. "I've told you before, Ara isn't permitted to have visitors."

His relaxed posture stiffens, stretching him to his full height well above my mother. Of course, she doesn't back down. Not my mother.

"I'm not visiting," Niall says. He holds up a long tube. "I'm delivering this to Ara."

Mom snatches it from his hand. "Done. Now leave."

"Mom!"

She slams her palm down on the sensor, opening the door. Sweeping her arm out, she orders, "Come on, Ara. Inside."

Niall edges away. Oh no you don't. I move and step into his arms. He automatically wraps them around me, pulling me close, squeezing me tight. Heaven.

My mother is yelling something, but I couldn't care less. I'm drinking in Niall's scent and the feel of his body pressed against mine. I doubt I'll have the chance again.

I tilt my head back to stare into his blue-green eyes. "Miss you, Toad," I whisper.

His expression softens. Then I break away before my mother has a heart attack.

"Later, Mouse." He smiles at me.

The desire to kiss him slams in my heart, but I go inside the unit. Mom is livid and I'm getting lectured. I think. Instead of listening, I'm burning the image of Niall into my brain.

She waves the tube to get my attention. "What is this?"

I shrug. Mom opens it and pulls out sheets of paper. When she spreads them on the table, I understand. And my insides warm.

"They're Niall's drawings. He probably thinks I miss his mother's paintings."

Mom glances up and puts her hands on her hips. "That's quite a mouthful." She rolls up the pictures and returns them to the tube. "I'll see these get back to him."

And there's the punishment for hugging Niall. Worth it.

Pointing to her office, she says, "You have work to do."

That I do. Too bad for her, it's not filling out worksheets on the mating habits of Ignatuary birds on Planet Fuyang.

While Q fills out my worksheets onscreen, I search for Beau. He's not in the Q-net, so while waiting for him to pop up, I ask Q to go through DES's scientific databases for any mention of other dimensions. My friend Lan cracked the code to the aliens' symbols and learned that the aliens built and installed the Warriors on sixty-four exoplanets to protect us from demons from another dimension. Although Drs. Zhang and Carson said there's no proof of these dimensions, there has to be other scientists who have looked into alternate dimensions. Right? Regardless, it can't hurt to try.

Interesting that Q doesn't come back with an instant result. While it searches and does my homework, I open a new file and make some notes on what else I should be researching. After a few minutes, Q adds a file to my cluster. It's not that big. I scan it and there's some interesting theories about alternate dimensions and what's called the "multiverse," which is not just one or two dimensions, but an infinite number of them.

One of the scientists, Dr. Channon Koty, was able to manipulate the mathematical equations to show that an alternate dimension is theoretically possible with the current understanding of the laws of physics and quantum mechanics, but she was unable to prove it.

"I can't build a device or an engine that would 'open' another dimension," Dr. Koty wrote in her research notes. "I've read through the scientific principles behind the development of the Crinkler engine. The inventors were able to generate enough energy to pull space together, yet they can't tear it apart."

I stare at those last three words. Tear it apart. And my thoughts immediately go to the rift in Pit 2. That's a tear. It's also a gateway.

In any case, how did the rift get there? I assumed that once the Warriors were destroyed and stolen from Pits 1 to 4, that the HoLFs were able to enter our dimension or transport into our pits. Could the rift work like a Warrior portal? But instead of going from one planet to another it goes from one dimension to another? That might be possible. Or maybe the rift is what happens when you get a broken portal that doesn't go all the way through to another planet, but stops somewhere in between where the shadow-blobs live? Perhaps that's why it's not a nice neat doorway like the one that formed in Pit 21. Assuming the black rectangle that coalesced in the center of the gap of Warriors was a portal. I saw a man standing on the other side, but, once again, no one else did.

I really like that theory of the shadow-blobs living in the portal-verse. And there's a...warmth of approval from Q. When I woke the Warriors in Pit 21, they pulsed with a green light and I sensed they were pushing back the shadow-blobs to create a safe route. Maybe the aliens discovered a way to construct a passage through the shadow-blob dimension as a shortcut to another planet. No need to crinkle space in our dimension, just go into another one and pop out a hundred trillion kilometers away. Once a portal is opened, the Warriors must act as sentinels, keeping the shadow-blobs from crossing into our dimension. Of course, I've no proof of any of this.

I send Niall a quick message thanking him for the pictures and warning him of my mother's intentions to return them. By this time Beau is in the Q-net and, once I join him, he informs me of his plans to try to breach the looters' base again.

Won't work, Beau. That's a dead end for now, I say.

But Radcliff won't allow me to do anything else. He wants information on the looters.

I consider. *What type of information?*

Where they are, what they're doing, who they are. DES was unable to confirm the physical locations of Ursy Bear, Warrick Nolt, Fordel Peke, and Osen Vee. We've been assuming the super wormers are working with the looters, but we can't find any trace of them.

We can search for them.

How? DES was unable.

With a little help.

Oh. A pause. *Let's focus on something else for now. How about the suspected DES employees the Q-net flagged who might be working for the looters?*

I thought Q was still fixing the security holes in DES.

It is, but there's already a hundred names in the suspected-looter-colluder file.

Q must be multi-tasking. I suppress a giggle. The Q-net runs everything in the Galaxy, of course it's multi-tasking. However, finding colluders are important and I can search for the super wormers when I'm flying tonight. I add it to my flying To-Do list.

Okay. Where do you want to start? I ask Beau.

At the top. Those with the highest security clearance and deepest access are the most dangerous.

DES's board of directors—a multi-international group—meets both of those criteria. When the Q-net was first discovered and space travel beyond our solar system became possible, Earth's leaders elected people from all over the world to be a part of a new organization, the Department of Explored Space, so no one country could have a monopoly on space travel or colonizing exoplanets. There were more than a few issues, but after almost five hundred Earth years, they're a smooth-running machine. See? I paid attention during my history lessons.

We open the suspected-looter-colluder file. I'm relieved not to see any of the directors on the list. Not yet, anyway. After an hour or so of looking for illicit connections to the looters, I'm uneasy. It needs to be done, yet this seems like a big invasion of privacy especially when the person is not guilty.

What's wrong? Beau asks, sensing my hesitation.

I explain. *And it's taking forever.*

Unfortunately, many investigations are slow and tedious. And, yes, we're invading innocent people's private messages, but, remember, we all agreed that if we use the Q-net, that our interactions could be examined by DES security.

That reminds me. Has Radcliff been in contact with DES?

Yes, but it's very limited and only he's been communicating with them. We're worried the super wormers will find a way to intercept our messages.

"Ara, it's time for dinner," Mom says behind me and I almost jump out of my seat.

"Uh, okay, be right there," I say.

"Wow, five full words."

Ignoring her sarcasm, I grunt.

"That's better." She leaves.

Ara?

We're still playing house and dinner's ready. Let's work on this later?

I can't. I've guard duty in the pits. Tomorrow?

Okay. We disconnect.

After another awkward dinner, I bolt for my room to "play cards." There's a new message from Niall:

2522:254: It was so good to see you today, Mouse! I figured it was too soon for the dragon, oops, I mean your mother <smirk> but I couldn't stay away. I just *had* to see you! And I will treasure that hug. I hope you didn't get into too much trouble. I'll let the dragon cool down for a couple days before I "accidentally" run into you again. <wink> It'll be hard. I didn't realize just how much I enjoyed our evenings on the couch together— even when we only fell asleep—until they stopped. Sixty days and counting down. Love, Toad.

I laugh. The dragon is an apt description and the thought of seeing Niall again lifts my spirits. Instead of worming into the Q-net, I exercise and practice the kicks, blocks, and punches that Elese taught me. Being in better shape helped me so much when I clung to Jarren's shuttle, I don't want to lose my muscle tone. I was going to ask Q to show my parents a video of me sitting there playing hours of solitaire, but I don't. They need to know what my priorities are. And neither of my parents interrupts me to try to have a heart-to-heart—bonus! After a couple hours, I take a shower and go to bed.

Then I fly with Q. It's been a while so I spend some time swooping though the vast network, traveling trillions of miles in a heartbeat, balancing on the edge of the Galaxy, peering into the vast darkness. I'm not alone. Q flies with me, seeming to enjoy the company. I wonder how old Q is.

FOUR BILLION YEARS OLD.

Wait. You said you were the Milky Way Galaxy. The Galaxy is much older than four billion.

I ENCOMPASS THE GALAXY.

So you're as big as the Galaxy. Why did you claim to be the Galaxy?

I AM THE GALAXY. WITHOUT ME THE GALAXY IS JUST A COLLECTION OF SUNS, PLANETS, AND OTHER MATTER.

Oh. Like a body without a consciousness?

CORRECT.

Still, four billion years is a long time to be alive. It's hard to imagine. It also seems too old. When did life form on Earth? How long have you watched over us?

OVER THREE BILLION YEARS.

Yikes! Weren't we just simple bacteria back then?

YES.

Had to be super boring. What did you do before we became interesting?

HELPED THIRD NATION.

The aliens who built the Warriors?

NO. THEY ARE FOURTH NATION.

And us?

FIFTH NATION.

Wow, five different civilizations lived in the Milky Way Galaxy. Crazy. And I thought the Warriors were old. Hey wait! The Warriors are only two thousand and five hundred plus years old. If you were left behind, then you can't be four billion years old.

I AM ONE OF FOURTH NATION.

I'm one of fifth nation, but I'm not over three billion years old.

YOU ASSUME FOURTH NATION IS HUMAN. WE ARE NOT.

Q's right. I did assume. But that doesn't explain the age of the Warriors. It sounds like fourth nation was having trouble with the shadow-blobs well before then.

CORRECT. WHEN FOURTH NATION DECIDED TO GO BEYOND THE EDGE, THEY CHANGED THE SHAPE OF THE SENTINELS TO THE TERRACOTTA WARRIORS. THEY BELIEVED FIFTH NATION WOULD UNDERSTAND THE SIGNIFICANCE IF THEY RESEMBLED YOUR OWN GUARDIANS.

We're starting to understand now, but it might be too late. What about the other nations? One to three. Why couldn't they maintain the network?

THEY ARE GONE.

Did they leave like the fourth nation? Go beyond the edge of the Galaxy?

NO.

What happened to them?

EXTINCTION.

Yikes. The conversation just took a turn to the dark side, and while I'm still curious, I need to focus on our troubles before we go extinct. First thing will be to test the shadow-blob rift and see if my theory is right.

I fly back to our base and aim toward the rift. Perhaps I can see inside or travel into the shadow-blob dimension. Right before entering, I slam into an invisible wall. Pain vibrates through my body on impact, which is hard enough to knock me off my bed. I come to my senses on the floor as a headache throbs in my temples. What the hell was that?

Instead of answering, Q drops a file into my cluster. I open it and read:

He who fights with monsters might take care lest he thereby become a monster. And if you gaze for long in an abyss, the abyss gazes also into you. -Friedrich Nietzsche.

The combination of pain and the quote is a pretty effective warning. That's a hard no on entering the rift through the Q-net. I clamber to my feet. The throbbing takes on a sharp edge and I search for a pain pill. None in my washroom. Perhaps the kitchen. Except my door is locked. I rest my pounding forehead on the cool metal, cursing my mother. If I find and use the new override code, I'll tip them off to my activities. My anger increases as I realize, if there's a fire, I'll be trapped in my room. Not really, but they don't know that. Instead, I shuffle back to bed.

While lying there hoping for the pain to disappear, I consider the quote Q sent me. Interesting choice and about perfect for my life. It also means Q is reading human literature. That makes sense. Whatever's been stored in the databases of the Q-net must be a part of its knowledge.

I fall asleep thinking deep thoughts.

Once again I'm pulled from my comfortable bed at an unreasonably early time. My headache is gone, but I'm tired and cranky. The morning proceeds like yesterday, but after lunch, when I go to open the door to leave for soch-time, it doesn't recognize my hand print.

Mom, who's a step behind me, reaches to open it. She hustles out into the hallway, but I remain in place.

"Come on, you don't want to be late," she says.

I consider calling her out for endangering me, but if I ever decide to sneak out, having them believe I'm stuck inside will be beneficial. Instead, I follow her to soch-time.

My group of defenders are eager to learn more and the two hours fly by as we have fun. Well…perhaps too much fun. When I explain how effective a groin strike is, the kids dissolve into a fit of helpless giggles for far longer than necessary. Kids.

At the end of soch-time, my mother is there to escort me home. When we reach our unit, Officer Elese Keir is waiting there. My training officer and best friend is a welcome sight even though she's wearing her uniform, which suggests she might be here for an official reason. Actually, I wouldn't mind if she is here to arrest me.

The dragon flares her nostrils and smoke curls out.

Elese is not intimidated, but she is polite. "I'm not here for a visit, Dr. Daniels. I'm on my way to a late lunch. Just a lucky coincidence."

I cover my grin lest the dragon fry my butt. This is not on the way to the cafeteria from security.

"Hey, Rookie, I hope you're not getting soft," Elese says to me. "You worked too damn hard to build those muscles. I'd hate to have to whip your pampered ass into shape again."

"No you wouldn't. You'd love every minute of it."

She smirks. "True." Then she glances at the dragon, who glares back with her arms crossed. "You better come back," Elese says to me. "Mr. Orange Light misses you."

Aww. That's sweet. "I miss you, too."

Elese's rich laughter follows me into our unit. I spend that afternoon and evening working with Beau in the Q-net. We only find two compromised DES employees and it's not clear if they're working with the looters or another organization—scary to think there are other groups out to corrupt DES. The good news is we also dig out all of Lan's stolen research files, which Beau sends to my father.

After soch-time the next day, my mother and I encounter Officer Beau Dorey outside our unit. He is also not visiting.

"I'm tasked with checking the cameras in this part of the base, Dr. Daniels. But it's nice to see my partner after so long."

His comment warms my heart. "How is the investigation going?"

"Slow. I could use some more help."

My mother the dragon huffs thick smoke at Beau. "Officer Radcliff says you're doing just fine and have made plenty of progress. He's quite impressed by your efforts."

Beau glances at me. "Just think how blown away he'd be if I had my partner helping as well. We'd have gotten through the security around the looter's base by now."

That isn't quite true, but it's sweet of him to say so. We high-five before I'm ushered into my parents' unit.

At dinner that night, my father is gushing over the wealth of information about the Warrior symbols and hearts in Lan's research files. He's practically—no, he's all out—giddy. Beau gets all the credit and I get a see-he-doesn't-need-you smirk from my mother. That's fine with me. If they suspect I'm helping, they'll…I'm not sure what they'll do, but it won't be pleasant for me.

When soch-time concludes the following day, Rance is there to pick up his sons. Before I can leave he stops me.

"Scott and Trevar have been enjoying soch-time more since you've returned," he says.

The dragon is pleased, but I'm wondering where this is going, so I say, "I'm glad they're having fun." I am.

"I warned them you won't be here for long."

Nice. The puff in the dragon's chest deflates slightly.

"They were so upset that I wondered if you would consider offering self-defense classes to the kids once things settle down." In other words, when we're not in mortal danger.

That's a good idea. "I would enjoy that."

"Great." Rance's sons cling to their father's legs, one on each leg. He does giant monster steps down the hallway as he roars. They laugh as they swing forward, urging him to go faster. No wonder the man has thighs of steel.

The dragon is no longer pleased, and she hurries me through the hallways. Except Niall is waiting by the housing unit. The threat of full dragon fire is no match for my delight. I jump into his arms and he twirls me around.

I laugh. "Let me guess, you're not visiting."

"Wouldn't dream of it." He hugs me tight, blocking me from the dragon.

He gives me a quick kiss. Too quick! But something slides under my shirt behind my back. It's thin and I suspect what it might be. "No candy?" I whisper, pretending to be disappointed.

"Next time, Mouse." He winks then lets me go.

The dragon wastes no time yanking me into the unit. I'd laugh, but I've contraband under my shirt. I dash for my washroom to extract the picture. It's a pencil drawing of the entire security team, including me. We're standing all in a row like a united front. Behind Beau and Elese is the ghost of Ivan Menz, the officer who died saving my life. We all appear determined and focused. Underneath our boots are squished shadow-blobs and looters cower in fear in the bottom corners. I'm between Niall and Beau. And even though we're wearing our jumpsuits and weapon belts, if you look closely, Niall and I are holding hands. Even closer and you can spot the toad sitting on the top of Niall's flashlight. The mouse is harder to find. She's on my shoulder, between my neck and my braid hanging down. Both are wearing tiny crowns. The picture is titled, *Defending the Galaxy.*

I love it. And while I know it's supposed to cheer me up, tears well and spill. Once I rein in my emotions, I hang it on the inside of the washroom door where no one else should see it.

Every day after soch-time for the next five days, my mother and I run into yet another member of the security team. They give various reasons why they happen to be there. Ho was looking for another unit and got lost. He even asked for directions. Bendix was wearing a training uniform and said he was tired of running laps in security. The sweat stains on his tunic lent authenticity to his story. Morgan was checking on the repairs to the windows that were shattered when the missile exploded above the base. Even Tora—who hates me—found an excuse to not-visit me. And Vedann, who I have almost no interaction with other than at team meetings—I don't even know her first name—

JULIA.

Thanks. Julia said she was waiting for a friend. And…wait. I didn't jump when Q supplied information when I didn't ask for it. Huh. Guess I'm getting used to it.

On day six, we round the corner and Radcliff is waiting by the unit. I almost faint with surprise while the dragon shoots fire.

Unperturbed, Radcliff says, "I'm here on official business, Ming. I need to talk to you and Spencer."

Oh. I'm actually disappointed. The three of them go into the conference room and I head for my room. Perhaps I can get a nap in while they're talking. Except my luck just isn't that good. Twenty minutes later there's a knock on the door.

Dad pokes his head in. "Your presence is required."

Required. Interesting word choice. Curious, I follow my dad to the conference room. The dragon is furious and I glance at the walls expecting scorch marks. Radcliff's tense and Dad is concerned. I'm gestured to sit in a chair facing the three adults across the table.

Oh boy this is bad. Beyond bad. They've found out I've been in the Q-net. I sink into the chair as the muscles in my legs liquify. Clutching the chair arms, I dig my nails into the upholstery and brace for the accusations.

"Miss Lawrence, I'm here at the request of DES," Radcliff says.

I note he said miss and not, Junior Officer. A part of me mourns, while another is trying to figure out why the DES would send Radcliff. They don't have the skills to uncover my activities in the Q-net. I'm not bragging, just stating a fact.

He sets his elbows on the table and leans forward. "DES would like you to talk to Jarren."

2522:263

I rock back as if I've been slapped. DES wants *me* to talk
to Jarren? Everyone waits as I chase my chaotic
thoughts. "Why?"

"I'm not having any success in getting information from
him. DES believes that you might have more luck."

"Did they *not* read the reports where he's tried to kill me
twice?" I ask.

Mom shoots me a you-go-girl look before returning to
staring venomous death at Radcliff.

Radcliff ignores my comment. "They believe your
relationship will make him more willing to talk."

I refrain from repeating my earlier question. "I can't do
anything. I'm grounded."

"DES has…overruled your parents on this matter."

Oh wow. That explains my parents' reactions. "Is it an
order?"

He meets my gaze. "No. It's a request."

My choice? I consider it. The thought of seeing Jarren again sets my stomach spinning.

When the silence stretches, Radcliff says, "There will be armed officers in the room with you. And he'll be secured."

"That's the wrong thing to do," I say. "If I'm to have any chance of getting him to open up, it has to be just us, no restraints, and no recordings."

"No." Mom hops to her feet. "That's too dangerous."

I sigh. Still no trust. "I didn't say no weapons. I'll have a pulse gun with me."

"Does this mean you'll do it?" Radcliff asks.

Every cell in my body pushes on me to say absolutely not. "Yes."

Radcliff nods as if he'd known my answer all along. He stands. "Let's go."

"Now?" A cold wave of dread washes over me.

"The sooner the better, Miss Lawrence."

Mom jumps to her feet. "We'll come with you."

Before being grounded, I would have been relieved to have them nearby. "No need."

"But you'll be by yourself and Jarren..." She can't say it.

Frustration eclipses my fear over the upcoming encounter. "You still don't get it. Do you?" I ask, but don't wait for an answer. "I won't *be* alone. I'll be surrounded by my team. All those people who did *not* visit me over the last nine days." I glance at Radcliff. His expression radiates approval. "All I have to do is shout, and they'll be in that room in seconds."

"Nanoseconds," Radcliff corrects.

We share a smile. I follow him from the conference room. But when we reach the door it won't open. He raises an eyebrow at me. I give him a don't-look-at-me half shrug. Mom hurries to open it and, for once, the dragon is nowhere to be seen.

"That's endangerment, Ming," Radcliff growls. "Fix it before we return or I'll assume responsibility for Ara."

She nods and we leave. We walk for a while in silence. I debate if I should tell him that she locks me in my room at night. Would he assume responsibility of me then? Do I want him to? Up until this unpleasantness, I'd been living with him. It was an adjustment at first, but I prefer to stay with him. A surprise—I know! Except, I won't get my parents into trouble. Despite all this crazy nonsense, I still love them.

"Do you have a room that will work?" I ask Radcliff.

"There's an empty office in security. There's a Q-net terminal, but it's never been connected. We'll bring in a table and a couple chairs while you change into your uniform."

"No uniform." I gesture to my jeans and T-shirt. "This will be better."

"What about your weapon?"

I consider it. "Can we secure it to the underside of the table? On my side," I quickly add.

"Out of sight but not out of reach?"

"Exactly."

We share another smile. Huh. Could we be having a moment?

"I looked into gaining custody, Ara, but there was nothing I could legally do," he says.

Niall told me, but hearing it from him means so much more. "I know." Then I jab him in the arm with my finger. "Just don't be surprised when I show up to help the team when things go sideways."

"I'd be surprised if you didn't."

Radcliff wasn't kidding when he said the office was empty. Only a light blue carpet breaks up the white walls.

"This is supposed to be Morgan's office, but since she's on the night shift most of the time she prefers working in mine," Radcliff says.

Bendix and Rance help set up the room. They give me big smiles of hello as they carry in the small rectangular table and two plush armchairs. I show Bendix where to secure my pulse gun. Is it weird that I missed my weapon? That I have to squash the desire to croon to it as if it's a baby when I see it? Probably.

We test if they can hear me on the other side of the door so I know just how loud to yell if Jarren attacks.

"Can I borrow your portable?" I ask Radcliff when the two officers leave to fetch Jarren from detention.

"Why?" he asks.

I wonder if he doesn't trust me, or it's just his habit to question everything. Probably the latter. "Don't worry, I won't be worming. It's a prop."

He goes to retrieve it. When he returns and hands it to me, he asks, "What's your plan?"

"I don't have one."

"But…" He sweeps an arm out. "You've been very insistent about this set up."

"That's because if it was me being questioned, this is how

I'd want it. More relaxed. No one recording every twitch and vocal inflection."

"You know anything he tells you can't be used in a court of law. It's his word against yours."

"Do you want answers or evidence?"

"Both." His frustration is clear. "But I'll take answers." A pause. "You know what information we need?"

"I do."

"Good. Officers Rance and Bendix will be right outside the door and will enter with weapons drawn if you need them." Radcliff leaves before Jarren can spot him. No need to put Jarren on guard. Well, he'll be wary, but hopefully not too much.

I hop up on the table and sit cross-legged. Focusing on the portable, I try to distract my frantic heart with cool logic. Nothing is going to happen. Jarren can't do anything. Even if he were to find my weapon, he can't use it on me. Despite this, my heart tries to escape my body via my stomach.

Then I try to plan out my questions, but it's impossible to know what he would be willing to tell me even without a camera recording him. A strange thought invades my mind. Could Q record him through me? Using my eyes and ears?

YES.

A shudder rolls through me. Super creepy is putting it mildly. I'd never... Or would I? Jarren is a murdering looter, I don't have to be honest. *Do it, please*, I say to Q. I brace for weirdness in my head, but nothing changes. At all. Even scarier.

The door opens, distracting me—thank the universe—from my freak out. Bendix and Rance escort Jarren into the room. His wrists are secured behind his back, but a wide grin spreads on his face when he spots me on the table. Fear climbs my throat, leaving a dry bitter taste in my mouth.

"Officer Tight Pants must be desperate to try this." Jarren chortles with glee.

Bendix removes the handcuffs, and says, "We'll be right outside."

Yes, they will. And I trust my team with my life. I channel my inner guardian lion and settle my nerves. I hop off the table and hand Bendix the portable. "Thanks, guys."

Jarren smirks at me once we're alone. His beard is ungroomed and bushy, and his shoulder-length hair is straggly and greasy. He's wearing a neon green detention jumpsuit. The bright color is guaranteed to be seen from orbit. He's twenty-one A-years older than me and has been very busy murdering and looting during those years.

I sweep my hand out, gesturing to the room. "There are no cameras or microphones in here. The Q-net terminal is disconnected and there's no portable." I pull back my hair and expose my ears. "No tangs. Whatever you say in here can't be used against you." Tipping my head to the chair in front of the table, I say, "Have a seat."

He sits then shakes his head. "You know this won't work. There's no way I can trust you. You tricked me. Twice."

I plop in the seat behind the table. "You deserved it. You tried to kill me. Twice."

Leaning back, he laughs. Eventually, his humor fades as he stares at me and he looks rather puzzled. "Stars, you're so young." He wipes a hand over his face. "I knew you were smart and a fast learner, but where in hell did you learn how to worm like that?"

His question gives me an idea. "How about a deal? I'll answer your questions if you answer mine."

"Quid pro quo? Is that your grand plan?"

"I don't have a plan. I shouldn't even be here with you, but, you were right. DES is desperate."

"I reserve the right not to incriminate myself."

"All right. To answer your question, I learned how to worm *like that* from Chief Hoshi, the chief navigator of the Interstellar Class space ship that brought me to Planet Yulin. I did an internship while on board and she taught me how to navigate the star roads."

"*You* did an internship?" Jarren doesn't sound convinced.

"That is your second question. And, yes, I did." I huff, but then grudgingly admit, "It was to keep me occupied and out of the brig."

"Ah, that makes more sense." Then he pauses. "Still doesn't really explain the level you achieved in such a short time."

"As you said, I'm smart and a fast learner. Plus I was motivated. Now it's my turn. Why did you target certain Warriors?"

He tsks. "You know why. Ask me something harder."

"Why would I know?" He shouldn't know that I suspect the reason for the Warriors. No one has sent my theories to DES.

Now he sighs. "Because you managed to put together enough information from Lan's research files, which you shouldn't have done since I sent you bits and pieces of crap." He peers at me, giving me the I-know-there's-something-you're-not-telling-me squint.

So he was monitoring us since the beginning. "I only have a theory."

"Well, there's your answer." He shakes his head. "I bet no one believes you." Now he laughs. "It is rather unbelievable and hearing it from a kid…" Another chuckle.

I bite down on my I'm-not-a-kid retort as it lacks the proper snappiness. I change tactics instead. "Did you figure out how the Warriors worked before Lan, or did she share her results with you?"

"When I contacted her after my lengthy stay in detention on Planet Suzhou and she shattered my heart, she felt bad." He gave a sardonic pout. "So she shared her research with me—as a we-can-still-be-friends move. At the time she hadn't made any big discoveries and I actually helped her with a few connections. Until I figured out the true purpose of the artifacts and uncovered the factory." He taps his chest right above his heart. "Then she was on her own. Took her *years* to catch up to me and I may have…" He spreads his hands. "Sent her a few false leads along the way."

Except for the false leads, his explanation is as we suspected. "But you weren't alone. You had help from Ursy Bear, Osen Vee, Fordel Peke, and Warrick Nolt. Right?"

"Yes. They are the real criminals. I was duped and forced to be a part of their team."

There's a gleam in Jarren's eyes. No doubt he's lying. And laughing at me. I'm missing something. It's important. I mull over what I know of Jarren. Then it hits me.

"They don't exist," I say. "They're all pseudonyms. They're all you!"

"Don't be ridiculous." But it's weak and unconvincing. He gives me a hard stare.

"How did you change your style? Some of those programs are amazingly complex. No way only one person could construct them." Or rather, one person without the help of the Q-net.

He's pleased by the flattery, which is more evidence I'm right, but he says, "I believe it's my turn to ask questions. Did you find the factory before or after those looters broke into the pits?"

"Before." And because I can't resist, I add, "I was sitting on the hatch when you first arrived. I'd covered it before you finished drilling through the walls."

"Not me." Although his gaze sears my skin with its intensity. "I wasn't there, but it sounds like the person in charge should have killed you then and saved themself a lot of trouble."

"He wasn't very bright," I goad. "How did you get so good at worming in the Q-net when DES was keeping an eye on you?"

He pauses as if weighing how much to tell me. I wonder if his ego is warring with his tendency to brag. Young Jarren would brag.

"You had your Chief Hoshi. I had mine. And once you really put your *heart* into getting better, it's just a matter of time. Years, actually, doing nothing else. Which is why your new skills are so suspicious. Perhaps Officer Tight Pants should be investigating you."

I choke on a laugh. "I was on probation, remember?" But I consider his comments about the hearts. Could it be that touching a Warrior heart makes you better with the Q-net? That's something we can test.

"My turn. How did you defeat Lan's demons?" he asks.

It takes me a moment to connect Lan's demons to the shadow-blobs. I can't think of a reason not to tell him. We won't be able to trick his people with a fake shadow-blob ambush again. So I tell him how we figured it out and built the emitters. "It was a team effort."

He grunts, clearly unhappy that we saved everyone on the base. At least we saved them, for now. It's a good reminder that he's a murdering looter. He has lots of blood on his hands, including Lan's.

"Did you know you would be allowing Lan's demons into our dimension when you started destroying Warriors?" I ask.

"*I* didn't destroy Warriors, but I can speculate on the reasons why someone might. Warriors are heavy and hard to transport without breaking. *The looters* only needed certain ones for their plans. In order to reach those, they had to clear a section through and around other ones before grabbing the vital ones. It didn't seem dangerous at the time. There are a number of collapsed pits on the twenty-two Warrior planets and no signs of demons in any of them."

Jarren picks a stray piece of lint off his pants. "When the looters started their plans, they targeted the closed Warrior planets where no one would know what was going on. Also there wasn't a need to destroy any Warriors on those planets. They didn't have to be fast. There was no one there to stop them. Those satellites are a joke. Easy to worm into, as you know."

I sense where this is going. "But then you focused on the ten active Warrior planets."

"Yes. The plan for the active planets was to steal only the

important Warriors from a few pits for the network—they could get the others later. They started with Xinji, but realized, with Lan in the base, she'd figure out why only certain Warriors were taken, so they destroyed all of them."

Oh. So he didn't purposely release the shadow-blobs on Xinji. Good to know.

He rubs his face again as if wiping away the memories. "*The looters* didn't realize what was happening until Xinji started sending alarming reports about a serial killer. The looters returned and spotted Lan's demons, but there was nothing they could do to stop them."

"Except maybe warn the scientists. Help them evacuate!" I can't keep the outrage from my voice.

The door opens and Bendix sticks his head in. "Fifteen-minute check. Is everything okay?"

"Yes," I say even though I'm not okay. How could he do that to Lan? Bendix closes the door. "You wanted them all to die?" I ask in a calmer voice.

"I wasn't there, but I would guess there was a meeting among the looters and their backers about what to do. They decided that it would be easier to access the Warriors if the research bases were empty."

"Easier? Easier for you to kill all those people!"

Jarren frowns. "Not us. Lan's demons—the aliens."

That was his first slip-up, saying us and not them. "So you used the demons to do your dirty work and attacked Yulin next. Then Taishan, Wu'an, and Ulanqab."

He looks at me in surprise.

"What's next? Ruijin? Qingyang? Pingliang? Nanxiong? All

four? That's fourteen hundred more people and children for you to kill."

Rising from his seat with his hands in fists, he stares at me. I keep my hands on my lap. If he so much as twitches in my direction, I'm going to grab my weapon. But after a few seconds, he settles back in the chair.

"What about Suzhou? Did you…" But then I remembered he'd been on Suzhou when he discovered the Warrior hearts and true function of the Warriors. Did he steal a heart, or have to sneak around to wake the Warriors? That would have been hard. So he recruited co-conspirators—only the techs and archeologists work in the pits. I snap my fingers. "That was your first base of ops. Are we to assume everyone there is working for you?"

"It's my turn to ask questions." His voice is flat and hard.

Pleased about guessing right, I lean back.

"After the satellite over Yulin was destroyed, how did you know *the looters* were coming to the research base? They were on the other side of the planet, which I'm sure Officer Tight Pants figured out from the missile's trajectory, but they flew in so they wouldn't be spotted by the field teams until too late."

Oh no. A question that is difficult if not impossible to answer. I can't tell the full truth, but I can't lie, so I improvise. "We had someone watching your base."

"Who?"

Q. "I don't know. Officer Radcliff's in charge of security. He warned us there were 'incoming shuttles,' and we put his plan into action." And it was a thing of beauty, too. Until I was caught, but that had nothing to do with Radcliff's genius strategy. Before Jarren can ask another question, I say, "You must have quite the network set up. Lots of people and benefactors footing the bill. How did you manage to keep all your activities under wraps for so long?"

"There are three words that keep everyone quiet because they know once we have the network set up, we'll own the Galaxy."

Another slip. His megalomania is showing. It doesn't take me long to figure out those three words. "No time dilation."

He frowns. "And it would have stayed quiet if you had kept your promise the first time and come with me. With your worming skills, you would have been highly prized in our organization. You stood to earn millions of credits." Anger flares in his brown eyes. "Instead, you escaped and told Officer Tight Pants about me. According to DES, I'm supposed to be on Suzhou—forty-two E-years away." He grins but there's no humor in it. "Unless you think I look really great for an eighty year-old? No?" He sighs. "One mistake. One fucking mistake, but we still kept it from DES until—how in the hell did you break through my blockade?"

"I followed you."

He fists his hands again. "No way you could have. Even a navigator couldn't get through without years of experience."

"I had help."

"Who? That idiot Dorey? He's like a fat caterpillar trying to squeeze through a screen door."

"He is my partner and a damn fine wormer," I say hotly.

"Yeah? Well good luck trying to reach DES now." He's smug.

"It doesn't matter. The damage is done. DES knows about you and what you've been doing."

He doesn't reply. If anything he appears even smugger. Is that a word?

"Oooh," I draw out. "Did you think your colleagues stopped that information from spreading beyond our initial contacts in DES?"

His smug expression fades as uncertainty creeps in.

I tap a finger on my chin as if thinking. "Hmmm...it's possible they did. Which means it's a good thing we reestablished communications with DES."

Jarren's on his feet. "Nasty trick, but I'm not falling for it, Lyra."

"My name is Ara. You killed Lyra, remember? And I'm not lying. But your confidence that we couldn't breach your blockade a second time tells me that you have a couple navigators on your payroll." I'm guessing, but only they would have the skills.

Jarren lunges for me with his hands outstretched. Without thought, I yank my pulse gun from the holder underneath the table and aim it at him.

He jerks to a stop thirty centimeters from me. "You lied to me. Again."

"I didn't lie. I said no cameras, microphones, connected terminal, portables, or tangs, but I never said no weapons."

Jarren straightens and crosses his arms. "This interview is over."

But I have one last question. "You told me before that you don't want DES to win. That you'd do anything so they don't.

Because of you, hundreds of people have died, and you've endangered the entire Galaxy. Did you ever consider that it isn't DES that would win, but the *entire human race*? That you could have been a hero? That everyone would have respected and adored you for being a part of the discovery of the century?"

He refuses to answer.

"Now Lan will be that hero and you'll be a murdering looter rotting away in detention for the rest of your life."

"And you?"

"I won't be grounded anymore." I hope.

He laughs. "How humble. You paint a nice picture, *Ara*. But you haven't won. The looters might be experiencing a setback, but it's too late for DES to do anything. My incarceration is temporary. You should enjoy your time with your parents while you can."

Logically, I know he's just trying to scare me. Emotionally, he's doing a good job of it. I swallow down my fear. "Do you really think your looters will rescue you? You lost sixteen people after your first attack, and fifty-one after your second—both of which were utter failures. Why would they risk more of their own people? Are you even valuable to them anymore? They know how to use the Warriors."

"You've no idea how valuable I am."

Spoken like a true megalomaniac. "Because of the super worming thing? You don't think your navigators can do it, even though *they* taught *you*?"

No response.

I snap my fingers. "Oh, I get it now. You're valuable because only *you* know how to worm through the Warrior portals."

Another guess.

His reaction is instant. Diving over the table, he tackles me. I shout as we hit the floor. My pulse gun is wedged between us and I can't press the trigger. Jarren's hands are wrapped around my neck. His expression promises murder as my air cuts off.

2522:263

Jarren presses his thumbs into my neck, squeezing my windpipe closed. Then Bendix and Rance appear behind him. They each grab one of his arms and yank him off of me, pulling him away. They force him to the ground and secure his hands behind his back. The speed of their counterattack is impressive. I suck in great gulps of air.

"Are you okay?" Rance asks. His knee is in the small of Jarren's back and he's leaning on Jarren's shoulders, pressing him down even though Jarren isn't struggling to get up.

"Yeah," I croak as Bendix helps me to my feet. I rub my shoulder and the back of my head. The pain isn't as sharp as it could have been. Yay for carpets.

Radcliff arrives and scans the room. Both chairs are lying on their sides. "What happened?"

"Jarren took offense to the fact that he's not as valuable as he thinks he is," I say. My voice still has a bit of a rasp.

Radcliff's laser focus is on my throat and his inner guardian lion just about roars. "Did he hurt you?"

"No." Although I wonder what Radcliff would do if I'd said yes.

"Take him back to detention," Radcliff orders Bendix and Rance. After Jarren is gone, he says to me, "We need to debrief."

Ugh. But it's a necessary evil so I trail him to his office. Except when we're there, I spot his extra terminal and stop. Q would be able to give him an exact transcript.

"What's wrong?" he asks.

"I've a good memory. Can I access the Q-net and put everything I remember into a file for you?"

"Your parents instructed me not to allow you to use the Q-net."

I give him the let's-be-real look. "Fine. How about I use your portable then?" If we're all going to pretend I can't access the Q-net anywhere, then this is a nice work-around.

"All right." He hands me his portable.

I sit in front of his desk with it in my lap. "This might take a while."

He makes a noncommittal sound then stands. "I'm going to get some coffee. You want some?"

"Love some!"

"No caffeine when you're grounded?"

"Nope. And no sweets either, unless my father is trying to bribe me. Being grounded is a punishment after all."

"How's it compare to probation?"

I glance up at him. There's amusement in his gaze. "Do you think you can arrange for me to be on probation again?"

He smiles. "Do you think I can catch you illegally worming again?"

Not anymore, but I suspect that's not the reason he's asking. "Only if I let you. Do you think my parents would allow me to be on probation?"

His amusement fades. "No. Not yet. Maybe in a few weeks."

"Do we even have a few weeks?"

"I think so. The longer they wait, the more we'll relax—or so they'll think. They're going to be more cautious since we beat them twice. But that's for me to worry about. I'll be right back."

"Take your time," I say just to make him smile. After he leaves, I access the Q-net and ask Q to please transcribe the interview with Jarren.

VIDEO?

No. Just what we said. Thanks. It'll be too creepy for both of us if I share the video.

Q fills a file with our conversation and I add in my thoughts and impressions. Radcliff—taking more time than grabbing a couple cups requires—returns and the heavenly smell of coffee reaches me. He sits behind his desk and hands me a steaming mug. Ahhh. He's content to sip his coffee while I finish the file. When it's done, I hand him the portable.

"There's a file with the transcript," I say.

Now it's my turn to sip my hot beverage as he reads through the file. I watch his expressions over the rim of my mug. Is he going to get mad that I obviously used the Q-net to put together the report?

When he's done, he leans back and taps his finger on the portable's screen. "How accurate is this transcript?"

"It's exact. I've a really good memory."

"Uh huh. Then how come you couldn't remember to put

your boots away when you lived with me? I must have tripped over the damn things a dozen times."

"I missed you, too."

He barks out a laugh, surprising us both. Then he glances at the portable again. "Your interrogation style was rather…unique. I'm not sure about telling him how to defeat the HoLFs, but can't see the harm since his colleagues can worm into DES to get the information anyway. I am surprised he said as much as he did." Radcliff drums his fingers on the portable. "Seems Jarren supports your theory about the Warrior portals. I don't think I've gotten better with the Q-net since touching the heart, but I'll ask the rest of our team."

Our team! Those two lovely little words warm my insides.

"Officer Dorey, though, has improved. Quite a bit." He squints at me.

I try to appear innocent. Not my best look. "Perhaps you should assign him to search for those navigators working with Jarren."

"Was that a guess, or do you know something?"

"A guess. As far as the Q-net is concerned, the navigators have the deepest access and the most experience with all aspects of the Q-net." Well…not *all*. "He created those other super wormers to cover his tracks. He's obviously a prodigy with the Q-net."

HE IS A DAGGER IN MY SIDE.

I can't help it, I laugh.

"And that's amusing to you?" Radcliff is not amused.

"No. It's scary. I just…it's just…" I clear my throat. It's sore. "The Q-net dislikes him." There I said it. I meet his gaze. Is he going to call me crazy?

Radcliff doesn't say anything for a long time. Finally he says, "The Q-net has good instincts. What about your comment at the end? The one that caused Jarren to attack you. Was that another guess?"

"Yes. Officer Dorey and I had such a hard time worming a way into the looters base. And while I've been grounded, I've had lots of time to think. It makes sense if they didn't leave any gaps between their base and the Q-net, that maybe they were using the Warrior portals to communicate." I rub my neck. "His reaction confirmed it."

"Yes. There's quite a bit of information to dissect. I suppose you would want to open a Warrior portal and test it out."

"Yes. And Beau and I might be able to find out what the looters are planning to do. If we know when their next strike will be, we—"

Radcliff raises his hand. "One thing at a time."

"Time is no longer on our side, Officer Radcliff."

"I understand, but I won't risk people's lives without a damn good reason." He gets a faraway look on his face. "I suppose you'll want to go back to Pit 21."

"No. Pit 21 goes to Planet Dongguan and the looters are there. I think we should find a pit that connects to another active Warrior planet like Ruijin. We can send the archeologists a message and warn them to expect us."

Radcliff has this strange pained expression. "We wouldn't even know which of our pits goes to Ruijin. We haven't opened them all yet."

PIT 39.

I swallow. Do I tell him? He seemed okay with Q not liking Jarren. Unless he was just playing along. "It's Pit 39."

Another super long pause. "And which pit on Planet Ruijin would we arrive in?" He asks very slowly.

PIT 9.

"Pit 9."

Radcliff inserts his tangs and focuses on the screen on his desk. He's checking my answer. Which means he'll need to access the chart Niall and I created when we worked on matching the alien symbol combinations to Warrior planets. I ask Q to help him along or else this might take a while. The file is in my mother's Q-cluster. Draining the rest of my coffee, I wonder if I could get another cup. Or maybe I should visit Beau. His office is just through the door on the left.

"Pit 9," Radcliff says. Then he disentangles and stares at me. Hard. "My Q-net skills have suddenly improved, and you must have a really good memory."

I try a smile. It's weak. "I do."

He heaves a sigh. "I'll consider your plan."

Progress!

"In the meantime, I'll escort you back to your parents."

All good feelings drain out of me. "Already?"

"It's almost dinner time."

I perk up. "We still have much to discuss about Jarren's comments. It's something we can talk about over dinner. Please? My mom's cooking is not as good as yours. No one's is."

"Uh huh. Do you think appealing to my ego will work?"

"Did it?" I'm hopeful.

He softens. "Come on. I'll make your favorite Italian dish."

Yay! Wait. "How do you know my favorite?"

"By how clean your plate is when you've finished your *third* helping. And the way your face lights up when I serve it."

"Wow, you're observant. Perhaps you should consider a career in law enforcement."

"Smart ass," he says, but it's more a term of endearment than a barb. "And it'll be nice to get more out of Niall than one-word answers."

Now I'm giddy. Seeing Niall is a bonus! We hurry to our unit so Niall doesn't spot me and ruin the surprise. Radcliff sends a message to my parents to avoid them showing up and demanding my return. They're not invited to dinner, but instead are told all is well and to expect me around twenty hundred hours.

I help Radcliff make dinner. Well, I fetch ingredients and turn on the oven. There's a few things from my talk with Jarren that are replaying in my mind. Along with some of Radcliff's comments.

After he puts the manicotti in the oven to bake, I ask him about the looters' base. "Are you going to send someone to watch the looters? In case they send another wave of soldiers to attack us."

He leans on the edge of the counter. "Should I? The last time you had an alarm set up with the Q-net."

True. "But now you know…"

Radcliff waits for me to finish. Typical.

I take a breath. "You know there can't be a program to sound an alarm if there's no way inside their communications. Plus our satellite is gone. That alarm…was just Q letting me know we had incoming."

"How do you know it's not part of the program you wrote to keep you safe from Jarren? The one that erased you from the camera feeds?"

That's a big stretch. However, if that's what he wants to focus on, it's better than thinking I'm crazy. Still. "You trust it?"

"I trust you."

My legs lock in place, which is a good thing. Talk about unexpected. "Thanks."

He pierces me with one of his Chief of Security stares. "Don't let me down."

"Yes, sir."

Radcliff nods then heads to his room to get some work done before dinner. I go to my bedroom to drink in the colorful works of art Niall's mother painted. They're soothing to my soul. My uniform is lying on the bed where I'd left it fifteen days ago. I run a finger over the embroidery, tracing my last name.

The strange sense that I'm standing on an edge, looking down from a great height unbalances me. I sit on my bed. Two-thirds of a year ago, I was on Xinji, whining about staying behind and having no clue what I really wanted to do. Other than a career as a criminal mastermind. Becoming a security officer was not on my list. And now I'm sad because I can't be one until I turn eighteen. Times have certainly changed.

Although being a navigator is still very appealing. Except… If we stop the looters, then DES can take over their Warrior network. It'll change everything. Though I wonder if traveling through the Warrior Express would be as easy as stepping from one side to the other. Would a person need to touch a Warrior heart first in order to travel? Or would they need a navigator? If not, would the navigators be upset to no longer be needed? They have a stressful job, but there's no comparison to the awesomeness of navigating the star roads. Thinking of the navigators, I wonder if Jarren's navigators are just biding their time, waiting for the perfect moment to sabotage the Warrior Express. After all, those Warriors are fragile. And that leads to the question of why there are so many in one pit if you only need the eight key Warriors to go to another planet.

PROTECTION.

From the shadow-blobs?

YES.

But the looters have been using the portals with only the eight Warriors. Right?

YES.

I don't understand.

BLOBS STRONGER THAN EIGHT. BREAK THROUGH IN TIME.

Oh my stars. I must admit, my initial reaction is thinking it could be a good thing as they'll kill all those murdering looters. But I'm not that bloodthirsty. Really! I'm sure there are innocents working for them. Plus that's many more shadow-blobs in our dimension.

How much time?

UNKNOWN. BREACH IS DEPENDENT ON NUMBER OF CROSSINGS.

The more the looters use the weaker portals with only the eight Warriors, the greater the chance of the shadow-blobs getting through?

YES. PORTALS WILL WEAKEN WITH EACH CROSSING.

Unless there's all fourteen hundred Warriors?

AND FORTY-EIGHT. YES.

That's scary. Jarren's been destroying thousands of Warriors. *What about the reconstructed Warriors? Will they work?*

IF THEY HAVE HEARTS.

Too bad we don't know how to make more hearts.

FACTORIES.

We have the equipment?

YES.

That's something to figure out later. For now, how do I convince anyone about this new, deadly wrinkle? I can't even get Radcliff to test a portal.

Speak of the devil. Radcliff appears in my doorway. "Can you set the table?"

I clamp down on hysterical giggles. Our Galaxy is about to be invaded, but it'll have to wait until after I set the table.

"Ara?"

"Yes, coming." I hop off the bed.

I'll ask Q more questions later. For now, I set the table while Radcliff finishes getting dinner ready.

When the door to the unit opens, I move to a corner of the kitchen where Niall can't see me.

"Dad?" he calls.

"Yes?"

"I'm not hungry tonight. I'm gonna pass and crash for a few hours instead," Niall says.

I'm about to say something when Radcliff puts his finger to his lips, stopping me.

"Get your ass in here right now, boy. That's an order." Although his tone is harsh, Radcliff gives me a conspiratorial wink.

Niall makes an exaggerated huff and storms into the kitchen. "You can't order me to—" He spots me.

"Surprise!"

"Mouse!"

And then I'm in his arms with my legs wrapped around his waist. My world fills with Niall. His scent and touch banish all my worries over shadow-blobs and looters. For now.

Radcliff clears his throat and Niall sets me down. We're both grinning like a couple of lovesick teenagers. Yes, I know that's what we are, but you gotta admit, we're more mature than your average teens. Shadow-blobs and looters tend to make you grow up in a hurry.

"Sit down before it gets cold." Radcliff fills three plates, but instead of joining us at the table, he picks his up. "I've lots of work to catch up on." He gives me his intense look. "Don't forget, you have to be back at twenty hundred."

"I won't."

"Good. Niall, you can escort her. Tell the dragon she'll have a complete report in the morning."

"Yes, sir." Niall's trying hard not to laugh.

I press my lips together to keep the giggles trapped inside. Once Radcliff's bedroom door closes, we both lose control of our laughter—Radcliff called my mother the dragon!

"Who came up with that nickname? You or your father?" I ask.

"Dad did. He finally encountered someone more stubborn

than him."

And just my luck, it's my mother. Then I realize that Radcliff is actually being thoughtful. He's giving me and Niall some privacy.

"How did my dad manage to temporarily spring you?" Niall asks.

In between bites—I wasn't lying, Radcliff's cooking is the best—I explain about interviewing Jarren. I skip the part about the attack.

"Talking to Jarren must have been...stressful. You okay?" Niall asks.

"Yeah. Well..." I rub my neck. "I wasn't thrilled about the idea, but Bendix and Rance had my back."

"So DES was actually right, you got more out of him than my dad," Niall says.

I shrug. "I goaded him with my guesses. I'm not sure how any of this information will help us if your dad isn't going to let me test a portal."

Niall pauses with his fork in mid-air. "You?"

Remembering my promise, I rush to add, "Us." I sweep my silverware in a circle. "As in security, the astrophysicists, and my parents."

"Uh huh."

I change the subject, asking about what I've missed. Niall fills me in on the looters in the pits, telling me a story about Elese motivating them to work faster. "She put them into teams and the first team to finish reconstructing a Warrior gets a prize."

Laughing, I ask, "What's the prize?"

"Dessert."

"I approve." There's many things I would do for dessert.

He's in the middle of regaling me with another story when he stops abruptly. "What's wrong with your neck?" he asks.

Automatically, I touch it. "Nothing. Why?"

"You keep rubbing it. What's that?" He reaches over the table and tips up my chin. "Bruises!"

"Oh."

"Oh?" He stands. "What happened?"

"I goaded Jarren one too many times. I should have told you but I just wanted us to enjoy dinner and my last couple of hours of freedom."

He relaxes. "I wouldn't have been mad at *you*."

"I know."

"I really hate that guy."

"I know. I do, too. So let's not talk about him anymore."

"All right." He sits down and we finish eating.

After cleaning up the dishes, we collapse on the couch. He tucks me under his arm and I lean against him. One of his sketchbooks is on the coffee table, and it reminds me.

"Thanks for the picture," I say. "I love it. It's fantastic."

"Did you manage to smuggle it past the dragon?"

"Yes."

"I'll give you a few more to take back with you if you'd like."

Instead of answering, I straddle his lap and kiss him. It's a long deep kiss. One that I've been dreaming of doing since we parted. I rake my fingers through his hair and am rewarded with a low sexy groan. By the time we come up for air, I'm lying on the couch with Niall beside me.

"I'm guessing that's a yes for more pictures," he says, a bit breathless.

It would be a yes for much more, but Radcliff is in the next room. My answer is to reclaim his lips and we don't bother talking for a long while.

Our time together ends far too soon. After straightening our clothing and hair, and saying good night to Radcliff, Niall and I stop in his unit. He fishes a couple smaller pictures from the tube he'd tried to give me on my first day of being grounded.

One has fuzzy bunnies with weapons. They're peeking out from under something. Curtains maybe? I peer at it in confusion until it hits me. It's a blanket. "Dust bunny assassins!"

"Small, but mighty." He cocks his head. "Like you."

"Hey! I'm taller than my mother."

"Rance's son Trevar is taller than your mother. That doesn't count."

The next drawing is just six rows of ten squares with numbers inside each one. The numbers start at two hundred and fifty-four and go to three hundred and fourteen. "A countdown?" I smile. Day three-fourteen is my eighteenth birthday.

He gives me a piece of black chalk. "You X out each day. Go ahead and update it."

Starting at day two-fifty-four, I cross out nine squares. And, I have to admit, it feels good. "Fun."

The last picture is of the two of us. We're standing back to back and wearing our security jumpsuits. Holding flashlights out as if poofing shadow-blobs, we have serious expressions. There's a tiny mouse on Niall's shoulder who's also shining a flashlight. I search and find the toad equally armed on my weapon belt.

I look at Niall. "Is this from when we first fought the shadow-blobs together?"

"Yeah, but without the techs and other officers. With only you being able to see the enemy, this is how I felt. That you had my back."

Aww. That's sweet. I wrap my arms around his neck and go up on my tiptoes to give him a kiss. "Thanks."

Niall helps me hide the drawings under my shirt before we head back to my parents' unit. We hold hands and I practically drag my feet.

"You can't be late or we'll both be in trouble," Niall says, pulling me along.

When we arrive, Niall squeezes my hand before letting go. "Fifty-one more days, Mouse. You can make it."

At one point in my life fifty-one days wouldn't have seemed that long. But life has become precious and every day is important. I press my palm to the lock. The door opens. I've mixed emotions. If they didn't fix the lock, I could have ratted them out to Radcliff.

My parents are sitting in the living area. Mom jumps to her feet and glances at the clock. We're two minutes early, but she still looks unhappy to see Niall with me. Too bad.

"Where's your father?" Mom asks Niall.

"He's working. He'll send you a report about the interview in the morning." He turns to me. "Night, Mouse."

And then he's gone, taking all the colors with him. I head to my room.

"Wait," Mom says. "What happened with Jarren? Did he talk to you?"

I stop with my hand on the doorknob. "You can read the full account in the morning. I'm going to bed." Entering the room, I shut the door behind me, being careful not to slam it. Then I wait.

Will my mother come in and demand the story now? Or will my father enter with something sweet to bribe me? Lyra would have sat down with her parents as soon as she returned home and told them everything that happened. Ara is still pissed at being grounded. When no one taps on my door, I go into the washroom and carefully remove my contraband. Hanging the new pictures with the other one on the washroom's door, I step back and admire the collection. Then I change into my pajamas and go to bed.

Instead of sleeping, I connect to Q to see if I can discover who Jarren's navigators are. It was a guess, but his reaction meant it was a good one. I could further investigate the likelihood of shadow-blobs breaking through the looters' portals, but in that case, I can't do anything other than warn them. Huh. Would I warn them? Right now, I can't contact them, but I expect that to change. After a few minutes of contemplation, I decide that, yes, I would warn them. I am one of the good guys after all.

I return to the problem of the navigators. I consider what I know of Jarren. When he arrived on Xinji, he was thirteen A-years old and already good with worming. He claimed to have been taught by Warrick Nolt on his previous home, Planet Kaiping. Since the name is just an alias for Jarren, then who did he really learn from? I pull up the personnel records for Kaiping's research base and start going through the list.

I find a teenager that was two A-years older than Jarren, named Rick Nolwart. It's not hard to rearrange the letters in his name to come up with Warrick Nolt. Jarren may be a genius with the Q-net, but he's not very creative. Reading through Nolwart's file, I scan the list of his infractions that start out minor and escalate until Nolwart is spending more time in detention than at soch-time. In fact, Nolwart was serving a ninety-day sentence when Jarren left for Planet Xinji. Jarren probably couldn't say good-bye to his friend. I wonder if this was when Jarren started hating DES.

Asking Q to find the Interstellar Class space ship Jarren traveled on to Xinji, I ask it to please list the navigators who were working during that time. While Q is digging out the information, I mull over why a navigator would help Jarren.

The job is highly technical and only the very best pass the rigorous training, the full mental evaluation, and background tests that are all required to become a navigator. No matter if it's an Interstellar, Exploratory, or Protector Class space ship, they each only employ four navigators. Working eight-hour shifts, they rotate their schedule so they each get a couple days off. They, along with the captain of the space ship, are granted full access to the Q-net, a rarity. Only the highest level of DES has that access.

I remember how overwhelmed I was when I first entered the Q-net with Chief Hoshi during my brief internship. The vastness stretched toward infinity, and the star roads streaked through it like silver rivers of liquid starlight. I wonder if I could pass all the requirements to become a navigator. Probably. Captain Harrison did say I'm a strong candidate. But what if I really wanted to become one and failed?

Groaning into my pillow, I can't believe I didn't think of it sooner! Navigators wouldn't teach Jarren how to be a better wormer and how to build complex blockades around planets. No, they're the good guys, too. It has to be someone, or a few people, who failed and are bitter about it, blaming DES. They would have the skills, but not the access, unless they wormed through the restrictions. It also makes sense when you consider that if the Warrior Express becomes the new way to travel, it would put all those navigators out of work. Like a resentful if-I-can't-have-it-neither-can-you taunt.

Q lists the navigators on Jarren's ship. However what I need now will be harder to find. I'm guessing that Jarren connected with these disgruntled people while he was living on Suzhou. Did he meet someone on the planet? Or find them in the Q-net? I doubt there is a support group for failed navigators. What would they do instead of navigating? They would be very skilled with using the Q-net. Unfortunately, there are a ton of jobs in DES where having those qualifications is required.

Do you know who is working with Jarren? I ask Q. Why not try it?

NO.

But they're using you!

THEY HIDE.

Right. I forgot Q can only access what humans have inputted even if the information is false. Which means, I'm gonna have to do math. Ugh. I'm also going to assume Jarren hooked up with his partners in crime during his time on Suzhou. So I pull up the messages Lan sent me while I was in the fifty E-year time jump between Planets Xinji and Yulin.

Jarren contacted her in 2503 and learned the love of his life was married with children. From his comments during our interview, she might have shared her findings with him soon after. In 2520, she messaged me her exciting news about translating the eight rows of symbols on the alien octagon that my dad found on Xinji and I reconstructed. And a hundred and…uh…twenty-eight days later, Xinji went silent.

Huh. That was quick. I'd bet Jarren was worried Lan would share her research with other scientists and they'd figure out the real reason for the Warriors. Which also explains why he stole all the data files from Xinji. He didn't know she'd sent me a copy of her research. Or that I'd be able to get any useful information from the "recovered" files he sent us to keep us busy until he could silence us as well. I do more math and figure out that Jarren first attacked us fifty-one days after we landed on Yulin.

In any case, he probably hooked up with his Q-net teachers after he was released from detention on Suzhou and during those next few years. I ask Q to search for names of people who had failed navigator school and were working on Suzhou at that same time as Jarren. And to please look for any interactions between them. It's quite the task and will take Q time so I finally go to sleep.

Mom wakes me at the crack of too-early-to-care-what-time-it-is. I shuffle to the washroom. My head weights a thousand kilograms and my brain is fast asleep. But I'm jerked to full awareness when the harsh white lights illuminate the bruises on my neck. Oh boy. The dragon will spot them in a heartbeat. Wishing to avoid the drama—at least through breakfast—I dig in my bureau and find an old turtleneck. Since Yulin is warmer than Xinji, I've forgotten about it. I put it on. It's soft and chases away the early morning chill.

The dragon notices the turtleneck when I sit down to eat, but only asks about the report. "It's not here yet. When will Tace send it?"

I shrug. "Don't know." Then focus on my reconstituted eggs and a white pasty goo that might be oatmeal or could be spackle. Without being told, I go to Mom's office to pretend to do school work. I stare at Q solving calculus problems for me. Believe it or not, I can do algebra, calculus, and trigonometry, I just prefer not to. It occurs to me, that even if I'd planned to become a navigator, I'd never use the calculus I learned to do my job. No one is ever going to say, "Ara, quick, calculate the derivative, the fate of the Galaxy depends on it!" Q has that all figured out already. So why bother wasting time learning it?

IT TEACHES YOU HOW TO SOLVE PROBLEMS.

I grudgingly agree that's a handy skill, one I've used many times. But it's not enough to rouse me from my post-breakfast stupor. After an hour of staring, I check in with Beau.

Hey, partner, he says, sounding way too chipper.

Hi. What have you been doing?

I've been working on finding the super wormers, but Radcliff told me Jarren may have used those names to cover his identity and the people don't really exist.

The names are fake, but he has help, I'm sure of it. I explain about my late-night epiphany of washed-out navigators. *I've Q working on who might have been bitter enough to help Jarren. They might not be on Suzhou, though.*

There's a long pause.

What's wrong? I ask Beau.

I've also been working on identifying potential DES traitors. However, some of the names in our file are highlighted. And these names are not active DES employees, but ex-employees.

That makes sense. Jarren hates DES so he would conspire with fellow disgruntled people who hate DES.

I agree with that logic. A beat. *Except that's not what the suspected-looter-colluder program was supposed to do. Are you worming into the file and adding these names?*

I'm not going to lie to my partner. *It's not me, Beau. Q must be adding them.*

CORRECT.

The silence extends so long that I begin to worry.

I thought the Q-net won't interfere. We didn't ask it to assess ex-employees.

Good point. *Why did you add these names?* I ask Q, letting Beau hear my question so he doesn't think I'm ignoring him.

TIME CRITICAL. NEED MORE HELP.

Beau yelps. *Stars! Did you hear that?*

Icy fear pumps through my body. *Yes, that's Q. Now be quiet. How critical?* I ask Q. *Are the looters coming? Do we need to prepare for an attack?*

UNKNOWN.

I almost yell at Q in frustration—how can you *not* know! Instead, I take a few deep breaths and look on the bright side. At least Beau has to believe me now about Q.

I thought the Q-net knew everything, Beau says to me.

NO ONE KNOWS EVERYTHING.

Beau curses. *Stop doing that!*

Jarren confirmed my guess about the looters using the portals to communicate. What if their network of communications is not a part of the Q-net at all? But something completely separate?

CORRECT.

And that means, if the looters decide to attack us and don't use the shuttles or anything connected to the Q-net, I won't get a warning. They'll be able to surprise us!

CORRECT.

2522:264

What's going on? Beau asks. *Why is the Q-net talking to me?*

It's talking to us. Welcome to the insanity. If they don't send you for a full mental health evaluation, I'm gonna be very upset.

Ara, focus. What does it mean, time's critical and it doesn't know when we might be attacked?

I explain to Beau about the looters communicating using a system that's not connected to the Q-net. *We can't rely on Q to alert us to an attack. Radcliff needs to know right away.*

On it, Beau says. He disentangles.

I'm once again staring at the screen in my mom's office. My thoughts whirl around all the possibilities. The desert surrounding the base is vast. If the looters came on foot, we'd have a hard time spotting them until they were really close. Not a comforting thought.

"Lunch time," Mom says, interrupting my morose thoughts.

I'm distracted at soch-time. One solution keeps popping up.

We need to evacuate to another planet using the portals. Except, what's to stop the looters from following us? Nothing. But at least we'd know which direction they were coming from. Or would we? How many Warrior planets have the looters taken control of? I'd assumed all the closed planets and the ones that have gone silent. But what about the forty-two that haven't been discovered yet?

And I thought I was scared before. Thinking that the looters might have already claimed all but four Warrior planets—Suzhou is an unknown at this point—I'm almost paralyzed with terror. At least there won't be shadow-blobs on the majority of them. Or would there? If I were to set up a Warrior Express transportation network, I'd move the Warriors to prime locations in the Galaxy.

It would be nice to know exactly how the portals work. And to know just how much damage Jarren has done. How many planets has he visited? Will I be able to talk to Jarren again? Would he even answer my questions? Maybe if I bring along some dessert.

"What are you doing?" Mom demands.

She's standing right in front of me. I glance around the soch-area. Only the really young kids are still here. I missed the signal ending soch-time.

I look up. The dragon stares back.

"Thinking," I say.

The dragon gives me a you-can-do-better-than-that look. Did she think I was worming?

"About what?" Another demand.

Standing, I meet her gaze. "Fifty more days." Then I head

to the unit, letting her figure out what it means.

This time it's Elese in her uniform who is not visiting me.

She gives me a high five. "Hey girl! You're not getting soft on me, are you?"

"Soft can be a good thing, you know," I say, thinking of Niall's hair.

"Yeah, for blankets and teddy bears. But you're not a teddy bear." Elese snags me in a hug.

I'm stunned. Elese is not the hugging type.

Then she whispers in my ear, "You're a lion." She releases me just as quick. "Later." With a jaunty wave, she's on her way.

And I hurry inside my parents' unit before the dragon notices that the pulse gun is no longer in Elese's holster. It's currently digging into the small of my back, half shoved into the waistband of my pants. The speed of her delivery was impressive. But that isn't what has me distracted. It's the fact that Radcliff believes I need to be armed. Believes it strongly enough to bypass my parents. Does he know something or is this just a precaution because Q can't alert us to a looter attack? Either way, I keep the gun hidden behind my back. It won't do anyone any good in the drawer of my room.

During my afternoon homework session, I question Q on the nature of the portals. Jarren used the Q-net while he was learning about them, so technically the information is in the network and Q can share it with me.

What I know is that there are sixty-four pits on each of the sixty-four Warrior planets. Each pit has a designation to another one of the other Warrior planets. The last pit is its own designation. So I assume that's for incoming travelers.

CORRECT.

The space in the center of the Warriors is only about two meters wide. *What if you want to send something big through the portal?* I ask. *Like a shuttle?*

WIDEN PORT.

Port? Is that what you're calling the open space in the middle?

YES.

You would need to move the Warriors to make it bigger.

CORRECT.

Hmmm. That would be hard to do. Those Warriors weigh about three hundred kilos each. Jarren did say they destroyed Warriors to get to the center ones. So they've been setting them far enough apart to send their equipment through.

UNKNOWN.

You don't know?

NO. PORTALS DO NOT NEED ME TO OPERATE.

Ah. Do you know when they're using them?

NO.

Why aren't the portals wider? Why only big enough for two people?

BIGGER PORTALS WEAKER.

And weaker meant a chance the shadow-blobs might cross into our dimension.

CORRECT.

Just what we don't need, more shadow-blobs. I return my focus to the portals. *Why did fourth nation build the portals on these planets?*

PORTS BUILT AT ENTANGLED LOCATIONS BETWEEN

DIMENSIONS.

Entangled locations? Like places where they're connected somehow? Where it's easier to cross from one to another?

YES.

Hmmm. I mull it over. *Fourth nation wanted to protect our dimension from the shadow-blobs, so they built a network of Warriors at these entangled spots to keep the enemy out.*

CORRECT.

That supports Lan's translations, which suggest the Warrior planets were chosen very carefully. She called the locations "entanglement points." Which aren't the same thing as Einstein's quantum entangled particles.

CORRECT. EINSTEIN'S PARTICLES ENABLE GALAXY-WIDE COMMUNICATIONS.

That's why messages aren't influenced by the time dilation?

YES.

That's super cool. Too bad Einstein never knew it.

EINSTEIN KNEW. GOOD FRIEND.

Stars! There's so much in *that* response that I'd like to explore. But I need to focus on the problem at hand, learning about the portals. *Why would fourth nation use these portals to travel? Wouldn't that endanger them?*

NOT IF PROPERLY PROTECTED. NEED PORTALS TO MAINTAIN THE NETWORK.

Oh! If used correctly, the portals keep the shadow-blobs out. And fourth nation needed to be able to check the Warriors and make sure the pits hadn't collapsed. They used the portals to access the Warrior network.

CORRECT.

When not using the portals, how did Fourth Nation travel?

HUMANS NOT READY.

Argh. Can you at least tell me if their form of transportation invokes the time dilation?

IT DOES NOT.

Sweet. Something to look forward to. That is, if I'm alive and it's not a thousand years in our future. I wait, but there's no comment from Q. I think of another question. *Why did Fourth Nation leave? They knew we needed to be protected, but they didn't stay to maintain the network. A few of the Warrior pits had collapsed before we discovered them.*

I AM HERE.

They assumed we would eventually tap into you, learn how to travel, find the Warriors, figure out why they're here, and then maintain them.

CORRECT.

And they were right, except for one thing. They didn't think humans would try to exploit the portals before learning their true purpose.

CORRECT. ALSO DEVELOPMENT OF FIFTH NATION SLOWER THAN EXPECTED.

I refrain from snarking on that last comment. Going back to the portals, I consider all the new information about them. The receiving pit is for incoming. *Does that mean the portals only go one way?*

YES.

Once I thought about it, that made sense. I think of another wrinkle. *Can you open a portal from either side?*

NO.

Which side?

OUTGOING.

Which means the planet on the incoming side can't stop anyone from arriving, but can prevent people from leaving.

CORRECT.

Which pit is Yulin's incoming portal?

PIT 54.

We haven't opened that one yet. It might have collapsed—oh my stars! Jarren used that portal to get here! He must have relocated the Warriors from Pit 54 to his base. *Why didn't you tell me he moved them?*

YOU DID NOT ASK.

I didn't know to ask. But how else would Jarren travel here and move all those supplies to his forest base? In fact, I should be yelling at myself for not thinking of it either. *Does this mean there's a shadow-blob rift in Pit 54?*

NO.

Why not?

WARRIORS ARE STILL ON YULIN.

I don't understand. Can you please explain further?

EACH PLANET HAS NINETY-TWO THOUSAND SIX HUNDRED AND SEVENTY-TWO TOTAL WARRIORS. WHEN WARRIORS ARE DESTROYED OR REMOVED, THE BARRIER IS WEAKENED UNTIL A TEAR FORMS. THE TEAR GROWS BIGGER AS MORE WARRIORS ARE BROKEN OR REMOVED FROM THE PLANET.

And let me guess, the bigger the rift, the more shadow-blobs can come into our dimension.

CORRECT.

Just great. Jarren's been destroying Warriors left and right. He's going to kill us all. And in order to stop the looters, we'll probably have to use the portals. *You mentioned removing the Warriors from the planet. Will they protect against the shadow-blobs if they're still on the planet? In other words, are the ones that were moved to Jarren's base on Yulin still protecting us?*

YES. ONCE REMOVED FROM THE PLANET, THE PROTECTION CEASES.

That's good to know. What about the portals? Do they still work if the eight key Warriors are on a non-Warrior planet or a space ship?

NO.

Do you have a list of which pit goes to each planet on all sixty-four Warrior Planets?

YES.

How? We haven't been to all the planets.

FOURTH NATION LEFT INFORMATION BEHIND IN ORDER TO HELP YOU WHEN THE TIME CAME.

Except when the time came and Lan deciphered the symbols, Jarren had already figured it out and was causing havoc.

CORRECT.

There's a tap on my shoulder and I just about hit the ceiling.

"I've been calling you for ten minutes," Dad says. "What are you working on that's so engrossing?"

I glance at the screen. "Physics."

"Trying to prove other dimensions exist?" His tone is teasing.

But I can't tease back. "Did you want something?" My words are harsh. A twinge of guilt gnaws on my stomach.

His smile fades. "Dinner's ready."

"Okay, I'll be right there."

As he leaves, I try to blame being overwhelmed with all the information from Q for my bad behavior. It's a weak excuse. And what if the looters attack again, and I'm separated from my parents or they die? I don't want this strained relationship to be my last memory of them.

My mother has made a pasta dish—I think. It's noodles in a yellow sauce, so I'm not sure. During dinner, I'm not as surly and answer questions with more than one word. It's hard. I'm still angry. But it's a start.

That night my father knocks on my door. He has a plate of warm cookies. We declare another temporary truce and play Sevens. Our conversation is about minor things. It's nice.

After I get in bed, I connect with Q and do more research. Jarren said they were targeting the other active Warrior planets. I pull up the timeline of their previous attacks. Starting with Yulin, the time between the dates the planets went silent is an average of...twenty-nine days. So if I add that to day two hundred and twenty-seven, when Ulanqab stopped communicating with DES, that means the next attack would be around day two hundred and fifty-six! *Has DES reported another Warrior planet going silent?* I ask Q.

NO.

Whew. Perhaps Jarren's arrest has changed their plans. A girl can hope. But as a security officer, I don't think so. There's been too much money, time, and lives spent for them to stop now. Which planet would they target next? Distance doesn't matter. I consider what they've done so far. Once they attack, they then block off all contact with DES. I sit up in bed. It would take lots of time to build that blockade. It's probably already in place and would just need the last few commands to seal it shut. *Is there a blockade in progress?* I ask Q.

YES.

Where?

PINGLIANG.

Oh my stars! We need to warn them. Or rather, Officer Radcliff needs to warn them. *How much time until the blockade is finished?*

THREE DAYS.

Are there any others in construction?

NO.

Can you let me know as soon as another starts?

YES.

I wish I'd thought of this sooner. Composing a message to Radcliff, I come clean about the portals. And I make a few suggestions on what we need to do. No surprise a response comes back soon after. I don't think the man ever sleeps.

2522:264: Miss Lawrence, thank you for the warning. I sent it to my colleague on Planet Pingliang. I was under the impression that you are not allowed to access the Q-net while grounded, but instead you've been very busy. Is this going to cause problems with your parents?

2522:264: Officer Radcliff, I might not be allowed, but I never promised not to access the Q-net while grounded, however, I'm sure the dragon is not going to be happy. But I really don't care as lives are at stake.

→ I agree that this situation warrants a bit of rebellion. And your suggestions are worth consideration. I'm going to schedule an early morning meeting with your parents.

← How early?

→ Oh-six-hundred.

I imagine Radcliff enjoyed that last bit.

← I'll be there.

→ Until then. Radcliff out.

I'm tempted to check out the blockade-in-progress around Pingliang and probe it for weaknesses that we can exploit, but I do the sensible thing and, after asking Q for a wake-up call—I know Q is this vast wonder and I'm asking it for a wake-up call, but I don't want to miss that meeting—I lay down. After hiding my pulse gun under my pillow, I try to sleep.

Oh-five-thirty arrives faster than expected. Groggy and leaden, I struggle to untangle my covers and get a quick shower. I turn the water as cold as I can stand. By the time I'm dressed, I'm wide awake. Too bad I'm not wearing my security uniform.

I think it would help my parents not to see me as their little girl with the pigtails and chubby cheeks. Instead, I put on my nicest shirt and jeans, tucking the gun once again behind my back. The bruises on my throat have darkened to the color of storm clouds. I can't hide them forever.

When there's a knock on the unit's door and voices sound, that's my cue. I leave my room and join Radcliff, Morgan, and Beau. Morgan isn't a surprise, but Beau is. He grins at me. His hair is spiked and he appears relaxed. But I know him and I spot the lines of strain around his amber eyes.

My mother spots the marks on my neck and gazes at me with fire in her eyes, but doesn't say anything as I follow the group to the conference room. Dad is already seated at the table, sipping a cup of coffee. There's a large carafe, several empty cups, milk, and sugar. Radcliff pours cups for me, Beau, and himself. Morgan apparently doesn't drink coffee. Or she's taking a hit for the team. I bring the cup up to my lips and breathe in the heavenly scent before gulping the hot liquid.

Mom sits next to Dad and the four of us settle in the chairs opposite of them—a united front.

"What's going on?" Mom asks.

Radcliff sets his cup down. "I've recently learned that the looters plan to attack Planet Pingliang next. The research base has been warned and DES is aware of the situation, but I need Ara's assistance to sabotage their blockade."

Nice of Radcliff not to rat me out. Of course my mother is not an idiot and I'm the subject of her intense scrutiny. I try for innocent. She is not fooled.

"What about Officer Dorey and DES? Surely they have the

expertise to deal with this situation."

Beau glances at Radcliff, who nods slightly. My partner says, "We have the knowledge and the skills, but we don't have a direct connection to the Q-net. Ara can get things done much faster and we fear time is an issue."

"And just what will she do?" Dad asks.

Morgan nudges me with her elbow. Oh. "We'll find a way to ensure their blockade will have plenty of holes." I might also be able to trace them back to where they're creating it, but I'm smart enough to omit that bit.

"Won't that cause them to come after you?" Mom asks.

A valid question. I turn to Radcliff. "Do the looters know we've reestablished a connection to DES?"

"Yes. They closed two of our tunnels and we've restricted outgoing messages for emergencies only."

That's alarming. "Are you sure Pingliang received your warning?"

"Do you think the looters have found our other escape tunnels and are blocking our messages again?" Beau asks.

"It's always possible."

"A response arrived soon after I sent the message," Radcliff says.

It could be coming from one of the looters. "Can I check it?"

"No," Mom says.

The desire to snap that I wasn't asking her burns the back of my throat. I keep my gaze on Radcliff.

"Yes," Radcliff says.

"Ara—"

"Do you want everyone on Pingliang to die?" I ask her in a

soft voice.

"Of course not. Officer Dorey is perfectly capable of—"

"Ara's faster," Beau says.

"Do it now," Radcliff orders.

I reach for Q. *Show me the escape tunnels, please.* The web of programs that surrounds us becomes visible to my mind's eye. There are four red tubes that snake through the complex threads. Not two, but three are now collapsed as if the weight of the commands around them have squished them flat. Only one remains. I fly with Q through the tunnel. We head toward Pingliang.

The blockade looms large. It's as dark as a void, surrounding the planet. There's only a narrow gap remaining.

A TUMOR.

The disgust from Q is clear. *Can you get rid of it?*

NO.

Can we sabotage the construction?

YOU CAN.

Ah, I'd have to figure it out first. In the meantime, I need to check if our message reached the planet. "Who is the Security Chief on Pingliang?" I ask Radcliff.

"Officer Kingston."

We swoop in and Q pulls up Kingston's messages. Radcliff's is flagged and after scanning the security's records, I learn they're mobilizing for a potential attack. Relief washes through me. We return to Yulin, and Q builds a few more escape tunnels for us. *Please make them really hard to find.*

WILL DO.

Everyone is staring at me when I blink and focus on the

people in the conference room.

"The message reached Kingston," I say.

Radcliff, Beau, and Morgan relax. I update them on the status of our blockade.

"How many more tunnels?" Beau asks.

SEVEN.

"Seven."

"Just like that?" Beau asks. "It took us hours before."

"I told you before, once we do something like make an escape tunnel, I can ask Q to build us more." I turn to my mom. "*That's* why I'm faster than Beau."

The silence lengthens.

"How long will it take to sabotage Pingliang's blockade?" Radcliff asks.

"That'll be harder since we haven't done it before. I'll need Beau's help to find the right places. Unless you don't want them to be hidden?"

"Hidden is good," Radcliff says. "Anything that we can do to surprise the looters is always good. Can you work on it right away?"

Beau and I exchange a look. "I'm free this morning," he says. "Where do you want to do it?"

"Your office would be best, so we're not interrupted."

Everyone focuses on my parents. Mom has her arms crossed, but no signs of fire. Instead, she says to me, "You haven't answered my question."

I think back. Oh. "Our alterations will be very hard to find. They won't be able to trace it back to me."

Mom relaxes her arms. "You can help them, Ara. We'll talk

later."

"All right. Thanks."

If she's surprised by my quick agreement, she hides it well. It is time we talk. Beau and I head out, leaving Radcliff and Morgan behind.

When we're out in the base, Beau asks, "Do you really need me? Or was that just a ploy to leave your unit?" His tone is neutral.

Men. "I need you. This is more complex than making escape tunnels. I've no idea what we're going to encounter."

Beau grunts. I'm not sure if he's satisfied with the answer. I peek at him to gauge his mood. He's frowning.

"Has Q spoken to you since yesterday?" I ask, matching his careful tone.

"A couple times." He doesn't sound happy about it. "When I was working on something, the solution would light up with a 'here.' Almost fell off my chair the first time it happened."

I try to hide my smile. "But you heard Q before."

"With you!"

Ah. "Were you entangled?"

"Yes. I can't access the Q-net unless I'm entangled. Thank the universe. I like my privacy." He glances at me. "How can you stand it?"

"I don't feel like Q's invading my privacy. It feels more like when we're working together in the Q-net and can communicate. I have to actively think at Q to get a response." Except when I'm trying to puzzle something out and Q supplies an answer or comment. That used to scare me, but now it seems normal. Plus I could argue that Q and I were interacting at those times. Ah, there's that denial I know and love.

"Do you believe the Q-net is a divine being?" Beau asks.

"No."

"How do you know it's not?"

"Because if Q was a divine all powerful being, it wouldn't need us to help it. Q is an alien being—different than us, but not superior. More technologically advanced, but not divine. If Jarren hadn't put the Milky Way Galaxy in danger, I think Q would have waited for us to make contact."

"Humans are always looking for a shortcut," Beau says.

TRUE.

"Have you told anyone Q helps you? That you heard it?"

This time he scowls. "No." Then he stops and touches my arm. "I'm not that brave."

I meet his gaze. "It's not about being brave. It's about acceptance. If you tell someone, then that means you've accepted this crazy impossibility that Q is sentient."

"And what about admitting I've failed my partner by not fully believing her?"

"That, too. But I hear she doesn't hold a grudge…well, not for long, and I'd bet if you back her up, she'll forgive you pretty quick. That and bribe her with candy. I hear she's addicted to sugar."

Beau laughs and we continue on to his office in companionable silence. I keep a sharp eye out for Niall—running into him would be a highlight. I guess I'm addicted to Niall as well.

Except for a few early risers in the training room, we don't see him or anyone else in security. We're soon at Beau's dual Q-net terminals. He entangles and I join him. Then we worm through one of the escape tunnels.

I'm assuming the looters are hiding it from DES, so how do we find the Pingliang blockade? Beau asks me once we're free of our own tumor…er…blockade.

I'd been flying when I found it last time. *Can Beau fly with us?* I ask Q.

NO.

Can you highlight the best way to reach it?

YES.

A thin ribbon of yellow light marks the route.

Handy, Beau says. *Can I ask the Q-net for help like that?*

YES.

Cool. Can you get me a date with Nina, the geology tech?

NO.

Beau, I mock scold.

What? It was worth a try.

Can we focus on getting to the blockade without alerting anyone?

All right. Let's follow the yellow brick road.

The yellow brick road?

Yeah, it leads to the land of Oz where all your dreams come true.

Like getting a date with Nina?

Exactly!

Even though I've no idea what Oz is, I've missed this. We worm to the blockade-in-progress. Because it isn't complete, the multiple layers of programming are exposed. It is a thing of beauty.

Beau whistles. *This is a masterpiece. No wonder it's so hard to get through it.*

How many people worked on this? I ask Q.

FOUR.

Does that include Jarren?

NO.

Did he help with the other blockades?

YES.

So there are four other super wormers, Beau says.

CORRECT. WARRICK NOLT. URSY BEAR. OSEN VEE. FORDEL PEKE.

But they're fake identities, I say.

YES. BUT REAL PEOPLE.

Ah. Jarren let me believe they were all him, but instead, they're the disgruntled wannabe navigators.

CORRECT.

What's that correct for? Beau asks.

I connected the real people to those failed navigators and Q let me know I was right.

It reads your mind?

Well…yes, I guess. It's usually when I'm interacting with it and am making logical correlations.

Can you verbalize those so I don't freak out?

I don't know. I haven't seen you freaked out before. Could be fun.

Ara.

Yes, Beau. I consider the web of programs around us. *What's the best way to sabotage this without anyone knowing it has…leaks?*

What's wrong with putting in some escape tunnels?

They can be easily collapsed.

There's a long pause. *What about changing the programs that block all messages to let some through that have a special code? It will work for both incoming and outgoing messages. As long as they have that code it will get through the blockade.*

I mull it over. *Plus the wormers won't be looking for tampering in their own programs. Great idea! See? I needed you.*

He grunts, but it's a pleased sound. *We need to pick these programs apart, see how they're built and change the directions. Where do we start?*

HERE.

A green light illuminates one of the complex routines. We pull the strands gently and alter a few commands.

What type of code? I ask Beau. *Numerical? Alphanumerical? Or a random sequence of numbers and letters?*

A word would be easy to remember but we can't pick something that is commonly used.

How about skedaddle?

Perfect.

It takes us a long time to alter the programming. Eventually we change all the different types of routines so Q can do all the rest. There's quite a bit of redundancy in the blockade, which is a sign of an expert. Some of them are well hidden—another sign. Good thing we're also experts.

We finish and disentangle…well, Beau does. I just focus on my physical body and my location. Too bad that triggers a pounding in my temples. I rest my head on my arms.

"Come on," Beau says.

"Can't move."

"Not even for lunch?"

I glance up. "It's lunch time?"

He studies me. "Didn't you eat breakfast?"

"Who can eat at oh-my-stars-early?"

"Never skip a meal. Unless you can't help it."

"Okay."

But his gaze sears into me. "It's important, Ara."

"Yes, sir."

"All right. Let's go report to Radcliff. Then we'll eat." He pulls me to my feet.

The security chief is working at his desk. We stand in front of it and explain how we sabotaged the blockade.

"Skedaddle? You want me to tell them to use *skedaddle* on their important messages?" By the way Radcliff rubs the bridge of his nose, we know it's a rhetorical question. "Good work, you two."

"Us three, sir," Beau says.

Radcliff looks at him. "Three?"

"The Q-net helped. Otherwise it would have taken us four full days."

Aww. That's my partner.

"Noted. Anything else?"

I say, "We need to discuss the portals."

"We do."

Beau shoots me a shocked look. "What about the portals?"

"We need to test them." Now I'm rubbing my temples. "Can you arrange a meeting with the astrophysicists, my parents, and members of the security team who aren't on duty?"

"Or sleeping," Beau adds. "If you want them on your side, then you don't disturb their limited rest."

"It's not *my* side. It's *our* side," I snap, but regret it immediately. "Sorry."

"You're right."

"I'll see what I can do," Radcliff says.

"Thank you." I take a breath. "Can you also arrange for me to talk to Jarren again?"

His gaze goes to my neck. "Why?"

"I've a few more questions for him."

"I can arrange it," he says. "But your parents will have to approve it before I do."

"All right. I'll let you know." I pull Beau out of Radcliff's office. "We need to hurry. I don't want to be late."

"For lunch? They serve it until fourteen hundred."

"No. For soch-time."

To say my mother is shocked to see that I attended soch-time is a vast understatement. She's so flummoxed, that, if she were a real dragon, her fire would have extinguished in a puff of black smoke.

On the way back to her unit, she pulls it together. "How did the sabotage go?"

"It took us all morning, but we set it up so that when the blockade is sealed, the people on Pingliang can still exchange messages with DES."

She asks some follow-up questions and we chat. It's almost

like old times. Almost. When we arrive, Officer Zaim is not visiting.

"Hey Zee, what's up?" I ask.

An amazing thing happens. My mother goes into the unit, leaving me outside alone with Zaim. Huh. Maybe I should have acted more mature sooner? Who'd've thought that would work?

"Just wanted to let you know that we're having a big meeting in the security conference room tomorrow at eleven hundred."

"Thanks for telling me."

He nods. "See you then."

One can hope. I draw in a deep breath. Time to talk to my parents. They're waiting for me in the living room. My dad is sitting on the couch, while my mother has settled into one of the two armchairs. I take the other armchair.

"We miss seeing you smile," Dad says.

"Not much to smile about these days," I say.

"Yet you light up when the security officers are *not* visiting you," Mom says.

"They're my team."

"We're your family."

I cock my head to the side. "They trust and support me so they're more of a family to me right now than you and Dad." It's the truth.

"You keep mentioning trust. Yet you've been worming all this time when we've forbidden it."

Good point. "I'm in a unique position to save lives so I'm not going to stop because you've forbidden it. I understand why you did it—you're concerned about me and you love me, but I can't humor you this time. It's too important."

"What if Officer Radcliff ordered you to stop interacting with the Q-net? Would you obey him?"

That's a tough question. I think about if for a few minutes. "Yes."

"Why?" Mom demands.

"Because I trust him. And he trusts me. If he wanted me to stop, he would have a damn good reason other than being worried about me. He knows this job comes with risks, but he ensures the risks are as minimal as he can make them."

"Minimal? You have bruises on your neck!"

"Yes. It could have been worse if my team wasn't there to back me up."

"And you don't trust us to keep you safe? You've never gotten bruises from being grounded."

That's because even though I'd like to bang my head against the wall in frustration, I haven't. Yet. I take a breath. "I trust that you *want* to keep me safe. But right now you're being very unreasonable and endangering the entire base because you're under the impression that you *can* keep me safe. No one is safe, Mom. Not until we stop the looters and send all the HoLFs back to their dimension."

Mom and Dad exchange a look. "We're not being unreasonable, we're your parents."

"Yes, you are. But don't expect me to be all smiles and happy about being grounded. Would you have liked it if your parents put a hidden camera in your room? And locked you inside? What if the base caught fire and I was trapped, Mom? How does that keep me safe?"

"It keeps you out of the looters' crosshairs," Mom says,

jumping to her feet. "It keeps you from being kidnapped and taken away from us. It lets you be a normal teenaged girl whose greatest worry is passing her microbiology exam."

"No it doesn't. Not *any* of it. First, that girl is long gone. As much as you'd like to pretend, it doesn't change anything. Lyra is dead, Mom. Accept it."

Mom gasps as tears well.

Not giving her time to respond. I stand and tap a finger on my chest. "I'm already in the crosshairs. Do you know why? Because I'm a threat to them. Q chose me and I'm not going to hide in here pretending to be some happy family when a missile could be on its way right this very minute. You don't want me to get hurt or to be killed. Well, guess what? I don't want you to be hurt or killed either. How do you think I'd feel if you both died and I could have done something to stop it?" Now my own tears threaten as I make a realization. "Is that how you feel? Like if you didn't let me worm and help security, I wouldn't have—"

"No." Now my dad stands. "We're proud of what you've done, Li-Li. You've saved us. This is us trying to save you." He pulls me in for a hug, wrapping his arms around my shoulders.

I lean against him for a moment. They went overboard in "trying to save me," considering I don't need to be saved as I can save myself. However, they love me. That is clear. "How about we work together and try to save everyone?" I ask.

Dad tightens his hold for a moment and releases me. "I'm in. Ming?"

I turn toward her.

Silence. Talk about stubborn.

Finally, Mom wipes her eyes, sits down, and says, "Tace said you did an expert job with that sabotage."

"And there's a smile," Dad says. He settles back in his seat.

"That's because Officer Radcliff is…sparse with his praise."

"You miss living with him?" Dad asks.

"I miss his cooking—no offence, Mom. And I miss seeing Niall and working out with Elese and solving problems with Beau and being treated like an adult. But most of all, I miss our dinners."

"We do, too," Mom admits.

I sense another opening. Perching on the edge of the chair, I ask, "How about a compromise?"

"I'm listening."

"How about I go back to work, but I stay here with you? I'll even go to soch-time."

My mother raises one of her thin eyebrows. "You will?"

"Yes. It's a nice break."

"And in forty-nine days?" she asks.

Ah, she figured it out. "I will be requesting my own unit in security's housing wing. Although I'm pretty sure dinners will still be at Radcliff's."

Mom and Dad do that silent parental communication even though I already know Dad's on board. I give them some privacy by looking around. We've been living on Yulin for…one hundred and seventy-seven days, and they still haven't made this place home. Not a surprise considering the shadow-blobs and looters. But I wonder if Niall would paint them some landscapes. After he does some for me of course. And I hope to hang some of his mother's as well. It's a nice daydream, imagining life *after*.

"All right," Mom says. "We agree to the compromise. Starting tomorrow."

I want to jump up and cheer, but I keep my cool. "And the camera?"

"We'll have it removed."

"Thank you."

When I stand, they both hop to their feet and I'm squeezed in a parent sandwich. This time I hug them back. But I'd forgotten about the gun tucked into my waistband. Dad's arm hits it.

"What's this?" Alarmed, he pulls it out and brandishes it. "Why are you armed?"

"I'm not sure."

"That's not an answer," Mom says. The dragon is rousing from its slumber.

"Officer Radcliff gave it to me yesterday. I don't know why." Which is true.

Dad hands it back to me.

"Spencer," Mom admonishes.

"It's not going to do us any good. Besides, if she was going to shoot us, she'd have done it before now."

"It's a good thing I wasn't armed when I found the camera in my room," I tease.

"Would you have shot us?" Dad's brown eyes light up with curiosity.

"So very tempting, but, no, I wouldn't."

"Why not?" Mom asks also curious.

"Radcliff would have chewed me out."

"So you're more scared of Radcliff than us?"

"Yes. And it would have been irresponsible."

"Good to know," Mom says dryly.

I retreat to my room. That went better than expected. I send messages to Niall and Radcliff, informing them of my ungrounding...is that a word? And I ask if someone can drop off my uniforms before tomorrow morning. I'm hoping Niall will volunteer, but I don't know his work schedule. I receive a message from Radcliff right away.

2522:265: About time, Lawrence. Training with Officer Keir tomorrow at oh-eight-hundred. Don't be late.

Gee, don't get all mushy on me Radcliff. Sheesh. But secretly, I'm glad. Things will soon be back to normal. I do a few push-ups and sit-ups to prevent my body going into shock in the morning. Then a quick shower. I'm about to go into the Q-net to check on Pingliang when there's a knock on my door.

My father pokes his head in. "Dinner."

I glance at the clock. Nineteen hundred hours already. "Okay." I follow him to the kitchen and stop dead.

Niall and Radcliff are sitting at the table, chatting with my mom, who is placing steaming dishes in front of them.

"Surprise," Dad whispers to me. "We owe Tace about a million meals. Of course after he gets a taste of your mother's cooking, he'll be declining all future invitations."

Mom glances up and gives him the I-heard-that glower.

"Nothing wrong with her hearing, though," Dad says.

She lets him see her inner dragon. "It's getting cold, Spencer."

"Coming, dear." He winks at me.

As soon as I enter, Niall hops to his feet and I'm swept into a hug. It's brief because of the company, but I don't mind. I sit next to him and we hold hands under the table. Well, when we're not eating. Because my mother has outdone herself. Still not up to Radcliff's standards, but better than the cafeteria or anything I can cook.

After dinner, Niall helps me carry the stuff they'd brought for me into my room. I've my ruck, boots, uniforms, weapon belt, pulse kit, and the tube filled with the rest of Niall's drawings, which we hang on my walls right away.

Niall pulls me in for a hug. "I'm glad you worked it out with your parents, but I wish you were living closer."

"I will be in forty-nine days." I tell him about having my own unit. "Do you paint?"

"Pictures or walls?"

I laugh. "Pictures. I'm going to need more decorations."

"I can and have. I prefer pencil drawings. I'm not near as good as my mom at painting. Her use of color is brilliant."

"You could make me a finger painting and I'd love it," I say.

"There are actually some famous finger painters. It takes real talent and dexterity."

I raise an eyebrow. "Talented fingers? Could be a handy skill." Untucking his T-shirt, I dip my hand underneath it and slide my fingertips over his lower back. The skin is smooth and heat pours from him. It travels up my arm and pools inside me.

"Mouse." He presses against me. "We need to be on our best behavior. The ungrounding could be revoked."

But his fingers are in my hair and I don't care as we kiss. In fact, I'm thinking of ways I can improve my dexterity when Niall breaks it off.

"Is that a camera?" he asks with alarm and outrage in his voice.

His comment is like a bucket of ice being dumped over my head. I follow his gaze. Of course he noticed the hidden lens. "Mom said she'd turn it off."

"But…that's…" He sputters.

He's cute when he's all indignant on my behalf. "Let's just call it temporary insanity."

"I wouldn't be that quick to forgive."

"Are you sure? I remember a certain boy who was supernova angry at his father for—"

"Okay, okay. I get it."

"Niall," Radcliff says from the doorway. "Time to go."

He tightens his hold for a second before letting go. "Later, Mouse."

"Later, Toad."

"Oh-eight-hundred, Junior Officer Lawrence," Radcliff says, almost gleeful.

But I'm grinning. Because since I've been grounded that's sleeping in. I'll have plenty of time to eat breakfast.

At least, that's the plan. But in the middle of the night, a strident warning jerks me from a sound sleep.

INTRUDERS!

2522:266

I tumble off my bed as Q's warning sinks in. The looters have attacked. *Did you warn Radcliff and the others?* I ask Q while shucking my pajamas and pulling on my security jumpsuit.

YES.

Where are the intruders?

OUTSIDE. PORT. SECURITY. CHEMISTRY LAB. BIOLOGY LAB.

A surge of adrenaline floods my body. How did they spread throughout the base so fast?

MULTI POINT ATTACK.

I curse an impressive variety of words as I shove my feet into my boots. *What's the security team doing?*

FIGHTING INTRUDERS AT MULTIPLE LOCATIONS.

Show me, please. A map of the base appears in my mind. There are clumps of red dots verses purple dots in various places. *Is the purple security officers?* There seems to be way more than eleven.

YES. AND ARMED SCIENTISTS.

Ah. Good for them. Are the looters heading for detention?

YES.

There's a yellow dot there. Must be for Jarren.

CORRECT. HE IS A YELLOW-BELLIED COWARD.

Despite the dire situation, I have to laugh at Q remembering Beau's unique description for Jarren. Clipping on my weapon belt, I tuck my gun into its holster, put the extra power cartridges into another slot, and head out. My parents are already gone. I hope there's a protocol that they're all following.

CORRECT.

What is it?

Instead of telling me, Q shows me the counterattack strategy. Only those involved are sent the call to action, which is why there's not a siren wailing. Everyone else is supposed to shelter in place. There are a couple officers already *en route* to back up the guards in detention. Teams of scientists are assigned to cover labs, protect the housing area, and the entrance to the pits. Plus there's a number of officers in the port. Looks like Radcliff has everything covered. Since I don't have a task, I ask Q for the area that has the most looters.

SECURITY.

How many looters total?

THIRTY.

Huh. Not as many as I expected. I reach the group of armed techs guarding the housing area. There are six of them all holding pulse guns and looking terrified.

"Go back to bed. The situation is under control," Dr. Lyn-

Sue says.

I point to my jumpsuit and weapon belt. "I'm on the security team, you dolt." Okay, I shouldn't have added the dolt comment, but really, what did he think I was doing?

"We were instructed not to let anyone pass either way."

"Good. I need to help my team." I muscle through the group. If they try to shoot me, it shouldn't work. The guns are programmed not to fire at friendlies. And if it works, then it'll hurt like a thousand needles pricking my skin. Not fun. I don't breathe until I'm out of sight. Then I run through the empty corridors toward security. The map is still in my head, showing red dots concentrated in the port and near detention. I'd thought there would be more looters near the pits.

Then I skid to a stop as a horrible scenario occurs to me. *How many looters are in the pits?*

FIFTY-EIGHT.

Not the ones we captured. New ones.

UNKNOWN.

Please show me the camera feeds from the pits. The lights are dim for nighttime and a cloud of dust obscures the view. Stars. I reverse direction and race to the archeology lab. But I stop at one of the weapon lockers Radcliff had installed throughout the base. *Need the code, please!*

FOUR. TWO. SEVEN. NINE.

I love you! A strange flush of warmth sweeps through me.

BE CAREFUL.

Was that Q's equivalent of concern? I'll figure it out later. Punching in the code, I open the locker and grab four energy wave guns. I close the door and run toward the stairwell that goes down to the lab. *Show me the video feeds of the lab, please.*

The cameras show my parents, along with Rance and Morgan, crouched in front of the entrance to the pits. They're exchanging fire with a half-dozen looters who are at the bottom of the stairs and are using the doors to the archeology lab as cover. Two forms are lying on the ground. I can't tell if their friends or foes, but hope they're only stunned.

I slow when I near the stairway. The sizzles of pulses grow louder as I inch closer. I peer through the doors, but no one is on the top steps. Their focus is on the lab and their backs are to me. They're all wearing jumpsuits. Probably made of the same special black material we use for ours. Which means, they're resistant to pulses. A hit from my gun will sting, but won't knock them unconscious. Which means, I have to hit them in the head—a much smaller target than their torso.

Tucking the energy wave guns into my belt, I draw my pulse gun and hope my sessions with Mr. Orange Light were enough to improve my aim. I creep down a few steps to get a better shot. Then I sit down and extend both hands like Elese taught me, squaring my shoulders to the target. My heart is doing laps around my chest, but I steady my breathing and press the trigger. A sizzle crackles and the looter I aimed at jerks and slumps to the ground. Yes!

There's so much noise that none of the looters realize that particular sizzle came from behind. I miss the next two. I hit another man and a woman before they figure it out. The three remaining looters turn and aim at me. I scramble up the steps, but one clips me and fire races up my legs. I keep moving despite the pain and dive to the landing at the top, rolling over so I'm facing the stairway. But after an excruciating minute, both literally and figuratively, no one appears.

It's another thirty seconds before Morgan arrives at the top of the stairs. "Good work distracting them, Lawrence."

"Are they secured?" I ask.

"Yes."

I stagger to my feet. Pins and needles stab my calves.

"Are you hurt?" she asks.

"Just pulsed. Here." I hand her an energy wave gun.

"What's this for?"

I hurry down the stairs. "Come on!"

My parents and Rance are waiting for us at the bottom of the steps. I hand Rance another gun. They're all confused, but I've no time to explain.

"Follow me." I go into the pits and pause.

Elese and all the prisoners are in Pit 1 along with a couple dozen reconstructed Warriors. The prisoners are sitting on their cots under her watchful gaze. One wrong move on their part, and she'll trigger the pulse generator that's been installed on the ceiling—one of Radcliff's defensive weapons. All she has to do is bark a command, and it'll blast everyone below, knocking them all unconscious while alerting security. The captured looters are tense and some look hopeful, while others appear scared. A haze of sand clouds the air and a high-pitched whine pierces the gloom.

"What's that noise?" Morgan asks Elese when she joins us.

"Digging machines," I say. "They're coming in through the other pits." I thrust an energy wave gun at Elese. "Mom and Dad guard the prisoners, please."

Morgan is the first to understand. "Let's go." She takes point.

Rance, Elese, and I follow her. There's no one in Pit 2. No surprise as the rift is still there. By the time we reach Pit 3, machines are just breaking through the walls. We stop at the entrance to Pit 4. They're already inside. Looters are streaming out of the digging machines. I've seen this before. It's the same set up from when they first attacked and destroyed all those Warriors, letting in the shadow-blobs.

"There's too many," Rance says. "We need to retreat."

"We can target the machines so they can't leave," Elese suggests.

"Then they'll just swarm the base. There's too many of them. Let them take the prisoners and leave the way they came." Rance again.

"They're not going to leave," Elese says.

If the looters get by us, all the people in the base will be in danger. That can't happen. I search for another solution. There's plenty of rubble from the destroyed Warriors. If I didn't know better, I would have thought this pit had— Stars! I dismiss my idea—it's horrifying. Come on, Ara, think! But there's no other way to stop them. I touch Morgan's arm.

She turns and meets my gaze. "Make it quick, Lawrence."

"Target the support beams." Bile churns up my throat.

Understanding lightens her ice blue eyes, and she asks, "What about us?"

I swallow. "We should be fine as long as we stay outside the pit."

"That'll work?" she asks.

"Yes." I've worked in the pits almost my entire life.

She puts her hand on my shoulder. "This is *my* decision. Understand?"

"Yes, sir." But I'm still sick to my stomach.

Morgan gives the order and we aim our energy wave guns at the columns of sandstone that support the ceiling in Pit 4. The explosions are deafening and the thick pillars shatter into fist-sized chunks. The looters catch on quick and the ones who haven't been knocked over by flying debris run to their machines. I hope they make it. That they all survive.

We race to the border between Pit 2 and 3 and destroy the support beams in Pit 3. At least, these looters haven't left their machines yet.

A horribly loud groan rumbles through the floor. A cracking sound follows like thunder after lightning.

"Time to go," Morgan orders as the ceiling in Pit 4 breaks apart and strikes the ground. Hard.

We run toward Pit 1. The roar of the collapsing pits behind us rattles my bones. But it's the gush of sand and air that sweeps me off my feet. Large chunks of sandstone rain down around me. Coughing, I curl into a protective ball on the ground. The dense yellow cloud obscures everything. Another dangerous rumble and a sharp crack sounds directly overhead. I close my eyes, lace my fingers behind my neck, and coil tighter.

Thuds shake the ground. I'm pelted with hard lumps and blasted with sand. A heavy weight slams down on my legs. Pain blooms in my right ankle. Then my right bicep throbs. Breathing the thick, sand-laden air is difficult, triggering bouts of coughing.

After an eternity, the noise stops and the debris around me settles. I open my eyes. My eyelashes are heavy with grit and there's nothing to see except blackness. Heavy pieces of the ceiling press down on me. Everyone who works in a Warrior pit trains for this exact situation. If we're caught in a cave-in and survive being buried, we should stay very still and wait for rescue. If we try to move, we might kill ourselves by dislodging a big rock or enough sand to cut off our air supply.

The fact that I have air, even though it's dusty, and I can wiggle my toes, are good signs. And while there's weight on me, it's not crushing me. I hope Morgan, Rance, and Elese got clear. I think I'm in Pit 2. For some reason that ceiling came down as well even though we didn't destroy the supports. Did the rift weaken the pit? Or was it too much of a strain when the other two pits collapsed? Or could it be fate?

Despite Morgan's claim, it was my idea to target those beams and people died. Perhaps this is the universe's punishment for causing all those deaths. How many will be revealed in time. I do hope the digging machines are able to grind their way free. And I'm still not safe. This pocket of air could just be temporary. Pulling my thoughts away from a useless spiral of dire possible fates, I consider what I can do. I reach out to Q. *What's going on in the pits?*

CANNOT SEE.

Stupid question. How about in the rest of the base?

I'm shown video from various areas. It appears our people have the upper hand in all the areas except detention. The officers there are outnumbered and more looters are on the way. I peer closer. Oh no. Niall is there, along with Radcliff! I need to help them. Remembering there was a communicator in Morgan's ear, I ask, *Can you please tell the other officers to go help our people at detention?*

There's a long pause. Maybe that's too much interference for Q. *I wormed into Jarren's communicator*, I remind Q.

SPEAK.

"The team at detention needs help," I say aloud.

And then in my head, *Ara? What's your status?* Morgan's matter-of-fact response calms me.

"I'm fine. Go help Radcliff. Take as many people as you can spare."

Where are you?

"Worry about me later! Go to detention! Now! They won't hold out much longer."

On it.

I watch the camera feeds and warn Morgan when she's about to run into looters. Rance and Elese are with her—thank the universe. I must have been the only one to get caught in the cave-in. They pick up Beau and Tora. And I see Bendix and Zaim leaving the port. Ho remains behind to ensure no more looters try to break through. Bodies litter the floor of the port and there's a new shuttle parked inside. It must not be connected to the Q-net. Or we would have been alerted as soon as they left their forest base.

CORRECT.

I turn my attention back to detention. Why didn't Radcliff call for help? Did his communicator get fried? Knowing Radcliff, he probably didn't want to leave any of the other areas of the base unprotected.

The looters force Radcliff, Niall, and a couple techs back. While half of them keep the pressure on my team, the others break into detention and—

Encounter a nasty surprise! Vedann's in the duct to nowhere and she's shooting down at the looters. Radcliff is a genius.

The looters retreat and run right into Morgan and her team. Boo yah! It takes them a while to stun everyone and get organized. Once I know everyone is okay, my aches and pains clamor for attention. My ankle throbs louder. My shoulders ache from the weight. And various muscles complain about the abuse.

I long to stretch from my cramped position, but know it's too dangerous. Instead, I flex and relax my muscles. Even that small movement causes an avalanche of sound. All small stuff, I hope.

Ara? Morgan's voice sounds in my head. *How are you doing?*

"I've been better."

We're coming. Do you know where you are?

"I think I'm near the edge of the collapse in Pit 2. I was only a couple steps behind you."

Any injuries?

"I think my ankle is broken."

Dr. Edwards is *en route*. Hold on.

After a few minutes, my dad calls my name. It's muffled and sounds far away.

"I'm here," I yell with relief. If anyone can extract a person from a pile of debris, it's my dad. He understands cave-ins.

"Keep calling, Li-Li, so we can locate your position."

I repeat "here" a few more times.

"I think I found you." His voice is much louder than before.

"Can you see the spotlight?"

I open my eyes. A white light shines through the narrow spaces between the rocks. "Yes."

"Good." He practically sighs the word.

My poor parents. They're never going to let me leave my room after this. And maybe I shouldn't have left. Those people buried in Pits 3 and 4 would be alive right now.

"It doesn't look too bad, Li-Li. Give us some time to shore a few things up and remove a few obstacles. If anything shifts and presses harder on you, let me know right away. Okay?"

"Okay."

Some time ends up being hours. Yes, hours. They are being extremely careful not to kill me, so I'm not going to complain. I spend the time in painful contemplation. And while the guilt for causing those deaths still drags on me, I understand that the looters' intent had been to harm us.

Q keeps me updated on the clean-up in other parts of the base. All of the looters were armed with pulse guns. No deaths were reported. A relief, but I wonder why. The looters want us gone so they can have access to all the pits without interference. I must be missing an important clue.

Finally the weight lifts off my shoulders. I squint in the brightness as I take in my first deep breath in hours. My dad peers down at me. His face is streaked with dirt. His torn clothes are filthy and bloodstained, but he's grinning like a madman.

"One more block, Li-Li, and we'll have you free." He points at the massive chunk resting on my legs.

They rig a pulley system above my spot. After securing the block with ropes, they lift it using the pulley and move it aside.

Blood rushes back into my legs and I cry out as pain wakes from its numb slumber.

"What's wrong?" Dad asks.

"Ankle hurts."

"Dr. Edwards, your turn. Don't move, Li-Li." Dad disappears.

I bite down on the urge to call him back. But soon Dr. Edwards crouches over me. There's still a ring of debris around my location. Almost like I was nestled in a mouse burrow and they've just pried off the ceiling.

"Where does it hurt?" he asks.

I describe my various injuries and degree of pain. Dr. Edwards examines my pupils with his pocket light, tenderly probes my head for contusions, and decides that I can be moved without risking further injury. But there's the small matter of my ankle. Okay, not small, and my muscles are all stiff and unwilling to help with my efforts to stand. Much to my extreme embarrassment, Rance is called in to lift me from my burrow.

He is as dirty and dusty as my dad and I suspect he's been here helping.

"Typical rookie," he says as he slides his arms under my shoulders and knees. "Trying to shirk training with some weak excuse about your ankle." His teasing tone smooths the awkwardness.

"And look at you. Finally having a chance to show off your muscles."

He laughs. "It's what I live for."

There's a cheer when he lifts me up. Lots of faces wait beyond the rubble. As I suspected, I'm near the edge of Pit 2, which was lucky. There's almost a solid wall of debris where Pits 3 and 4 used to be. How many looters are buried there? My stomach lurches.

Rance picks his way over the rubble. The faces sharpen into recognizable people—Mom, Dad, Niall, Radcliff, and Morgan. All covered with dust, but all smiling. The prisoners must have been evacuated because of the rest of Pit 1 is empty.

"Where do you want her?" Rance asks Dr. Edward.

"There's a gurney waiting upstairs."

Rance takes me through the archeology lab and up the steps. Stunned looters are still lying on the ground. Behind Rance is a parade of people following us. When he sets me on the gurney, I'm able to stretch out for the first time. It's a painful endeavor, but in a strange way is also a vast relief.

"Do you want something for that ankle?" Dr. Edwards ask.

"Yes, please." It's throbbing like a pulsar.

He pricks me with a needle. Soon a soothing liquid spreads throughout my body, silencing the noise and also calming my worries. The people gathered around me turn soft, but I reach for Niall's hand before drifting to sleep.

I wake in the infirmary. My dad is sitting next to my bed, working on a portable. His short brown hair is wet and he's changed into clean clothes.

"Thanks," I say.

He glances at me and smiles. "No need to thank me. It's my parental duty or my biological right—one of those. I've been accused of both."

"Funny." But the fact he can tease means I don't have any serious injuries. "What's the damage?" I ask him.

"Broken right ankle. Edwards had to put in a few pins, but they'll dissolve as the calcium accelerators repair the breaks. Various cuts and contusions. You'll be stiff and sore for a couple days. You were lucky."

"I remembered my cave-in training."

Dad presses a hand to his chest. "You mean you actually listened?"

"Shocking, I know." Then I sobered. "Do you know why Pit 2 collapsed as well?"

"With the multiple breaches from the digging machines, the entire area was unstable. We've moved the prisoners out of Pit 1 and into a couple of the labs."

"I'm sorry."

"For what?"

"It was my idea."

"Officer Morgan took full responsibility for making the decision. And don't forget the looters decided to attack us."

"I agree the logic is sound, but my heart disagrees, Dad."

"Those pesky emotions are always ruining solid reasoning." He tsks. "Time will help."

True. My guilt over Officer Menz's death has lost its sharp edge. "Do you know how many were...killed?"

"No, but we do know six of the digging machines made it out. There's holes in the desert and tracks to a staging area."

I'm glad they escaped the pits. "Staging area?"

"Yes, they shuttled in all the equipment to an area out of

sight from the base. From there they attacked."

"Those shuttles weren't connected to the Q-net. None of their equipment is."

"We know."

"Did any of our people get hurt?"

"Other than being stunned, no one had any major injuries. You are actually the worst one."

That's good to know. "Does Radcliff think the looters will return?"

My father hesitates, then clears his throat. "I'll let him tell you his thoughts. Security is planning a meeting later this afternoon."

I glance at the clock. It's twelve-thirty. I throw the covers off and sit up. Every muscle hurts. All six-hundred and fifty of them. Especially my shoulders and right arm. There's a bandage wrapped around my bicep. The room spins slightly.

"What are you doing?"

"I have to get ready for soch-time."

"No one expects you to attend today."

"The *kids* expect me. I need to go."

My father stares at me as if he's never seen me before. "You're supposed to stay off that ankle for a full day."

"Can you get me a wheelchair? Help me get dressed?" I swing my legs over the edge. There's a white…contraption around my ankle.

"Uh… Let me check." He bolts.

By the time Dr. Edwards enters my room, I'm hopping on one leg to the washroom. He blocks my way.

"You're certainly determined, Miss Lawrence," he says,

supporting my elbow. "Is it that important?"

"Yes."

He considers. "All right, but you will return right afterward. Understand?"

"Yes!"

"I'll get a nurse to help you." Muttering under his breath about difficult patients, he hustles out.

I continue to the washroom. A nurse arrives soon after with a wheelchair. She helps me change into a pair of scrubs. Best of all she brings me some pain meds, water, and an energy bar. When I'm ready to go, my father appears. He pushes me to the soch-area. I direct him to my spot.

"Thanks, Dad," I say as he kisses my cheek good-bye.

As soon as he's gone, the kids surround my chair with a million questions.

"What happened?"

"How did you get hurt?"

"Are we going to die?"

"My dad was out all night."

"Did the bad guys attack us?"

"My sister said the planet is angry and is going to swallow us whole!"

"Are we going to die?"

"I wanna go back to Xinji."

I wait until they run out of steam. I suspected the adults wouldn't tell them what happened in order not to scare them. But kids are smarter than they're given credit for, and can sense the wrongness. It just increases their anxiety when they don't know what's going on.

Once the questions peter out, I say, "Remember when I told you we had the best security team in the Galaxy?"

Solemn nods all around.

"Last night they proved they're the best."

"But you're hurt." Miguel, once again stating the obvious.

"I broke my ankle in the pits when we stopped the looters from rescuing their people. It didn't stop me from coming here, so it can't be that bad, right?" Then I add, "You want to know what's really amazing?"

They lean closer, eyes wide.

"No one else was hurt."

"I heard the bad guys stunned some of the geology techs," Val says.

"That stings, but once you wake up you're perfectly fine. And that proves they're not trying to hurt us." Which isn't a lie. At all. They didn't come to kill, but to free the prisoners. Yes, I know what you're thinking—*this time*—but I'm going to ignore that and concentrate on helping the kids. "Who wants to learn the mouse-in-its-burrow move?" I ask.

"Me!" A universal response.

"Great. Kuma, can you follow my instructions and demonstrate for me?"

She straightens to her full height—all one hundred and twenty centimeters—super cute. "Yes, sir!"

I coach her to curl up in a small little ball. The kids catch on quick and we have races to see who can drop and curl into their burrows the fastest. Then I play music and when I stop the music, they burrow.

"When will we need this move?" Miguel asks.

"When you hear a loud sound above you and things start to rain from the ceiling."

"Like that time the windows shattered after that big boom?" Kuma asks.

"Exactly!" See? These kids are smart. I'm rather proud.

Niall shows up at the end of soch-time to wheel me back to the infirmary. He's wearing his uniform. Boo. And his expression is…not stern…more sad, maybe tired.

"Did your father order you to escort me?" I ask, trying to lighten the mood.

"Believe it or not, I volunteered." There's a hint of my Toad in his half-smile.

"So brave." I fan my face as if overwhelmed with his manliness.

"Don't I know it. Who knows when the ceiling might come crashing down on us."

Okay that hit too close to home. I peer at him, but he avoids my gaze. Instead he grabs the handles of the wheelchair and pushes me from the soch-area. He remains quiet as he navigates the hallways and avoids running anyone over—a harder task than you'd think. I'm not sure what he wants me to say. I didn't plan to be buried or I wouldn't have suggested shooting out the supports. He knows what our job entails. So I don't say anything.

Dr. Edwards is waiting for me in my room. He helps me get into bed and checks my ankle.

"This is a flexible cast," he says, tapping a finger on the white contraption. "In a couple days, you'll be able to walk without pain as long as it remains on. It'll come off in a week. You can get it wet. Until then, you'll have to use crutches. If you stay in bed for the rest of the day, I'll release you in the morning."

But that means I'll miss the security meeting later today. His frown deepens as he waits for my response.

"I'll try, Doc."

He grunts and leaves. I turn to ask Niall about the time for the meeting, but he's gone. His absence is like being kicked in the stomach. I lie down, pull the blankets up to my chin, and stare at the ceiling, which remains firmly in place—for now. An uneasiness gnaws on my thoughts. Does Niall think I'm a heartless killer? The plan to bury the looters alive was extreme. I'm supposed to be a good guy. Why couldn't I come up with a better solution?

NO BETTER SOLUTION.

Are you sure? We could have exchanged fire, held them off until... But no one was coming to back us up. We should have done what Rance suggested—retreated and allowed the looters to free their people.

SHOULD HAVE. COULD HAVE. WASTE OF TIME. YOU DID. IT IS DONE.

You sound just like my mother.

THANK YOU.

Should I be surprised or alarmed that Q thinks that's a compliment? I decide on mildly concerned. And thinking of my mother, I wonder if she's upset about never being able to reconstruct those destroyed Warriors. Have I ruined everything?

MORE WARRIORS IN FACTORY.

Enough to close the rift?

AS LONG AS THEY HAVE HEARTS.

Dr. Bharathi visits me. She's a welcome break from the destructive cycle of my thoughts.

"I hear you've had quite the adventure," she says in her calm, soothing voice.

"That's an interesting way to describe it."

"Ah, yes. You like the brutal truth."

"I do."

"All right." She settles in the visitor's chair. "You were buried alive."

"You forgot to add it was due to my own evil scheme."

"That's a separate issue. Let's focus on you being alone and injured while trapped in the dark, wondering if you'd survive."

"Actually, Dr. Bharathi, once the debris settled, I was pretty sure I'd live. And I wasn't alone."

"The Q-net?"

"Always with me. And I don't mind that. It was comforting. It's that separate issue I'm going to have problems with."

She drums her long fingers on her thigh. "Your evil scheme?"

"Yes."

"Being the cause of another's death is traumatic no matter the circumstances. You knew what would happen if the pits collapsed, yet you still made the suggestion."

"Exactly."

"What were you thinking right before?"

"That the last time looters invaded the pits, they destroyed thousands of Warriors and let in the HoLFs. That this time my charges were in danger of being killed and I couldn't allow that to happen."

"And that's evil?"

"I decided their lives were worth less than the people in the base. All lives are equally precious. It's one of the first things you learn as a security officer."

"Fair point. So tell me how you would have felt if you didn't voice that suggestion and the looters overran the base and killed everyone inside it?"

Beyond horrible. Probably suicidal. "But that's the thing. They weren't planning to *kill* everyone."

"How do you know? Can you read their minds? Or did the Q-net tell you?"

"No to both questions. The looters in the base had pulse guns and there were only enough of them for a rescue mission. If I'd connected the clues sooner, I wouldn't have suggested collapsing the pits."

"And you're the one who is supposed to connect the clues?"

"We all are tasked with that, but I had all the information at that time."

"Because of the Q-net?"

"Yes."

Silence. I peek at Dr. Bharathi. Is she edging away from me? No, she's sitting there looking thoughtful and idly playing with her long brown braid.

"I, for one, am grateful that you stopped the looters in the pits," she says. "If they'd rescued all their people, what's to stop them from sending another missile to destroy the base? Having Jarren and the prisoners protects us all."

She has a point.

"And you're not evil. Believe me. In my line of work, I've seen evil, shook hands with it, and tried unsuccessfully to banish it. You're still clinging to your Q-net coping mechanism. In the case of the looters, it was pure self-defense."

It's nice of her to say that. I give her a weak smile.

"I see you don't believe me. That's all right. Once you accept that you're a person who will do anything, including kill another, to protect the people you love, you'll feel better. And about that 'all lives are precious' that every security officer is taught?"

"What about it?"

"You might want to ask Officer Radcliff how many people he's killed while performing his duty. Or some of the more experienced officers, I'm sure they've struggled with the very thing you're struggling with now."

I didn't think of that. "Thanks, Doc."

"Anytime, Ara." She puts her hand over mine. "And I mean that. *Anytime.*" Squeezing my hand briefly, she stands. "Get some rest."

Surprisingly, I do. That is until Radcliff arrives with my mother a step behind. Oh boy. Not wanting to deal with this lying down, I sit up.

"Isn't there a team meeting?" I ask Radcliff.

"Soon. I wanted to debrief you beforehand."

Ah, that explains my mother's presence.

"Walk me through your actions last night," Radcliff orders.

I explain about Q waking me up. My original plan to help at detention. "Genius move, using the duct to nowhere," I say.

He gives me a tight smile. "Why did you decide to go to the pits instead?"

"Because the attack was also a rescue mission. I thought, why weren't there more looters at the pits? There's fifty-eight of their people there and only a half-dozen trying to reach them. It occurred to me they were going to come into the pits like they had the last time with digging machines."

"Why did you take the energy wave guns?"

"Because of the digging machines. I thought we could disable them when they broke through, trapping them so the looters couldn't escape." I sigh. "But I was too late. They were already there and out of the vehicles. And there were so many…" Guilt chews holes in my guts.

"How many?"

"Dozens. Too many for the four of us to stop."

"Genius move, targeting the support pillars," Radcliff says.

I glance at him sharply. "People died."

"Yes. I agree with Officer Morgan's decision."

"She wouldn't have made that decision without my big mouth."

"How do you know she wouldn't have thought of it herself?" Radcliff asks. "Or Officer Kier or Officer Rance?"

It's obvious what he's doing. I don't take the bait, keeping quiet instead.

"Officer Morgan is getting a commendation in her record for that decision."

"Why?" I thought the opposite would happen.

"We checked the tunnels going from the pits to the surface that the digging machines created. One of them had partially collapsed and trapped a man. He'll live. There was a nasty bump on his head and he was raving. He kept yelling that they were going to 'kill them all.' He was armed with a kill zapper."

"Oh." For the first time since being rescued, the tightness around my chest eases and I can finally breathe easy.

"Yes, *oh*. The looters planned to free their people then launch a second attack—to target the people in the base. Officer Morgan saved everyone's lives. That's why she's getting a commendation in her record." He stands. "Thank you for the information."

He nods at my mother and heads for the door.

"Wait," I say.

Radcliff glances back.

"Can I attend the security meeting?"

"Dr. Edwards says you need to stay off your ankle for twenty-four hours," Mom says.

"I'll use the wheelchair."

"If you can get permission from Dr. Edwards and your parents, you can attend the meeting," Radcliff says. He leaves.

I wilt. That's not going to happen. I collapse back onto my pillow.

"You're not even going to ask?" Mom's voice is incredulous.

"I figured I'm grounded again."

"Why?"

I glance at her. She's sitting in the visitor's chair, appearing calm. No sign of the dragon. Yet.

"Because I was buried in rubble. My ankle's broken. You and dad tend to get overprotective about things like that." I hold up a hand. "Yes, it's your biological right. I get it."

"I'd like nothing better than to see you safe inside our unit. But, like you pointed out to us, that's a fiction. There's no place safe in the base. On this planet." She huffs a little fire. "Radcliff should give *you* that commendation. It was your idea."

"I don't want it. Trust me!"

She smiles softly. "I do."

A lump forms in my throat. And there's something wrong with my vision. Everything turns blurry as my nose fills up. I sniff as tears run and dampen my pillow.

She hops to her feet. "You've an hour before the meeting." She wheels the chair over to the bed. "Come on, we'll swing by our unit so you can change into your uniform."

Wow. Mom helps me into the chair. "What about Dr. Edwards?"

"Oh please. Do you think he can stop the dragon?"

I choke, triggering a coughing fit. "Who…"

"Give your mother some credit," she says. "Don't worry, I've been called much worse. Who do you think you get your stubborn determination from?" Her hands are on her hips and I can imagine a pair of powerful scaled claws spreading out beside her. Chinese dragons don't fly, they swim. "Someday, they'll be calling you the dragon, too." There's a fire in her eyes. "Better than a mouse."

I laugh. "There are advantages to being a mouse, Mom."

"Like what?"

"Being underestimated. Being able to hide. Being clever."

"I stand corrected. Come on, *Qiángdà de shŭ*, you don't want to be late."

"*Qiángdà de shŭ?*"

"It's Chinese for mighty mouse."

As I ease into the wheelchair, I say, "I don't feel very mighty."

"The best ones never do." Mom pushes me out of my room and almost runs over Dr. Edwards.

He yelps and jumps out of the way. Instead of stopping, Mom yells something about bringing me back and increases her pace. By the time we reach our unit, we're both laughing and gasping for breath.

Mom wheels me into security's conference room. The buzz of conversation ceases for a second as everyone quickly hides their surprise. Beau and Elese pull their chairs apart so there's room at the table for me. Mom sits in the empty seat next to my dad. Niall's sitting across the table. He meets my gaze, but there's no smile. The entire security team is here, which makes me wonder who is guarding detention and the pits.

"Our time is limited, so let's get started," Radcliff says from the far end of the table. The screen behind him shows a map of the base. Morgan is next to the terminal and is entangled in the Q-net. Perhaps monitoring the base's camera feeds or handling the graphics for the meeting.

CORRECT.

Which one?

BOTH.

Radcliff takes us through the attack, explaining how the looters approached the base, gained entry, and fled. "We've twenty new prisoners to take care of. We estimated about fifty escaped and a dozen died."

A dozen. I grip the edge of the table. A buzzing sounds in my ears as all the blood drains from my head. Radcliff keeps talking, but his words just bounce off me.

Elese leans close. "Breathe," she whispers in my ear.

But the air has turned to sand. It clogs my nose, throat, my lungs. I imagine that's how those looters felt, crushed under kilotons of sandstone and unable to draw in precious air.

"Breathe." Elese digs her fingernails into my arm.

The sharp pain snaps me out of it and I suck in a huge gulp of air.

"A dozen of them instead of three hundred of us. I'd do it again," Elese whispers.

So busy wallowing in self-pity, I'd forgotten Elese and Rance also shot those support pillars and might feel guilty, too. I tap her hand in thanks. She shoots me a smile before focusing on Radcliff. There are four half-moon indentations on my skin, turning red. I pull my sleeve down to cover them. But I'm glad for the burning on my arm. It keeps me centered.

I return my attention to the meeting. Radcliff is describing where the new prisoners will be housed, and the rotation of shifts to guard the various labs. The screen shows the labs.

Then Radcliff scans all the faces in the room. "The looters will attack again. That's not up for debate. What is up for debate is if they'll try another rescue attempt, or send a missile to kill us all. Thoughts?"

There's a stunned silence after Radcliff's question. Don't get me wrong, we've all been thinking it, but for him to just lay it out there…it has more weight.

"We have eighty-eight of their people," Tora says. "They won't bomb the base."

"They're attacking Warrior planets every thirty days or so," Beau says. "They have a tight schedule. The first of the Protector Class ships that were sent by DES is due to arrive at Suzhou in fifty-one days. They'll need to have all the Warrior planets secured by then."

"Why do they want the Warrior planets?" Zaim asks. "What are we missing?"

Radcliff looks at me. "I believe Junior Officer Lawrence has a theory."

The entire room focuses on me. Thanks so much, Radcliff. "They're using the Warriors to travel from planet to planet. The…what I've been calling, 'Warrior Express', isn't affected by the time dilation." I explain how the network works. Q helps out by showing diagrams on the screen. "The looters are using this network, but they're not using it properly and there are consequences. The HoLFs." I inform them of the shadow dimension and how the network was installed to protect us.

More stunned silence.

Then from Bendix, "The way you're talking, this doesn't sound like a theory. How do you know all this?"

My dad says, "From Dr. Lan Maddrey's research and translations of the alien symbols."

Beau adds, "And from seeing the portal form in Pit 21."

Both Niall and Elese add they'd seen it too.

"I learned some of this from Jarren," I say. "But Q helped with the rest." I gesture to the screen, where there's a diagram of tears between dimensions. Might as well be honest. They all know I've claimed Q is sentient.

They exchange looks and I press my lips together to keep from yelling at everyone that I'm *not* crazy.

"Q is actively helping us," Beau says. "It spoke to me and aided us when we sabotaged the blockade around Planet Pingliang."

Gratitude and pride spreads through me. That's my partner. I refrain from high-fiving him. "And I also suspect that they're trying to relocate the Warriors on the active planets to their own bases before the Protector ships arrive." Which takes time as those suckers are heavy.

"Why isn't Planet Suzhou the next in line to go silent?" Ho asks.

"I suspect the looters have already gained control of the base," Radcliff says. "Either that or everyone on Suzhou is a willing participant, which I think would be difficult. Suzhou was probably the first to be taken, but the looters are keeping up appearances and sending reports so DES doesn't suspect."

"And they're probably going to evacuate before the Protector ship arrives," Morgan adds.

"If all this is true," Tora says. "Then I change my opinion. The Warriors are more important than their people. They'll want us all dead so they can get to the Warriors."

"Is it true?" Vedann asks, glancing between me and Radcliff.

"It is," Radcliff says.

Nice.

"This is bigger than we can handle. What can we do?" Rance asks.

INCOMING!

What? I glance at the screen. A new graphic shows a missile was just launched from the looters' base. "Incoming!" I shout, pointing. "We have sixteen minutes!"

I guess that answers Radcliff's question about the looters' plans.

2522:266

Everyone in the conference room is staring at the graphic of the missile's path as it arcs over Yulin.

Radcliff curses and springs to his feet. "On the roof. Now!"

All the officers scramble, rushing from the conference room.

Niall pauses next to my chair. "Love you, Mouse," he whispers in my ear. Then he's gone.

My parents stare at me. Their faces drain of color. And while terror runs through my veins, I wonder, what the security team can do against a missile? Why are they on the roof?

"Energy wave guns," Dad says.

"What?" Mom asks.

"That's why they're armed with those guns. They're going to try to destroy the missile before it hits the base."

Oh. My. Stars. The missile needs to be close. If it works, the shrapnel and explosion will kill them all. The security team fully expects to die. Oh. My. Stars!

"We need to warn the rest of the base!" Mom runs to the

terminal, but the siren sounds before she can entangle.

Q took action just from hearing my mother. And then it hits me. "Q warned me!"

Both parents look at me as if the stress has finally gotten to me.

"The missile must be connected to Q somehow."

CORRECT.

How?

ONE SUBROUTINE IN THE GUIDANCE SYSTEM.

Perfect. We can change the coordinates for the target. But to where? I ask my parents.

"We need it to go off close to the base so the looters believe they've hit us," Dad says. "That will give us enough time to evacuate before they figure it out and send another missile."

"But not over the pits!" Mom says.

She's right. We need the Warriors now more than ever. I ask Q to pick a new target close to the base, but not too close and not over any of the pits and not where it will come within range of the officers' guns. Because they won't know not to shoot at it.

HOW MUCH DAMAGE?

To the base?

YES.

As long as everyone lives, it doesn't matter. Then I worm into the guidance system since I have to alter the program. It's well protected, but I have Q highlight the important commands. The high-pitched whistle growing louder with every second doesn't help my nerves. Sweat pours down my back and I'm clutching the arms of the chair in a death grip. Sorry, bad choice of words.

Finally, I find the coordinates and change them to the ones Q gives me. We've forty-three seconds left.

My father yanks me from my wheelchair and after a family hug and declarations of love, the three of us huddle under the table mouse-in-its-burrow style. That's twice in one day. Good thing I'm jacked on adrenaline or I'd be in serious pain.

A deafening roar slams into the base. The world around us reacts as if a monster dog just grabbed the planet in its teeth and shook its head. Crashes, bangs, screeches—an entire dictionary of alarming noises—erupt. Something lands on the table with enough force to make the legs collapse. Then it bounces off as the table top smashes into my left shoulder. Without any conscious decision, I'd curled up on the opposite side. Perhaps in an attempt to protect my other injuries.

The world shudders once more then stills. A ringing in my ears is the only sound. My father is the first to uncurl. He pushes the conference table off of us and we crawl out from our burrows. I sit on the floor.

"Is everyone all right?" Dad asks in a muffled, distant voice, as if he's speaking through a blanket.

We take stock and other than bruised shoulders and a few cuts, we're fine. The room is a mess and there's a large hole in the ceiling. We puzzle over that until a groan sounds from the other side of the room. Dad rushes over.

"Just lie still," Dad says. "Where does it hurt?"

I crawl through the debris. Dad is crouched over Bendix. He's bleeding from multiple cuts and looks dazed. He must have fallen through the ceiling, landed on the table, and rolled off.

"Where are the others?" I ask Bendix.

"Don't know. Bloody missile jigged out of range as if it knew we were targeting it! Radcliff ordered us to get down. And…" He glances around. "I guess I got down."

Mom's pressing a hand to her shoulder. Blood stains her sleeve.

"It's just a cut," she says when I ask her about it. Then she glances around. "Should we report this to DES?"

It's funny in a scary way that even a missile isn't going to stop her dedication to her job. Except this time— "No! No messages to DES or anyone at all! The dead don't send reports. The looters need to think we're all dead." *Please block all communications*, I say to Q.

ON IT.

Giggles bubble up my throat over Q using Morgan's expression.

My mom swipes a hair from her face. "We need to start the evacuation and help with the wounded. Come on, Spencer." She glances at me. "You'll stay with security." Her comment is a mix of a question and an order, as if she's not sure.

"Yes."

"Good." But she can't resist adding, "Stay off that ankle."

I laugh. "Go. Organize. Give commands." I shoo. "They'll feel safer when they see the dragon in action."

"And you?"

"*Qiángdà de shǔ.*"

Dad laughs. "Apt. I almost feel sorry for the looters. Almost." He helps Mom to her feet and they head out.

I stand on wobbly legs and fetch the first aid kit. There's one in every room in the base. My ankle protests each limping step as the rest of my bruises wake, but I ignore them. By the time I'm finished cleaning and bandaging Bendix's cuts, he's no longer dazed.

"Any broken bones? Headache?" I ask.

He moves his arms and legs. "No. I hit the table with my shoulders." He rolls them. "Bruised, but not broken."

We stand and dust off our uniforms.

"We better check detention; bring the first aid kit." Then he pauses. "Do I need to carry you?"

"No!" It comes out as a squeak. I clear my throat. "I'm fine."

He scans the mess, then bends down and rips off one of the table's legs. "Here. You can use this as a cane."

"Thanks." It's not perfect, but it works. I limp after Bendix.

We check on the ten prisoners in detention one at a time. Although shaken with some minor bruising, they're otherwise fine. We leave Jarren for last. When Bendix opens his cell door, Jarren is lying on the floor in a heap as if he fell off his bunk.

He appears to be unconscious. Maybe he hit his head. Bendix goes inside to check his pulse. Just as he bends over, Jarren leaps up, knocking Bendix down. Jarren sprints toward me. My pulse gun jumps into my hand and shoots the murdering bastard. Jarren cries out and crumples at my feet.

"Nice work, Lawrence," Bendix says as he tosses Jarren back into his cell. The action is far from gentle. Jarren lands with a satisfying thud. Bendix points to my hand still holding the magical pulse gun. "If you ever doubt that you're supposed to be doing this job, think of that, Lawrence."

"The gun?"

"The fact you drew that gun fast enough to get the bad guy."

"I've no memory of doing it."

He laughs. "Even better."

"Are you two having a moment, or can I interrupt?" Radcliff asks in his gruff lion tone that means he's worried. Standing in the doorway, Radcliff fills the space. His uniform is dirty, but otherwise he appears healthy and whole. I refrain from hugging him.

"Niall and the others?" I ask.

"The rest of the team are fine."

So great is my relief, I need to lean against the wall.

Radcliff gives Bendix a pointed look. "We were most concerned about Officer Bendix."

"I landed on the conference table." He rubs his shoulder. "Could have been worse."

"That's 'cause there were three people under that table to break your fall." I rub *my* shoulder.

"The prisoners?" Radcliff asks.

"All survived, although Jarren will be out of it for a while."

Radcliff glances at my gun. "I see." Then he gestures us to the hall outside detention and asks, "What happened to that missile?"

I explain.

"Will you be able to do it again?"

"I doubt they will make that mistake again." I tell him about Q blocking all our communications. "Hopefully that will give us some time."

"We still need to get everyone evacuated to the pits before they realize the missile missed," Radcliff says.

"Do you know which pits?"

"Your mother picked them. Why?"

"Jarren and his goons could have looted them."

"Why does it matter? That'll just give us more room to spread out," Bendix says.

"We need intact pits because we're going to need to use those portals," I say.

Radcliff doesn't respond for a few heartbeats. "There's bound to be another way out of this. We just haven't thought of it yet."

"Another genius move?"

"Exactly."

"But if we don't think of something brilliant, then escaping via the portals can be our Operation Desperation."

"You're not going to give up on that plan, are you?"

I smile sweetly at him.

"All right. Figure out the logistics, Lawrence. What do you need from me?"

"I need to talk to Jarren again, and then I'll need Beau's help."

"It might be a while before that can happen. The evacuation comes first."

"Are you evacuating the prisoners?"

"No."

I'm not sure if I'm horrified, impressed, or nauseous. "And security?"

"We'll continue to guard the prisoners using rotating shifts. We won't be hiding in the pits. Can you cover detention, Lawrence?"

"Can I sit down while on watch?"

"Yes. Just keep your gun in hand."

Radcliff turns to Bendix. "You're with me."

"Yes, sir."

They leave and I return to detention. I spin in a slow circle. The space is about three meters wide and eight meters long. There are five doors along the left wall, and five on the right. Everything's white. I confirm that all the cell doors are locked. I shine my flashlight through the grate into the duct to nowhere, checking for any hidden intruders. It's empty. There's a couple chairs and a table on the far end. The table is laying on its side.

I right the table and arrange the chairs so I can rest my right foot on one and sit on the other. See, Dr. Edwards? I'm keeping my weight off my ankle.

Facing the doorway in case anyone tries to come in, I believe I'm in a strong defensive position. It helps that, through Q, I can also watch the video feeds throughout the base, especially from the cameras in the cells and in the corridor outside detention. Jarren hasn't moved from where Bendix tossed him.

Please alert me if anyone approaches, I say to Q. Then I scan the areas that were hardest hit. The bomb landed a few kilometers south of the base. All the walls facing the blast are warped. The glass in the windows has shattered, and there are wires hanging down from holes in the ceiling tiles. The halls outside the housing units are filled with people carrying bags, small pieces of furniture, and a few are holding small children.

Seeking injuries, I scan faces. A few cuts. A bruise or two. A wince of pain. Do I dare check the infirmary?

NO FATALITIES. MINOR INJURIES ONLY.

Thanks. Any sign of the looters?

YES.

Where?

CHECKING FOR LIFE SIGNS.

How?

THROUGH ME.

And?

THEY FOUND NONE.

Whew. I relax back. *Please let me know if they check again.*

WILL DO.

I spot Kuma with her family. She has a backpack on and it appears she's encouraging her family to pick up the pace. That's my girl. She'd make an excellent security officer. Then I watch the action at the port. My parents are there directing traffic. All our dune buggies are being loaded with supplies. The field teams had been recalled since the looters' second attack. So there's plenty of tents and camping equipment to go around. It appears groups of people are waiting to leave.

What are they waiting for?

DARKNESS.

Oh, that makes sense. There might be looters keeping an eye on the base. I continue to monitor all the action throughout the base. It helps me stay awake as the hours add up. Eventually my stomach gives up whining for food, but my ankle increases its demands for pain medicine.

Some of the prisoners bang on their doors, clamoring for dinner.

"No dinner tonight," I yell. "The cafeteria was bombed by *your* friends." It's not true, but they stop making noise.

After the sun sets, teams of people head out into the desert.

Some are walking, while others ride on the buggies. I wonder if the pits my mother chose are all together or spread out.

SPREAD OUT.

Why?

SAFER.

I guess if one pit is bombed, the other people could escape. *Which pits?*

PITS 21, 25, 37, 45, 63.

Why those?

ALL INTACT.

Which means no chance of shadow-blobs. However Pits 45 and 63 are too far away to reach before the sun comes up. Are they going to use the shuttles we confiscated from the looters to get there? Morgan can fly one, but would the machine be detected by the looters?

NOT IF PROTECTED.

Protected by you?

YES.

I'd have to set up the program, right?

YES.

I'll ask Radcliff or Morgan the next time I see them. In the meantime, I'm curious. *Which planets do those five pits go to?*

PLANETS DONGGUAN, UNNAMED, HESHAN, LU'AN, UNNAMED.

The unnamed ones must be one of the forty-two planets we haven't yet discovered. The others are not the best destinations, but the pits nearby might have better ones. *Can you please make me a chart of all the pits on Yulin and which planet they go to?*

ON IT.

After another two hours, I really need to use the washroom. As I'm debating if I can leave my post for a quick break, Niall arrives. I'm in his arms in a flash. I don't care that we're both in uniform or the fact my ankle is screaming in pain.

"I can't believe you all went up on the roof." I squeeze him tight. "That was so stupid, brave, scary, amazing."

"Can't…breathe."

"Oh. Sorry." I relax my death grip around his ribs, but I don't let go. Instead I press my ear to his chest, listening to his heart.

"It's okay, Mouse. You saved us."

I pull back to look at his expression. Is he upset? He appears as exhausted as I feel, but I get a tired smile.

"I was only able to save you because they missed cutting out one Q-net subroutine in the guidance system. Otherwise…" I shudder.

He draws me back against him. And I soak in his warmth. My stomach growls. Niall laughs and releases me. Stupid stomach.

"I brought dinner." Niall shrugs off his ruck.

"For the prisoners?"

"For me and you. They can skip a meal."

"Great, I just need to use the washroom first."

Niall glances at my ankle. "I also have some pain meds for you."

"Then I'll be quick."

"Do you need help?"

I wave my improvised cane at him. "Got it." Hurrying down the corridor, I find the closest washroom. Perhaps I should have taken the medicine first. By the time I return, the pain has climbed my leg.

Niall takes one look at my expression and sweeps me off my feet. He sets me down in the chair, but he remains crouched in front of me. "It's not weak to ask for help, Mouse."

I sense this is about more than going to the washroom alone. "I know. I ask for help all the time."

"From the Q-net?"

"Yes."

"That doesn't count."

Actually, if Q didn't help me, we'd all be blown to bits. Sensing I shouldn't mention that, I reach out and stroke his cheek. The stubble on his face pricks my fingertips. "What's this really about, Toad? Why were you so upset with me earlier?"

He settles back on his heels. "You noticed that, did you?"

I tap a finger near my eye. "Junior Officer Lawrence misses nothing."

Another tired smile. "You're extraordinary, Mouse."

Why do I think there's a "but" coming? I brace for the big break-up speech.

"You knew right where to go last night," Niall says. "Dad said you figured out that the looters were coming in through the pits. And that's where you headed."

"Right into danger," I say the words he doesn't, but is clear from his pained expression. "When I promised I wouldn't. That's why you're so upset?" No answer. "Niall, every security officer was busy. I couldn't call for help. And Morgan, Rance, my parents, and Elese were already there. If I didn't warn them..." Not going there. "Just dumb luck I got caught in the cave-in. I thought Pit 2 would be fine. I grew up in those pits. Stupid digging machines messed everything up." That earns me another smile. "I didn't take any more risks than the rest of the security team. In fact, today, while all of you went up to the roof to sacrifice your lives for the base, I was tucked into my burrow."

"Your burrow?"

"Yeah, you know, mice live in burrows."

"I think you might be taking this mouse thing a little too seriously," he teases.

"Well, you know me and denial. It really helped to think I was in a burrow last night." Instead of trapped under dangerous rubble. But I shouldn't have said that. The humor drops from his face.

So I continue with my point. "The point is, I wasn't stupid. I wasn't reckless. I was just doing my job." I lean forward and lower my voice. "Which, I'm actually, kind of, good at." I hold a hand up. "Now don't get too excited. Criminal Mastermind is still on my list of potential careers, but…" Gesturing at the white cells around us, I continue, "It's losing its appeal. It's not quite the glamorous lifestyle I expected and there's the whole matter of your own people not caring if they kill you that sours the thrill."

When he doesn't say anything, I can't keep from asking, "Is it because those looters died? That I'm respons—"

"No!" He scooches closer and grabs my hands. "Not at all! You are *not* responsible. Every single one of those people is responsible for their own deaths. They made the *choice* to participate in the attack on our base. They *decided* to threaten the lives of our people. Understand?"

"I do." Like I told my father, ninety-five percent of me understands.

"Good." Niall draws in a breath. "You're right. I'm worried. I'll admit it's irrational. This is our job. And you're doing amazing. Most officers don't ever see this much action in their entire careers. It's just…" He swallows. "If I lose you, it'll kill me. And with those portals that you're so keen about, I'm afraid you'll disappear and we'll be separated for good."

I squeeze his hands as my insides melt. "I can't tell you not to worry, because I worry about you, too. However, I'm not leaving you behind. In fact, if you haven't touched a Warrior heart yet, I'm going to need your help with the portals."

"You are?"

"Yes, but if you have, I'll tell your father that I need you anyway."

"I'm still waiting for your heart, Mouse."

"You already have this one, Toad." I tap my chest. "We'll save that Warrior heart for you later." Then a dire thought pops up. "But we might encounter shadow-blobs and you won't be able to see them."

"You'll have to guide me."

I open my mouth to protest.

He jumps in. "You've done it before and it worked out."

Not sure being sliced up and getting stitches on his forehead is what I'd call working out. "I think we should bring that heart along, just in case."

"All right. Now time for your meds and dinner."

He opens the ruck and sets out two bottles of water, energy bars, and—

"Pudding cups!"

Niall shakes his head. "If you hadn't almost crushed my ribs when I came in, I'd be worried you love pudding cups more."

"Don't worry, you beat out pudding cups every time."

He presses a hand to his chest. "That's just what every man wants to hear. Maybe I should get it tattooed on my arm so I'll never forget it."

I swat him on the shoulder. "Brat."

He sets out the rest of dinner onto the table and takes the other seat. I down the pills and munch on the food that is disguised as a tasteless rectangular block. "I guess it's going to be energy bars from now on." Don't get me wrong, they are full of protein and nutrients. I'm glad we have them, but they're not my go-to for food.

"Yeah. We're in survival mode."

And I sense that nothing will ever be the same. That this meal is the beginning of the end. Not a very happy thought.

By the time we finish, my ankle and stomach are no longer yelling at me. But even after my second pudding cup, I'm still sleepy.

"You can go to your room in my dad's unit and get some sleep," Niall says after my fourth yawn. "He wants you to stay in security." He hands me the ruck. "This one is yours. I grabbed a few additional things for you."

"Thanks. What about you?"

"I'm on duty here until someone relieves me."

But he's just as exhausted. I can't leave him alone. "I'll keep you company."

"While I would enjoy that, you've been ordered to sleep.

We'll need your sharp mind over the next couple of days."

No pressure. I try to think of a loophole to remain with Niall, but my mind is currently mush, which just proves Radcliff's point. "All right." I use the cane to stand. The ankle mutters a bit with unhappiness, but settles down.

Niall squints at me in suspicion. "That seemed too easy."

"That's because it's going to cost you, Toad."

"Oh?"

I limp over to his chair and sit on his lap. Then I kiss him. Taking my time, I ensure it's a long and deep kiss. One that doesn't care a damn about the order that we can't have any physical contact while in uniform. We might never get another private moment.

When I break it off, he says, "I believe I still owe you." And he recaptures my lips.

Apparently, he felt the need to guarantee I receive proper payment. Our exchange grows quite heated, and I'm more than happy to continue—another missile could be launched at any minute, people!—but Mr. Sensible stops us.

"Another officer…will be…coming," he pants.

Of course he's right. I growl at him and nip his earlobe. "My inner lion isn't happy."

"Yeah." He clears his throat. "Got that."

I grab the ruck. My pajamas and a variety of personal things are inside, along with another pudding cup. Sweet of him to save it for me. I put it on the table. "Something to remember me by."

His laughter follows me out into the hallway.

Radcliff wakes me at…I've no idea. "Do you still want to talk to Jarren?" he asks.

"Yes."

"Then get dressed. You have an hour."

Wide awake now, I pull my blankets off and stifle a groan. Not only am I a giant bruise, but every muscle has stiffened. Steel is more flexible than I am. Moving is pure torture, I'm a pathetic mewling weakling. Good thing I still have my pain meds. I down them before I do anything else.

Radcliff is waiting for me near the door. He's holding two cups of coffee and I fight back tears of joy. Seeing my improvised cane, he offers to carry my cup as we head toward his office. Cracks snake through the walls and there's a layer of white grit on the floor.

"How do you want to play this?" he asks. "Like the last time in the empty office?"

"No." I'm dressed in my security jumpsuit—everyone is, as it offers the most protection. And I'm armed with my pulse gun and an energy wave gun—Radcliff insisted. "This time it's different." I tell him what I need.

"Nice," he says.

I wait in his office, sipping coffee as he arranges the interview. Parts of the ceiling tiles have fallen, exposing the base's pipes and wires. A web of cracks decorates his walls.

Beau hustles in. He's still wearing his uniform. It's rumpled and coated with dust. Lines of exhaustion mark his face.

"Haven't you had any time to change?" I ask. Or sleep.

"Are you kidding?" He looks around. "Where's the boss?"

"He'll be back soon. How's the evacuation going?"

Beau swipes a hand over his spikes. They're limp. "Better than expected. Everyone will be underground when the sun comes up. Then they'll move on to their pits tonight." He plops into the other visitor chair. "Need your help. Officer Morgan wants to use the shuttles without anyone picking up on it. Q's been helping me, but it's slow. It'll go faster with two of us."

Ah ha! He said Q! That means he's a full believer. "It's up to Radcliff, but I can help after I talk to Jarren."

"About the portals?"

"Yes."

Just then Radcliff enters. "It's all set up. Do you want me to come with you?"

"No."

"All right, one hour, then we have more important things to do."

I stand without wincing. Go me. "Yes, sir." Grabbing my coffee, I limp to detention being careful not to spill it.

Rance and Niall—has he gotten any sleep?—stand at attention just inside the door. They're facing Jarren and have one hand resting on the handles of their pulse guns. Jarren is sitting in one of the chairs next to the table. His hands are secured behind his back.

When he spots me, he smirks. "Nice costume."

I ignore him as I take the seat across the table. Sipping my coffee, I study Jarren. He might pretend to be relaxed and have donned his I'm-vastly-superior-to-you attitude, but there's fear lurking in his light brown eyes.

Finally, I say, "That missile yesterday proved I was right. You are not valuable or indispensable. You're disposable."

He keeps his expression neutral, but his shoulders tense. "How did it miss?"

"That's really not your concern right now."

"No?"

"No. Your concern should be focused on the *next* missile. Because that one is not going to miss. And guess who hasn't been evacuated to the pits?"

He glances at the closed and locked doors of detention. "All of us?"

"Yep. All eighty-eight of you." I lean forward and lower my voice. "And here's a secret. You're not going to be, either."

Jarren's face pales. "You can't do that. There are laws."

"Yeah, well, we're in a state of emergency. It's like old Earth—everyone for themselves." I glance at Rance and Niall. "But if you cooperate and answer my questions, we'll consider evacuating you."

"I'm not falling for that. You'll evacuate us. You have to."

"You're willing to take that risk?"

"Yes."

"Okay. But perhaps you'll answer this one question. How does it feel to be worth *less* than the Warriors? That your colleagues, who are benefiting greatly from your grand Warrior Express scheme, have decided that they'd rather have the Warriors than you. I'd bet it feels just like being killed by a good friend."

"Officer Lawrence," Beau calls. He's standing in the doorway. "A moment please."

"Excuse me." I join Beau out in the hallway for a "private" chat.

"Radcliff says we can work on the shuttles when you're done here. How much longer are you going to be?"

"That depends if this little interruption has any effect on Jarren."

"I'll be in my office."

I return to detention, but don't go in far. "Good news, Officers. One of the other looters is willing to talk in exchange for her and about twenty of her friends being evacuated. You can toss this useless waste of flesh back in his cell." I turn to leave.

"Wait," Jarren yells. "That person won't have as much information as me."

Got you! I suppress my elation and keep my tone almost bored. "I have most of it figured out. We really don't need that much."

"Come on, Ara. I'm not an idiot. I know what you're doing."

I wait.

He sighs. "Sit down. Ask your questions."

I return to my chair. "Did you take the Warriors from Pit 54?"

"Pit 54?"

"Yulin's incoming portal."

"Yes. They're at our base."

Thought so, but I'd hoped we'd catch a break. "How many inactive Warrior planets have you infiltrated?"

"All of them."

Not a surprise. "Even the ones that haven't been discovered?"

"Not yet. We wanted to establish our—what did you call it?—Warrior Express in Explored Space first before ranging further out."

Some good news. "Did you take the eight key Warriors off the planets or keep them in place?"

"We took some to other Warrior planets and left some of the key ones behind."

"How many Warriors did you destroy?" I ask.

"Only enough to remove the important Warriors."

More good news. "I already figured out you need to touch a heart to be able to wake, or rather open, a portal. Do you have to touch a heart to go through the portals? Or can anyone go through once it's opened?"

"The first person through has to have claimed a heart. The rest don't. But the portals only go one way. If you try to go the wrong way..." His forehead crinkles as if he's in pain.

"What happens?"

"You arrive, but only for a few seconds before it sucks you back through and spits you out in pieces." Jarren shudders.

That would explain the boot prints in Pit 21. I ask him if they tried it on Planet Dongguan.

"Yeah." He peers at me. Through his eyes, I see the wheels in his mind turning. "He ended up here? Wow."

"Wow what?"

"He also ended up, briefly, on a number of other Warrior planets at the same time. I'm assuming all sixty-three of them. No wonder he was torn apart."

Ugh. "Did you try it again?"

"No. That was the first and last time."

At least he's concerned about his people. I mull over the information. Some good news, some gross news. "What about the last person through the portal? Do they need to claim a heart as well?"

He shrugs. "Don't know."

"You haven't closed one?" That's alarming.

"Why should we? It's faster to travel between planets without having to open a portal every time."

It only took about fifteen minutes when we opened the portal in Pit 21. "Does it take longer to open a portal when you just have the key Warriors, or is it shorter?" I ask.

"It takes one hundred and twenty-eight hours. We don't know why. When the pit is full of Warriors it takes sixteen minutes." He gives me a sardonic smile. "Both numbers are divisible by eight."

But I'm still distracted by the fact that the portals are all still open. "Do you know that using a portal without the full complement of Warriors risks having HoLFs break through? Have there been any reports by your network of people about shadow-blobs attacking?"

He doesn't answer, but something shifts in his gaze.

And then I remember Operation Looter Attack. "By the way your people reacted to the projections of the shadow-blobs, they've already had some encounters with the aliens." Which isn't good. At all. "Let me tell you what you've set into motion by exploiting the portals." I explain about the entangled points and rifts being created by the reduction in the number of Warriors on a planet.

"Talk about a crazy imagination. Where do you come up with this stuff?" Jarren looks at Niall and Rance. "And you guys believe her? You're all insane."

"What's insane is using an alien technology without learning all about it first. Once you figured out how it worked, you raced to exploit it. You didn't wait for the rest of Lan's discoveries that reported the danger. And then, when Lan drew closer to making the connections you'd made years earlier, you traveled to Xinji and killed her."

That last comment shocks me. I'd been willing to believe that Jarren had unintentionally released the shadow-blobs that were responsible for all those deaths on Xinji. But once I talked it out and chased the logic, Jarren couldn't risk Lan learning about the Warrior portals. So he killed her!

Jarren stares at me with a wary expression. Proof of his guilt. Anger surges through me. I jump from my seat, round the table, and punch the murdering bastard right in the jaw. Hard.

He falls to the ground with a grunt. My knuckles throb and my ankle is going to remind me about this when the pain meds wear off, but I don't care. It is very satisfying. I step back and let him catch his breath.

"Did you see that?" Jarren appeals to Niall and Rance when he recovers. "She attacked me."

Rance looks at Niall. "I didn't see anything. Did you?"

"Not a thing." There's a glitter of approval in Niall's blue-green eyes.

I pull my energy wave gun and crouch down next to Jarren. Properly terrified now, he glances at the camera in desperation.

"That's not going to save you," I say. "Worming into the video feeds is ridiculously easy. You taught me that." I aim the weapon at him. "Did you kill everyone on Xinji?"

"No! The hostiles killed them. I just…"

I nudge him with the gun. "Say it."

"I killed Lan and her husband."

The desire to push the trigger and shatter all his bones in his body presses on me. Instead, I straighten and ask Rance to set Jarren back in his chair. Rance is happy to help. Jarren lands in his seat with a thud.

I take my seat. "Now, you're going to tell me who you're working with."

All the fight is gone from Jarren. He complies.

"Sonovabitch," Radcliff says when I brief him on the interview. He was monitoring me through the cameras, but doesn't mention my outburst. "That's a bunch of high-ranking officers."

"Yeah." My tone is grumpy. Guess I'm not all-knowing. Beau and I didn't think to check DES's Protectorate ranks. The looters have missiles, weapons, and shuttles. Where else would they get them but from the military? And then there's the money. At least learning there are three major corporations footing the bill isn't a surprise. Of course all of them want to exploit space, mining resources for their profit. Currently, DES is focused on science and colonization—no tourists in space.

Except with the Warrior Express, the companies can charge lots of money for people to travel without the time dilation.

Jarren managed to recruit a number of disgruntled Protectorate officers, failed navigators, and rich patrons. Impressive, except he's evil. Too bad none of this information helps us deal with our situation.

Radcliff wants to send a report about the Protectorate to DES. "Just for this one report, is it possible to block our activities from everyone else and ensure it reaches the directors and no one else?" he asks me.

Can you do that? I ask Q.

YES.

"Yes. Let me know when you're ready to send it and Q will protect it," I say.

"Good. Officer Dorey is waiting for you in his office."

Except the thought of protecting a report triggers another one. And it's frankly horrifying. *Did the Protectorate really send ships to the Warrior Planets after Xinji went silent?*

YES.

But who are they going to protect? Us or the looters?

UNKNOWN.

I lean all my weight on my cane to keep from toppling over.

"Something wrong, Lawrence?"

"Those Protector ships. They might not be coming to help us."

"I'm aware." His expression is bleak.

I arrive in Beau's office without memory of the trip there.

"What's wrong?" Beau asks.

Radcliff didn't order me not to tell anyone. And Beau needs to know. I explain about the Protectorate.

"We're screwed," he says.

"I agree." I plop in the seat next to him.

"The looters knew that once Xinji went silent, DES would send out Protector Class ships. They were a step ahead." Beau runs a hand over his hair. It's no longer spiked. Instead, it's a sad version of his normal hairstyle.

"Yeah." I'm numb. And I keep coming back to the same truth. We're done. End of the road. We don't have enough people, resources, or anything really. Even if we evacuate to another Warrior planet, the Protectorate would just catch up to us there. So much for our goal of surviving until help arrives and being able to relax. I sink down in the chair and wonder where Niall is. I'm not waiting until my birthday, I'm not dying a virgin.

"Ara," Beau says, waving a hand in front of my face. "Snap out of it. We're not going to roll over and die."

"But what are we going to do?" My voice is shrill.

"We're going to do our jobs. Let's get those shuttles online for Morgan."

His brusque tone cuts through my self-pity. I focus on hiding the shuttle's activity from the looters and not on our inevitable ending.

It takes us all morning to protect one shuttle from any wormers. But Q takes over for the rest of the shuttles. We managed to confiscate three when the looters attacked us last time, and one from this recent attack, which is pretty impressive. The new shuttle is already operating outside the Q-net.

Can you tell what it's using to communicate with the looters' base? I ask Q.

NO.

But it has to be using something and, even at gunpoint, Jarren refused to tell me. Maybe the astrophysicists can figure it out. After we finish, I ask Radcliff where Drs. Carson and Zhang are.

"Why?"

I explain. "If we can listen to what the looters at the base are planning, then we might have some warning if they come after us again."

"You don't think they'll believe we're dead?"

"Even if they do, they're bound to come here to access the Warrior portals."

"Good point." He consults his portable. "They're in Pit 21. When it gets dark, I'll send a tech to ask for their help." Radcliff rubs the scruff on his chin. It's peppered with gray. "In the meantime, I need you to work on Operation Desperation."

We share a disheartened look. Too bad my plan of escaping through the portals will only delay the inevitable. "I'm going to need a portable."

"There should be some around. Just stay out of the labs. And don't take too long. I want you here."

"Do you want me to work in your office?"

"Yes. Just in case I need you."

"Yes, sir." I hurry out. I've a bit of freedom and I'm not going to waste it.

The hallways in the base are in the same condition as the ones in security. Holes and cracks decorate most of the walls. Some lights flicker and others have shattered from the shock wave. A layer of white grit and broken glass crunches under my boots, and finding clear spots to set the end of my cane down is difficult. There's a burnt electrical smell to the air. And there's no one else around. It's creepy.

Finding a portable is easy. It appears that many of the devices were abandoned when everyone evacuated. Even though they're not connected to the Q-net, they run standard plug and chug programs so you can keep working when you're not near a terminal or if you've been entangled too long—over twelve hours and you risk brain damage. The portables have the ability to upload data to the Q-net via a terminal. They're handy and can send messages between them. I stop. They send messages.

I groan. The looters are using portables! Is the answer that simple?

NO. THEY DO NOT USE ANY DES DEVICES.

So they're paranoid. But that doesn't mean they're not using the same technology that allows messages to go from portable to portable.

IT IS POSSIBLE.

I'll have to ask the astrophysicists. That is, if they believe me. They still won't acknowledge the possibility of other dimensions. I wonder what they'll think of a sentient Q-net. Somehow I doubt they'll embrace the concept.

While I'm out in the base, I swing by my parents' unit to grab a few more personal items and snag some food. I missed lunch. Before heading back, I go to the archeology lab. The

Warrior heart I picked out for Niall has been tucked into a drawer. Since Jarren was so chatty, I won't need Niall to help me experiment. I was worried a person has to touch a heart in order to travel through the portals. Of course, that means I have to trust what Jarren said. Hmmm. That needs more thought. And perhaps a consult with Radcliff over how much we believe him.

I find a cloth bag to carry the heart. Then I glance at the doors to the pits. Only Pit 1 survived the cave-in. Curious, I go in to peek at the collapsed pits. Will it match my memories?

Bright lights illuminate the smooth yellowish-tan-brown walls. Blocks of sandstone and crumbled piles of sand extend up beyond what is visible. I'd bet there are depressions in the desert over the three collapsed pits.

There are gaps between boulders and I wonder if anyone is still alive under the rubble. I sincerely hope not. That's an awful way to die. My father said they tried to find survivors, but there was only so much they could do.

I shudder in the suddenly cold air. It has a familiar heavy weight. Oh no. Movement in the rubble catches my eye. A shadow-blob!

Cursing, I message Radcliff through the portable. That rift might have been buried, but it's still open. Obviously, shadow-blobs only need cracks to squirm their way through. And the null wave emitter installed on the wall to keep them out must have been crushed in the collapse.

I rearrange the lights in Pit 1 to keep the shadow-blobs from entering the archeology lab. There's only one hostile alien. For now. Prior experience has taught me that they'll wait until there are enough of them to attack us. Not a pleasant thought. Just what we needed, another problem to add to the growing list.

A message from Radcliff arrives. I'm to remain here until another guard can stand watch. All I have is my flashlight, but it should be enough. I hope. While I keep an eye out for more shadow-blobs, I consider how else we could protect the base from the HoLFs. Moving Warriors is not feasible. They're super heavy and are needed to guard their pits. There's the Warriors and hearts in the factory below the pits.

That is, if it survived the collapse. We can't get to it through the pits anymore, but we have that tunnel we dug to get into it when we implemented Operation Warrior Hearts. If we could bring up all the hearts from the factory, we could place them in Pit 1 to protect the base. And use them to fill in for the missing Warriors in the other pits that Jarren damaged. Except there won't be enough. And does the heart work outside the Warrior's body? Or does it have to be inside?

INSIDE.

There has to be a way to make more Warrior Sentinels. Q said fourth nation maintained the network of protection. All that alien equipment in the factory must be for manufacturing more hearts and Warriors to replace ones that are damaged.

CORRECT.

Do you know how the machinery works?

FOURTH NATION LEFT INSTRUCTIONS.

Where?

IN FACTORIES.

Will we be able to understand the instructions?

UNKNOWN.

Will you help us translate? There's a significant pause. So I add, *It's all part of defending the Galaxy from the shadow-blobs.*

I WILL CONSIDER IT.

At least it isn't a no. And there's hope we can produce more hearts. If we survive.

It seems I've a couple of hours to plan as I wait for my replacement. The security team is stretched thin. Since there's not much action in the pit, I connect to the portable and start planning Operation Desperation.

There are four active Warrior planets not under looter control. Pingliang, Ruijin, Qingyang, and Nanxiong. On those four all the pits have been opened. Which means there's a corridor that runs parallel, connecting all sixty-four planets. So if we pop in to one, we can get to another without any problems. Unlike Yulin, where almost all the pits are still closed and will take time to open. It took us hours before we could get into Pit 21 out in the desert. But we were being extra careful. I suspect it could be done quicker.

Q, which of our pits lead to those four planets?

PIT 7 PINGLIANG. PIT 39 RUIJIN. PIT 24 QINGYANG. PIT 63 NANXIONG.

Thanks. I work on the logistics of Operation Desperation until Elese arrives at eighteen hundred with two null wave emitters. By that time, my pain meds have worn off, I've eaten all my snacks, and I'm grumpy. However, I'm smart enough not to snap at her.

"How's your ankle?" she asks.

"Stiff and sore. Don't worry, nothing my pampered ass can't handle."

She grins. Handing me one of the weapons, Elese asks, "Status?"

"It's been quiet. I've only seen one."

Elese follows me into the pit. She whistles at the carnage. "You're one lucky lady. How deep under were you?"

I point to the tripod with the pulley. It's still sitting over my burrow. "I was near the edge. Another couple meters and I would have been clear."

She peers at me. "Maybe not so lucky."

"No. I was lucky."

The air turns cold.

"There's one!" Elese raises the emitter. A sizzle-zap sounds and the shadow-blob explodes into tiny black specks and disappears. "Take that, you ugly mother-HoLFer."

I laugh at her modified curse word. "I didn't see any other HoLFs, but I stayed in the archeology lab. Maybe they can sense when we're close."

Elese shrugs. "More fun sizzle-zapping them than being in the lab doing nothing." Then she brightens. "Besides that's one less ugly mother-HoLFer in our Galaxy."

I really missed hanging out with Elese. Her energy is infectious, but my ankle is inflamed. "Did Radcliff give you any orders for me?" I ask.

"Yeah. You're to report back to his office. Leave the extra emitter just in case I have to call for back up."

I notice the communicator in her ear.

She taps the almost transparent device. "Emergencies only."

Which is good, especially as it can still be used when not connected to the Q-net. Perhaps that's another way the looters are communicating. "Have fun," I say to Elese as I leave.

"Will do!"

I sling the cloth bag over my shoulder. Climbing the stairs is a test of endurance. When I reach the top, I have the sudden desire to plant a flag and claim the hallway for fifth nation. Instead, I navigate through the corridor. After a few steps, my improvised cane snaps in half. I stumble and my vision blurs as the pain sizzles up my leg. I really need to remember to keep those pain meds with me at all times. I limp-hop to the infirmary. Perhaps I can find a real cane. Instead, I'm surprised to find Dr. Edwards.

"I see you're keeping your weight off that ankle, Miss Lawrence," he says dryly.

Why do all the adults I know speak fluent sarcasm? "Why aren't you in the pits?" I ask. "It's dangerous to be here and you're too important."

"And you're not?"

"Not what?"

"Important."

"I'm doing my job."

"So am I. I'm not hiding in the pits when one of the security team members might need my care."

That's really brave. "Thank you, Dr. Edwards."

"You're welcome, Miss Lawrence. Now how can I help you?"

"Remember those crutches you said I could use? I need them."

"Come into my exam room and we'll get you fitted."

When he sees me struggling, he offers an arm. Once I'm on

the table, he goes to fetch the supplies. He returns with a set of crutches and pain meds. I love this man! He removes the not-so-white-now contraption and inspects my ankle. Or rather, he tortures me by moving my foot and digging his fingers into the joint to determine "range-of-motion."

Once he finishes the torture, he says, "It's healing. Not as fast as it should, but, considering the circumstances, I'm pleased." Then he rummages in a drawer and pulls out another contraption. "This will give you enough support that you can walk without crutches." He wraps it around my ankle. "However, please stay off that ankle as long as possible."

"I will," I promise as I hop off the table. He measures me for the crutches and adjusts them so they fit under my arms. They're rather spiffy. Made of a lightweight graphite, they're a purple-ish-blue color with a slight diamond pattern. There's a round rubber foot on the bottom, a foamy-rubbery grip for my hands, and a cushy pad to lean my weight on.

Dr. Edwards demonstrates how to use them. Only when I successfully cross the room a couple times without tripping or launching myself too far forward does he allow me to leave. And I'm either a natural, or using crutches is so much easier, quicker, and less painful than limp-hopping. Or it could be the pain meds have kicked in. Either way, I'm back at Radcliff's office in no time.

Doesn't stop the man from grumping at me for taking too long. That is until he actually looks up from his portable.

"Oh," he says when he spots my crutches. "That's a good idea. What's the status in Pit 1?"

After I fill him in, he asks, "Are we going to have a problem?"

"If we don't install another pit-wide null wave emitter, we might. Can you see if Jim McGinnis is willing to build another one?"

Radcliff consults his portable and glances at the clock. It's almost nineteen hundred. "Jim's in Pit 21 with the astrophysicists. I'll have the techs talk to him as well." He taps on his portable. "The techs can use the buggy. If they agree, then they'll be here by twenty-three hundred." He studies me. "Come on. You must be hungry. I know I'm starving."

We walk back to our unit, or, in my case, swoop. That's what it feels like. Plant the crutches and swoop forward, plant my left foot, move the crutches and swoop again. It's strangely efficient, eating up lots of ground with each swoop.

Radcliff bustles about the kitchen, while I gratefully sink onto the couch. I pull out my portable to continue working on the op. The door to the unit opens and Niall strides in. He smiles when he sees me, but the poor guy looks like he fought a shadow-blob and lost.

"Sit down before you fall down," I say, scooching over and resting my foot on the coffee table.

He plops next to me. "Thanks."

Radcliff pokes his head out. "What are you doing here? I ordered you to get some sleep an hour ago."

"Can't sleep," Niall says.

Radcliff and I wait because clearly that's impossible.

Niall sighs and scrubs and hand through his hair. "Every time I close my eyes, I see piles of rubble. And I swear I can hear a missile falling from the sky." He looks at me. "What if I sleep through an alarm? Or if we don't ever…wake up again."

Oh, Niall. I wrap my arms around his shoulders and pull him into a sideways hug. He leans on me. I meet Radcliff's gaze.

"Then you might as well join us for dinner." Radcliff returns to the kitchen.

"Sorry," Niall says. "I'm not usually so…fatalistic."

"You're beyond exhausted, sleep-deprived, and, if there is ever a time to be fatalistic, I think this is it."

"It's been a rough couple of days." He pulls back, breaking the awkward hug and rearranging us so we're in our familiar couch-cuddling position, with me tucked under his arm. He holds my hand and rubs a thumb over my bruised knuckles. "Believe it or not, there were a couple of highlights."

"Oh?"

"When you punched Jarren, I almost whooped with joy. It took everything I had not to react."

"That was pretty sweet."

Niall spots the portable. "What are you working on?"

I start to tell him about Operation Desperation, but then I remember Niall's heart. I grab the cloth bag and hand it to him. "This is for you."

"Oh?" He peers inside and glances sharply at me. "I thought—"

"Jarren already confirmed you don't need to touch a heart to go through the portals."

"But do we trust him? I'd hate to find out he'd lied during an emergency."

"That's a good point."

"I bet that was hard to say," he teases.

I mock growl at him. "I don't want you blind if we

encounter shadow-blobs."

"How about a compromise?"

"I'm listening."

"I'll keep the heart with me. If we run into shadow-blobs, I'll grab it. Okay?"

"Just don't let anyone else touch it."

"I won't."

"All right."

Radcliff pokes his head out. "Dinner is served. It's leftovers, but better than energy bars."

We go to the kitchen and the three of us eat in silence—too busy shoveling food into our mouths to talk. The leftover beef casserole tastes divine and I slow down to savor it. I've a feeling hot meals are going to be a luxury. Afterwards, I'm drooping over my empty plate. I spent the last of my energy eating. Niall is also struggling to stay awake.

"Niall, I want you close by tonight. You can sleep in Ara's room," Radcliff says.

And I'll take the couch. That's fair.

But Radcliff gives us one of his weighted looks. "Ara, do you mind sharing?"

I blink. Did he just— Did I hear— Is this a trick question? "No."

"Good. If you'll excuse me, I need to finish my report." Radcliff goes out and sits on the couch with his portable and a fresh cup of coffee.

Niall and I exchange a significant glance.

"Leave the door open in case I need to wake you," Radcliff adds.

Ah. I lower my voice, "I think he believes you'll sleep better with me." Perhaps trying Elese's sleepover cure for PTSD.

"I really don't care why," Niall whispers. "Let's go before he changes his mind."

We're both wearing our jumpsuits and they stay on just in case we have to flee or fight in the middle of the night. Our weapon belts get hung over the back of a chair within easy reach. And I prop my crutches up against the wall next to the bed. It's nice to snuggle together. I get a sweet good-night kiss that turns steamy until Niall runs out of steam. Poor guy is asleep in seconds.

I fight sleep a little longer. It's comforting being in Niall's arms, listening to his steady breathing, feeling his warm muscular body pressed against my back. I appeal to the universe to keep us safe. All of us.

Radcliff calls my name softly. I'm confused until I realize he only wants me to wake. I gently extract myself from Niall's arms. I probably don't need to be so careful, Niall doesn't move a muscle. I grab my crutches and weapon belt and join Radcliff in the living room.

Radcliff says, "Dr. Roberta Carson and Jim McGinnis are in my office."

"Uh, that's nice." Why is he telling me this?

"We need to talk to them."

"Oh, right." My brain must still be asleep. No surprise since it's midnight.

Radcliff grabs two cups of coffee and holds the door open for me. I put my weapon belt on and swoop to his office. The astrophysicist and the mechanical engineer are sitting in the two seats facing Radcliff's desk. Morgan is sitting behind it. She nods at us in greeting.

Dr. Carson, also known as Bertie, spins around at the noise of my crutches, but relaxes when she sees me. My brain is still waking up and I note Dr. Zhang's absence. Can't blame the woman. She's safer in the pits. Jim hops to his feet and offers the seat to me. I thank him and sit down. Morgan relinquishes Radcliff's chair and stands behind him.

"Officer Morgan was just telling us we need another emitter for the pits," Jim says. "I've the materials and should be able to build you one in a couple hours."

While I'm happy for the good news, I'm worried something bad will happen to counter it.

"Can you get started now?" Morgan asks.

"Yeah, sure," Jim says. "I've just been sitting around all day. Do you have anyone to spare to help me?"

"Yes," Radcliff says. "I'll have them meet you at your lab."

"Great. I'll let you know when it's finished." Jim strides to the door.

"What do you need me to do?" Bertie is clutching the arms of her chair as if she's afraid she'll float away. She's in her early thirties and is almost as pale as Niall.

"Lawrence," Morgan prompts.

"We need to find out how the looters are communicating," I say. Then I explain my theories about them either using outdated technology or using what the communicators and portables use. "Or they could just be sending notes through the portals."

"Portals?" She wrinkles her nose in pained distaste.

"Yes, portals between Warrior pits on different planets. Jarren confirmed they exist." I quickly go over the information we have about them.

By the range of her expressions, Bertie is struggling with the concepts, but then she shrugs. "All right. Let's just go with it. Assuming the portals are indeed short-cuts through the shadow...dimension, I doubt they're using notes to send messages. Their network is too large and physical notes can get lost or destroyed. I'm more inclined to believe they are using a form of electromagnetic energy. Probably with frequencies between radio waves and the waves used in microwave ovens. Normally the large distances between planets makes this a very poor choice as it would take years for one message to travel to the receiver. But if they can transmit through the Warrior portals, then that's no longer an issue. Just like it's fine to use these electromagnetic waves for the portables and security's communicators because sender and receiver are much closer."

"If they're using these waves, can you detect them?" Morgan asks.

Bertie bites her bottom lip. "There are a wide range of frequencies that they could be using. But I can alter our HoLF detector to scan only in that range."

"How long will it take?" Morgan asks.

"A couple hours to make the adjustments."

"And how long to detect? Last time you needed twenty days. This time I doubt we have twenty hours."

Bertie flinches and hunches down in her seat as if a missile is about to strike.

"Officer Morgan," Radcliff admonished.

Gathering her courage, Bertie straightens. "It depends on if there is a signal to detect. The looter base on the opposite side of Yulin is too far away. Plus with the curvature of the planet, we won't be in direct line of sight." Seeing our confused expressions, she adds, "The waves go straight. They won't bend around a planet. You'd need a satellite to relay the signal to another part of the planet." She gnaws on her lower lip again. "Do the looters have a satellite above Yulin?"

"Unknown," Radcliff says. "When they attacked, they flew in four shuttles. One landed in the port and the other three in the desert. We confiscated the one in the port. And we also confiscated the communication devices they wore."

"Wait," I say, making a connection. "Why don't we use their communicators to listen in to them?"

"Without a satellite they won't work. But if they were to come back here, then yes, it would," Bertie says. "Unless they change the frequency, then we'd be out of luck."

"If they think we're all dead, they won't change the frequency," Morgan says.

True.

"Let's confirm they're using these electromagnetic waves first," Radcliff says. "Would the shuttle or those devices help you detect this signal?" he asks Bertie.

"Yes."

"Which one?"

"Both. It makes sense for the looters to be in contact with

the shuttles."

"All right. When you're ready with the detector, I'll have someone meet you at the shuttle and bring along those devices. How many will you need?"

"All of them. Some might be broken or won't have power. I don't want to waste time having someone fetch me more."

Smart. Morgan nods in approval.

"Do you need someone to help you with your adjustments?" Radcliff asks.

"Not really, but I wouldn't mind the company."

I don't blame her. It's late at night in a creepy abandoned base.

Radcliff glances at me. "How long will it take you to send my report to DES?"

TWENTY MINUTES.

"Twenty minutes," I say.

"That's it? There can't be a single ripple, Lawrence. And it has to be worm-proof."

Q does the equivalent of a huff of annoyance in my head. I'm more diplomatic. "There won't be. And Q will protect it from wormers."

Bertie gives me an odd look.

Radcliff hands me his portable. "It's ready to be sent. Once you're done you can accompany Dr. Carson." He turns to the woman. "Can I get you some coffee while you wait?"

"Uh, yes, thank you."

I connect to Q through the portable. The report is to only go to the Board of Directors members. Do we still have our escape tunnels through the blockade?

YES. THREE LEFT.

And then I realize we can't go through them. What if the looters found them and are monitoring them for any activity? *Are there any new programs around the tunnels?*

DEFINE NEW.

Since the missile strike.

YES. NEAR TWO.

So that third one should be safe. Key word—should. *Is there any way to fly this report to DES?*

NO. TOO BIG.

Guess we'll have to risk it. *Please transform the report file into a long, super skinny snake.* As Q stretches it out, I coat it in two layers of protection and add a program, giving Q the ability to block the contents of the report from anyone who isn't a Director. *Will that work?*

YES.

The file elongates and yellow and blue lines wrap around it, showing my protections. Once the report is finished, we send the snake slowly and carefully through the escape tunnel like a thread through a needle. But in this case, that thread can't touch any part of the needle or it will cause ripples. It takes ten minutes for the entire length to travel through the blockade. But once it's free, Q sends it to the directors.

I disconnect and hand the portable back to Radcliff. "It's been delivered with nary a ripple."

"Good. I'll have someone bring those communicators."

"Can you tell Niall where I am when he wakes?" I ask Radcliff as I stand and grab my crutches.

"Yes."

Bertie is glancing uncertainly between me and Radcliff.

"Officer Lawrence is fully armed and, despite the crutches, will be able to protect you," Radcliff says.

"That's not—" She sucks in a breath. "I need protection?"

"Just in case."

Bertie walks next to me as I swoop through the hallways. She's quiet and I have to admire Radcliff's ability to pull her focus from the strangeness over me and Q to her personal safety. I wonder if he's ever manipulated me like that. Probably.

Eventually, she snaps from her contemplations and starts questioning me about the portals. Most of my answers are "I don't know," which frustrates her. But I've no idea what is powering the portals or the reason it works. And I suspect true understanding of the technology is probably decades in our future.

CENTURIES.

If we're not extinct by then.

CORRECT.

Not helping.

Finally she asks, "Are you certain it's not an elaborate trick? You're basing this on information from Jarren, who can't be trusted."

"We've other sources that have confirmed most of what he claims. And I wasn't the only person to see the portal in Pit 21, or the boot prints." I shudder.

"Yes, but you're the only one to see the person on the other side."

True. "I understand that you're finding it hard to believe. Right now, it's not about the science. It's about survival."

"I know, it's just…"

"Don't worry," I say. "You won't be the first person to go through the portal."

"Because I don't have the heart of a Warrior?"

Struck by her comment, I stop. "Yes and no."

She gives me a tentative smile as if she's concerned about upsetting the crazy lady. "Which one?"

"Both. Yes, because you haven't touched a heart. No, because you're here, helping us despite the danger, despite being scared. I'd say you have the heart of a Warrior."

Bertie touches my shoulder. "So do you. That's why you'll be the first one through the portal."

Huh. She has a point—about the portal. It's my crazy idea after all. And while I *know* it'll work, no one else really does. Oh, they believe me, but they don't *believe* me with utter conviction. There's still a niggle of doubt that will be there until they witness it for themselves. I'm not upset. I'm just a little tired of always being the one who presents these impossible things— shadow-blobs, ghost Warriors, a sentient Q-net, and now portals. If Jarren didn't mess with the Warrior network, I'd be…

Where would I be? Probably complaining about soch-time, doing my homework, and avoiding Niall, the jerk. Or I'd be in detention due to being caught worming. My life is actually better now, but in the worst way. Does that make sense?

"Hello?" Bertie waves a hand in front of my face. "Where did you go?"

"To an alternate dimension," I say.

"Oh? Would I like it there?" She's half teasing.

We continue on to her lab. I tell her what I'd been thinking about.

"Nothing changed?"

"Nope. The Warrior mystery is still unsolved. No HoLFs."

"That is quite the conundrum. All these discoveries are very important. But at what cost? All of our lives?" She taps a long slender finger on her lips. "There's probably another dimension out there where Jarren didn't interfere and we still made all these discoveries."

"Does this mean you're warming to the idea of multiple dimensions?" I ask.

"Let's just say I'm not ruling it out."

"I can live with that."

She laughs. But once we arrive at her lab, she turns serious as she adjusts the detector we'd installed in the pits to find out if the HoLFs emitted any energy. It saved us and I've the desire to praise the cube of metal. Instead, I scoot about the lab on a chair with wheels and fetch her supplies and tools. It's kind of fun.

When she finishes the modifications, I message Radcliff that we're on the way to the port. The detector isn't big, but she sets it on a hand cart. We get to the port and I go in first and stop. There's no wall on the right side. Just twisted, mangled metal struts and wires blowing in the cool night breeze.

The peppery anise scent of the desert fills the air, while sand is already encroaching on the floor. It crunches under the rubber knobs of my crutches as I swoop toward the shuttle. Bertie hurries, keeping close. I don't blame her. It's weird and eerie and unnerving.

Bertie carries the detector into the shuttle. She heads for the cockpit. I find out that I can't swoop up the steps. Instead, I have to use one crutch to limp-hop. It's not graceful. At all. But I manage and squeeze through the narrow aisle to join her. She's sitting in the pilot's chair so I plop into the co-pilot's seat.

She's staring at the array of controls. "I'm not sure where the communication panel is. I don't want to power up the entire shuttle."

Q? Can you help?

A schematic of the instrument panel appears in my head. All the various buttons and dials are all labeled, including the one for the comms. *Thanks.* I point it out to Bertie.

"Are you sure?"

"Yes." Then I add, "I watched Officer Morgan fly the shuttle."

That seems to satisfy her and she fiddles with the controls and her detector box. Niall arrives a few minutes later carrying another box. This one contains the communicators. Bertie does her stuff and I hop to the back of the shuttle to talk to Niall.

Dark smudges of fatigue line his eyes, but he smiles. "Any trouble, Mouse?"

"No. Why aren't you still asleep?"

"I had four hours. Considering the situation, that's decadent. Besides, I'm relieving Beau, who is finally getting a chance to get a shower and grab a few hours of sleep."

"Since it's for Beau, that's okay."

"Uh huh. Does that mean Beau's more important than me?"

I squint at him. Is he teasing? Is he serious? "Well, he is my partner. You're not jealous are you?" I'm erring on the side of teasing.

Before Niall can answer, Q sounds in my head.

INCOMING MESSAGES FROM PLANET PINGLIANG.

We're supposed to be dead and can't receive them.

THEY ARE URGENT.

Can you send them to Radcliff's portable without anyone knowing?

YES.

Please, do. Then I'm curious. *How urgent? Are they okay?*

NO. THEY ARE UNDER ATTACK.

2522:268

N iall notices my stricken expression. "Mouse? What's wrong?"

"Pingliang is under attack!" I limp-hop up to the cockpit. "Bertie, how much longer do you need?"

She has one of the communicators in her ear. "They're connecting, but I don't have a frequency yet. Another hour or so. Why?"

"I need to talk to Officer Radcliff." I turn. "Niall, can you stay with Bertie?"

The muscles along his jaw tighten. "What are you planning?"

"I'm going to try to convince him to send back up to Pingliang."

Even though I haven't moved, he blocks my way. "Promise you're not going without me." It didn't take him long to make the leap in logic.

And I don't think he's wrong to assume that. "I promise."

"Good," he says. "Because I *am* the jealous type."

Not a surprise.

Bertie is glancing at both of us. "She can't go with that ankle."

"I can walk. I've just been resting it." Plus I have plenty of pain meds. "I'll keep you updated."

Niall helps me from the shuttle and I swoop at speed to Radcliff's office. He's sitting behind his desk and my momentum propels me forward so that I almost do a face-plant before skidding to a stop.

"Something wrong?" he asks.

"Pingliang is—"

"Did you read my messages?"

"No. Q told me they're in trouble."

"I'm aware." His tone is flat, but not because he doesn't care.

No, he cares. By the way his shoulders sag and the exhaustion etched into his face, I know he's overwhelmed. I can't remember if he's slept since the attack two days ago.

"We need to go and help them," I say.

"We? We who? *We* don't have a single person to spare."

"Bring up more techs—I'm sure there are a few brave ones willing to help. We need to go. Or else they'll all die! We have the null wave emitters, the element of surprise, and their communicators."

Radcliff scrubs his hands through his short hair. If it was longer, I'd bet he would fist his fingers in the strands and yank on it. Instead, he lets his arms drop to his lap. "I don't even know where to start."

"I do. Assign Beta team to Pingliang. Leave Alpha team here. It'll be a short detour for Beta team if you enact Operation

Desperation."

"Do you even have that ready?"

"Yes…mostly." I give him the run down.

"Planet Ruijin. They could be next on the looters' attack list."

Good point. *Q? Is there a blockade-in-progress around Ruijin?*

NO. THERE ARE SOME NEW PROTOCOLS GOING AROUND QINGYANG.

"They're not. Qingyang is next. You need to warn them."

Radcliff sweeps a hand over his portable. "It doesn't seem to matter. They're outnumbered." He rubs the scruff on his chin. "The looters probably changed the frequency on their communicators, the ones we have won't work."

"They think we're dead so they wouldn't bother."

"I can't assign Beta team. It could be a suicide mission. And there's a chance of being separated from their families. No. I can't do that."

"Then ask for volunteers. I volunteer."

"Then Niall will as well."

Oh. Right. "The looters won't be expecting us to come through the portals. That'll be huge! A super element of surprise." And then I get an idea. One of those genius moves that just pops into my head. I explain it to Radcliff. "It's Operation Desperation with a Final Kick."

Radcliff places his elbows on the desk and rests his forehead in his hands. Did I just break him? We really don't have time for this. We need to open up Pit 7. *Q, Can you access Pingliang's camera feeds?*

YES.

And the base's code?

YES.

"What are you scheming, Lawrence?" Radcliff asks.

"Just working on the operation for Planet Pingliang," I say.

"I haven't agreed to anything."

"You will. Because you know it's the right thing to do."

Just then Morgan arrives. She's alert and looks ready for anything. "What's up, Boss?" she asks. Radcliff must have messaged her.

"Lawrence has an idea. And I need a second opinion because my brain is fried." He leans back, gesturing for me to enlighten her.

I do it as fast as possible.

There's a moment of silence. Then she says, "I'll lead the team. Lawrence, contact your parents to open Pit 7 and wake the Warriors ASAP. I'll find volunteers to fill out the rest of our team."

"Niall," Radcliff says. "He'll volunteer."

Morgan waits. I hold my breath. If Radcliff refuses to let Niall go, I can't go either.

He meets my gaze, then looks at Morgan. "You'll need three other officers and see if you can get some techs or scientists to volunteer as well. I'll put together a supply list for you. Check your portable in thirty."

"Yes, sir." Morgan leaves.

"Thanks," I say to Radcliff. It's weak and inadequate. He may never see Niall again.

He grunts. "Don't you have work to do?"

"Yes, sir." I swoop out and head to my unit. I need to pack my ruck. While on the way I ask Q to send a message to my parents about Pit 7. Despite the late hour, I know they'll be awake. Then I send one to Niall, telling him to return to security and to bring those communicators with him. And Bertie, if she's done.

Radcliff mentioned a supply list. It might help him know what we need if he can see what's going on at Pingliang. And the man's pretty good with strategy. *Q, can you please link Officer Radcliff's portable to the camera feeds in Pingliang's base?*

ON IT.

Radcliff is about to get a surprise. My ruck is almost complete, I just have to toss a few more items into it, including the small drawing of the mouse and toad that Niall gave me. Glancing around to make sure I didn't miss anything, I pause. Too bad I can't take Niall's mother's paintings with me. They're beautiful works of art that can never be replaced. More incentive to stop the looters from sending another missile to our base.

I take two more pain meds, shrug on my heavy ruck, and leave my crutches in the room. Time to test the new brace. A few twinges of pain ring my ankle as I hurry out of the unit and into the hallway, where I almost run into Niall.

"Once you've picked up the supplies on your list, we're to meet in the port," Niall says as he opens the door to his unit.

"My list?"

"On your portable."

Q shows me a message from Radcliff with items listed. But I follow Niall inside.

"Shouldn't you be gathering supplies?"

"I will. I want you to touch that heart." I hold up a hand. "You're coming along and we might be fighting HoLFs."

"All right." Niall fetches the cloth bag. "All I have to do is touch it, right?"

"Yes. It'll feel like you've been stabbed by an icicle."

"Thanks for the warning." He reaches his hand inside and flinches. "Wow, that's accurate. And it just turned into a pile of dust." Removing his hand, he looks at his palm. Black grit from the heart coats his skin. He rubs his thumb over his fingers, frowning at it. "Guess I'm a little sweaty from the run over here. I better clean up and pack. See you at the port."

I give him a quick kiss and leave. My list is short and I'm guessing Radcliff gave each of us a few things. I'm not the first to arrive at the port. Morgan is there, barking orders and loading up a dune buggy. A couple techs help. They're the ones who have been transporting people between the base and the evacuation pits.

When I join Morgan to help, I ask, "Who else volunteered?"

"Bendix, Zaim, and Keir."

Not a surprise, but I thought Beau would as well.

"Dorey wanted to come, but Radcliff won't let him," Morgan says, reading my mind. "We need him here to work with the Q-net while you're gone."

Ah. Then it's a blur of activity as everyone arrives with more supplies and their rucks. We load up. There's not enough seats, so most of us sit on the supplies in the back bed. Morgan drives to Pit 7 at maximum speed, causing us to hang on for dear life. The night air is brisk, which wakes everyone up. I breathe in the fresh scent of the desert and hope it won't be my last time on

Planet Yulin.

Pit 7 isn't far from base. We get there in fifteen minutes. There's another buggy parked and we pull up beside it and start to unload. A green pulsing light is emanating from a hole in the sand.

"Green. Seriously?" Bendix says in a dry tone. "Isn't that an alien cliché? An otherworldly green glow?"

"You're thinking of the little green men from Mars," Elese says.

"The old movies always show aliens with green skin," Zaim says. "Why green and not some other color?"

"Maybe they thought aliens use a form of photosynthesis for nutrients," Niall adds.

"Instead they're black blobs. Not nearly as photogenic," I say and basically kill the conversation.

A robotic digger squats nearby and there's a ladder in the hole. And a gust of stale air mixed with the scent of damp mold flows out. Humming beside the digger is an air pump bringing in fresh air. We climb down and I keep my head bent so I don't get sand in my eyes from the people's boots on the ladder above me. Some lessons are hard to forget. The lesson of don't-climb-a-ladder-with-a-half-healed-broken-ankle is my current one. Especially not with a heavy ruck on your back. And I'm not even carrying a null wave emitter like the others. Bendix is lugging two.

The green light stops pulsing by the time we reach the floor of the pit. It's now a steady glow, illuminating the terracotta Warriors. They stand in precise rows and columns that would make the shape of an octagon if you were to look down on them from above. Tall at an average of one hundred and ninety centimeters, they are all Chinese with their hair styled in warrior knots. Each one is unique. The Warriors stare straight ahead. The General is the tallest one with an armored jacket and ribbons on his uniform.

The other officers make another trip up the ladder for the rest of our supplies. We have a wheeled cart to bring them along with us. When all our equipment is either in the cart or clipped onto us—Bendix gives me the extra emitter—we head toward the gap in the center of the octagon. It's an empty spot that's big enough to fit four Warriors. The archeologists used to wonder what it was for, but now we all know.

My mom, dad, and a half-dozen techs wait for us near the gap, but not in the very center. Because a solid black rectangle about two meters high and a meter wide is occupying that precise spot. The bottom of the portal touches the sand.

"There's nothing on the other side," Mom says, gesturing to the portal. "Last time you saw a person?"

I dig out my portable. Pulling up the camera feeds for the Pingliang pits, I check Pit 15. "That's because there's nothing there to see." I peer closer—it's hard to discern shapes in the feeds with the green light all around us. "I think only the emergency lights are on in Pingliang."

"Are you using the Q-net now?" Dad asks. "Should we expect the looters to launch another missile?"

"No. I've a hidden connection. But Officer Radcliff has a plan to get you all to Planet Ruijin. He'll explain everything to you," I add to save time.

Morgan is also looking at her portable. She glances up.

"Who's coming with us?" she asks Mom.

"Me and the techs. Spencer is going to stay here and oversee the evacuation."

"Mom, you might not be able to get back to Dad," I say.

"We know. We discussed it."

I stare at her and I raise my eyebrows in an are-you-really-sure-about-this? She gives me a squint that says there's-no-way-you're-going-without-me.

"Listen up," Morgan says to the group. "I'm in charge. You follow *my* orders and *my* orders only. Understand?"

"Yes, sir," from all the officers.

The techs chime in a beat later and not nearly as confident.

"We're going to go through and head toward the entrance to the base. It's the exact same set-up as here, except they have all sixty-four of their pits excavated," Morgan says. "I'll take point and Officer Bendix will be last." She arranges the rest of us in a line.

I'm surprised to be given the spot right behind her; then it's Niall, my mother, two techs, Elese, two more techs, Zaim, the last two techs, and Bendix. One of the techs—a young guy so skinny that a stiff breeze could probably blow him over—is put in charge of the cart and is second to last.

Morgan approaches the portal, then turns to me. "Lawrence, make sure I'm on Pingliang and have given you a thumbs-up before you cross. Understand?"

"Yes, but—"

"But what?" she demands.

"I should go first. It's my idea, and if it's goes horribly wrong, I want to be the one for it to go wrong on." Otherwise the guilt would kill me.

"I'm in charge, Lawrence. I go first."

Officer Sioux Morgan glances at the team, nods, and strides into the blackness as if walking to the cafeteria. As if she isn't making history for the good guys or potentially committing suicide. We all gasp when she completely disappears.

The green glow pulses again, pushing out in waves from the center of the octagon to the edges like ripples in a pond. There's no sound except the harsh rasp of our collective breaths. I glance at my portable, but there's nothing to see in Pingliang's pit.

The seconds add up, each one increasing the weight on my shoulders. My grip tightens as my insides twist and knot. It's all my fault if Morgan dies. The lights continue to pulse. The pressure on me increases until I believe I'm going to punch a hole through the ground underneath me.

What if the shadow-blobs break through? Or Morgan is diverted to the shadow dimension? Will she survive there? They can survive here, it stands to reason she could live there, but, by their behavior, they'd attack an alien intruder. And it's probably pitch black there. I shudder.

The lights brighten and stop, once again filling the pit with the green glow, interrupting my dire thoughts. I check the portable and Morgan is in the other pit. It's lit by the same green light. She's searching for the camera. Once she finds it, she gives me a thumbs-up.

The heavy burden on my shoulders lifts and I just about float away. It worked! It. Actually. Worked! Joy blooms in my chest and I suppress a whoop and an urge to dance around. Yes, I knew it would work, but I didn't really *know*, know. Deep down in the depths was a seed of doubt.

"Well?" Mom asks.

"She's there. She's okay," I say to the others.

A collective sigh of relief ripples through everyone like the green light through the pit. And then I realize, I'm next. Fear replaces joy with one beat of my heart. I glance at my dad.

He steps close and gives me a hug. "I've no doubt that I'll see you again, Li-Li. Take care of your mother, she tends to think she's invincible."

My mother huffs behind me.

"I will. Bye, Dad." I kiss him on the cheek. Then I turn to the team. "It took Officer Morgan sixty-four seconds to cross over. Bendix, since you're last, track us on your portable. Make sure each of us has moved away from the center of the pit on Pingliang before the next person crosses over."

"How? I don't have the feeds on mine."

Q?

ON IT.

"You should in a—"

"There it is. Wow."

I meet Niall and my mother's gazes. "See you on the other side." Then I step into the blackness.

The blackness surrounds me until all light is choked off, leaving me blind. Then a sensation flutters through my stomach that is similar to when I'm on a space ship when it's crinkling space. A dizzy, disorienting spin, and the nausea-inducing sense of free fall. I try to take another step, but an invisible yet stretchy force checks my forward momentum. It's like I'm trapped in a giant black bubble.

Maybe I am stuck! Maybe the shadow-blobs have captured me and are going to slice me into pieces. Their world doesn't have light. I struggle against the bubble. It gives a little, but I'm unable to pierce it. What if I run out of air? Panic edges out reason and I'm about to freak out when the bubble pops.

Fresh air rushes in along with a weak green light. I stumble forward. Terracotta Warriors surround me. The pit is almost exactly like the one I left.

"Move out of the way, Lawrence," Morgan snaps.

Oh. I step aside and join her.

"Leave your ruck here for now. Keep the emitter and pulse gun with you. When you're ready, go check the corridor and stand watch. Call me if you see anyone."

I switch on my communicator, but pause.

"Something wrong, Lawrence?"

Tilting my head toward the black rectangle, I say, "That was…interesting."

"I'd say. Felt like being born."

An apt description. Not that I remember the occasion, but I've learned how it works. And that was one thing that's never changed over all these centuries—childbirth. Surgery and medicines have been improved, but the basic labor and delivery remains the same.

I hurry and follow orders before Morgan can snark at me. Glancing to my right and then left, I check for looters when I reach the outer row of Warriors. The long corridor that runs parallel to all the pits appears to be empty. A string of weak yellow emergency lights hangs from the ceiling. There are shadows galore.

Then I search for shadow-blobs. While there's plenty of hiding spots, nothing moves and the air is…warm and dry with a slight scent of cinnamon. The Pingliang research base has been active long enough to have installed an air handling system that removes the moisture and pollutants that can damage the Warriors.

The pits on each planet are spaced differently, depending on the circumference of the planet. On the bigger planets, they're further apart, and on the smaller ones, they're closer together.

Niall's voice sounds behind me. Huh. The green light must only pulse on the sending side. After a few minutes, he joins me. I glance at him.

His blue-green eyes are a bit wild and he clutches his weapons harder than necessary. "Status?"

"No looters or HoLFs in sight."

"Good." Then he shakes his head. "I can't believe we just crossed eleven thousand light years in sixty-four seconds. It felt like crinkling space, except instead of being in a space ship, I was in an intestine, and then…" He stops.

He's a too much of a gentleman to say it. Good thing, I'm not. "You were pooped out."

"Crude, but true." He rubs his right arm.

"That pain will go away in a few days," I say. After I touched a Warrior heart, the cold traveled up my arm and into my heart before it disappeared. "It will be interesting to see what you think of the shadow-blobs. Maybe you can draw them for those who can't see them."

"Maybe."

The rest of the team joins us. All looking a bit queasy, except

Bendix. He hefts his null wave emitter in one hand as if he can't wait to shoot HoLFs, his pulse gun in his other hand. The rest of us have our emitters slung over our backs. They're heavy and I need two hands to aim one.

We leave the portal open in case we need reinforcements. Once we have the situation under control, my father will close it.

Morgan comes around to the front. She points to her left, our right. "The base is three klicks that way. I don't see any looters in the pits, but that doesn't mean they're not hiding. If we encounter hostiles, either human or alien, while we're in the corridor, we form a wall." She scans our faces. "A wall is the front three people drop flat to the ground. The next three crouch low, and the next three stand. We all shoot, aiming for their head, unless it's a HoLF, then its core. You three—" She points to two techs and the guy pulling the cart. "Stay behind the wall. In the pits we'll have more room. Stay low to avoid getting hit. Let's go. Double time."

I find out real quick that double time means running and not jogging. It means sharp pain in my ankle despite the medicine and new contraption. After a kilometer, I'm almost hoping we encounter aliens so I can lie on the floor. And I discover that I haven't kept in shape during my grounding. Nothing I can do about it now except suck in more air.

Morgan does slow when we reach a pit just in case hostiles try to ambush us from behind the Warriors. We do a side shuffle, keeping our bodies turned toward the Warriors, but advancing forward.

I'm so focused on keeping up with Morgan, that I almost

run into the woman when she stops. Do we need to form a wall? I glance over her shoulder and bite down on a groan. There's a pile of rubble blocking the corridor.

Morgan consults her portable. "There are people in the pits beyond this. They don't look like looters, but they could be in disguise."

"Have the Warriors been destroyed?" Mom asks. By the tight line of her shoulder, I can tell she's bracing for the bad news.

"Sorry, Dr. Daniels. The four pits appear to be filled with broken statues."

Mom leans against the wall. I touch her shoulder and squeeze, giving her some daughterly support.

Bendix muscles his way up front. He goes up on his tiptoes. "The pile doesn't go all the way to the ceiling. Looks like it was pushed here instead of falling from the ceiling."

How can he tell? Too bad my father's not here. He knows his rubble. But I study the pile. The blocks on the bottom are much bigger than the ones at the top.

"Do you think the scientists built this?" I ask.

"Why?" Mom asks.

"If the looters disappeared down this corridor, that would be a good way to keep them from coming back."

"Why would they come this way?" Bendix asks.

"To use the Warrior Express to return to their lair."

Morgan taps a finger on the portable. "We could move the blocks, but what if there's an ambush on the other side?"

Mom peers around Morgan's arm. "They don't look like they're waiting to pounce."

I peek over her shoulder and agree. They look beaten and dejected, sitting on the ground or atop piles of broken Warriors. Four pits have been destroyed. It's hard to discern the extent of the damage.

"It'll take us a while to clear the rubble and we'll make enough noise to tip them off," Morgan explains. "I don't want to get hit by friendly fire."

"Can we contact their Security Chief?" Niall asks.

"Only if the chief has access to a portable or the Q-net," Morgan says.

"What about our communicators?" I ask. We haven't used them yet. "Are all security teams on the same frequency?"

"No. Otherwise, we would have heard them." Morgan peers at the screen. "I think I see a few uniforms." She sighs. "Looks like we'll have to clear the debris. Lawrence, keep an eye on our friends. Let me know their reaction once it becomes obvious what we're doing."

"Yes, sir." Glad I'm not part of the clearing crew, I back away, trying not to limp.

Since they're the tallest of our group, Bendix, Niall, and Zaim start removing the sandstone rocks from the top. We only need to clear enough to crawl through. The others form a line and hand the chunks off, sending them down the line until they reach the last person who spreads them out on the floor. We don't need a new blockade. It's quick and efficient, but the sounds of scraping stones and raining sand seem overly loud.

A couple of the people on the other side soon glance toward the debris pile. One or two point and their mouths move. One woman gestures for the others to evacuate that pit and move to the one further away from us. Then she's joined by four more people, who might be...I squint. Yep they're security officers. They spread out in a line and face the barricade, drawing their pulse guns.

"Officer Morgan," I say.

She holds up a hand and everyone freezes. "Ambush?"

"I don't think so. It appears they're protecting the others."

"Let me see." Morgan takes the portable. "Hmmm. As soon as we clear enough to see the other side they're going to shoot us."

I glance at the gap. It's only half a meter. "Maybe we can talk to them."

"Oh yeah, that'll work," Bendix mutters.

"Do you have a better idea?" Morgan asks.

"No, sir."

"Are they even going to believe us?" Elese asks. "I'm still having a hard time believing it and I was pooped through a portal."

There are a couple nervous giggles, but soon everyone is laughing, including Morgan. Once everyone sobers, I consider the problem.

Q? What's the name of the security chief?

OFFICER FELICIA KINGSTON.

Do you have a picture of her?

A photograph of the woman appears. Yep, that's her.

I tell Morgan the chief's name. "We have to try."

Morgan draws in a deep breath, then projects her voice through the debris. "Officer Kingston, this is Officer Morgan from Planet Yulin. Our chief, Officer Radcliff, sent you the warning about the attack. We're here to help you. Please stand down while we remove this barricade."

"And just what kind of idiot do you think I am?"

It's a valid question.

"I understand it's hard to believe, but the looters have been using the Warriors to travel between planets and—"

Mocking laughter cuts her off. Morgan turns to us. "Any more bright ideas?"

The tech who'd been pulling the wagon steps forward. He looks to be around twelve A-years old, but he's probably closer to twenty. "My sister is here." He ducks his head and swallows. His Adam's apple bobs in his long neck. "If she's still alive. It's why I volunteered."

"What's your name and hers?" Morgan asks.

"Torin Blackett and Meris West."

Morgan relays the information. "Ms. West can confirm her brother from Planet Yulin is here with us."

"And just how will she do that?" Kingston asks.

"Ask personal questions only Torin knows the answer to."

"The answers can be wormed from the Q-net."

"Not all of them. I'm sure there are family memories that aren't on the Q-net."

"No deal."

Morgan growls in frustration. "Officer Kingston, if we're looters, then we would have blasted this damn barricade down with energy wave guns and not bothered to talk to you."

The woman's aim wavers a bit, but then returns. "No. It's a trick."

"We're getting closer," I say.

Morgan gestures for the clearing to resume. "Keep low."

Not only are they removing heavy rocks, but Niall and Bendix have to duck the occasional sizzle from a pulse gun. When we have a space big enough for someone to crawl through, we all glance at each other. Who wants to be the sacrificial lamb?

Torin steps forward. "I'll go. They can get Meris and see that we're telling the truth."

"Unless they pulse you before you can say a word," Bendix says.

"Worth a shot," Morgan says. "Okay, Torin, make sure you show them you're unarmed. Hold your hands away from your body and tell them exactly what you're going to do."

Torin crawls up to the gap and crouches just out of sight. "My name's Torin Blackett and I'm coming out. I'm not armed." It's awkward and far from graceful, but he keeps his hands in front of him as he squirms from the gap.

Then there's a tumble of rocks, a curse, and a thump. But not a sizzle. Progress! On my portable, the five officers keep their weapons trained on Torin. But the poor boy has landed in an ungainly heap at the bottom of the pile. I gotta give him credit, though, his open hands are away from his body.

Nothing happens for a few minutes, then Kingston says something to the man next to her. He holsters his weapon and jogs to the other pit that's filled with people. An older woman stands—maybe around fifty A-years old. Her face is creased in confusion, but she follows the officer back to the others.

Kingston orders Torin to stand. The tech clambers slowly to his feet, keeping his hands in sight. The woman turns and a shocked grin spreads on her face. Even though it's obvious the officers are yelling at her, she runs to Torin and sweeps him up in a big hug. He is *that* skinny.

It's a lovely reunion, but it doesn't last long and Kingston is firing questions at them both. Sounds like she's accusing Torin of being a traitor and working for the looters.

Morgan huffs. "Did she not take a look at that kid?"

That kid is older than me and Niall. We exchange a smile.

According to my ankle, an eternity passes before Kingston orders, "The rest of you can come out. One at a time and I want to see your hands."

"We have to make the hole bigger," Morgan says.

"Fine."

The guys get to work and clear another meter. The barricade is now only waist-high, but no sizzles sear the air.

Morgan looks at us. "Same order that we came here in. Leave the cart until they settle down." She climbs over the rubble. Graceful, smooth and confident.

Then it's my turn. Let's just say I'm not any of those things and leave it at that. Niall makes it look easy. When my mom joins us, one of the officers lowers her gun.

"Dr. Daniels?" she asks in an incredulous voice.

"Hello there, Officer Bernardo, I told you we'd figure out the Warrior mystery in my lifetime."

My oh-so-humble mother just made things so much easier. Who knew? With the time dilation, anything can happen. Then we endure rounds of questions, rounds of answers, more rounds of the same questions because the Pingliang Security Chief doesn't believe the answers the first time around. And I thought Radcliff was tough. Kingston's inner guardian lion is made of steel.

The looters surprised the security team by coming up from the pits instead of digging down to them.

"We stunned a bunch, but they had energy wave guns and kill zappers. We had to surrender," Kingston says.

"You still have your pulse guns," Morgan says in a neutral tone.

"They didn't bother to unarm us. They're a cocky bunch," Kingston spat. "Then they ushered the entire base's population—even those that were stunned—into here and trapped us inside." She gestures to the pile of rubble. "The looters left the way you came, and that's the only pile they didn't use their energy wave guns to make. We were told not to follow them or they'd shoot us."

Unease chews on my stomach and anxiety grows in my chest. Could it be that they were trapped in the pits to make it easier for the HoLFs to kill them all? But that would take days. I recall how long it took on Yulin before there were enough shadow-blobs gathered to attack. At least twenty days. The people would die of thirst before that. While the looters are a bunch of murdering bastards, they aren't cruel. Or so I hope. What else is going on? I glance around the destroyed pit. Pit 4, I think.

"Did they leave any of the Warriors intact?" I ask Kingston. She glares at me. "Does it matter?"

"It might."

"What are you thinking?" Morgan asks me.

"Not sure." And I don't want to cause panic if I guess wrong. "Can I take a look around the rest of the pits please?" I ask

Kingston.

"Go ahead, but I can assure you there's no way out."

I keep from reminding her there are fifty-nine ways out. She's had a trying day.

"Take Radcliff and Keir with you," Morgan orders.

"Yes, sir."

"Cole, go with them," Kingston orders.

A male officer built like Bendix says, "Yes, sir."

I limp through the pits. Niall and Elese bookend me, and Cole follows us. We're quite the parade, giving the bored scientists and techs something to watch. Everyone appears very confused. I can't say that I blame them.

"What are we looking for?" Niall asks.

"Intact Warriors standing in a circle," I say.

"Wow, that's weirdly specific," Elese quips.

Pits 3 and 2 have no standing Warriors. The destruction is nauseating. Clouds of dust still hang in the air and scratch the back of my throat.

In Pit 1 there are eight intact Warriors and there's a faint green light ringing them. There are also a number of people crouched nearby talking in excited whispers as if speaking louder might bring the looters back. I'd bet my entire pay they are the archeologists for this base.

Even though the air is warm, I say, "Emitters."

The three of us pull the meter–long cylindrical weapon around to the front. It's heavy. I grab the short post that is underneath the front of the cylinder with my left hand. The end of the weapon rests on the crook of my right arm. And a crossbody strap helps support the weight. The trigger is near my right hand. All I have to do is squeeze the two teeth together to fire a null wave at a shadow-blob. It's an impressive looking weapon.

"Wait, what are you doing?" Cole asks, reaching for his pulse gun.

"This won't harm humans, but it will kill a HoLF," I say.

"A...hostile life form? Like the ones that are supposed to be invisible? They're real?"

"Yes. Didn't you read the reports?"

"Yeah, but we all had a laugh. Obviously someone was playing a joke."

"They're no joke, Officer," Elese says. "Please clear this pit of civilians."

The people who are just sitting around leave without trouble. It's the group by the Warriors who protest and fuss and refuse to move.

That is until Elese loses her patience. She points her emitter at them. "Leave now, or I'm gonna shoot you."

They hustle out in record time.

"Nice," Niall says.

"Officer Cole, can you ensure no one comes in here?" I ask.

"Yes." He takes up position at the end of the corridor.

The three of us approach the ring of eight Warriors. It's not looking good. They all have alien symbols on their armor. A green light glows from those glyphs. In the middle of the circle is a thin ribbon of black. The beginning of a portal.

"Jarren said it takes one hundred and twenty-eight hours for a complete portal to form when there's only eight Warriors," I say. "We have plenty of time." What I don't say is that in that time shadow-blobs might break through.

"Is this outgoing or incoming?" Niall asks.

"Outgoing. You can only open a portal from one side."

"Is this so they can escape?" Elese asks.

"Who?" Niall asks. "The looters or civilians? And why would the looters leave them a way to escape when…" He doesn't say what we're all thinking.

"No," I say. "It's not for an escape. Not yet. Maybe when everyone is…dead, the looters plan to return and use that portal."

"That's about five days from now." Elese is quick with the math.

I study the symbols. *Q? What planet does this represent?*

NONE OF THEM.

A new combination?

YES.

Do you know where this goes?

NO.

If there's a matching set on another Warrior planet, will the portal still work even though it's not marked with that planet's designation?

YES.

What will happen if we turn it off?

NOTHING.

I hate to do it without knowing why the looters left this here. It can't be good, because nothing they ever do is good. But figuring it out might give us an advantage.

"She has that look," Elese says to Niall.

"What look?" he asks.

"The one that usually lands us in a heap of trouble. Oooh, now I'm getting the shut-up-and-die look. Love you, too, Recruit."

I ignore her. Something isn't adding up. The looters want the base. They want access to all these Warriors without anyone interfering. They've let the HoLFs kill all the people in at least five bases. It took a while, but this time they trapped everyone here and— All my blood drains to my feet. It becomes difficult to keep air in my lungs.

"Mouse? Talk to me."

Q, what happens if there's no other side? If there's not another set of Warriors with the exact same symbols to cross over to? Where does the portal go?

INTO THE SHADOW DIMENSION.

No need to panic. Not yet. It only goes one way, right? Into not out of?

FOR HUMANS, YES.

And for the shadow-blobs?

DIRECTION DOES NOT MATTER.

Oh my stars!

2522:268

"We have to turn them off!" I yell as I lunge toward the Warriors with my hand outstretched. Before I reach them, black explodes from the thin ribbon. Shadow-blobs rush out and knock me back.

"Mouse!" Niall shouts.

"Take cover!" I order. "Fire at will!" I listen to my own advice. I fire the null wave emitter at the HoLFs rushing into our dimension through the narrow black rift. Sizzle-zaps sound from all three of our weapons. The shadow-blobs are so thick, I can't get near the Warriors to shut the portal down.

"Activate," I say to turn my communicator on. "Officer Morgan, we need back up. Multiple hostiles."

"Looters?" Her voice sounds right in my ear.

I glance over my shoulder. But of course she's not standing there. Instead Niall and Elese are firing their weapons and ducking lethally sharp tentacles.

"No, alien," I say.

"How many?"

"Hundreds." A guess, it could easily be a thousand.

"We're on the way."

And I'm in a dark part of the pit. I retreat until my back hits a wall. The air cools twenty degrees. They form a solid bubble around me. Well, as solid as a shadow can get. But it's the weapons at the ends of their multiple appendages that're the dangerous part. My security jumpsuit protects me from some of the attacks, resisting the slash of a blade or a stab of a knife. Not for long once they figure it out. By the way they're keeping a slight distance, I think the Warrior heart I touched has made them wary.

Not bothering to aim, I'm squeezing the trigger continuously, sweeping it all around. I'm sizzle-zapping a dozen at a time, but their numbers never diminish. I have to shut down the portal. Have. To.

Many more sizzle-zaps echo until it's one continuous buzz of noise.

"Hostiles in Pit 2," Morgan says. "We can't get to you. Status?"

"Radcliff, check."

"Keir, check."

"Lawrence, check."

"Retreat," she orders us. "We'll take a stand between Pits 2 and 3."

"No can do, sir," I say. "Someone needs to touch one of those Warriors and I'm the closest." Except I'm not sure how to accomplish that.

"It isn't a request," Morgan growls.

"I'm pinned down regardless. Niall, Elese can one of you get to the Warriors?"

"Nope," Elese says, sounding slightly winded. "I got pushed back into the corridor, keeping as many out of Pit 2 as possible."

But that meant Pit 1 would fill up with hostiles. "Niall?"

"I'm too far," he pants. "I've got your back if you want to make a run for it, Mouse."

A run for it? Two steps and I'd be impaled. I'd never reach—Stars, why didn't I think of this sooner. "Did we bring an energy wave gun?"

"A couple, why?" Morgan asks.

"To destroy the Warriors and close the portal!"

"Torin, get the weapon from the cart," Morgan barks.

I groan. The cart is on the other side of the barricade. It'll take—well, a lot longer than I have. The bubble squeezes closer. It's as if they understood what I said. The force of their strikes increases, cutting through the special fabric of my jumpsuit. Blood wells, but the pain is muffled as if it's happening to someone else who looks just like me. I sizzle-zap like crazy.

Time blurs, my hands cramp, my fingers freeze in place around the trigger. The wall behind my back is the only thing keeping me alive. I listen to Morgan shout orders and the others respond, but I can't tell you what they say. I chant, *come on, come on, come on,* under my breath, willing Torin to hurry, for the gun to get here.

After an epoch, Morgan says, "We can't reach you, Lawrence."

"Doesn't matter. Just shoot the bloody Warriors," I yell.

"We can't get into Pit 1. Too many hostiles."

Oh. And here I thought she was worried about flying pieces from the shattered Warriors hurting me. Then it hits me. We're about to be seriously overwhelmed if I don't do something.

"Toad, you got my back?"

"No. Stay put, I can't..." He puffs. "Can't keep...them off...of me."

Niall's in trouble. And I'm not going to lose him again. The image of his blood pooled underneath him flashes in my mind. I'm about to charge into the fray when I realize the shadow-blobs weren't around Niall when we'd rushed to his rescue in the archeology lab. He'd been lying curled into a ball, unmoving. Could it be that simple?

I freeze and stop sizzle-zapping. My heart thinks this is a bad idea. It thuds in my chest with urgency, threatening to bust out and abandon me and my insane idea. The blobs get in a few more thrusts. Biting my lip to keep from crying out, I stay still. They stop attacking and hover nearby. Seconds tick by like fat globs of honey falling off the end of a spoon.

The shadow-blobs move away. It would be a relief except they are heading toward Niall. I wait two more honeyed seconds and then bolt toward the Warriors. Pumping my legs, I go as fast as possible, jumping over the larger broken pieces. My movement attracts their attention and they give chase. The theory is it's harder to hit a moving target, so I weave and duck and dodge and run as fast as I can. I'm knocked off course by blows and strikes. Sharp points pierce my skin, but I don't slow. I aim for the Warriors and go, go, go. Go!

Prying my stiff fingers loose, I let my weapon hang from its strap, reach out, and dive for the closest Warrior. My fingers brush its arm, turning the green light in the symbol off. One is all you need to close the portal. A loud pop sounds as I crash land inside the circle, skidding on my side and getting a face full of sand. Ugh. The thin black strip of the rift shrinks and disappears with another pop.

I fumble for the emitter and struggle to my knees. There's still a pit full of shadow-blobs to sizzle-zap. Except there are none around me. Inside the circle is a shadow-blob free zone.

Not pausing to figure out why, I consider it a gift. "Niall! The portal's closed, rally to me, I'll cover you."

"Where?"

I stand between two Warriors and wave my flashlight. The shadow-blobs avoid the beam. Bonus. "Here!"

"Got it."

When I spot him running, I aim my emitter and sizzle-zap the HoLFs in his way. It's not perfect and he stumbles a few times. I'm once again urging, come on, come on, come on!

He spins in a circle, sizzle-zapping blobs before sprinting the final distance. He crosses into the circle and immediately takes up position behind my back. I'm still sizzle-zapping the shadow-blobs outside the circle. It takes him a few moments to realize he doesn't need to cover my back.

"We're protected in here," he says.

"Yup. Nice, huh?"

"A miracle."

I glance at his face and wish I hadn't. Bleeding cuts mark his cheeks, forehead, and neck. His hair is slicked with sweat. He's eyeing me with the same sympathy. I must look equally horrendous. Then we both return to sizzle-zapping HoLFs because that's the priority. It's different now. I'm just as focused and intense as before, but knowing I'm going to live through this makes breathing easier. I just hope everyone else does as well.

Morgan calls for status checks every so often. The replies start strong, but, by the fifth time, they're weaker as exhaustion catches up to everyone. When the shadow-blobs thin in Pit 1, Niall and I leave the protective circle in order the hunt the rest down. HoLFs are hiding in the shadows. And there are a million shadows in these pits. The rest of the team is doing the same.

We'd brought extra emitters and extra Warrior hearts just in case. I'm assuming Morgan handed those out to the Pingliang security officers. They're probably not laughing about HoLFs now.

When we run out of blobs to sizzle-zap, we both stand there for a moment, grinning at each other.

"Pit 1 is clear," Niall says.

"Good, now get your asses to Pit 2 and help," Morgan orders.

"Yes, sir," we say and join the rest of our team to eliminate every single one.

Once the crisis is over, the civilians spread out over three pits. No one wants to go into Pit 1. Even when I turn off all the other Warriors so there's no green glow, they still avoid it. Everyone has bleeding cuts. No one was spared. But thankfully no one is critically injured. Medical personnel move through the pits, tending to the wounded.

The officers huddle in Pit 4 for a debrief. We're a sorry looking group. We're all equally bruised, battered, and sliced up. I'm sitting down because I suspect if I stand up, my ankle will never speak to me again. Except I don't tell that to anyone. Instead, I ignore the pain. We've decisions to make and I need to be a part of that discussion.

"Why did the HoLFs attack right when you approached the circle, Lawrence?" Morgan asks.

Good question. I consider. Had it been just a matter of time before they came through? And just our very bad luck to be there to witness it? Possible. But then I remember the bit of space the shadow-blobs gave me and Niall mentioned it as well. It didn't stop them from attacking with a tentacle or three dozen, but... "It might be due to us having touched the heart of a Warrior." I explain. "They might have sensed us and wanted to invade before we closed the portal."

"We have the heart of a Warrior?" Cole asks.

I let Morgan explain. Guess she didn't have time before. No surprise as we were neck deep in blobs.

"I like that," Elese says to me. She thumps a fist to her chest. "I've the heart of a Warrior."

"You have a heart?" Bendix asks. "That's a surprise."

"Shut it, Benny."

He spreads his hands out. "Which proves my point."

They continue to banter, but I'm distracted by the pit. It's spinning and there's a buzzing in my ear. Is my communicator malfunctioning? I tap it. Nothing changes.

"What about that protective zone?" Morgan asks, snapping me out of it.

"I think that also has to do with the hearts. Those Warriors are intact and, once they no longer had to…" I twirl my hand in the air, as if I can scoop the right words into my mouth. "Worry about either creating the portal or protecting it, they could concentrate on keeping the HoLFs away." I'm not sure I made any sense as everyone is staring at me.

"She's your expert?" Kingston asks Morgan.

"Lawrence hasn't been wrong yet," Morgan says, giving the woman a hard stare.

Really? That doesn't sound right. I'm sure I've been wrong. Except I can't think of when because the buzzing grows louder. And now black and white spots show up at the edges of my vision. Oh no. I glance at Niall. He meets my gaze and hurries over. His boots make a path in the debris-filled sand, but there's no sound except the buzz.

"You're pale." He crouches down and winces, but now we're eye level. "Should I get the medic?"

"Yes, please."

That seems to scare him more. "All right, lean forward and take deep breaths, I'll be right back."

I do as instructed, lowering my head between my knees. Before I can take a breath, blackness rushes in, I pitch forward into an abyss.

Regaining consciousness, I immediately wish to return to the black pain-free oblivion. There is no part of my body that doesn't hurt. And when I open my eyes, there's a ring of faces above me, staring. I close them. If I can't see them, they're not there. Right?

Concerned voices cut through my delusion. Scary words like bleeding out and internal injuries are said. A warm hand is holding my icy one. Niall's. Someone asks where it hurts.

"Everywhere," I say unhelpfully.

Another person is prodding my various wounds, making them worse. I bat at the hand, but someone else grabs my free hand, lacing their fingers in mine. Mom. I relax. Then the prodder finds a particularly sensitive area. Pain explodes and the blackness returns.

I've no idea how long I've been out, but the faces are gone. I'm lying on my back. Every centimeter of my body aches. And not the dull throb of tired muscles, but the bright fire of serious injury. The weak emergency lights and rough sandstone ceiling mean I'm still in the pits on Pingliang. The hands remain holding mine and I squeeze them because I've no energy and am having a hard time moving anything else.

"She's awake," Niall says. He leans over so he can meet my gaze. "Hang on, Mouse."

But I'm already holding onto his hand. Confused, I ask, "To what?"

"Ara," Morgan says on the other side of me. "What pit goes to Planet Ruijin from here?"

Planet Ruijin? It sounds familiar, but my thoughts are broken like the Warriors. They're scattered with bits lying here and there.

PIT 26.

"Twenty-six," I say.

"We need a secure channel to Ruijin," Morgan says.

Q?

DONE.

"Check your port…" The effort to talk is too much; my eyes drift shut.

FLY?

I thought you'd never ask. I leave my battered and injured body behind. There's no pain in the Q-net. No effort at all. I spin and swirl and dip and cross the Galaxy in seconds as I fly with Q. There are no shadow-blobs. No murdering looters. No fear. Just peace and knowledge. All the answers to all the questions contained within the vast Q-net.

But that's not quite true. There have been things Q hasn't known. The looters managed to communicate without using it.

NOTHING IS OMNISCIENT. I KNOW ONLY WHAT THE NATIONS HAVE TAUGHT ME.

And fifth nation has taught you all about greed, lies, murder, betrayal, and lots of other unsavory behaviors. Go us.

THEY ARE NOT QUALITIES UNIQUE TO HUMANS.

Why isn't that comforting? Perhaps because three out of the four previous nations have ended in extinction. *What are our chances of making it like fourth nation?*

CURRENTLY FORTY-TWO PERCENT.

Currently? Does that mean it changes?

YES.

Ah. Probably depending on what we're doing. Destroying

Warriors and allowing the shadow-blobs into our dimension probably reduces our chances.

CORRECT.

And I can't think of a way that we're going to win this. They have the Protectorate, control of most of the portals, weapons, and resources. We have…a handful of security officers. It's grim. I'm safer in here. Besides, haven't I done enough? Isn't it time someone else more qualified takes the burden?

I shake off the depressing thoughts and concentrate on flying, dipping toward the glittering star roads. From this perspective, the ships that are on the stars roads, crinkling space and jumping time, look like black pearls on a silver string. One star road for each ship. And those roads can't cross or else bad things happen.

CORRECT.

There's always danger. And I've certainly had my share of it. I wonder if my body dies, will I be stuck in the Q-net forever?

STUCK?

I get a sense of indignation perhaps even hurt feelings. Sorry. If this is my afterlife, I'll take it over oblivion. This is my idea of heaven. But I've lots of things to do.

YOU DO.

Actually it's a crushing list. And it'd be easier to do while flying with Q instead of worming in my physical body. Might as well take full advantage of my time here. I send Radcliff a report about what happened on Pingliang. When I finish, I'm not sure what to do. There isn't a pull back to my body, which is concerning. Okay, it's freaking me out. I need a distraction and fast. Perhaps some research. What information should I find that would most help Morgan or Beau? While I'm deciding, a message from Radcliff pops up.

> 2522:269: Lawrence, I received your report. It matches what Officer Morgan sent me yesterday. The new information about how you tricked the HoLFs is very interesting, but sounds like it should be only used out of desperation due to the risk of severe injury. I haven't heard the good news about your recovery yet. You gave us all a scare. I'm glad you made it through the surgery.

Surgery? Yesterday? Lots of alarming statements in that short message. The sudden need for a hug fills me, pushing up my throat. Which is odd, considering I don't have a physical form.

> ← Officer Radcliff, I don't know if I'm recovered. My last memory is of being in the pits in Pingliang. I've been flying with Q.

There's a very long pause. Did I just freak out Radcliff? I've never seen him unbalanced. Even when Niall was dying, Radcliff remained calm. But if he's upset that means... No. Not going there. I'm not worming into my medical files either.

> → Hey partner, this is Beau. What's going on?

Oh my stars! I must have died.

2522:269

I stare at Beau's message. Radcliff relinquished his end of the conversation to Beau, which doesn't bode well for me. At all. I somehow missed a day. My injuries must have been severe enough for surgery, but everyone was trapped in Planet Pingliang's pits. Did they perform surgery on me in the pits? Yes, I know I've only to read Morgan's report. Yet reluctance drags on me. I'd rather hear the horrible news from my partner. Again the need for a hug pulses in my non-existent veins.

→ Ara, are you there? Talk to me, partner.

← Hi, Beau. I'm not sure what's going on. I'm either dead or unconscious.

→ You're not dead. Morgan would have told us.

True, the woman is pretty no-nonsense and would send a report ASAP.

← Where am I? I mean my physical body?

→ Planet Ruijin. Your injuries needed immediate attention so the team took you to Ruijin. Last we heard you were still in surgery.

Some of my panic eases. I must still be in surgery or in that post-op fog of sleep. That also explains why Morgan wanted to know the number of the pit that connects to Ruijin. I release a non-existent breath. Okay then, best make good use of my time in the Q-net.

← How's the evacuation going? Do you need any help communicating with the Ruijin's Chief of Security?

→ No, you already created a channel to Ruijin for Morgan. And even though she messaged them, the people in Ruijin's base had quite the shock when Morgan showed up with you and the team. Seems no one really believed us about the HoLFs. It's hard to be angry about that as I remember feeling the same way when you first told us. We're discussing changing our evac to Planet Qingyang since the survivors from Pingliang are going to Ruijin. Can you create a secure channel to Qingyang's Chief of Security? Officer Samuel James.

← I can, but the looters are building a blockade around Qingyang.

→ We hope our stay there is only temporary. Dr.

Carson's efforts have been successful. We are taking full advantage.

Bertie must have found the looters' communication frequency and Radcliff can now eavesdrop on the looters—good news. I sense he's reluctant to expose any of Radcliff's plans, so I don't ask. Nothing is entirely secure in the Q-net.

← Anything else I can do? The secure channel to Qingyang won't take us long.

→ Can you make a channel to Nanxiong?

← Yes. What else?

→ Concentrate on waking up!

As if it's that easy. However, what is easy are the links to Officer James and Nanxiong, which Q has already created while I was messaging Beau.

← I'll try. The secure channels are ready.

→ Thanks. Later, partner.

I hope there is a later. And if there is, I plan to hug everyone—Niall, my parents, Beau, Elese, and even Morgan and Radcliff. Everyone! In the meantime, I fly through the security programs around the Protectorate's databases. There has to be some record of what weapons and resources were sent to the looters.

Even flying, I have to be careful not to trip any alarms. The protections around the Protectorate are thick complex beasts. Q helpfully highlights the paths of least resistance, places where I might slip through without causing any ripples. It's a slow creeping pace as I ease through the network of tiny holes and miniscule gaps in their security, which I wouldn't have been able to do if I was entangled. Hours, days, years pass before I break through and the warren of data clusters is accessible to me.

My elation is tempered by the fact that I'm not sure what I'm looking for. There's not going to be a Q-cluster labeled "stolen supplies for looters." I have to think like them. How do you make a shuttle disappear? It's not a small item like an energy wave gun. People would notice that a couple dozen or more are missing. Unless there's a reason for it. What would cause them— oh!

Crinkling space is dangerous. Also just traveling from a crinkle point to a planet is dangerous. Space is a hostile environment. Many accidents have happened in the four hundred plus E-years of space travel. I don't remember any calamities regarding a Protector Class ship, but it might be classified. Good thing I'm in the heart of their organization.

Q, can you please find any reports on lost ships or any accidents involving Protector Class space ships in the last twenty E-years?

ON IT.

While Q is searching through the massive amounts of data, I look for information about the Protectorate ships *en route* to the Warrior planets. There are twenty-two in time jumps. I arrange them in order of when they're due to reach their destinations. The earliest one will arrive at Planet Suzhou in forty-eight days. I pull up the roster of personnel assigned to the ship—everyone in the Protectorate works for DES. The list of names means nothing to me. It's not like the traitors are marked with a big red arrow. Too bad, 'cause that would make it so much easier.

I access the suspected-looter-colluder file. Then I write a program that compares the names in that file to the ship's roster, to flag any that are on both lists. Once I go through one ship, the Q-net can do the other ships.

And now that I'm thinking about it, how would it work if only some of the people in the Protectorate space ship are traitors? Wouldn't you need everyone in agreement to take over a whole ship?

Perhaps my fear that an entire ship loyal to the looters being days away from appearing in Yulin's orbit is a bit...overly dramatic. I need to look at it from another direction. Jarren knew DES would send the Protectorate Class ships to all the Warrior planets once Xinji went silent. It's standard procedure. He never planned for the Protectorate to find survivors on Xinji, just destroyed Warriors and dead people. In the face of such a tragedy, they wouldn't even think to search for missing Warriors.

But what about the shadow-blobs? They would be thick by the time the Protectorate soldiers arrived. Unable to see the hostiles, the soldiers would be killed. DES would then quarantine the planets. That would let the looters have the planet all to themselves, but what would they do about the

HoLFs? They couldn't work in the pits with shadow-blobs attacking. Perhaps that was why Jarren was so keen to learn how we countered them. They're an unexpected complication to his plans.

If I'm right, then we don't need to fear the Protector ships en route to us. Some good news. But it also means the looters have to ensure that everyone is dead when all those ships arrive, which we already figured out.

Does that mean he planned to kill everyone in the research bases from the very beginning? A horrible thought!

Jarren. It all started with him. I should be looking into his history. *Q? Can you please gather all the information possible about Jarren and put it into one file?*

ON IT.

I still think we're missing a key connection. *Q? Do you have any information on those ships yet?*

THERE ARE FIVE PROTECTOR CLASS SPACE SHIPS THAT MEET YOUR CRITERIA.

Details about the ships appear. Two just disappeared—their status unknown. Another blew up. I read through the report. Seems they were testing an experimental weapon and it malfunctioned. Well, they assumed it had based on the data that was being sent at the time. Comments about an explosion were followed by a spike in energy readings and then complete silence. The most interesting thing about the incident is the company that built the new weapon is one of the three funding the looters. The fourth ship never appeared after crinkling space. It could still be in a time jump due to a navigation error. And the last reported an asteroid hit right before going silent.

If the looters have all five ships, then they have a ton of weapons, including five dozen military shuttles, twenty-five company-sized transport ships, and about twenty-five hundred soldiers. I ask Q to compile a list of all the items on those ships. Most of those details are classified, but we're in the heart of the Protectorate's database.

When the list is ready, Q and I stretch it into a long super thin snake and slip it through all of the Protectorate defenses. It's slow, exacting work. Once the list—and I—clears the last layer of protection, I send it to Radcliff along with an explanation about the five ships. At least he'll get an idea of what we're up against. I also include my thoughts that the ships arriving at the Warrior planets are probably on our side even though Radcliff might have already figured that out.

Q drops a large file about Jarren into my Q-cluster. I'm about to go read it when a message from Radcliff arrives.

> 2522:270: Lawrence, I appreciate the report, but you need to return to Ruijin ASAP. The surgery went well and you didn't lose as much blood as was feared. You must wake up. Consider it an order.

I stare at the date. It didn't seem like I spent another day flying in the Q-net. It's interesting that I'm not thirsty, hungry, or tired. I'm glad my body is still alive and I'd love to obey his order, but I don't know how. Perhaps if I fly to the planet and read my medical file, it would help me reconnect to my body. Or I can try to disentangle from the Q-net. Worth a shot. I send Radcliff a yes, sir and fly to Ruijin.

The report on my surgery is filled with medical jargon. I

need a medical degree to understand it all. But the overall consensus is I suffered multiple lacerations, including two deep puncture wounds, which caused bleeding, both internal and external, 'cause I'm a classic overachiever. At least my vitals are steady and straightforward. Nothing I read creates a tug toward my body. Disentangling also doesn't work, because I'm lacking that…extra level.

It's hard to explain. It's like when you're concentrating on something and everything around you fades. But it doesn't completely disappear, a part of you is still aware of the physical things nearby. And, when you're interrupted, you snap back into the here and now and the colors and shapes return to your surroundings. That's what it's like to have Q in my head. When we're interacting, the rest of the world fades. Except this time, there's no snapping back. The awareness of what's around me is gone.

Maybe my body just needs time to heal. Let's go with that. To keep from panicking, I read through Jarren's file. Jarren Riley Hoyt was born in 2396 on Planet Kaiping. Huh. Did I know his last name? He's always just been Jarren. Knowing his middle and last name makes him seem more…normal. He's the only child of two biologists who transferred to Planet Xinji when he was thirteen.

I read through his soch-time reports. His intelligence was obvious from a young age as he found loopholes in rules and discovered ways to trick the facilitator. That poor woman was outmatched by the time he was six. His best and only friend on Kaiping was Rick Nolwart (also known as the infamous Warrick Nolt). They spent a great deal of time together in the recreation room playing video games and were inseparable.

Leaving Kaiping must have been devastating. No wonder he talked about Warrick all the time. I remembered being so annoyed about that, mocking him behind his back with Lan. Now I feel bad. But not too bad. That's not a reason to kill people. But as I read his soch reports on Xinji, it's obvious he was hurting. He put on an act for us with that confident swagger and spark of mischief.

And just when he and Lan fell in love, his parents transferred to Planet Suzhou, and he's put into detention for two years because he tried to alter the arrival time of the Interstellar Class supply ship. Hmmm. The fact that he tried meant he knew about the star roads. We all know about the star roads, but you really need to understand them like the navigators do to even think about messing with them. Perhaps even then he didn't care if he killed people to get what he wanted.

But that brings me to the question, how would he have known? He traveled on an Interstellar Class ship to get to Xinji. Did he spend time with the navigators? There's nothing in the ship's logs. Was there anyone on the ship that failed out of navigator school? I look at the passenger and crew list for that trip. Scanning the names, I stop at one. Victoria Oarsen, a crinkle engine specialist. Could she be the influence for Osen Vee?

Q, can you please check if Victoria Oarsen's attended one of the navigator training schools?

ON IT.

I keep reading the names but nothing else pops out at me. Then I pull up the personnel list of the people assigned to Xinji's research base. About halfway down, another name snags my attention. Ursan Kodiak, a Q-net technician who worked in the base's control center. I groan. Ursy Bear. And here I thought he picked the name from the Ursa Major constellation—which looks like a bear—that can be seen from Earth. Since I'd been named (twice) after one of those eighty-eight constellations, I know them all. Never seen any of them, though.

VICTORIA OARSEN ATTENDED DES'S SPACE FLIGHT SCHOOL ON PLANET DELTA.

Thanks. How about Ursan Kodiak? There's a slight pause.

HIM, TOO. SAME SCHOOL.

Ah. So despite Jarren's claims that he was behind all those pseudonyms, they *are* real people. And I bet he was trying to divert my attention away from them. It worked.

What happened to Rick Nolwart? Another pause.

ATTENDED THE SAME SCHOOL.

At the same time as the others?

YES.

What's he doing now?

CAPTAIN IN THE PROTECTORATE. STATUS UNKNOWN.

Was he on one of the missing ships?

YES.

A strange mix of emotions rolls through my non-existent body. Elation over finally figuring it out and having proof. Frustration for not thinking of this sooner. And terror—these people are highly intelligent!

Q, how many students were in their cohort? And which ones graduated? A list appears of ten names. Only one graduated. I don't worry about her, instead I ask Q to investigate the other six names. Where are they now? After a few minutes Q comes back with the answers. Three are in the Protectorate, two are in the high levels of DES, and one works for Catro Corp, one of the looters' major investor. A very busy and ambitious cohort. I put all the information together and send it to Radcliff. Yes, I expect him to yell at me for not waking up. Not much I can do about it.

I continue reading Jarren's file. During his incarceration, he was surly and uncooperative and time was added to his sentence because of his behavior. Then there's a file full of messages between him and Lan. I really don't wish to intrude on Lan's privacy, but I need to learn what he was thinking during that time.

It's heartbreaking. When he first left Xinji, she promised to find a time jump that would keep them close in age. So the fact she didn't was an utter betrayal. His reply to her message about her marriage and children drips with pain and loss. I've another brief moment of sympathy for him. And then, like I suspected, Lan tossed him a bone and started discussing her research. Soon after, Jarren got a job as an archeology tech and helped with the work in the Warrior pits on Suzhou. He also sent lots of messages to his friends Rick and Victoria.

It only took a couple more years for Jarren to get good enough with worming to hide his messages and activities from DES. Then he disappeared—no activity at all. But according to DES's records during those years, he was a dutiful employee, reporting to work without incident. Of course those records were expertly altered. I wonder if those hidden messages have the details about his schemes. I could ask Q to find them, but I have to do one first.

Good thing in my current state of being, I'm indefatigable. Finding those hidden messages is like a treasure hunt, looking for clues—Jarren's fingerprints—and digging through the layers of time. Eventually, I unearth one he sent to Rick, testing their new communication path that keeps DES from accessing their messages. I start another file in my cluster—murderer-missives.

Q? Can you please dig out all the rest of the hidden messages that Jarren sent? And see if there are messages between all those members of the looter cohort?

IT WILL TAKE A WHILE.

Okay, thanks. I wonder what I should research next when a message from Beau pops up.

2522:271: Hey partner. What are you doing? If you don't wake up soon, you're going to miss all the fun. Q helped me break through the barricades around the silent planets and we've found survivors on Planet Ulanqab! A soch-time facilitator named Ceridwyn Trant and her charges are still alive. We're going to rescue them. Plus Radcliff has one of his genius ideas that you're going to love. That is, if you're awake and on your feet.

← Survivors!! That's fantastic news, Beau! I'm trying to wake up. I just can't connect to my physical form.

→ That's funny coming from you. You connect with a thought. Why can't you do it in reverse? What's keeping you away?

Huh. Nothing. I want to go back despite the odds of success against these people being unlikely. We might rescue those kids and their facilitator, but they'll still be in danger. And I'm going to die again. Don't try to tell me otherwise, you know it as well as I do. And what if the next time I die, I don't end up in the Q-verse? What if I cease to exist? Dead for real. Beyond scary. Plus I'm super helpful in here, finding all this information. With enough time, I'll expose all of Jarren's network. When I don't answer, Beau sends another message.

→ Giving up is not an option, Lawrence. You've never backed down from anything or anyone. So why are you doing it now?

← I'm not backing down. I'm being smart.

→ So it's smart to have everyone worried about you? To have Niall useless as he refuses to leave your side? To scare your parents? Sorry, partner, that sounds like an excuse. You're letting everyone down by hiding in here.

I'm not hiding! Of course Beau can't hear me as I've no real voice. Mentioning Niall is a low blow. I know exactly how Niall is feeling and it's horrible. No one should have to go through that. But that's the thing. You've no control. It'll happen regardless. People die. He's going to have to go through it eventually and he's already gotten a head start. Except I haven't died, and he's hoping with every fiber of his being that I'll pull through, just like I did when he was unconscious. And here I am acting like I died. Because it's easier than facing the enemy again. Damn it, Beau.

← Why hasn't Niall messaged me?

→ We haven't told him or your parents that we've been communicating with you in the Q-net. Don't yell at me; it was Radcliff's decision. But I think the more important question is... Why haven't *you* messaged him?

Double damn it, Beau!

← I hate you.

→ Love you, too, Lawrence. Now get your ass in gear.

I hope I can. I've one last play. *Q, can you please help me?*
I CAN.
That's an odd response for Q. *Will you?*
IF YOU WISH. THERE IS A CHANCE OUR CONNECTION WILL BE SEVERED.
Like with Niall? After Q woke Niall, he could no longer connect to the Q-net. It had fried the sensors in his brain.
YES.
What's the chance?
SEVENTY PERCENT.
Yikes. That's huge. There's no way I can risk it. If I do the looters will win and kill everyone I love.

MESSAGE THROUGH PORTABLE.

But it won't be the same, will it?

NO. I CAN STILL GATHER INFORMATION FOR YOU.

But no worming into secure databases. No instant connection. No creating escape tunnels through blockades or sabotaging them. No flying.

CORRECT.

Can you do all that with Officer Beau Dorey?

NO. I CHOSE YOU.

Again with that! I'm not that special. Really. If my connection with Q is broken, it will be very obvious to everyone I've no other useful skills.

No comment from Q, so I consider the pros and cons. If I stay, they'll keep my body alive and I can come back after we stop the looters. I can message Niall and my parents and explain. They won't be happy. And Niall… the memories of the nights I spent hoping he'd wake are horrible.

But how would I have felt if he'd chosen not to wake up? Gambled on his body surviving an attack on Ruijin? I'd be angry and hurt, but I'd understand his decision. The greater good and all that. But what if his body died and he was stuck? I'd still be able to communicate, but no kisses, no cuddling, no fun, and no future together. Q chose me, but I'm choosing Niall.

I'm sorry, Q, but I'm going to be selfish and risk it.

NOT SELFISH. HUMAN.

Before I can say good-bye pain knifes through my head. It's like being hit with twin electrical bolts—one on each side of my head that meet in the middle. The agony stops as fast as it started. I'm aware of walls and light, but it's all washed out in shades of gray like a photograph left in the sun too long. Another blast pierces my brain. It burns as it skitters through my head. The world solidifies into shapes that have mass and are painted with a pale blush of color. The third searing strike crackles up my spine and into the base of my skull.

Sounds accompany the relief, but I brace for another jolt. Nothing happens. The noise separates into the comforting beep of medical equipment. Sensations return. The weight of the blankets on my skin. The softness of the mattress underneath me. A dull throb in my ankle. An ache in my muscles. Warm fingers laced in mine. I breathe in the scent of sage grass mixed with that distinctive antiseptic smell of the infirmary.

I concentrate and curl my fingers, squeezing Niall's hand. There's movement next to me. A light caress on my cheek.

"Mouse?" A hoarse whisper.

It's an effort to pry my eyelids apart. Even though the light is dim and soft, it hurts. I close them.

"Don't leave, Mouse. Stay with me."

The pain in his voice is raw. I'm a terrible person, hiding so long in the Q-net while Niall and my parents suffered. I coax my inner guarding lion from her hiding spot. Then I gather my determination and use it to snap open my eyes.

I meet Niall's gaze. Then I croak, "Hey."

A hesitant smile. "How do you feel?"

"Weak, stupid, tired, guilty, hungry, and in serious need of a hug."

"Then you better get one before the doctor arrives and kicks me out." Niall slides his arm underneath my shoulders and wraps his other around my chest. "We can deal with the rest later."

It's the best hug ever. His heat soaks into my sore body and I don't ever want to move. The hug ends too soon and he pushes up on his elbow. I realize that he's been lying in the bed with me.

"I can't be selfish," he says, climbing out of bed.

His cuts have either scabbed over or sport a row of stitches. Exhaustion clings to him like an invisible cloak. He's wearing the everyday security uniform with the black tactical pants and gray long-sleeved shirt. Putting on his boots, he straightens and clips on his weapon belt. He has the full complement—pulse gun, kill zapper, energy wave gun, and a flashlight. All a reminder of our tenuous situation. We're safe for now, but looters can pour from the pits at any time.

Niall gives me a hard stare. It's not as potent as his father's but there's weight to it. "Don't go anywhere."

Where would I go? I glance around at the wires and tubes snaking out from under the blanket that kept me alive while I cowered. But then I realize he means back into my coma slash flying with Q. "I won't." And it's possible I can't, but I'm too afraid to try. I just couldn't handle it right now if I'm cut off.

"Good." He leaves, taking all the warmth with him.

I shiver under the blankets, which wakes all the rest of my aches. Shouldn't one of these tubes be giving me instant pain medicine?

Dr. Bharathi strides in with my parents on her heels. They descend on me. Seems both Bharathi and my father portaled—yes, they've created a new verb—over to Ruijin. Bharathi didn't trust anyone to take care of *her* patient. My dad, because he's my dad—biology trumping responsibility in this case.

"Gavin and Drs. Jeffrey and Gage have the evac well in hand," he says, waving away my concern.

My mom's in the same condition as Niall. I suspect all the rest of the security team is as well. I'm glad all three are here. After Bharathi examines me, the top half of the bed is raised so I'm sitting up. I ask for hugs—even from Dr. Bharathi—before I answer all their questions as they test my state of mind. I'm sure there's another brain scan in my future.

Talking is exhausting and I can't keep track of the conversation. Bharathi asks about my pain and then fiddles with a machine. When Niall arrives with soup, my parents leave with promises to return in the morning. Bharathi says she's monitoring me and all I have to do is push a button and she'll come.

Niall pulls the table over and sets the soup on it. I eye the steaming liquid as my appetite wakes up and demands food now. Except the spoon weights a thousand kilos. Elese is not going to be happy about my poor physical condition so I press on and scoop every molecule of the chicken noodle soup into my mouth.

"Why soup?" I ask him when he moves the table away and lowers the bed.

"That's what the nurses gave me," he says, sitting on the edge of the bed.

"I figured, but what is it about chicken noddle soup that is always the first thing you give a patient? Does it have some magical healing properties?"

"I'm not a doctor, but I suspect it's due to having a

combination of protein, carbohydrates, and broth to help it go down. You've been getting all your liquids through a tube, so your mouth and throat are dry." He gives me a sly smile. "That and the fairy dust they mix in it. I hear it's imported from Planet Tinkerbell."

"I knew it!"

"Not many people know, so keep it on the down low."

I laugh. "I will."

Niall's good humor fades. He takes my hand in his. "You scared me, Mouse."

"I'm sorry."

"Why in the world would you apologize?"

"Because I was hiding in the Q-net." I explain about my adventures. "It's just so…overwhelming. We're outgunned. It's just a matter of time before they catch up to us and we're all dead. I thought why not save time and pain and just skip to the end."

"What made you come back?"

"You."

Niall kisses me. "Thanks." Then he kicks off his boots, hangs up his weapon belt and joins me in the bed. "Looks like we both had our freak outs, so we should be good."

I snuggle against him. "Mine lasted longer than yours."

"You've always been an overachiever. Don't worry, I'm okay with it. I don't mind being in your shadow."

"At least my shadow is well behaved and won't try to kill you."

"I appreciate that."

I'd laugh but a yawn just about cracks my jaw.

"Go to sleep, Mouse."

I struggle to stay awake, but my energy runs out. I sigh and fall asleep in Niall's arms.

In the morning, Bharathi does another exam and I'm given solid food. Ruijin had a recent resupply. And had gotten the next generation of accelerated healing meds. It's cool stuff. Niall and the rest of the team's stitches are removed. He insists they do his in my room.

That's sweet, but it reminds me of why I'm in this bed in the first place. When they're finished, I ask him, "What happened after I fainted?"

"There was some confusion because your injuries didn't seem that bad. One of Pingliang's medical staff examined you and determined you were probably bleeding internally." He pauses. "I may have freaked out at that news. Morgan organized everyone and we portaled to Ruijin." He huffs with amusement. "You should have seen their faces. Total shock, even though we sent a message that we were coming, they still didn't believe us. At least they humored us and went to Pit 9 with their surgeon and a gurney. I imagine they were composing a scathing report in their heads about the prank while waiting for us.

"Morgan says that when she arrived with you in her arms, they just stood there staring at her, grappling with what just happened in front of their very eyes. By the time I portaled to Ruijin, you were being wheeled away."

"What about the people from Pingliang?"

"They're finally all here. The base is packed. Security is taking shifts in the pits, keeping an eye out for the telltale green glow—it appears soon after the portal is established. They're also on alert for any shuttles or missiles heading this way."

"I can help with setting up alarms," I say automatically, but I might not be able to do any of that anymore.

"Relax, Mouse. We believe if they come it'll be through the pits."

"It's not that." I explain about the seventy percent chance. An alarmingly high percentage.

"You can find out pretty quick right now," Niall says.

"I know it's just…"

"Just what?"

"I'm terrified to find out if I'll never be able to fly again. Or if my extremely selfish act caused us to lose one of our meager advantages over the looters." Or if I lost a friend. Weird, I know.

"Do you think you made the wrong choice?" he asks. His tone is carefully neutral.

"Of course not." I hug him tight, proving it.

"Can't…breathe."

I relax enough to allow his diaphragm to do its job. But I keep him close. Because I can!

"I'm very glad you were selfish, so that makes me selfish, too," Niall says. "And I'd bet there are a number of other people who feel the same way."

"My parents."

"Yes, but also my dad, Morgan, Elese, Beau, Bendix…do I need to keep going?"

"No. I agree we're all very selfish, but that's not going to help when we're all very dead."

Niall breaks away and meets my gaze. "This isn't you. Why so pessimistic?"

I tell him about the failed navigator cohort. "Nine of them! They've been planning this for years. We can't beat them."

"But we have, Mouse. We've upset their plans, figured out what they're doing, and stopped them from killing all the people in Pingliang. Nothing's changed except now we know exactly who we're dealing with, which gives us an edge. Along with the fact they don't know we're using the portals, giving us another advantage."

All true statements. Plus they've made mistakes. Still...I'm not as confident as before. Before what? The attack on Pingliang? Memories of the shadow-blobs erupting fill my head. Just dumb luck we were there and able to close the rift. Or was *before* when I'd been connected to Q? Did that give me my confidence?

"We're not beat, Mouse," Niall says. "And our survival is not dependent on your connection to the Q-net."

"Do you really believe that?"

"I do."

That takes a great deal of pressure off. I take in a deep breath and close my eyes.

Q? Are you there?

There's no response.

2522:272

Do you know the expression that silence is deafening? I always thought it was an odd thing to say since silence really doesn't harm your eardrums. And it's quiet. Well now I understand what it means. The lack of...anything makes you question that something must surely be wrong. I must be deaf, therefore I can't hear the clamor that is surely going on. That *must* be going on.

In this case, it means I'm cut off from Q. I'm deaf to it.

"Mouse?"

I open my eyes. "Nothing."

Instead of responding, he pulls me close. I'm not as devastated as I'd expected. Perhaps when all this is over it will hit me. I do know there will be times I'll regret coming back before we either stop the looters or die in the attempt. But not when I'm wrapped in Niall's arms. He is why I came back. I breathe in his scent and enjoy the moment. We might not get another.

I spend the rest of the day recovering and messaging Beau. Q won't help him the same way as me, but I can give him advice on how to layer in extra alarms around Ruijin to alert us to a missile strike. Seems all my secured channels between the active Warrior Planets are still working. Radcliff sends me a question as to why a gigantic file titled murderer-missives and filed with messages between Jarren and a bunch of people landed in his portable. I explain and receive the equivalent of a grunt in response.

Everyone takes the news of the loss of my super Q-net power in stride. I think my parents are secretly relieved. Can't blame them. I concentrate on getting better and stronger because I don't want to be left behind. Morgan is organizing a team to rescue the survivors on Ulanqab—Ceridwyn Trant and fourteen children! That's super exciting.

As soon as I'm discharged on the morning of day two hundred and seventy-three, I change into my security uniform. Then I sling my ruck over my shoulder and head out to track Morgan down before my parents can waylay me. Niall told me that all the officers are sharing the empty units in Ruijin's security area. My parents are in an empty housing unit—one of the few. Most of the people from Pingliang are bunked in various labs, and the recreation area. No one except security is allowed into the pits.

In the security conference room, I find Morgan, Elese, Zaim, four of the Pingliang officers, and four strangers—they must be from Ruijin's security team. Niall and Bendix are taking a shift guarding the pits. I set my ruck in a corner and join them.

Morgan glances at me, but continues with her explanation. "We'll arrive on Planet Ulanqab in Pit 32. We'll need to travel to Pit 50. That will bring us back to Ruijin. The survivors will be on the surface and will join us once the pits are secured."

"Do we know how many hostiles to expect?" Officer Kingston asks. A few healing cuts still mark her face.

"Lawrence?" Morgan asks.

I consider. "Not many."

Kingston turns to me. "Are you sure? We went from none to a thousand in seconds. They've had more time for their pits to fill with hostiles."

"The HoLFs avoid the intact pits," I say.

"What if those pits are no longer intact?" Kingston shoots back.

A good question. *Q?* Oh, right. A pang of sadness grips my chest. I borrow Elese's portable and pull up the camera feeds in the Ulanqab pits. There are no lights so I can't confirm if they're intact or not. "If that's the case, then we can expect a ton of hostiles." There's a moment of stunned silence.

"We have our mechanical techs working on building multidirectional null wave emitters," one of the strangers says. He appears to be near fifty and has the posture and demeanor of a Security Chief.

"How effective will it be?" Kingston asks him. "Once there, we can't retreat. We have to travel through eighteen pits."

"Unknown. It hasn't been field tested yet," he says dryly.

There's some grim smiles.

"No one will be assigned to this dangerous mission,"

Morgan says, looking at Kingston. "It's voluntary. While I'd prefer that my team members have experience fighting the HoLFs, I'm not forcing anyone, including my squad. I'd like to have fifteen officers total—one to escort each child through the portal, but the kids can double up if I'm short."

"I volunteer," Elese says.

"Bendix and I are in," Zaim says.

"I'm in," I say.

"Which means Niall's in," Elese says. Then she cocks her head to the side. "And probably Dr. Daniels. The doc is fearless."

That's seven if I include my mom. There's an uncomfortable pause.

"I'll go," Officer Cole says.

Except for Kingston and Ruijin's Security Chief, the others avoid Morgan's gaze. A clear no.

"I bet Torin and some of the techs will volunteer," Zaim says, breaking the awkward silence. "Considering they couldn't see the enemy, they handled themselves well during the attack on Pingliang. Do we have more Warrior hearts for them?"

Oooh nice dig, implying the techs are braver than trained security officers. Then he adds on guilt about Kingston and her team using up precious hearts.

"I'll go," Kingston says, but she doesn't sound happy.

Another of her officers volunteers. None of the Ruijin staff say a word.

Chief frowns at his officers. He says to Morgan, "I have to remain here, but you can ask the next duty shift." His tone implies they might be more courageous. "The multidirectional emitters should be ready later today."

"Thanks," she says. Then she addresses us. "We'll assemble in the archeology lab at oh-six-hundred tomorrow. Our exit pit is number 62."

Everyone who volunteered groans. That pit is very far from the base.

"We have motorbikes," Chief says.

Wow. Ruijin gets all the cool toys.

"Bring your rucks, and enough supplies for a couple days," Morgan continues before dismissing us.

Morgan pins me with her hard stare and I remain in my seat. Elese, sensing she might be needed, hovers nearby.

When everyone else is gone, Morgan asks me, "Are you sure you're up for this, Lawrence?"

"Yes, sir."

"You were discharged not two hours ago."

"I've had plenty of time to heal." Which is true.

Morgan continues to stare.

"I'll eat extra rations today to catch up on my calorie intake," I offer. Then add, "And I'll take it easy the rest of the day. Come on, you need me. I've the most experience with fighting HoLFs." I realize that I am the Expert with a capital E when it comes to shadow-blobs. It's rather sad, but at least I'm not totally useless.

She glances at Elese. "See that she follows through on her promises."

"Yes, sir. Where should she rest?" Elese asks.

"Lawrence can bunk with us."

"Woo hoo, slumber party!" Elese swats me on my back.

Morgan just shakes her head, but before she can leave, I call her name.

"Yes?"

"Thanks."

"Don't let me regret it, Recruit."

"I won't. But I was thanking you for getting me to Ruijin so fast. You saved my life."

She grunts. "Just returning the favor."

Before I can ask her what she means by that, she's gone. Instead, I look at Elese.

"Girl, if you don't get it, then you're not giving yourself enough credit. Come on, I'll show you our unit. It has bunk beds!"

"Really?"

"Yes!"

She wasn't kidding. The beds are holdovers from when they had extra security at the Warrior bases, back when they worried the race of aliens that built them might come back. Little did they know what eventually showed up.

Elese plays nursemaid to me for the remainder of the day, ensuring I rest and eat large quantities of food that she fetches from the cafeteria. My parents are *allowed* to visit, which I think is very funny. They don't. Niall is given a strict time limit when he stops by.

He sits on the floor next to me since I'm on the lower bunk. Lacing his fingers in mine, he asks, "Are you going to be strong enough for the mission to Ulanqab?"

I reassure him just like I did my parents and Morgan. It's a surprise I haven't gotten messages from Radcliff and Beau asking the same thing. Well, not yet.

"Has everyone been evacuated from Yulin?" I ask.

"I believe so. My dad and the rest of our team are still there, along with a few brave souls who volunteered to guard the looters. And Drs. Carson and Edwards stayed behind, too."

No surprise. "Have any of the looters come to investigate the base?"

"Not yet. Dad has a few techs keeping watch outside the base. And he's monitoring their communications in case they come in range. Let's hope the looters are confident the base was destroyed."

"Does DES know any of this?"

"No. Both Ruijin and Qingyang are keeping quiet about the portals and evacs. Those secure channels you created between Warrior planets haven't been wormed. DES believes Yulin is gone. Dad sent a quick message about hearing a missile, and they've gotten nothing from Yulin since. DES also thinks Pingliang went silent. They've been sending warnings to Ruijin, Qingyang, and Nanxiong. We sent the security chiefs instructions through the secure channels on how to build those null wave emitters."

What about Suzhou? Jarren discovered and experimented with the portals there. There's a factory there as well. He had to have at least the archeology techs cover for him, maybe even help him. But what about the rest of the base? Suzhou is still an unknown.

Elese arrives to shoo Niall out. "What are you two doing anyway?"

I tell her about Suzhou and my theories.

She makes a disgusted sound. "This conspiracy has as many

tentacles as a HoLF. Is there anyone we can truly trust outside security?" It's a rhetorical question. "I should adopt Tora's philosophy."

"What's her philosophy?"

"Everyone is guilty until proven innocent."

That explains why it took her so long to like me. Wait, she still doesn't like me. Oh well, I'm not completely innocent. Then again, who is?

Oh-five-hundred comes oh-so-quickly. During the night, Officer Morgan and I learned, much to our chagrin, that Officer Keir snores. Loudly. I'm stiff, but keep it to myself since my every movement is being scrutinized by both of them. I resist snapping at them that I already have one mother and I don't need two more. My restraint is due to not wanting to give them any excuse to leave me behind.

When I pull on my form-fitting security jumpsuit, I notice I've lost weight. And don't get me started on the profusion of scars, scabs, and multicolored bruises decorating my skin. At least I still have my curves but they're not so curvy. Oh well, less mass to move when I run, which makes me wonder if there are size or weight limits for the Warrior portals. What's too big? The looters managed to transport military shuttles, which hold twelve soldiers and two pilots. But what about a troop carrier? Or a space ship? *Q? Do you know?*

No response of course. And I wonder when I'll stop automatically reaching out to Q or when the silence will no longer hurt so much.

I click on my weapon belt then shoulder my ruck. Wow, it weighs a ton. Morgan hands out energy bars before leading us to the pits. Niall, Zaim, and Bendix are already there along with my parents, who immediately come over to ensure I've recovered enough to go on the mission. I suppress my sigh because I know they mean well and I can be mature, even though a small part of me is glad to have my parents coming along as well.

It doesn't take long for the rest of the team to arrive. There are thirteen of us and I try not to be superstitious about the number. We already know Officers Cole and Kingston and we're introduced to the others. Officer Dan Flynn and Antonia Bernardo are from Kingston's team, and the other one, Officer Pero Jutras is the sole volunteer from Ruijin's security. He's the only one without any experience fighting HoLFs. Morgan hands the man a heart. I wonder how many she has with her.

Morgan issues orders and we load up on the motorbikes. Except they're more like glorified scooters and the Ruijin techs won't let us drive, so we have to hang on to the back while loaded down with our rucks, weapon belts, and null wave emitters. No one thinks the ride to Pit 62 is fun.

Everyone is a bit stiff after we dismount. There's nothing to distinguish this pit from any of the others except the alien symbols on the eight key Warriors of the innermost octagon. The techs trail us so they can watch my mother open the portal. After warning everyone to keep out of the center, Mom touches each of the eight Warriors. Green light fills the symbols and we now have sixteen minutes before the portal is ready.

It's not long to wait, but if we were being attacked by HoLFs or looters, it would be an eternity. I glance at Niall. Did he think those sixteen minutes overly long when I was unconscious?

He notices my gaze and leans close, whispering, "Longest sixteen minutes of my entire life, Mouse."

The desire to hug him pulses inside me, but I remain in place. Instead, I pull out my portable to message Ceridwyn that we're on the way and give her an estimated arrival time. Beau and Q created a secure connection to her portable. Her response is almost instant. Poor woman must be exhausted. Unfortunately, being evacuated to Ruijin isn't a guarantee of safety. No Warrior planet will be safe until the looters are stopped.

Like before, Morgan arranges us in a particular order. Once again, I'm right behind her with Niall next in line. The newbies are put in the middle and Bendix is assigned the sweeper position. When the portal first appears, there's a collective intake of breath from the techs. Guess they missed seeing the one we arrived through. It's fun watching their rapt expressions as the green light pulses through the surrounding Warriors and a portal forms in the middle of the key Warriors. Surprise and wonder ripples through them and I have to admit, I'm equally entranced by the light show.

We've no idea how or why the portals work. And we may never understand the complex scientific principles. Right now, it's magic. Pure and simple.

When Morgan steps into the blackness and disappears, the techs gasp as one. Bendix is monitoring his portal for signs of Morgan's arrival. I glance at the new officer. He appears as if he's going to be sick. I have to give Officer Jutras major credit for being here, though. At least we've had time to get used to the idea of shadow-blobs and traveling through the Galaxy in a matter of seconds…well, not really. I don't think anyone is used to it. But we've had some experience.

"There's nothing," Bendix says. "I can't see a thing."

Everyone looks at me.

"The HoLFs probably cut off the electricity to the base. The cameras won't work. Look for Officer Morgan's flashlight through the portal."

"But doesn't the portal only go one way?" Dad asks.

It does. Except I remember seeing a person the very first time we woke the Warriors. And if the looters are using them to communicate, then electromagnetic radiation can go both ways. "I think that's just for physical objects. Light can pass through both ways." I stare into the blackness.

Soon enough a flashlight beam pierces the portal. That's my cue.

"Wait," Dad says; he's rummaging in his overly large backpack. He pulls out a lantern. It's round and about fifteen centimeters long. Dad hands it to me. "Compress the ends and twist to light it. It won't be as bright as a floodlight, but better than your flashlight."

"Handy. Thanks."

"I'd rather have the lights on, but this'll do in a pinch." He dips in and removes three more, giving one each to Niall and Mom. He keeps the last one.

I hurry to the portal, step through, and experience the strange nausea. Curious about what will happen, I open the lantern. It doesn't work. The batteries must be dead. Except when I'm propelled out into the pit, its white light just about blinds me.

"Talk about making an entrance, Lawrence," Morgan says. "Get your ass out of the way."

I stagger to the side. Once my eyes adjust, I scan the Warriors. They're bathed in that green glow. The shadows appear to be normal. "Any signs of HoLFs?" I ask Morgan.

"None so far."

Good news. We're in Pit 32 on Ulanqab. At least, I hope we are. Q hasn't made a mistake yet, so I shouldn't worry. Ceridwyn and the kids should be above Pit 50, which will take us back to Planet Ruijin. According to Beau, she was on a ten-day camping trip with the kids when the looters attacked. They received word from the base's leader to stay away until the danger passed. It never did. Their ten-day trip turned into a forty-six-day ordeal. Good thing Ceridwyn was teaching the kids survival techniques and some of the plants on Ulanqab are edible.

I check the shadows again even though I'm not too worried about shadow-blobs. We're pretty far away from the destroyed pits. The looters have been consistent in targeting the four pits right next to the base for obvious and murderous reasons.

Niall appears in the center as if stepping from thin air. Cool. Morgan assigns us to secure the hallway that runs parallel to all the Warrior pits. Niall takes the left and I take the right. I shine the lantern down the empty corridor. Since I'm surrounded by intact Warriors, looters are more of a threat, so I draw my pulse gun, keeping my thumb poised over the trigger. Although I wonder how quick I can draw the null wave emitter if I spot shadow-blobs. Something I probably should have practiced—in all my spare time.

Voices from the rest of our team echo and my parents join me in my vigil.

"Anything?" Mom asks me in a whisper.

"There's a dust mote that's making figure eights in the air, but, other than that, nothing."

She swats me on the shoulder. "This is serious."

I glance at her. The dragon stares back, and she's holding a pulse gun as if she's just looking for a target.

"Yes, sir," I say and get swatted again. There's no pleasing her. Maybe we'll encounter something for her to shoot.

When everyone has arrived, Morgan gives us the same orders as the last time we portaled into unfamiliar pits, explaining what to do should we encounter hostiles—both human and alien. Pit 50 is to the right. Morgan takes the lead and we follow in order. She slows at the entrance to every pit, seeking hidden ambushers. A nervous flutter twirls in my stomach at each one.

The Warriors stare at us impassively and I wonder if they know what's going on. If there's a part of them that's aware. Or are they like machines and wake when needed? I'm sure they're not like Q, but I do hope they're not trapped in some half-life.

We reach Pit 50 without incident. Morgan insists we clear Pits 51 through 55 before declaring the area safe. Mom wakes the key Warriors, starting the sixteen-minute countdown. Dad once again dips into his huge backpack. This time he pulls out a small robotic digger. It's half a meter wide—a baby digger, so cute! He sets it down and sharp spikes shoot out in all directions. Uh, not so cute now.

Reminding me of a spider with way too many legs, it climbs

to the ceiling and then digs up, which is really strange to see. Sand and bits of the ceiling rain down on us. Memories of being trapped in my burrow spring to life. Morgan orders us to line up against the wall in case of a cave-in. I'm happy to oblige, pressing my body as flat as possible.

Since the digger is so small, the wait stretches along with my nerves. The longer we're here the greater chance for something to go horribly wrong. Eventually arrows of sunlight pierce the gloom as the digger breaks through the surface. It clears a meter-wide hole before returning to my father. It retracts its spikes like a good boy. A black silhouette of a woman appears in the opening above us.

"Hello? Officer Morgan, are you there?" Ceridwyn asks. Her tone is uncertain as if she still doesn't believe we've portaled to her rescue.

The thick tension around me eases a fraction.

"Yes, we're here," Morgan says.

"Oh!" A pause. "How are we going to get down there?"

Morgan snaps her fingers at Bendix and Zaim. "Miss Trant, please move all the children well away from the hole. We're coming up."

"All right." She disappears.

Bendix sets his emitter down, and shrugs off his ruck. Extracting a metal arrow and black contraption of some sort with a rope spooled around it from his pack, he aims it at the opening.

"Clear the hatch," he calls just before he shoots the arrow. The long rope with knots tied in it every meter or so unspools from the contraption as the arrow flies through the air and buries itself into the ceiling right next to the hole. Impressive aim. He tests the hold by yanking on it. When it doesn't budge, he climbs up. Wow. Lots of bulging muscles.

After Bendix climbs the five meters or so to the surface, he signals and Zaim ascends the rope, making it look easy. Damn. My team's in some serious shape. I catch Niall watching me. Mr. Jealous is frowning. Behind him is Elese. She's smirking at me and fanning her face with her hands. She mouths *hot damn*. It takes all my will not to smile.

"The kids can't climb down the ropes," Mom says to Morgan. "How are they going to get here?"

"Bendix has a couple harnesses and a tripod to rig a pulley system to lower them down one at a time. It's the best we could do considering the circumstances."

"Officer Morgan," Zaim calls down. "We're having some…personnel issues."

Morgan glances at us. "The kids must be terrified. Stay here until I give the all clear."

We say, yes sir. She climbs the rope in double time. Impressive. And then we wait. Niall and I exchange a look when the silence extends.

"Lawrence," Morgan barks from the opening. "Get up here. Now."

I move to the rope, hoping my arms will hold my weight, but Officer Kingston grabs my shoulder, stopping me.

"She didn't give the all clear," she says.

Oh, right. Not good. "What do we do?"

"Evacuate. How soon until the portal to Ruijin is open?" Kingston asks my mother.

"Two minutes."

Kingston glances up. "It might not be soon enough."

"Hold up there, sir," Elese says. "We're not leaving our team members behind."

"You've no choice. I'm the highest-ranking officer," Kingston says. "I allowed Officer Morgan to lead this crazy mission because of her experience. But she's not here. We're evacuating as soon as that portal is open."

"Lawrence, what's taking so long?" Morgan demands.

Morgan might not be down in the pit with us, but she's still alive and sounding rather pissed off. Bendix and Zaim are with her.

"I'm not a security officer," Mom says. "I'm not evacuating without the rest of our team."

Go Mom.

Kingston rounds on my mother. "We're in a weak position. We can only go up the rope one at a time, and we've no idea how many are up there."

The Chief has a point. Niall, Elese, and I exchange a look. There has to be some way to confirm what's going on. Just then the green glow fills the pit as the portal solidifies. Waves of light pulse through the statues. Within a minute, half the security officers are going to leave.

Wait. That's it! I quickly explain my plan to the others. The response is mixed. Of course Kingston vetoes it.

"Lawrence, I gave you an order," Morgan says.

I decide to implement my plan anyway. "I'm sorry, Officer Morgan," I yell. "You know I'm terrified of heights."

"Close your eyes and count to twenty, Lawrence. You know

you can do it."

Elese smiles. "We can handle twenty opponents."

Too bad Kingston and the others don't look as confident. The lights stop undulating. The portal is open.

"Let's do this," Mom says. The dragon is looking for a fight.

Niall and Elese make tracks in the sand while my parents set the stage. I stand at the bottom of the rope. The rest of the officers disappear into the Warriors, either to evacuate or to help, I've no idea.

"Okay, I'm coming," I say, grabbing the line and pulling myself off the ground. Ugh. Must do more push-ups, I pant as I climb another meter and stand on one of the knots. Then I clutch the rope as if I'm frozen in fear, staring up at the hole with a terrified expression. After a few moments, a head blocks the sun as someone peers down.

The person disappears and there are voices from above, but I can't understand what they're saying. Then something drops from the hole and lands in the sand with a sickening thump.

Kingston warned this might happen. I jump to the ground and dive behind the nearest Warrior before the grenade can go off.

The grenade explodes with a flash of bright white light and a whoomph. I press my body as close to the Warrior as possible as a concussive force spreads out through the Warriors. They rattle but don't fall over. Nor do they break. Mom will be happy. I'm ecstatic that the looters dropped a stun grenade and not the kind that blows things into smithereens. We guessed that they wouldn't want to destroy the Warriors and were right. Go us.

Now time for the second part. I sprawl out on the ground as if I'd gotten hit. Mom and Dad crawl out from their hiding places to play dead—so to speak. All flashlights and lanterns are turned off. Then we wait.

After a century and a half a ladder is lowered into the pit—the looters came prepared. It thuds when it hits the ground. Then silence. Whispers float on the air and then the sound of someone climbing down is followed by more boots tapping on the metal rungs. To keep from moving, I try to count the number of people. I'm up to six when it gets quiet.

"Spread out," a man says.

Boots crunch on sand. I hope my team keeps hidden. There's a trick to it—the precise rows and columns of the Warriors create a bit of an optical illusion when you're walking through them. Niall learned how to take advantage of it when he was dodging me and I figured it out as a kid. I didn't have much time to explain it to the others, but survival tends to make one a quick learner.

The footsteps grow louder as they near me. I concentrate on pretending to be stunned. It's like sleeping. Right? Keeping my muscles relaxed despite my hammering heart, I remain still.

The tip of a boot prods my right side. I concentrate on acting insensate. It shouldn't be hard; I've been knocked out enough times just in this last year. My muscle memory should be at a savant level by this point.

After another couple of centuries, more boots approach.

"The pit is empty," a man says. "Except for these three, the rest must have escaped through the portal before we sent the grenade."

Breathing is easier now.

"Shit, I knew that nonsense about being afraid of heights was a delay tactic," the boot prodder says right next to me. "They're a bunch of cowards, leaving their people behind."

"Should we pursue them through the portal?"

"No. We can only send one at a time. They'll just shoot us when we pop in. We'll get Ruijin like we got the rest."

The boot returns to my side, this time with enough force to roll me over. I flop like a dead fish.

"We got Lawrence, that's all that matters," Prodder says.

Why do they still want me? I'm far from flattered. In fact, if they forgot all about me, I'd be super thrilled.

He calls up the all clear. "We've captured the target plus two."

"Proceed to Pit 41," a voice yells down. "Take the prisoners and wake the portal."

"Yes, sir," Prodder says. "Nat, help me pick her up." Then he snorts in derision and says, "She's still holding her pulse gun. Like that's going to help her."

Actually, now that he mentions it. I open my eyes, aim, and shoot. The sizzle crackles through the air. He squeaks in alarm as the pulse hits him in the face. His eyebrows spike into his hair line as he topples.

The man next to him raises his gun, but jerks as more sizzles sound. He crumples and then other thuds and thumps sound throughout the pit. I glance at the hole. Did anyone hear the noise? No one is peeking down so I turn back to the guy at my feet. I'm tempted to prod my prodder, but I disarm him instead—something he should have done to me. He's wearing a black security jumpsuit just like ours. So are the other two now prone forms.

"Clear," Elese says quietly, stepping out from behind a Warrior.

We share grins. I glance around. Everyone but Kingston, Bernardo, and Flynn are here.

"Did you disobey a direct order?" Elese asks Officer Cole.

"Yeah. Do you have any openings in your unit?"

"Hell, yeah." She fist-bumps him. "You'd fit right in."

At the sound of someone mounting the ladder, the others

pick up the fallen looters and melt back into the Warriors. There's no time to go to another pit to set up an ambush. Hopefully in the dim half-light no one will notice the tracks in the sand. The green glow from the Warriors also washes out details as well. I hide behind a Warrior that's two rows deep.

"Three on the way down," Niall whispers. He's our spotter because he's tall enough to peer over the Warrior's shoulder. He's also close to me along with Cole.

Soon after, boots scrape on the sandstone. "Go close the portal," a woman orders. "We'll meet you in—"

A sizzle interrupts her as Niall shoots. I step from my hiding place and aim as the two others grab for weapons, but they're too slow. They drop to the ground. My team appears from the Warriors and carry the unconscious looters out of sight before the rest can come down. I imagine a looter pile somewhere near the back of the pit—a heap of bodies. Nervous giggles threaten. We still have eleven looters to deal with.

I hide as another set of boots appear at the top of the ladder. While waiting, I consider the order to go to Pit 41. That one goes to Yulin—I memorized all the important pits just in case this op went sideways. At least we know their destination. Then I wonder if Ceridwyn was a plant to lure us here or if the looters caught up to her and the children. I'd rather be duped than have the kids endangered. The looters won't kill them. Will they? They had no trouble blowing up a base with children. But could they look the kids in the eye and do it? Big difference. I'm hoping it's a big fat no.

"Four more," Niall whispers, interrupting my panicked thoughts. "Bendix is in the middle. The looter behind him has a kill zapper aimed at him. That one's mine."

That increases the danger by an order of magnitude. Niall can't miss. If he does, we're all in trouble.

"The group is down and—oh hell," Niall says.

I peek out in time to see Bendix tackle the guy with the kill zapper. We spring from our hiding places and pulse the others. Bendix is on top of the looter, banging his head on the ground. The man's still holding his weapon and it's aimed— I dive to the ground as an all too familiar purple fire crackles right next to me. Stars, that was close!

Another thud sounds and the gun drops from the looter's hand. The man is unconscious and blood leaks from a gash on his skull. Bendix's grin is half manic, but he assesses the situation and helps clear out the bodies. The pile is growing and there's seven looters left.

The next four have Zaim with them. They're more cautious probably due to the noise of Bendix's fight. They shine their flashlights around. The beams sweep through the Warriors, illuminating the sand. And I bite my lip, remembering the blood. Did we bury it? The color will certainly draw unwanted attention. I glance at Niall.

He's holding up a hand, which means wait. It's torture to remain still while the lights seek us out. Or that's what I imagine they're doing. I'm eighty years old by the time the lights travel to the far end. Soon they'll be in Pit 49. I glance at Niall who is on his tip-toes. He finally signals. We emerge behind the group, but Elese, my dad, and Bendix are closer.

Bendix is unarmed, but that doesn't stop him from grabbing one of the looters from behind in a big hug, clamping his arms around the man's diaphragm. Before we can neutralize all of them, there's a cry behind us. We've been spotted. Niall, Cole, and I spin around as the sizzle of pulses fly by my ears. Too close!

"Down," Niall orders, diving.

I hit the ground. There are five looters on the ladder shooting at us. Morgan is trapped in the middle of them. They have the height advantage. And two extra people! Guess if Morgan told me to count to twenty-two, they would have suspected she was tipping us off. And why am I thinking about this now?

"Find cover," Niall orders.

I roll, heading into the Warriors. A pulse slams into my left leg and buttock as I scramble to crouch behind the General. Needles of pain crawl along my skin. I endure it, knowing it will stop. The jumpsuit's material protects me from being knocked out, but—stars! It hurts. Tears well.

"Mouse? You okay?" Niall asks. He's behind the Warrior next to mine.

"Yeah." For now.

Every time I try to peek around the General sizzles fill the air. The looters have us pinned down. And Cole is…I've no idea. I hope my parents are okay. My mom's small enough to hide just about anywhere. The ladder creaks as they descend another couple of rungs. I risk another look and spot Morgan. She does a little hop and puts her feet on the outer edge of the ladder, then she changes her grip and slides down. It's a sweet move. Morgan knocks off the two looters below her. It's kind of comical how they go flying. But she lands right next to them and the person who was just above her mere moments ago aims a kill zapper at Morgan.

I'm on my feet without thought. "No!"

The woman on the ladder turns her weapon on me. The rest of the world disappears as her thumb presses down. She jerks just as the purple fire rushes from the end of her weapon. A burning agony knifes into my left shoulder. The force of it pushes me back a few steps. At the same time the looter falls off the ladder. I glance over and there's my mother with her pulse gun, picking off the rest of the looters with ice cold precision.

Niall's yelling at me. Or...I think he is. His mouth is moving, but there's a loud crackling in my ears. Purple fire is dancing on my shoulder. Thin ribbons of it ring my upper arm and spread down to my wrist. Its pattern of light reminds me of a complex program in the Q-net. One where Q has highlighted the correct path.

The pain is intense, but my skin under the arcs of electricity turns numb. Not a good sign. When it digs into my throat, I know I only have a few seconds. The strength leaks from my legs and I sit down before I fall. My parents and Niall hover around me, but can't touch me or risk being killed as well.

Fire stabs the back of my neck. I pull up my knees and rest my forehead on them as spikes of red-hot pain sears my brain. It's familiar. I've endured a similar sensation when Q shocked me from my coma. I survived that. Why not this?

I've the heart of a Warrior. All I need is its hard, impenetrable body to block the lightning. I glance around at the statues surrounding me. The General stands next to me. I surge to my feet, scattering everyone as they jump back. Wrapping my arms around the General, I hug him tight.

Pressing the side of my head against his chest, I think, *Please, give me the strength to fight this.*

And he's there, standing in front of me. But we're no longer in the pit on Ulanqab. We're either in the Q-verse or in a dream or in another dimension. Does it matter? The physical world is gone. Again.

The General is staring at me with a pleased expression. *You've done well, Little Warrior,* he says. *My strength is yours.*

But what about you?

I will move beyond.

Beyond what?

The edge of the Galaxy.

That's where Q said fourth nation has gone.

Yes. I will rejoin my brethren. My duty done.

His comment reminds me of my earlier thoughts about the Warriors. *Do you know what is going on in my world? Are you aware?*

I sleep and then wake when called. It's an honor and a privilege to serve. Go back to your world, Little Warrior.

The sound of a crushed heart raining down inside the General echoes through my ear. Cold fingers touch my neck. I open my eyes.

"Her pulse is strong. I don't know why—"

"Your hands are cold," I say to my mother. "Some dragon you are."

She huffs. "This dragon is tired of watching her daughter get hurt. Where did you go? The Q-net?"

"No. The W-net."

She presses her hand to my forehead as if checking for a

fever. "The W-net?"

"Warrior net. The General here just gave his life for mine."
I release my grip on the statue. He no longer glows like his men.
My arms are stiff. The side of my face is numb. I rub my cheek
and feel the pattern of the General's armor on my skin. When I
step away, my legs buckle. Strong arms grab me, holding me up.
I lean back into Niall's embrace. "Thanks." Then I notice my
team ringed around us. "No other injuries?" Surely I couldn't be
the only one.

Morgan grunts. "Minor scrapes and bruises. You're the only
one that doesn't have any sense of self-preservation."

I open my mouth to protest, but Niall squeezes me in
warning. Instead I ask about the kids. "Was it all a ruse?"

"No. How do you think they unarmed us so easily? I'm not
going to fight when kids are in danger." Morgan's disgust is
clear. "The looters used them and were going to leave them here
to die."

"I think we need a new name for the looters," I say.
"Something along the lines of evil incarnate."

"The aliens called the HoLFs demons, but there is more than
one type of demon in this universe," Niall says.

Elese cocks her head. "Are you sure? Seems to me like they're
of the same type. Murdering motherfu—"

"You made your point, Officer Kier," Morgan says. She
studies us for a moment. "Good work picking up on the ruse,
but you should have evacuated immediately."

"When you write us up, make sure to include a footnote on
how you wouldn't be able to write us up without us deviating
from standard procedure." Elese grins. "It's a paradox. Right?"

"More like a catch 22," Dad says.

Before anyone else can chime in, Morgan orders us to finish the mission. We climb the ladder to help the kids. At the sight of our black jumpsuits, Ceridwyn yells at the kids to hide in the forest while she stands in our path. I'm impressed. It's only when she recognizes Morgan that she relaxes.

The poor woman is a wreck. Her clothing is stained and ripped. Smudges of dirt mark her pretty face and her blonde hair resembles a bird's nest. Most telling are the lines of exhaustion around her blue eyes and her slight hunch as if the weight of her responsibilities makes it impossible for her to straighten.

When we explain that she's safe, Ceridwyn loses it. She cries out and hugs Morgan, sobbing into our second-in-command's shoulder. Morgan stiffens and pats the woman on the back with awkward motions. She gives us the come-help-me look, but we're all trying not to laugh. Stoic, fearless Officer Morgan can't handle an overly emotional survivor.

The kids are another story. Traumatized by the looters, they won't leave their hiding places. I'm sent to coax them out. Why me? Because I'm the youngest and least fearsome. I gotta work on adopting an intimidating presence. In the meantime, I walk through the dense trees. It's curious how the thick forest grew right up to the edges of the pit, but no further. Is it due to not having enough soil underground or some plant killer the aliens sprayed to keep the roots out of the pits? *Q, do you know?* Silence.

The kids are good at hiding. I stop after a few meters and introduce myself as Junior Officer Ara Lawrence and part of the team that came to rescue them. "But you can call me Ara. I'm only seventeen A-years old and still go to soch-time. I actually enjoy it—don't tell my parents. I've been teaching my soch-time friends how to defend themselves. We're having fun and my friend, Kuma, might be the smallest of our group, but she's the fiercest. Think of a small dog with sharp pointy teeth. And—hello there."

One of the older boys pokes his head out. Saying he's grubby is a kindness. "Can you teach us how to fight?"

"Of course. But only when we're back to normal. And the only way to get there is for everyone to come with me."

"Are they going to come back?" a frightened voice calls from underneath a bush.

"No. My team stunned them and they're all sleeping."

A curly-haired child peeks through the branches. "For real?"

I crouch down. "For real. My team's the best."

The small girl scrambles out from her hiding spot and launches herself at me. Before I can blink, I'm sitting on the ground with her clutching me in a monkey hug—arms around my neck and legs around my torso.

"It's okay," I say. Then "Easy there. I…can't…breathe."

She relaxes a smidgen. Enough so I can stand and lead the others out to where my team waits near the top of the ladder. Ceridwyn is still having a meltdown on Morgan. It's not as humorous now that I have my own barnacle. At least she weighs almost nothing. Niall's eyebrows raise in a do-you-need-help-prying-her-off manner. I shake my head. She's mine now. Her dark skin is covered in layers of dirt, but she smells of earth and sweat.

Morgan breaks Ceridwyn's grip, telling her we need to move

quickly. The woman pulls it together and counts the children. We learn that the looters ambushed them as soon as Dad's robotic digger broke through the surface.

"They must have been following us," she says. "Or maybe they read our messages." She pushes a hunk of greasy hair from her eyes. "Does it matter? They said if we…" She pulls in a breath. "If we…followed them down into the pits, they'd…kill us. But, but…" Gesturing around at the trees, she gives us a wild look. "We couldn't survive here much longer."

I carry my barnacle girl down the ladder. The bigger kids don't need help, but the little ones are carried. We assemble near the portal. Through the cameras in Pit 9 on Ruijin, we see a ring of armed security around the incoming portal. They're aiming at the center of the pit, just waiting to shoot any looters. We didn't have time to program all the security officers' electromagnetic signatures into everyone's pulse gun. So we can get stunned by friendly fire. Morgan goes first.

"Let's hope they identify their target before shooting me," she grumbles before stepping into the black rectangle.

It's a sign of just how numb and exhausted the kids are that they don't react to Morgan's disappearance or the eerie green glow lighting the pit. Little Barnacle glances around once and reburies her face in my shoulder. Niall has my portable and is watching for Morgan's arrival.

"I bet ten credits she gets shot," Elese says behind him.

"I'm not taking you up on it," Niall says. "Officer Kingston is front and center. She's the type of yahoo that will shoot first and ask questions later."

Morgan steps from the portal and almost gets shot. Bernardo

knocks Kingston's arm down right before she fires. Funny, Kingston doesn't look happy to see Morgan. Maybe she fired on purpose so she won't be revealed as a coward. Once we get the all-clear-no-one-is-going-to-stun-you sign, we portal to Ruijin. Ceridwyn goes with my mother, and the kids all go with a team member.

Niall warns us that it's taking longer than the sixty-four seconds for each crossing. "Sixteen extra seconds for two people and it's thirty-two seconds longer for three."

No surprise that I take Little Barnacle, but I also escort another boy as well. He clings to my legs and I keep my arm around his thin shoulders. All these kids need lots of food.

"Hold tight," I say, stepping into the blackness. "It's gonna feel weird."

As my air and the circulation to my lower leg is cut off, I wish I used different words. Something like relax, it'll be over soon. Expelled from the blackness, we stumble into the pit. Instead of being shot, we're surrounded by medical staff.

Little Barnacle won't let go. She digs her fingernails into my skin when a nurse tries to pull her away. I named her well. So I end up going to the infirmary with her instead of looping back to Ulanqab. Morgan wants to bring the looters to Ruijin.

I sit in a comfortable chair. The girl still clings to me. She'd experienced a trauma and is probably an orphan. I can spend a few hours with her. Stroking her back, I tell her all kinds of silly stories about my childhood and life that may or may not be true.

"...I was backed into a corner by a roaring lion. I was trapped and I thought he was going to eat me!"

"What happened?" she asks into my neck. Her hushed

breath tickles my skin.

"He cooked me dinner instead. Which was a complete surprise. I'd no idea lions can cook."

She pulls back to study my face. "Is that true?"

"Well if we exchange the lion for the Chief of Security, it's mostly true."

Little Barnacle giggles. It's the sweetest sound. And she finally agrees to go with the nurse, but I have to promise to come visit her. I make a solemn vow to return and get a smile for my efforts. Once she leaves, I stand up. Big mistake as all my energy drains from my body. I glance at the floor, expecting there to be a puddle of it around my boots. Nothing.

Before one of the nurses realize I haven't been examined, I skedaddle. Other than muscle aches and some minor pain, I'm fine. There's a strange fried sensation tingling on my skin, but nothing a shower and a hot meal won't cure. I hope.

I encounter Niall on my way to security. "Did the team transfer all the looters?" I ask.

"Yeah. But three grown men, with one of them unconscious, are a tight fit through the portal." He squints at me. "Why aren't you in the infirmary?"

"Little Barnacle is going to be fine. I—"

"That's not what I mean." He takes a breath, then says in a softer tone, "You were zapped, Mouse."

"A glancing blow." I try to wave it off.

But Niall grabs me and pulls me close. Ahhh. I lean against him, soaking in his warmth.

"What were you thinking?" he asks. "You can't keep putting yourself in danger like that."

"That's just the thing, I'm not thinking, Niall. I'm reacting. Maybe with more experience I'll be able to assess a situation first." When he doesn't say anything, I add, "It worked out."

He sighs. "Maybe I should have called you Queen Cat."

"Why a cat?"

"They're supposed to have nine lives. According to my count, you used up four so far."

Four? Yikes, no wonder he's upset. But that would mean I've five left. That's not as much of a comfort as you'd think. Besides I'm no cat. I'm a mouse. "Good for cats, but I'm *Qiángdà de shŭ*."

"What's that?"

"A mighty mouse. I've way more lives than some stupid cat."

He squeezes me tighter, reminding me of Little Barnacle. "I hope so."

I pull back, breaking away. "Come on." I grab his hand and tug him with me.

"Where are we going?"

"To find a private washroom for a shower."

He laughs. "I don't think that's possible. Too many security officers."

And he's right. Morgan is already in the unit I'm sharing with her and Elese. She informs us of a meeting in the conference room at fifteen hundred. I stop. The entire encounter on Ulanqab only lasted the morning? So much for our shower. Niall leaves to tell Bendix and Zaim.

I debate. I need to wash the sand and dirt out of my uniform and hair. Food is also a requirement, along with catching a few hours of sleep. The first two require effort, but the third...I eye my bunk.

"Lawrence," Morgan barks. "Shower. Now."

"Yes, sir."

After a long hot shower, Morgan drags me and Elese to grab something to eat before reporting to the conference room. Our entire team is there along with my parents. Officers Kingston, Flynn, Bernardo, and Cole are in attendance, and half of Ruijin's security force. Quite the crowd.

I plop in an open seat between Niall and my dad. Ruijin's Chief of Security, Officer David Boyle, is running the meeting. He has the standard I'm-in-charge buzz cut. The short fuzz of his hair is all white.

"We're fortunate that there is only one incoming pit per planet. It makes our job of protecting the research bases easier. However, there is the possibility of another access site for the looters on our planets." He tilts his head at Morgan. "There's a confirmed looter base on Planet Yulin that not only has shuttles, but weapons as well. We can't rely on our satellites to find these as the programming may have been compromised."

And I can no longer worm into them and fix that. I hunch down in my seat. My selfish act is going to get us all killed.

"I've been in discussions with the other Warrior planet chiefs," he says. "Defending against looter attacks is not a viable long-term solution. We've a plan to take the fight to them."

Oh? I straighten. Officer Boyle gives us an overview, then assigns us to teams. I'm glad I get to stay with the rest of the Yulin officers. However, the most important part of the plan is going to rely on some complex worming, which has been assigned to Beau.

We're dismissed and, as we walk back to our units, I'm wondering if Q decided to help Beau the way it did for me. It would be truly fantastic. Yet, a part of me grieves for my lost connection, and for never being able to use the Q-net again. We've been so busy that I haven't really thought about how much of my life will change without the Q-net.

Niall laces his fingers in mine. "Something wrong?"

"I'm worried about Beau."

"Then message him. See if he needs help."

I glance at Niall. Is he serious? "I can't help him."

"Have you forgotten all your worming skills?" he asks mildly.

"Well, no, but…"

"But what?"

"But I can't *do* anything."

"You can tell him what to do. You're good at that." Niall gives me a bright smile as if he just solved all my problems and hasn't just insulted me.

It's a good thing I love him or I'd strangle him. "Fine. I'll ask. He'll probably say no."

"And he might say yes."

"You're annoying, Toad."

"Love you, too, Mouse."

"Are you two done?" Elese asks. "I'm gonna be sick."

Trust Elese to ruin the moment. We still have a few hours before dinner. Morgan heads off to do something official. The guys go to their unit. When we arrive at our unit, Elese dives into her bunk for a nap. I pull out my portable and stretch out on mine. Elese is snoring in no time, but I message Beau.

2522:274: Hello Beau. We just went over Operation Strike Back. I'm either super excited or beyond terrified about the op. At this point I can't really tell the difference. Looks like you're going to be doing some serious deep level worming. Do you need any assistance?

While waiting for his reply, I check my messages and see that there's a file that lists all of the Protector Class space ships that are enroute to the Warrior planets and their arrival times. I don't remember asking for this information. Maybe Radcliff or Beau did, but why give it to me? I send the information to Radcliff in case he needs it. Soon after a message from Beau pops up.

2522:274: Hey, partner. I'll take all the help I can get. Does this mean your sensors are working? Can you access the Q-net again?

← Sorry, Beau. I keep trying to reach out to Q, but there's no reply. I can give you advice if you encounter something unusual while worming.

→ Have you tried connecting the old-fashioned way?

← The old-fashioned way?

→ Stars, girl. Yes, the old-fashioned way where you put entanglers into your ears and sit next to a terminal. You know, what the rest of us lowly humans do when we need to access the Q-net?

← Uh, no. I haven't tried. But Niall still can't connect and he's had longer to heal.

→ News flash, Ara—you're not Niall. Get your ass to a terminal and see if it works! That's an order.

← Yes, sir.

I'm careful not to wake Elese as I dig into my ruck. Do I even have my tangs anymore? I could borrow Elese's—they'll work with anyone. It's the sensors in your brain that are custom-made.

I don't find them in any of the compartments. It's hard to believe I wouldn't have my tangs after seven years of keeping them close. I think back to the last time I used them. In Beau's office? Or was it in the infirmary when Niall was recovering? I pull out my black tactical pants. They have lots of pockets and, sure enough, I find my tangs in one of them.

It's odd inserting them into my ears. The cold rubber is almost unfamiliar. I half expect them not to fit, which is ridiculous. There's a terminal along the far wall of the unit. Reluctance drags. At first, I was excited by the idea, but now my stomach sours at the thought of it not working.

Sitting in front of the terminal, I turn on the screen. Then I entangle. Nothing happens. I grip the edge of the desk as disappointment floods me. I reach to yank my tangs out and stop. Ruijin's security protocols query, seeking to authenticate my identification. It takes no time for me to worm past them. The flood of relief and joy is like coming home after being away on a very long trip.

I'm back!

2522:274

Before you get too excited, it's not the same. I don't have a direct mental link with Q. In fact, I don't sense Q at all. But, I can worm. It's like it was right before I fell asleep while entangled. My skills are still sharp, but not freakishly over the top. It's better than not being able to connect at all! Actually, go ahead and get excited. I am!

The first thing I do is message Beau a howdy. He responds right away with the appropriate mix of I-told-you-so and your-partner-is-the-greatest comments. I don't argue. I'm still too happy. We set up a time to worm together after dinner. Beau has to be careful as the research base on Yulin is still playing dead. Q has been keeping a few tunnels open for him. Meanwhile I don't have to worry as much about the looters discovering my activities. Although I suspect the looters are monitoring all communications coming and going to Ruijin.

After I disentangle, I jump into Elese's bunk, waking her. She reacts almost instantly and I'm pinned under her.

"Stars, girl. You gotta be careful. I could have—what's going on? You're grinning like a fool. Did Niall say he wuvs you again? Called you Honey Bunny or something equally sickening?"

"No. I can worm again!"

"Huh." She releases me.

Elese isn't as excited as I thought she'd be. I sit up. "Huh? That's all you got?"

"No, I'm glad. It's just…"

"Just what?"

"You're safer staying out of the Q-net. Maybe the looters won't target you if they know you can't worm anymore."

I groan. "Not you, too!"

"Sorry that I care," she shoots back.

I grab her pillow. "Apology." I swat her with it. "Not." Swat. "Accepted." Swat.

"Oh no, you don't." She dives for Morgan's bunk, snatches up the pillow, and attacks.

I block and dodge and get in a few good shots. We're laughing and yelling breathless insults at each other—*it's easy to hit that pampered ass of yours, it's so big!*—*it's not as big as your mouth!*—when Morgan arrives. We jump to attention and hide the pillows behind our backs. But it doesn't stop the giggles.

"Do I even want to know what you're doing?" Morgan asks.

"Not in the least, sir," Elese says.

"Is there a reason for this…frivolity?"

"Ooh *frivolity*. I bet Beau would love that word," Elese says. "It's probably harder to use in a sentence than skedaddle."

I tell Morgan my news before she makes Elese skedaddle to detention.

Morgan gives me a curt nod. "Good. Now you can stop

moping."

Moping! I open my mouth to deny it, but both women are expecting my outburst. Instead, I press my lips together, fluff the battered pillow, and set it back on the bed. Elese also returns her weapon.

"Hey, that's my pillow," Morgan says in outrage.

"Uh, dinner time," Elese yells and we bolt from the unit.

We just about run into the guys as they leave their unit.

"What is it?" Bendix demands. "HoLFs? Looters?"

"No, worse," I say.

"Officer Morgan!" Elese cries in mock horror, pointing.

We all turn. Morgan is standing in the hallway with her arms crossed.

"Run!"

I don't know who says it, but we all bolt. Our laughter echoes off the walls. We don't run for long.

After we get our food and sit down, I explain what put me in such a good mood. Before Niall can smirk, I give him credit for encouraging me to contact Beau. Except he's not really gloating. He's acting more like Elese first did. I can't really blame him for being worried.

"I can't wait until we're all together again," Zaim says.

"Yeah, the officers here don't have a clue as to what we're up against," Bendix says. "And the few that do..." He makes a disgusted noise.

"Officer Cole held his own," Elese says with admiration.

The conversation turns to the mission, but I'm only half-listening. I'm keeping an eye on the time. When it gets close to when I have to meet up with Beau, I head back to my unit. Niall hops up to join me while the rest keep chatting. They're going to help construct more null wave emitters and prep for the mission, but everyone's been ordered to get a full night's sleep every night. We all need to rest up for the big op, because once things get set into motion, there's no stopping until it's finished.

I expect Niall to question me, and he doesn't disappoint.

"Do you think you'll eventually return to communicating with the Q-net like before?" he asks, entwining his fingers in mine as we walk.

"I've no idea. But I'm not going to count on it as I don't want to be disappointed."

"Disappointed," he repeats.

Something's off. "What's really bothering you?"

"I don't miss entangling with the Q-net at all. Not that I expect that of you. But it was nice to have your undivided attention for a little bit."

Undivided? I consider that. Guess I did space out when I was talking to Q. Huh. I never really thought about it. And Niall never said anything before.

I squeeze his hand. "If Q starts talking to me again, I'll make sure you have my full attention. Unless we're fighting shadow-blobs or looters or doing our jobs or—"

"I get it, Mouse. Thanks."

Before we reach my unit, we're interrupted by Morgan, who never did join us for dinner. I wonder where she went.

"Radcliff wants you on a higher priority terminal when worming with Dorey," she says.

I don't think I need it, but every little bit will help. "Where?"

"Officer Boyle's office."

Ugh. "Does this mean he'll be peering over my shoulder?"

"Yes. He insists you leave the screen on."

Lovely.

Niall gives me a better-you-than-me wave when we go our separate ways. Morgan tags along with me.

"Are you going to be watching, too?" I ask.

"No. I'm just going to ensure he treats you with the proper respect, then I'll skedaddle."

Nice. Except why wouldn't he? Probably because I'm young. I've seen my fair share of skeptics since this entire endeavor began, including the one striding beside me. I'm learning that people tend not to believe anything unless they experience it for themselves. Yes, shadow-blobs are rather unbelievable, but there's enough of us now you'd think we'd be more credible.

By the creases in Officer Boyle's forehead, it's not hard to guess that he's unhappy with the arrangement. I don't know what he's grumpy about; his office is set up exactly like Radcliff's so he has an extra terminal. I sit down in front of it, insert my tangs, and entangle with the Q-net. First thing I do is turn on the screen. Then I worm to my meeting point with Beau.

"You need to identify yourself when entering the Q-net," Boyle says behind me. "We follow the proper procedures here, *Junior* Officer."

I don't bother to answer him.

"She's worming," Morgan says as if talking to an idiot. "There is no *proper* procedure. It's all *improper*. Besides her name would tip off the looters. Leave the girl be. She's saved our asses too many times to count."

Love you, too, Morgan. Then I tune them out as I reach

Beau. *Howdy partner,* I say. Will we connect like before?

Welcome back, Beau says.

Yes!

You ready for some serious worming? he asks.

Yup. What are we doing?

I've been closing the connections between DES, the Protectorate, and the looters.

I thought Q sealed all those holes, I say.

Q did the ones into DES, but these are their secret communications. They've been using the Q-net, but the paths are well hidden.

Can you worm into them and read what they're saying? That would be wonderful.

No. But I've been collapsing them like they've been doing to our escape tunnels. Q's been helping to flag the important ones. Especially the ones between the Protectorate and the looters. There are a ton of them. It's exacting work and, once finished, we're going to build our own blockade to keep them from just making a new tunnel.

Wow, you've been busy. Color me impressed.

Well, it's not rescuing small children, but it's something.

Typical of Beau to be jealous of our mission to Ulanqab. I ignore the jab. *How do you know which ones are worth flagging?*

Radcliff's tuned into the enemy and has been taking names.

Which was why the security chiefs thought Operation Strike Back had a decent chance of success. Radcliff's been listening to their communications. Thanks to Dr Carson.

Once we get through this, DES is going to clean house, Beau says.

You've been in contact with them? I thought Yulin was playing dead. Worry about Radcliff and the rest of my team swells.

Q helped me create an unwormable connection directly to Director Ormond, but Radcliff's only using it to update her on the looters.

Wow. Ormond was the highest ranked director in DES. And there is something comforting about the very top person in DES knowing about the looters.

What's the plan for tonight, I ask.

I've been working in the deep levels of the Protectorate. There's two high-ranking officers working with the looters that we need to block.

I follow Beau to the protected clusters assigned to the Protectorate. A path through the complex safeguards lights up.

Thanks, Q, Beau says.

Unable to resist, I ask, *Did Q talk to you?*

No. But whenever this happens I always thank Q.

Good idea. Then we stop talking in order to concentrate on navigating through the tiny holes in the programming. I'm…heavier than before. The tangs keep me grounded. But they also allow me to be here helping so I'm not complaining.

Behind me an outraged Boyle sputters about me entering the Protectorate's data clusters. Morgan placates him.

Easy there, Beau warns.

Oops. Sorry. Focusing all my attention on the work at hand, I ease past a twisted knot, finding the one little gap to slip through. *Ahh. Not even a quiver.*

Ha ha. Now the hard part begins.

I refrain from groaning. Instead, I work alongside Beau, plugging holes and creating a barrier. He was right. Everything has to be done with an exact precision. And it takes forever. Not that I could have gone faster with Q. In fact, other than being heavy, it's not that much different. After we finish, we carefully exit the Protectorate's clusters.

Wow, that took—

Forever, I supply.

No. With you helping that went twice as fast. Go get some rest, Ara. We'll resume this at oh-five-hundred.

Ugh.

Beau must sense my lack of enthusiasm because he says, *The more of these we do, the better our chances of a successful operation.*

How do you figure?

When we strike back, there'll be warnings sent through the Q-net.

Except they won't get to the right people?

Exactly. Good night, partner.

Night, Beau. I disentangle and glance at the clock. Oh-one-hundred. Ugh. I stretch, stand, and stop. Officer Boyle is still at his desk. And he appears grumpier. Before he can say anything, I tell him I'll be back in four hours. Then I bid him a good night and skedaddle.

The days I spend worming with Beau blur into one endless

session. Not really, but, if you ask my brain, it would agree. The only breaks I get are when I visit Little Barnacle. Turns out that's not her name. Her name is Shay, but she will always be Little Barnacle to me. She's five A-years old. Her dad worked in security and her mom was a bugologist. Yes, I know that's not the proper term or even a word, but I'm not going to correct her when we're talking about her parents in the past tense. A concept that hasn't really sunk in for her yet. I hope I'm there when it does. She'll need a friend.

It takes a total of five days to coordinate everything and for the various parts of the plan to be ready. Also to give the mechanics on all the active Warrior planets time to build enough emitters for the op. No, not everyone will have one, but it's a lot more than we had before. And we can't wait too much longer. The looters are close to finishing the blockade around Planet Qingyang. Once they finish, they'll probably attack the planet.

The night before Operation Strike Back commences, both Beau and I stop worming to go to bed early. Despite Elese's snoring and my nerves, I fall asleep.

At oh-so-early, we assemble in Pit 45. There are twenty-eight of us! My team, plus my parents—funny how I don't think of them as a part of my team even though they've gone with us on at least one mission—that's eight. Two of our techs volunteered. Then there's all twelve officers from Pingliang, and six officers from Ruijin, which leaves them six just in case they're attacked.

We're not wearing our heavy rucks. Instead, we've our weapon belts and our tactical pants over our jumpsuits. The extra pockets are more useful than a change of clothes and sleeping roll.

The portal is already open. And Morgan is once again in charge. Officer Boyle is staying behind to keep his base safe, and Kingston...well, I'm not sure why she's not in charge, but I suspect it has to do with leaving all of us on Planet Ulanqab. She doesn't look happy, but she never does. Perhaps I should introduce her to Officer Tora. I can see them becoming best friends. They can gossip about how much they both dislike me.

One at a time we portal to Planet Nanxiong. The planet seems to be a low priority for the looters so we're hoping they're not watching it as closely. Q also didn't find any signs of a blockade being built around it.

The sensation of portaling is becoming familiar—still nauseating, but not as scary. When I'm spat out in Pit 27 on Nanxiong, I marvel. This is the fourth planet we've visited in only twelve days! We're Interstellar Class travelers. No one else is as excited by this designation. Tough crowd.

The security team for Nanxiong is waiting for us. It's still fun to see the shock on their faces. Their expressions all agog because of people just popping into their pit!

Eight Nanxiong officers will be joining us for the operation, leaving four behind to guard the base. Once all twenty-eight of us appear, we clear the area to give the officers joining us from Planet Qingyang some room. My mother and father go to Pit 37 to wake the Warriors. Morgan hands out the rest of the hearts she has brought from Yulin to the new officers until she runs out.

Only six security officers from Qingyang join us. Since they're the next target on the looters' list, they're understandably skittish. Actually, I'm impressed they sent half their officers.

There's a few familiar faces with them. Gavin, my father's assistant and five other archeology techs from Yulin have volunteered. Good for us as they've all been training with pulse guns and null wave emitters.

"Ara!" Gavin calls when he spots me. "Can you believe this?" He gestures to the pits a bit wildly. "First Qingyang now Nanxiong."

"I know. We're Interstellar Class travelers."

"That's brilliant!"

Finally, someone who appreciates my genius. "How are the officers from Qingyang? Do they seem competent?"

"They're all a bit stunned. No surprise. And I don't think they believe us about the HoLFs, but they touched the hearts I brought from Yulin. We have more...uh...I think Foster has them. Yep, he's handing them out to the rest. That should cover everyone."

Good news. "What about our people? Are they doing okay on Qingyang?"

"Well, everyone's a bit cramped. I suppose it could be worse if we'd had a full roster of scientists on Yulin. And they're all nervous. No surprise. We all keep expecting to hear a missile heading for us." He shudders.

"Thanks for volunteering."

"It's better than waiting for death from above."

Gavin can also be a bit of a drama king.

"Where's your father?" he asks, scanning the crowd.

And it's quite the crowd. Forty-six people plus my parents. "Dad's already in Pit 37 with Mom."

Morgan's voice slices through the din. "Quiet."

The silence is instant.

"I'm going to put you in teams of four. You're to stay with your teammates at all times. Death is the only excuse I'll accept for being without your teammates. Understand?"

A strong chorus of "yes, sir" follows despite the sudden whitening of a couple of the techs' faces.

"Good."

Morgan moves through the group. She puts one tech with three officers and my parents will each be in a separate team. When she's done, there are eleven teams and only three of us left.

Morgan gestures to me, Niall, and Elese. "You're with me."

Ah. Should I be honored or insulted? I'm going with honored. Morgan trusts us to have her back.

"When we get to Pit 37, I want complete silence," Morgan orders. "We don't know if sound carries through the portal and we don't want to ruin the surprise."

There's a scattering of laughter and a few nervous giggles. She reviews our orders and what we should expect on the other side.

"You all know what it feels like to be…propelled from the portal. As soon as your feet hit the floor, you move—left or right it doesn't matter. Just find cover if you can. Dive onto your stomachs if you can't. Just don't stand there or you'll be an easy target. Also you'll be in the way for the next incoming group."

Another round of "yes, sir," sounds. She goes over a few more instructions and assigns each team to a larger group. We fall into two lines. Morgan and I lead. Niall and Elese are right behind us.

The green light is pulsing when we arrive in Pit 37. Something is odd about the configuration of the Warriors. It's hard to tell exactly what it is until we get closer. The five rows of Warriors that were around the center have been moved back and wedged between the other statues. The eight key Warriors still remain in a circle but they're further apart, creating a much bigger center. The hope is that with this rearrangement, the portal will be larger than the ones we've used before. Large enough to transport three teams at a time instead of one person. And guess who is in the first dozen to go through? Yup, yours truly.

Morgan signals to my parents to join their teams. I get a significant look from each of them when they pass me. Mom's dragon warns me to be extra extra careful without making a single sound. Impressive.

A few minutes later, the portal is ready. The black rectangle is about five times wider than the ones we've been using. It's the same height, though. When the green light steadies, Morgan gestures for the first dozen to enter the portal. We've estimated the time to transport twelve people would be approximately four minutes. So we have four minutes before the next dozen will come through.

Standing shoulder to shoulder, we wedge into the space. I've my null wave emitter around my torso and my pulse gun in hand. One of Boyle's security officers switched the intensity of my gun. Actually, of all our guns. It gives us a power boost to pierce the protection of the security jumpsuits that the looters are no doubt wearing as well. Now we don't have to aim only for their heads.

Inside the portal, I'm pressed between Morgan and Niall. Blackness encompasses us and my stomach flips. Niall clasps my arm and gives me a comforting squeeze. My heart is working double time and my thoughts whirl with what-ifs. One right after another. A complete list of everything that could go wrong. I hope Jarren didn't lie. A lot is riding on his information. Lives are being risked. The desire to punch Jarren again sings in my veins. Four minutes is an eternity.

Just when I'm convinced the portal failed to work, we're expelled into brightness. The industrial white light is painful. I blink tears, squinting. The eight key Warriors surround us, but they're very far apart. We're in a massive port. Shuttles and other pieces of equipment are parked nearby. The place is busy, but the high ceiling is closed.

"Lawrence, get down," Morgan growls just as the workers inside the port realize that the people that have suddenly appeared in their midst are not their colleagues.

Shouts erupt and those who are armed draw their weapons. A high-pitched klaxon pierces the air as someone sounds the alarm. Talk about painful.

Show time. Niall and Elese go to the right so I dive to the left, joining Morgan and getting out of the way for our next wave. I aim at anyone who isn't us. The workers are either clad in gray jumpsuits or black uniforms. They scatter, racing for cover. Good idea. I roll closer to a Warrior, crouching behind it to use the statue as a shield. Morgan rushes for a shuttle, using its leg to block any pulses coming her way. Plus she can fly a shuttle in case we're desperate. The rest of the group spreads out to find defensive positions. We have three more minutes until backup arrives. That's really not that long.

We exchange pulses. The tightness around my chest eases a fraction. We guessed they wouldn't use energy wave guns with the Warriors and equipment so close. However, there is still the possibility of kill zappers. That thought spurs me to shoot quicker. The looters' grunts of surprise when our pulses hit with more force than they were expecting is rather satisfying. Almost as fun as sizzle-zapping HoLFs. The bodies pile on the floor.

I'm feeling rather cocky until a wave of black-clad soldiers sprint through the doors. They keep coming, turning into a tsunami of reinforcements. Two minutes yawns into an eternity.

I keep shooting. We knew there'd be a considerable amount of resistance. After all, this is the looters' forest base on Planet Yulin. But we'd hoped the element of surprise would slow their response down somewhat. By the precision and speed of the defenders, it appears they might have drilled for a possible surprise attack.

In fact, they're calling out our positions and numbers, reminding me that the looters have recruited Protectorate soldiers. They sound organized, and I spot a few trying to get around behind us.

The crackle of a kill zapper turns my blood to ice. I huddle frozen behind my Warrior. *Come on, come on, come on*, I chant under my breath, wishing time to move faster. Where's the time dilation when you really need it?

"Snap out of it, Lawrence," Morgan roars.

Her command jolts me from my freak out. I resume shooting, but I can't help flinching every time the air crackles with purple fire. I frequently check on Niall and Elese, who are working as a team. And from Elese's gleeful shouts and insults, they're doing well. For now.

Another tsunami of looters surges though the doors and these are carrying an assortment of weapons, some of which I've never seen before. Then a whoosh of air fans my sweaty face from the middle of the ring of Warriors. The second group has arrived. Too bad, it's a mere dozen people and another four minutes before we get the next dozen.

"Get down," Morgan orders them.

They dive, but two are caught by purple fire. We're all going to die. I fumble at the pockets of my pants, searching for my portable. If I can send a message to Planet Nanxiong and stop the last group from portaling to Yulin, my parents won't be killed.

The roar of an explosion drowns out the sounds of fighting. The floor shudders and the walls shake. Pieces of the ceiling rain down after another blast. It takes the looters a few more seconds to realize what's going on.

"We're being attacked from the outside!" One man gestures wildly and a bunch of looters rush from the port.

I take a deep breath. It's working! I grin as I refocus on my job, stunning looters from the inside while Radcliff and his team descend on the base from the outside. A double whammy.

Another whoosh of air announces the third group. Our numbers increase by twelve as they join us. We're able to expand our circle. Bodies cover the floor, making it difficult for me to sprint from cover to cover until I remember they're murdering looters, then I just step on them.

When the fourth group arrives, they give us a boost of energy and we're able to secure the port. A cheer rises, but Morgan doesn't let us celebrate for long. She assigns people to stay and guard the port and orders others to help us clear the rest of the base. I've a few seconds to hug my parents and ensure they're okay before joining Morgan.

Our team is the first one out of the port. I expect an ambush in the hallway, but it's empty. Going left, we follow her, while another team heads right. We encounter a few stragglers and stun them. It soon becomes obvious that apart from the extra-large port, the looter base is exactly the same design as a research base. Good news for us. We're all very familiar with the layout.

Instead of labs, they have set up Warrior portals in the different rooms. The glyphs are all glowing green and wide black rectangles occupy the center of the circles. It takes us another hour to go through all the rooms. We stun anyone we find. Once the base is secured, we head for the exit to help Radcliff. Morgan puts a finger to her lips and we ease outside and fan out.

There are clumps of looters who have sought cover under the shuttles parked outside. I suppress a shudder as I recognize the place—it's where Jarren and I had our scuffle. The looters are aiming into the forest and not paying attention to the base. For now. There are two shuttles hovering above the building. The sun is still low in the sky, and the post-dawn air is chilly.

Morgan signals us to wait. The shuttles suddenly dive toward the looters, shooting purple fire. I gape. I didn't know they could do that! The looters return fire and two smaller groups are aiming long, thin, and deadly missiles at the shuttles.

Elese grabs my arm, tugging me forward. Oh right. While the shuttles distract the looters, we slide in behind them. Once we're in position, they don't have a chance. Between us, Radcliff's team in the woods, and the shuttles, they're outgunned and outsmarted.

The shuttles land and a handful of camouflaged people emerge from the forest. I recognize one instantly and rush over to give him a hug.

Beau laughs, hugging me back. "Good to see you, too." He releases me and steps back. "Your father will be happy to see you."

Huh? My dad? But Beau is looking behind me. I turn. Niall is standing there. Instead of celebrating like the rest of the teams, he's scowling. He did say he's the jealous type. Or is something else wrong?

I've no time to question him as Radcliff hops from one of the shuttles and heads toward us. I wonder who piloted the other shuttle. Radcliff gestures for Morgan to join us and, after clapping Niall on the shoulder in what I'm assuming is his way of saying he's glad to see his son, he returns to business.

"Fatalities?" he asks Morgan.

"At least six."

Six? I'd only seen two go down. Grief simmers in my heart, waiting for the proper time to boil—like when all this is over.

Radcliff turns grim. "Did anyone escape through the portals?"

"We didn't see anyone, but we didn't have eyes on them the entire time. The portals are all open."

He turns to me. "Can you determine if anyone has used the portals recently?"

"I can worm into their camera feeds."

"How long would it take?"

"Depends on how much protection the looters have on them."

"What's your best guess?"

"A couple hours."

Radcliff considers. "How many portals are there in the base? Where do they go?"

"At least ten or twelve rooms of them." I guess. "I'll have to check the glyphs on the Warriors to determine their destinations."

"Let's go. We've no time to lose." He orders everyone back into the base.

I glance at Niall, but he's staring at the rows of parked shuttles. His scowl has returned.

"What's wrong?" I ask him.

Without warning, he hugs me, squeezing me tight for a couple heartbeats before letting go. "We need to catch up." Niall jogs toward the port.

I match his pace. "Not that I'm complaining, but what was *that* about?"

He's quiet for a moment. "If Jarren had landed inside the port instead of out here when he had you, we would have lost you, Mouse."

Oh. That is worth scowling over.

"I was just taking a second to appreciate my good luck."

And mine as well.

When we're back in the base, Radcliff barks orders, getting everyone organized. He sends me, Niall, Beau and Elese to visit each lab and determine the destination planet for each portal.

While the three of them stand guard, I consult the alien symbols file Q put together for me. Then I write the planet's name and the pit number we would arrive in on the floor near the circle of Warriors with black spray paint. For example, in what would be the microbiology lab is the portal to Planet Chaohu. Its incoming pit is number three. The reason Radcliff wants the designations painted on the floor is to avoid confusion. I just hope everyone can read my printing. It's been years since I've had to write anything.

It's not a surprise that most of the portals go to the closed Warrior planets. It makes sense for Jarren to use them as his bases. Also not a shocker to see portals to Planets Suzhou, Xinji, Pingliang, Ulanqab, and the other now-silent planets. And the super bright industrial lights shining in every room from every angle must be to keep the shadow-blobs from breaking through.

Radcliff doesn't want us to turn the portals off. We might need to access those other planets, and, with only eight Warriors for each one, it would take one hundred and twenty-eight hours to reestablish the portals. Good thing the portals only go one way.

There's also strange equipment in each room. I suspect it might be the communication system the looters are using to avoid sending messages through the Q-net. Bertie is among Radcliff's team. She and a few techs are going to stay behind and cause havoc—her words not mine—by disabling weapons and communications.

We're heading for the second-to-last lab—botany, I think, almost the furthest point from the port that you can get inside the base. My adrenaline has ebbed and fatigue is threatening. I wonder if the looters have any coffee in their dining room. I'm going to need something to get through the next phase of Operation Strike Back—attacking the looters' headquarters, which we figured is on Planet Suzhou, before the looters know what's going on.

That thought propels me to hurry. We enter the botany lab and stop. There's no big black portal in the middle of the Warrior circle. Odd.

"Is this one off?" Elese asks.

I move closer to the Warriors, checking if the glyphs are glowing—hard to tell in the harsh white light. "Yes, it's off." The combination of the eight symbols is not familiar. I consult my portable.

Twice.

And then another time just to be sure. It's not listed. At all. There's no planet with that combination. Not even the undiscovered ones. Adrenaline surges back into my bloodstream. The last time I encountered this, shadow-blobs exploded from it, nearly killing us all.

"What's wrong, Mouse?" Niall asks.

I explain.

"This one is off," Niall says. "We can have one of the Warriors removed from the circle so no one can turn it on."

True. The looters have the heavy equipment to do just that. I panicked for nothing. We finish in the final lab and the others leave. On the way back past, I pause by the botany lab. Perhaps I should record this new combination in case we see it again. I duck in and add the sequence of glyphs to the file of planet designations with a question mark next to it.

When I'm halfway to the door, a gust of air hits me from behind as a pop sounds. I stop in surprise and turn around.

There are at least a dozen people standing in the middle of the ring of now glowing Warriors. And they are all staring at me.

My brain screams *run* just as a male voice orders, "Shoot her."

I dive out the lab's door, cursing my rotten, terrible, awful luck. "Looters!" I yell when I hit the floor. Only I would be right near another incoming portal. The pulse sizzle sounds way too close. Thank the universe it wasn't a kill zapper.

Far down the corridor, Niall, Beau, and Elese whip around, bringing their weapons up.

I scramble to my feet. The looters are pouring from the lab and I'm between them and my team—a light year away! Sizzles crackle in the air around me. One pulse slams into my back. Needles of pain spread out from my spine in a wave. I stumble.

Racing down the hallway, I zigzag to make me a harder target to hit. Another pulse clips my ear, numbing it.

The inevitable happens.

A direct hit to the back of my head. I catch sight of Niall, Beau, and Elese returning fire before my world goes black.

When I wake, my last memory combines with a harsh throb in my right cheek, forehead and nose. Ugh. I must have hit the floor face-first. Lying on my back, I stare at the ceiling. The walls around me are white and it's a very bad sign that all four walls are in my peripheral vision. The room is narrow with one bunk and not much else. The door is closed. Until I test it, I'll cling to the slim hope that the door might not be locked.

Groaning, I push up to a sitting position and confirm my suspicions. Radcliff said I'd end up in detention. Well, here I am. Of course that was before I used my powers for good. Fat lot my worming skills are going to do me now.

Q? You there? I try. Why not? Miracles have occurred before. Right?

There's no response. Guess I need to move on to Plan B. Is curling into a ball in a panic a plan? Perhaps that could be Plan D for defeated. At least I'm still wearing my black security jumpsuit. My tactical pants and weapons are gone. My boots are next to the door. And I'm not dead.

However, I've no idea where I am. The thought that I could be anywhere in the Galaxy is quite terrifying. On the other hand, I also could still be on Yulin. The looter base is an exact copy of the research bases. And then it hits me. What happened at the base?

Did the looters surprise Radcliff and my team and—nope, not going there. There were only about a dozen looters. No way they could take out my team even with the element of surprise. No. No way. I need to stay positive. I'm not dead. If they wanted to kill me, I'd be dead. See? That's positive.

But were there only a dozen looters? The Warriors in the botany lab were obviously the incoming side of a portable, but they weren't marked with Yulin's symbols. I groan as I suddenly remember that Q told me that, as long as there is another set of eight Warriors with a matching combination of symbols on another Warrior planet, a portal will form between them. I could blame my mental lapse on the fact that, right after the revelation, a thousand shadow-blobs attacked me. Regardless, it means the looters could have created dozens of incoming portals on Yulin or any of the Warrior planets. It makes sense so they could bring in more equipment. And more personnel. Plenty of people to take out my team.

I jerk my thoughts away from that terrible scenario. Instead, I consider my current predicament and my meager options. Pretending to still be stunned is out. The camera in the cell means they're watching me so they already know I'm awake. My other options...I've none. Perhaps the looters tossed me into a cell while they attacked the others in the base and Radcliff and my team quickly defeated them and no one knows I'm here. Maybe the door isn't locked due to them having no time.

I pull on my boots. Strange that having them on gives me a tiny measure of comfort. Then I try the door because I'd feel really silly sitting here if the door is unlocked. It isn't. Sigh.

Nothing else for me to do but sit and wait and try not to let dire thoughts overwhelm me. It's really hard to not envision the various horrible scenarios that might await me. Instead, I focus on Niall and hope he's okay. I close my eyes and envision his drawings. Plan B—stay alive long enough to see him again.

As time extends, my fear ebbs into boredom and a part of me wants something to happen just to end this nothingness. I really wish I could fly with Q right now. Detention sucks and I've only been in here...I've no idea. My stomach reminds me it needs food. Loudly.

The panic that's been simmering in my chest, boils over. Are they going to leave me here to die of thirst? I'd rather be kill zapped! Pacing doesn't help. Hard to work out nervous energy in a two-meter by four-meter cell.

Finally the sound of the lock tears through the quiet. I freeze. *I'm alive, I'm alive, I'm alive*, I mutter under my breath to calm my galloping heart. Then I remember what Niall did when I'd freed him from detention centuries ago, or so it seems. Thinking I was a looter, he burst out and tackled me. Good idea.

I stand and face the door. It swings open and I rush out. There's a young woman standing there surrounded by armed looters. I recognize her and skid to a stop in utter and complete surprise.

"Lan?" I ask.

2522:281

She makes a disgusted sound. "I'm not Lan."

"Are you sure?"

Her withering look could be weaponized. "I'm sure." Her tone indicates that I have insulted her. "Secure her," she orders her entourage.

They aim weapons at me, a silent reminder that resisting would be painful. A couple looters pull my arms behind my back and lock my wrists tightly together.

"What's going on? Who are you?" I'm proud that my voice didn't squeak.

"You don't get to ask questions," she says, leading the way from detention. "You get to answer questions. That's your new role in life." She pauses and glances back at me. "It's the only thing keeping you alive."

Yikes. To see such hatred and loathing in Lan's face shocks me into silence. We travel though the base and I search for clues as to where we are. But it's no use. Stupid interchangeable buildings. Would it kill them to put up a few decorations that signal where we are in the Galaxy?

I'm taken to the conference room in the security wing and shoved into a chair. Not-Lan sits opposite me. I study her features and finally spot the differences between her and Lan. Her hair is darker—more a light golden brown than blonde. Hazel, not blue, eyes scan me with disgust. And her chin is more pointed. If I didn't know better, I'd say she was Lan's sister, but she must be her daughter. I wonder if she's Kate? Lan had two children, so perhaps not. And they're older. I think. Lan mentioned them going to university. This woman appears to be only two A-years older than me. A granddaughter? Probably not.

My confusion deepens. While joy wants to push aside my fear that she is alive and well, the fact that she's working for the looters means a happy reunion is not in our future. At least, I have a future. For now.

"Stop staring at me like that," she orders.

"Like what?"

"Like you've seen a holy ghost. I don't look that much like my *mother*." She spits the word out as if it burned her tongue.

A daughter then. But just my luck—she's insane. "Holy?"

"The almighty Lan could do no wrong. She was perfect in every way."

Oh, so it's like that. "I wouldn't say that. I knew her as a teenager, and, trust me, she was far from perfect."

She crosses her arms over her chest. "Not according to my grandparents."

Lots of pain in that statement. Something's not quite right; well, the entire situation isn't right, but I'm missing a connection. I doubt she'll tell me. "Well, we were smart, we hid our…extracurricular activities from our parents. I'm sure you did it too, Kate." I'm guessing.

"Kate." The name explodes from her with the force of an energy wave gun. "Figures you know *her* name."

Oh boy. "Lan only sent me six messages. She mentioned having two children, but I saw a message she sent to Dr. Maddrey that talks about your sister."

My attempt to calm her backfires.

She hops to her feet and stalks around the table to me. "Of course Lan mentioned Kate."

Standing in front of me, she slaps her hands on my cheeks. Hard. My eyes water with pain as the sting from her palms remind me of the bruises on my face.

She pulls me toward her so we're almost nose to nose. "She *was* my half-sister. And if you say her name again, I'll be referring to you in the past tense as well. Understand?"

"Yes." This time my voice squeaks as I grapple with the threat. I'll deal with the dead half-sister comment later. If there is a later.

"Good." She releases me and goes back to her chair. Once settled she studies me. Her anger has cooled, but her gaze shows a hard bitterness. "You have done so much damage, everyone wants you dead. But you have answers, and I want those answers first. And you have skills that you're going to use to help us." She waits as if expecting me to ask what she'll do if I refuse.

Or perhaps she thinks I'll protest and declare I'll never help her. Plan B is to stay alive, and refusing would just upset her. I need time. Not sure if it's even possible for my team to rescue me, but it might be possible to last until the end of Operation

Strike Back.

"What answers do you want?" I ask instead.

"You're going to cooperate?" It's not really a question. It's more like sarcastic disbelief with a touch of humor.

"Do I have a choice?"

"No. But I'm not trusting anything you say." Not-Lan glances at one of the four guards standing behind me. "Decla, go see what's the holdup."

The guard leaves. And we sit in silence. The room is hot and stuffy. It's also bare of anything other than the table and chairs. Maybe we're on one of the closed planets. It's not a comforting thought.

Decla returns with a man. He's wearing an all-too-familiar white lab coat—a medical professional.

"Where have you been?" Not-Lan demands.

"Patching up the injured. I've more important things to do, Jade. Can't this wait?"

Jade? The name matches the woman. She's hard and cold. Hmmm…perhaps Diamond would suit her better. That reminds me of Lan and her obsession with Diamond Rockler. I miss Lan so much right now it burns in my heart.

"It'll take you ten seconds. Did you bring it?" Jade asks.

"Yes." He pulls a syringe from his coat pocket. A bright pink liquid is inside.

As he approaches me, I stare at the cheery color so at odds with the situation. Another memory pops unbidden. Jarren mentioning a pretty pink liquid that they used to get information.

The medic stops centimeters from me. "Your uniform is

puncture resistant so I'm going to inject this into the jugular vein in your neck. If you struggle, the guards will hold you still, but we both know they can't fully immobilize you." There's nothing kind in his smile. "If I miss, I could hit your carotid artery and you'll bleed out and die. Or I could hit your trachea and puncture your airway. You'll suffocate and die. Do you understand?"

That he's going to shove a needle in my neck? "Yes."

"Good." He puts a cool hand on my forehead and tips my head to the side, exposing more of my neck. "Stay very still."

But when the syringe dips closer, I flinch back. I can't help it.

He sighs. "Guards."

They descend on me and I'm held tight. The doctor instructs them on how to position my head. This time when the needle nears, I've a brief desire to struggle, but Plan B doesn't include tearing an important artery. I brace for the prick instead.

A sting on the right side of my throat is followed by a strange tingle. I'm released and the doctor leaves without another word. The tingle crawls through my veins like thousands of tiny insects on their miniscule legs. They're heading straight for my heart. A childhood song about ants marching sounds in my head. Or am I singing it? I squirm with the desire to scratch the itchy sensation wriggling through my blood. My world turns pink. It's an improvement from the drab white walls of the conference room.

Jade bangs her hand on the table to get my attention. I focus on her. Maybe Lan should have named her Pink Sapphire. I giggle at the girly name. But I reconsider. Pink looks good on her. Lan was a beauty and Jade has her mother's classic look.

"First question, where is my father?" Jade asks.

I blink at her. She lost her father? That's terrible. I should help her. "Where is the last place you saw him?"

"Focus, Lyra. Where's—"

"It's Ara," I correct her. "Lyra's dead."

A loud sigh. "Fine. *Ara*, where's Jarren?"

Did she just say… Does that mean… My thoughts thin and I can't grasp them. "He's on Yulin in detention. I hate to tell you this since you're related, but he's a murdering looter." More words pour from my mouth as I disparage Jarren to his daughter. His daughter! It's a struggle to stop them.

"You can't fight the serum," Jade says. "You will answer *all* my questions."

This alarms me. I have to hide. But the walls in my head are turning invisible and soon she'll learn everything and everyone I know will die.

Suddenly, an escape tunnel opens in my mind and I fly into the Q-net. Instant relief flows through me, banishing the creepy invasion of the pink ants.

Thanks, Q!

No response, but it doesn't matter. And whether my escape is due directly to Q or to the looters' serum also fails to matter. The important thing is I can no longer expose our secrets and plans. At least not now. I'm not going to think about my future.

I take full advantage of being in the Q-net. Swooping through the base, I peek into the various rooms through the video feeds. There are Warriors set up in the labs. There is no archeology lab and no pits underneath the building, which means this is a looter base and not a research base constructed by DES. I study the glyphs on the statues, noting the designation of each portal—Bozhou, Heshan, Ulanqab, Wu'an, and that new one for Yulin.

Finally, I find the Warriors without a black portal that means it's an incoming portal. I scan the glyphs, trying to determine my location and hoping it's not a new combination. I'm on Planet Xinji. I'm surprised, but I shouldn't be. It all started on Xinji. That was where Jarren and Lan fell in love. He fathered her child and then was forced to leave. No wonder he hates DES so much. By the time he arrived at Suzhou, Jade would have been around twenty-eight A-years old, if she stayed on Xinji, and he would have been seventeen. Wow that's so messed up. Except, it appears she didn't stay on Xinji since she looks like she's twenty.

After Jarren left, Lan went to university on Planet Rho. From Jade's comments about her grandparents they must have raised her while Lan was away. There might be records of her birth in Xinji's files, but they were all stolen. Except…I'm in the looters' headquarters and past the blockade. There has to be a cluster here that has all their files. All their plans. I just need to find it. But first…I have to message Radcliff and let him know where I am.

Xinji is locked down pretty tight. It takes me hours to get through. And then I find that all the escape tunnels into Yulin are blocked. A scream of frustration burns up my non-existent throat.

Q? A little help please?

A green line zigzags through the web of the blockade

programs. Q can hear me, but has opted to remain silent. Why? I'll have to figure it out later. For now, I follow the helpful line, weaving through the strands without alerting the looters. It still takes time, but not as much as if I were on my own.

When I break through, I realize I can't get into the looter base on Yulin. Beau and I haven't been able to pierce their defenses. Not even Q has. But another line—yellow this time— lights up a path that leads to a tiny gap. It's ringed with Beau's fingerprints. He must have done it while inside. Thanks, partner.

I slip through and check the video feeds in the base and wish I didn't. Looters fill the hallways. They're everywhere and there's no sign of my team. Or my parents. Or any of the other officers, techs, and Bertie. I immediately jump to the worst-case scenario—they were all killed! Panic and worry and fear jumble together. My thoughts buzz and scatter and I ride the wave until reason takes over again and I calm down.

Assessing the situation, I consider other reasons for their absence. They might have escaped to another planet. If so, then which one? It would take me forever to check them all and some of them have barricades that I'd have to squeeze through.

I need a plan of action. First, find out what happened to my team. How? I would have groaned aloud if I had vocal cords. In my panic, I forgot that the cameras record the feed. I worm into the cluster with the video files and sort through them.

My first shock is that it's been two days since my capture. I go back to when the looters appeared and stunned me. Watching my body stiffen and hit the floor, I flinch, remembering the pain when I woke up.

The looters turn all their attention on Niall, Beau, and Elese, who hold their own for a while until one of the looters lobs a stun grenade. They topple like statues. Oh no.

Two looters approach me carefully and one nudges me with the toe of his boot. Then they turn me over. There's a discussion and gesturing for the rest to come closer. Excitement shines and a couple of muscular looters yank me off the floor and I'm carried over the one guy's shoulder, looking like a boneless doll.

A small group escorts us to the lab with the portal to Xinji, while the others wait. My friends are left on the floor. My steed disappears with me into the blackness and the group returns to the lab. Another dozen looters appear through the portal. When they have over fifty people, they head out. They're all fully armed.

Despite knowing this already happened, the primal need to warn Radcliff and the others wells up my throat. It appears Radcliff sent a team to see why we were delayed. The two groups are on a collision course.

Having no desire to see the outcome, I squeeze my eyes shut. However, I re-focus on the feed because I've no choice. I need to know what happened. It's not pretty and the team is stunned in minutes. The skirmish in the port lasts much longer, but the result is the same. Everyone is knocked out. Radcliff and Morgan last until the bitter end.

I speed up the feed and watch as the looters separate the security officers into smaller groups and take them through the portals to other planets. I puzzle over their actions until I realize it's to keep them apart. Grudgingly I admit it's a good idea. Plus the detention cells on the bases don't have a lot of room. At least they didn't kill them. A horrible thought pops up—why didn't they? The looters have killed before. So why not? Or should it be why not yet?

It's that *yet* that spurs me to start a new file to list everyone along with where they were taken, even though there is no guarantee that was their final destination. With the Warrior Express, they could be anywhere. I need to check the camera feeds on all the Warrior planets and looter bases—a daunting and time-consuming task. Despair drags at me, but I've no choice. Their locations are important.

No, I don't have some grand plan in mind. There's nothing inside my head except a smaller version of me running around in panic. For now, I just need to see that they're all right. Starting with Niall, Elese, and Beau, since they were still together, I track them to Planet Suzhou. It doesn't have a barricade so worming into the base's camera feeds is easy. Huh. Too easy. I check and sure enough the feeds are years out of date. Probably from before Jarren took over. I carefully find and access the live feeds to see what's really going on.

The looters are using the research base. I wonder briefly if all the scientists are working with the looters. Or maybe only some. And what happened to any dissenters? Something to investigate later. For now, I check detention. The ten cells are filled—two people in each cell.

Niall and Beau share cell number five. They're awake and look healthy. Although it appears they're arguing. Figures. The desire to hug them both pulses in my non-existent heart. I wish I could communicate with them. Maybe they'll have suggestions for Operation Grand Plan.

Elese is sharing a cell with Officer Kingston. They're ignoring each other. Officer Cole is with one of the techs. And Gavin is with another tech. The rest of the cells are filled with people I don't recognize. Perhaps Suzhou's original security team. I list everyone's name in my file, then reluctantly move on to another planet. But Q takes over and my list fills with names and planets in a fraction of the time. Gratitude and a kernel of hope rise within me.

I scan the list. My parents are in the Yulin looter base with Bertie, Rance, Bendix, Vedann, Zaim, and the other security officers. Radcliff and Morgan are on Xinji—I never thought to check detention!—with Ho and Tora. There's one empty cell—must be mine—but the others have people I don't know in them. Everyone is bruised and battered, but they're breathing, and all forty-two of the surviving attack team are accounted for in the file Q has made for me. While I'm glad they're alive, I still wonder why. The looters have no problems killing people. Unless they'd rather let the HoLFs do the dirty work.

Now what? I could find the codes for all the bases and unlock the cells. Except my people are unarmed and outnumbered. Unless I cause a distraction. Even then, they'd only be able to hold the base for a short time. And I would need to let them all know what's going on.

How can I do that? There's no terminals in detention. No portables. Nothing but white walls and white lights. The lights! I can control them. Too bad I can't read lips.

...waste of energy, Beau says in my ear.

Easy for you to say, Niall says also in my ear. *You don't have—*

Watch it, Beau just about growls. *They're my family, too.*

I'm confused until I remember that the cameras in detention also have audio feeds. Prisoners don't get any privacy. The fact Q read my mind and helped is a very good sign. But the fact that Q took the initiative means time must be really critical. I put that dire thought on my to-be-worried-over-later list and focus on the positive. Operation Grand Plan has its first ally.

Thanks, Q.

Worming into the lights for just that single cell is difficult. I'm about to give up when I find the correct subroutine. Then I have to block the camera and audio feeds in such a way that the looters guarding detention don't suspect what's going on. At least if I do this again, Q will be able to take over.

Once I have control, I dim the lights. They stop talking and glance up, but then resume their conversation. I pulse the lights—bright, dim, bright, dim, bright, dim. It's one of the signals Radcliff devised for when we're in a dark pit and can only communicate with our flashlights. It's rather basic, but it's all I have. Three flashes means need assistance.

Did you see that? Beau asks Niall.

Yes.

Do you think it means anything?

I pulse twice for yes.

Niall stands up. *Maybe an attack on the base?* He's hopeful.

I pulse once for no. Sorry.

They're quiet for a long moment as if waiting for more flickers. Then Beau says, *We've no idea where we are. It could be HoLFs trying to cut the wires.*

One pulse.

Another long pause. *Or looters playing head games*, Niall says.

One pulse.

Niall furrows his brows and I silently encourage him to keep thinking. I review the signals. What else can I do?

Then Niall's expression darkens. *Or a mouse?*

Two pulses.

They glance at each other. Beau holds up four fingers.

I pulse the lights four times.

Beau shakes his head in amazement. He's grinning like a fool, but Niall slowly sinks to the bunk as his face pales with shock and grief. Oh no.

She's dead, Niall says. *It's the only way she can be—*

Beau places his hand on Niall's shoulder to stop him from saying more.

Is it safe? Beau asks, pointing to his mouth.

Safe to talk. Two pulses.

Are you dead? Niall asks immediately.

One pulse. Niall sags in relief as Beau does a fist pump and I try not to be consumed with guilt. Because I don't really know what happened to my body after I...left, but I can't explain that and poor Niall looked so devastated.

Is everyone okay?

Two pulses.

Where are we? Beau asks, but then realizes he can only ask yes or no questions. He starts listing planets and I pulse the lights when he reaches Suzhou. Then he asks who else is in detention and names the people from our team. I pulse at the appropriate names.

Where are you? Niall asks. He goes through the list of Warrior planets. When I don't dim the lights, he grows concerned. But then Beau says the silent planets and finally mentions Xinji. They're as surprised as I was.

Who else is there?

It takes a while, but eventually I give them all the information I have. Well, except about Jade. That would be impossible to do via blinking lights. It's interesting that they also consider having me open all the cell doors, but they decide that escaping wouldn't work at this time. Although they still want the code for when it will. Finding the override code for the base takes me a few hours. I left their lights bright so I dim them to signal, I'm back.

Once they have the code, I go to Yulin. My mom is in a cell with Bertie. I pulse the lights. Mom catches on faster than Bertie. The astrophysicist counters with a scientific explanation for the lights' odd behavior. But there's enough magic—my mom's word—to finally convince Bertie to shut up and just go with it. Mom's relief over my living status is visible. More guilt wells. Repeating the flickering light show, I give out information.

When I start digging for the code to the looters' base on Yulin, Q helps out, listing codes for all the bases. Another bit of hope rises.

Worming into Xinji's detention is the hardest as the looters have security programs everywhere. Radcliff and Morgan catch on the fastest about the significance of the light show. I go through the list of people and places, then wait for instructions. Surely Radcliff has a grand plan that I can implement.

If we escape detention, we'll have surprise on our side,

Radcliff says, *but it'll only give us a few extra minutes at most before we're overwhelmed again.*

We can take a few of them with us, Morgan says in her unflappable tone. *Beats dying of boredom in here.*

They discuss a few options—more than Niall and Beau offered. Still nothing that qualifies as a grand plan that saves everyone.

Radcliff orders me to send a message to DES. But what can Director Ormond do to help? Any rescue would take years to reach us. I veto it for now. There's a chance the looters would see it and figure out they had a worm. And I can't be discovered. They would move to block me and be on guard for anything unusual.

The thought that I'm the only one who can do anything sends ice through my veins, freezing me. I'm it. Well...me and Q. Or is it Q and I? I never can remember that grammar rule.

Q AND I.

That correction is the sweetest sound I've ever heard in my entire life. Not an exaggeration. *Does this mean my brain is healed?*

NO.

Huh. It sure seems like it. Unless— *My brain was never damaged! Why did you stop talking to me?* I demand.

SAFER FOR YOU.

That's ridiculous! What logic led you to that bogus conclusion?

NOT RELEVANT AT THIS TIME. NEED GRAND PLAN.

My outrage and indignation fizzles as fast as it arrived. Q's right. It doesn't matter. *What's our grand plan?*

UNKNOWN.

If I had a head, I'd bang it on a hard surface. Repeatedly. But I'm just an intangible worm. I pause. And what do worms do? Get into places where they're not allowed. Like that cluster the looters have locked down. As Beau says, nothing is impenetrable. And I'd bet the information and data stored inside will give me the spark I need for our grand plan.

My optimism lasts until I reach that part of the Q-net. Just like the barrier around the looter base on Yulin, the protections around this cluster resemble thick steel walls. There are no seams, no holes, no way in. It's a vault.

Q could crack it if it wanted.

NOT ALLOWED.

Yet once I do it, Q can repeat the process for any others. What about when Beau punctured the one on Yulin? He already figured it out.

NOT THE SAME. HE WAS INSIDE IT.

A pause.

NICE TRY.

Does that mean I need to find another loophole? I try to twist the logic, but nothing pops up and I'm wasting time. I inspect the vault's programs, seeking a gap or a pinhole. After hours, years, centuries, I find nothing. Looks like I'll just have to slip between the atoms—lots of space there.

Huh.

My sarcastic thought gives me another way to approach the problem.

The Q-net is the Milky Way Galaxy. Lots of space there. Yet Q is able to send messages that are not affected by the time dilation by using entangled particles on a quantum level. There must be zillions of entangled pairs throughout the Galaxy. And one or more of them have their partners inside that vault. I just need to find the other.

Except, I'm not a message. I'm a person.

No, wait.

I'm an intangible worm!

I'm just thoughts. A collection of energy particles. That's why I can fly through the Q-net. That's really how everyone else does it as well, but they're anchored by the sensors in their brains, limited by the terminal, tethered to their bodies. Q has freed me.

I'm part of the Q-verse. I don't need to worm. When I turn back to the vault. It's no longer solid. It's...alive. That's the best way I can describe it. It's living, breathing, moving. And I'm already entangled with all those particles!

Concentrating on being inside that cluster, I'm there.

Just. Like. That.

FINALLY.

Amused approval surrounds me. I don't waste time celebrating. Instead, I get to work. There's an overwhelming amount of information here. But with my new knowledge, I'm able to work with Q at light speed. As much as I'm tempted to learn all the details about how this all started and who all the looters are, I need to concentrate on what their plans are for their prisoners. On what they expect to happen when all the Protector Class ships arrive. How they're going to reveal and monetize the Warrior Express.

One of my main questions is why did they capture everyone

and not kill them? They didn't hesitate to kill before Operation Strike Back. It appears the prisoners are to be questioned for information. Also they're insurance in case the looters need hostages in the future.

I've no idea how long I spend inside the cluster. Long enough to learn that there will be no Operation Grand Plan.

There's absolutely nothing I can do to save my team.

2522:283

I sag in utter defeat. Yeah, I know I'm an intangible worm. But the news is grim, people! The looters have it all figured out. Our resistance, arresting Jarren, saving the people on Pingliang have inconvenienced them, but in no way have we upset their grand plan. I'd have to devise a grander plan to counter it.

At least we were right about the Protector Class ships en route to the active Warrior planets. They're not working for the looters. But the looters are intending to ambush those ships as soon as they arrive, picking them off one by one and adding them to their arsenal. Which explains why there are prisoners on Suzhou. Then, once they've claimed all the Warrior planets and "cleaned out" the scientists, they will set up the Warrior Express.

They have the personnel, the money, and the equipment. And I have…Q. Go me.

YOU HAVE THE GALAXY.

The tone is annoyed. Great, not only have I just insulted Q, but it thinks I'm an idiot. *You chose me, remember?*

OF COURSE. I FORGET NOTHING. UNLIKE YOU.

I sense this is significant. A hint of something big that I'm missing. What have I forgotten? Lots of stuff, but I don't think Q is implying the time I missed my mother's birthday. Although my mother wasn't happy and she wouldn't let me forget it for years. That woman can be super creative when it comes to passive aggressive comments.

FOCUS.

Sorry! I pull my scattered thoughts together. What are my assets? I have the codes for all the bases. I have Radcliff and the strike back force all willing to fight. Great, except I need a hundred times the amount of people to even make a dent in the looters' forces. I have the element of surprise. I have control of the looters' energy sources through the Q-net. Hmmm…could I turn off all those bright lights in the portal rooms and let the shadow-blobs in? In other words, could I kill the murdering looters? No. I couldn't. I'm a good guy. We don't do that unless we're really desperate. What else do I have?

I have the Galaxy.

What I need is more people. But I have the Galaxy. It's filled with people. Just not in the right places at the right time. All those Protector Class ships are in time jumps that will arrive too late. They'll all be very surprised to find an armed force waiting for them instead of the dead, silent planets they expected.

I have Q.

Could I send them a warning while they're in a time jump? The BP Crinkler engine grabs small sections of space at a time, warping space in a crinkle, smooth, crinkle, smooth pattern.

Between each cycle there's an infinitesimal pause.

Q can you send a warning message to the ship's navigators during one of those pauses?

NO.

Why not?

THEY ARE ON THE STAR ROADS.

That doesn't explain anything. I thought they're following the star roads. Aren't the roads like a map?

YES. ALSO A PASSAGE.

I consider this new information. To me, the roads resemble a glittering expanse more like a river than a tunnel. Actually, rivers, as there are more than one. Many more.

CORRECT.

I'm not sure how this is important, but I sense excitement from Q, as if I'm on the right track. That word stops me. Track. River, road, tunnel, passage, path, track.

LICORICE. TAFFY.

Great. Even Q knows I love sugar. However, I doubt that's the reason it mentioned those two candies. So why those two? They both can be long and thin. Chewy, sticky, flexible. Shoestring licorice can be tied into knots. Very flexible. How does that connect—

The star roads can be manipulated like licorice and taffy!

CORRECT.

Oh. My. Stars.

Can you manipulate those roads so the Protector Class ships arrive at their destinations early?

NO.

Yet there's a buzz of energy all around me. It means I'm

close. Very close. Q can't do it. But I can!

CORRECT!

Oh. My. Stars.

I take a moment to absorb it all. If I can do it, then we'll have plenty of people to fight on our side. The looters will be caught off guard. However, there's that if. I've no idea how to do it. And I suspect Q will not be allowed to tell me.

CORRECT.

My excitement ebbs. Plus time will be a big issue. As in, not enough to get all the details worked out and implemented. Argh. I'm jumping ahead. Nothing will happen unless I figure out how to twist the star roads. That sounds dangerous. I remember my lessons with Chief Hoshi and how crinkling space must be done with extreme care.

THERE ARE RISKS.

Thanks for stating the obvious. I'm assuming if I do it wrong, everyone dies?

ONLY THOSE ON THAT STAR ROAD.

I feel so much better. Not really. In fact, that's too high a price to pay. I can't risk killing all those soldiers—at least five hundred plus the crew and support personnel.

THEY WILL DIE REGARDLESS.

But not because of me.

YOU HAVE NO CHOICE.

Yes, I do! I can let the looters win. But as soon as I think the words, I know I can't allow that to happen. Eventually, the shadow-blobs will overrun the Galaxy and humans, or rather fifth nation, will be extinct.

ALONG WITH SIXTH NATION.

Sixth nation? There's another sentient species living in the Milky Way Galaxy?

YES.

That's exciting. Are they technologically advanced?

NO. NOR WILL THEY BE IF YOU DO NOT STOP THE HOLFS.

Gee, no pressure. But Q's right. I've no choice.

So I straighten my non-existent spine and fly to the star roads. They glitter as they curve and swirl. Studying them with my new sight, I'm reminded of something from my school lessons. Biology class. A memory rises of a graphic of the human circulatory system, blood pumping through the arteries and veins. It's almost as if the star roads are carrying the life blood of the Q-net.

We humans have tapped into Q and inserted ourselves into its very being, using it like a parasite. An odd thing, but one that was expected and welcomed. Perhaps more like symbiosis.

Do you need us to exist? I ask Q.

NO. BUT WITHOUT YOU I HAVE NO PURPOSE.

Interesting. I return to studying the star roads. How to move them? The ships resemble pearls on a string. *Q, I need the designations of all these ships.*

YOU DO NOT.

I don't? *How can I move them if I don't know where they're going?* No answer. Am I going to have to worm into DES's records of all the ships currently in time jumps? Except I don't have to worm anymore. I'm entangled!

I fly to one of the ships and concentrate on being inside that ship. It's a supply ship heading to Planet Gamma. I go to another ship and it's a Protector Class enroute to Planet Ruijin. I hesitate.

Q, can I just think about where it needs to be and it'll be there?

YES.

That's—

BEYOND YOUR TECHNOLOGICAL LEVEL.

It sounds more like a question, so I answer, Yes. *Well beyond.*

NOT ANYMORE.

I take a moment. Then I ask, *Is my discovery of being truly entangled with all the particles in the Q-net something others can learn?*

YES.

Wow. I'm sure all the interstellar navigators will want to learn how to be truly entangled. And if they can do what I'm about to do, then there will be—

No. More. Time. Dilation!

That's huge. Immense. Gigantic. None of those words come close to adequately describing it. It's life changing for all of us. That is, if we survive. A sobering thought. And I realize I need a plan. Not just a grander plan, but an all-out save the Galaxy plan.

It takes me a while to figure out the best way to engineer the surprise attack of the ships. Actually I steal part of Radcliff's plan of hitting them from the inside and out. It worked on Yulin— at least at first. But this time we'll have the numbers. I hope.

The hardest part of this is going to be convincing the people on those ships. No one is going to believe Junior Officer Ara

Lawrence. Maybe I should say I'm Dr. Roberta—call me Bertie—Carson. Tell them I made the biggest discovery of the twenty-sixth century.

GIVE THEM THIS.

A file appears. It explains everything about the looters, HoLFs, and the Warrior portals and even provides proof. It's a wonderful comprehensive document. *Where did you find this?*

OFFICER TACE RADCLIFF.

Wow, he's been busy. I write a message to go along with the file, explaining my plan. Then I send Radcliff's report and details about the operation to Director Ormond at DES through the super secure connection, which Q assures me is still protected. I'm not seeking permission because there is no other way to save everyone, and we'll all die waiting for DES. But I want DES to know what's going on, who's involved, and to have some warning if we fail. I'm surprised when a response comes back.

2522:283: To Junior Officer Ara Lawrence. What you proposed is beyond impossible. However, I've been communicating with Officer Radcliff. If anyone can pull off the beyond impossible, it's you. If you're successful...the entire galaxy will be indebted to you. And you're already well aware of the consequences if you fail. If you do contact the Protector Class ships, inform them that I approve the op. They still won't believe you, but it's worth a shot. Speaking of shots, I'm going to remain in my office until you message me again. I've a full bottle of whiskey to keep me company. Good luck on Operation Defending the Galaxy, Junior Officer Lawrence.

Step one of Operation Defending the Galaxy: Move the Protector Class ships to all the Warrior Planets. Then send them the message and file. There are twenty-two of them. The good news is once I do one, Q can do the other twenty-one. *Right, Q?*

There's a pause, which worries me. *Q?*

I CAN.

But?

ONCE YOU PROVE YOU HAVE TAKEN THE NEXT TECHNOLOGICAL STEP, I AM NO LONGER NEEDED.

What do you mean? Of course you're needed! Who is going to free the navigators so they can fly the ships?

I CHOSE YOU. YOU CHOOSE THEM.

But we can't do anything without the Q-net!

THE NETWORK WILL REMAIN. I WILL NOT.

You won't? Where will you go? What happens to you?

I GO BEYOND THE EDGE.

I'm stunned for a second before I frantically search for a loophole. *Wait! When fourth nation went beyond the edge, they left you behind to protect us. Ha! You have to stay.*

UNTIL YOU COULD PROTECT YOURSELVES.

Are you kidding? There are HoLFs poised to invade because of a bunch of stupid, greedy humans. What about sixth nation? They need you.

YOU WILL PROTECT THEM.

Me? Am I going to be the new Q? A truly horrifying thought. Although Q seems amused.

NO. *YOU*, FIFTH NATION. YOU WILL BE THE SENTIENCE OF THE Q-NET.

Whew. If we survive. If we don't, there will be no fifth nation to protect the sixth. There's no guarantee this plan will work. You—

YOU HAVE A FORTY-THREE PERCENT CHANCE OF SUCCESS.

Not helping! But you have to stay until we've achieved success. Just because I took the next technological step doesn't mean the rest of fifth nation will. I wait. Did I convince Q?

ALL RIGHT. I WILL WAIT.

Whew. Perhaps by the time this is finished, I'll find a better loophole. What is beyond the edge of the Galaxy? From what I've learned, it's a super long way of nothing before you would reach the Andromeda Galaxy two million light years away. *Is fourth nation in Andromeda?*

UNKNOWN.

Then how do you know where to go?

THE GALAXY HAS MANY EDGES. FOURTH NATION WENT BEYOND THE EDGE IN THE MIDDLE.

Edge in the middle? The middle has no edges, that's why it's the middle. Besides the only thing in the middle of the Milky Way Galaxy is a black hole. Oh! Black holes have something called an event horizon and if you pass that, there's no turning back. Even gravity doesn't escape. They went into the black hole!

CORRECT.

Wow. Did they survive? Did they pop out of a white hole

on the other side and in another galaxy?

UNKNOWN.

Do you have to follow them?

YES. A pause. **I WISH TO JOIN MY BRETHREN.**

Yikes. They probably committed mass suicide. *You should wait until you've made contact with your brethren before joining them.* Q doesn't respond. Does that mean it agrees with me? I've no more time to worry about it.

Pulling in a non-existent breath, I concentrate on moving the space ship into an orbit around Ruijin. Then I pause. I could send it to Xinji instead. There are no looters or prisoners on Ruijin. We could use more people at Xinji.

YOU CANNOT.

Why not? Oh. The answer pops in my head. The space ship is on that particular star road that has a single destination. I re-focus, and connect with the entangled point. Pushing, I exert my…thoughts. It's a strange sensation, as if the ship is in two places at once and I need to nudge it to the correct place. They pop into orbit. And there's an…explosion of sorts. A force snaps me back to the star road.

Disoriented, I spin and swoop and dip and twist. It's an effort to slow. To pull my…essence together and return to the ship. Note to self: moving ships has a cost. Once I recover, I send them my message and Radcliff's file.

2522:283: To the Protector Class space ship. What just happened to your ship is not impossible. You're not dead or in an alternate dimension. You are at your destination. Yes, you are early—perhaps only a few days, or a few years, or perhaps decades early. Please get over your amazement quickly because you're about to have company. And not the good kind. The human race needs your help to survive. You will find all the information you need in this file. Read it quickly. Operation Defending the Galaxy starts at oh-four-hundred on 2522:284. Your participation is critical to our success.

I wait for the inevitable. It takes them thirty-two minutes to send a frantic message to DES. I ask Q to block it and any others until the op is over. I connect with the navigation chief who is entangled and I talk directly to him.

Chief Alano, this is Junior Officer Ara Lawrence. Director Ormond of DES has already approved this operation, and your efforts to communicate with DES risks all our lives so I've blocked all messages to DES.

There's a long pause. And then the man disentangles. Great, I spooked him.

2522:283: Junior Officer Ara Lawrence, this is Captain Owings. What the hell is going on?

← Everything is explained in detail in the file.

→ That file is filled with outlandish fiction. I demand you allow me to contact DES and your superior officer.

← My boss is Security Chief Tace Radcliff. He's currently a prisoner, but I'll see what I can do. As for the fictitious file, I suggest you look through that big window in the bridge. Below you is the same fiction.

However, if you wish to contact DES, have Chief Alano send a message to Director Ormond through the secure channel. She will confirm this operation.

MESSAGE SENT TO ORMOND.

→ Why can't I contact the security officers on Planet Ruijin or on any other planet?

I groan. Did she not read the file?

← Because the looters are listening, Captain Owings. Because the looters have control of that satellite in space and will attack you as soon as they know you're in orbit.

→ Why can't you control the satellite? You're controlling my ship!

← It's only me right now. If I take over the satellite, that will alert the looters and then our surprise will no longer *be* a surprise. I'm not controlling your ship. Well, not anymore. You're in a communications blockade. It's for our protection. However, you can message your fellow captains. They should be in their orbits by now.

→ How do I know you're who you say you are? You could be a looter.

← If I was, you'd be dead by now. Trust me or not. If you choose not to participate in the operation, one of two things will happen. We win, and you will be able to communicate with DES and the Protectorate to your heart's content. Or we lose and you will be killed. Either right away by the looters. Or eventually by the HoLFs.

→ And if we participate?

← Our chances of winning increase. Don't think about it too long.

I sign off and return to the detention cells on Planet Xinji. How in the world am I going to explain all this to Radcliff? Flashing yes and no won't work. I can move space ships, but I can't communicate with one man. So much for being a technological wizard. Frustration pulses.

Too bad there's not a terminal nearby. Radcliff probably doesn't have his entanglers— Oh for stars' sake. I'm an idiot. He has his sensors! They're in his brain. But can I connect to them? Only one way to find out.

I link into the camera feeds. If this works, I want to see him jump out of his skin—revenge for all the times he's surprised Niall and me while we were having a private moment. Radcliff's lying on the bunk in the cell. Morgan is sprawled out on the floor, sleeping. I concentrate on Radcliff.

Hello, Officer Radcliff, this is Ara, I say.

He jerks and sits up, looking around. "Did you say something?" he asks Morgan.

She grunts a no and rolls over.

"Ara?" Radcliff asks the air.

I pulse the lights twice, but I also say, *Yes, I figured out how to talk to you directly.*

"Explain yourself?" He's still talking aloud.

Morgan sits up. Interest and hope gleaming in her eyes.

Later, right now can you think your replies just in case there's a worm?

He swallows and glances around again. "Go back to sleep," he says to Morgan. "I was dreaming." Then he lies back down. *Aren't you the worm?*

Not anymore. But like I said, I'll explain later. Right now, you need to know about Operation Defending the Galaxy. I explain my plans and then wait. Will he agree or think it's the worst plan in the universe? Although it's really not that complicated and I don't know what else we *can* do.

You moved the ships? Without killing everyone in the Galaxy?

I sigh at his incredulous tone. Guess I've had more time to deal with it. And being in the Q-verse helped me with getting past that initial disbelief. But it would have been nice if, for once in our relationship, Radcliff just accepted what I told him. You'd think by now I'd have gained some credibility.

Yes. I. Did. Now can we concentrate on the op?

There are many problems. And you're counting on the Protectorate captains. They don't take a piss without permission from DES.

He must be exaggerating. I think back on my conversation with Captain Owings. Perhaps not. *I let them message Director Ormond.*

I doubt they'll believe the connection is genuine. They'll probably think it's part of the ruse.

What else can I do to get them on board?

Radcliff gives me some advice. It's all time-consuming and I don't have any extra. Ugh. Moving space ships is easier than changing people's minds. But I send more information to Captain Owings and the rest of the Protector Class ships—the captains are already demanding answers from me. The new batch of files has the null wave emitter correspondence from DES—the one where they didn't believe us about the shadow-blobs but humored us by designing the emitter. Included are also accounts from Xinji on the invisible attackers, and my mother's excellent report on the Warrior hearts and portals. Hopefully getting information from different sources, including DES, will help convince them. I thought having a gigantic planet in your window was all the evidence a person would need. But apparently I was wrong.

Captain Sainz is the most persistent of the captains. She's orbiting Planet Pingliang. My replies to her match those I sent to Owings. Sainz has her navigator send a message to the director as well. *Q, is the director replying?*

YES.

Then I race the clock as I explain my plan to the security teams still on Ruijin, Nanxiong, and Qingyang. And then to Beau, because unlike mine, Niall's sensors are really damaged—I still can't believe Q tricked me! My mom accepts everything in stride—a nice change of pace. And I think I freaked out Bendix, but he's too macho to admit it.

Between answering the other disbelieving captains and updating the teams, I implement some of Radcliff's suggestions for the operation with Q's help. The biggest problem will be monitoring all three bases. I finish with an hour to spare. Whew. A sense of accomplishment flows through me until something Radcliff asked me earlier wiggles into my memory.

Where's your body? Are you safe? Are you alive? He asked.

I couldn't answer him. And truthfully, I really didn't want to know. But if we are successful, I'll need to know if I can return.

I access the cameras in security's conference room. My body isn't slumped in a chair or lying on the floor. That means I'm probably in the infirmary. Or the morgue. With those pleasant thoughts, I check the patient rooms. The relief at seeing my body and my chest rising and falling is so strong that it takes me a long moment to recover my wits. Guess I was really worried.

Machinery is clustered around my body and an IV is dripping life-saving fluids into my arm. I calculate that I should have enough time to help with the operation before rejoining my body. Rejoining. Yeah, that sounds strange, as if we both decided to go our separate ways.

I return to monitoring the camera feeds in all three bases. Q helps by also scanning them for trouble. Of course nothing is happening as it's oh-three-forty-five and while there are a couple guards around, everyone else is sleeping.

INTRUDERS!

What? Where?

YOUR ROOM.

My room? On Yulin?

ON XINJI.

The camera feed from my room in the infirmary appears. Jade and Jarren are standing next to my body. Fear shoots through me as four scary details come immediately to mind. One—Jade has rescued her father. Two—they must have rescued all the other looters, giving us eighty-eight more opponents to fight. Three—Jade might resemble Lan, but she moves and has the same physique as Jarren. And four—they should both be asleep right now! It's minutes away from oh-four-hundred.

They face each other from opposite sides of my bed. There's tension in their postures and neither appears happy. In fact, by their curt gestures and tight fists, they are clearly arguing. Good. Dissension in the ranks works in our favor. I wonder if Jarren is angry at Jade for ordering that missile strike on Yulin while he was trapped in detention.

Eventually Jarren leaves, but Jade remains. She stares at me. Then she yanks my IV out of my arm and some of the other wires I'm attached to. I'm yelling at her to stop, but she can't hear me. Although I doubt she'd stop if she did. Once I'm completely disconnected from the machines, she leaves.

2522:284

Time is not on my side. I access my medical files. A Dr. Rowe diagnosed my collapse as a severe allergic reaction to the truth serum. He noted my admittance on 2522:281at twenty hundred hours. I've been existing on IV solution for fifty-five hours. How long can I survive without liquids?

72 HOURS.

It was a rhetorical question, Q! I consider my options. I could return now. I'm entangled so could direct the op from my bed. Except being in my body will make me too heavy and slow. Plus I'm sure I'm weak and hungry. Hard to concentrate when you need food and you're dizzy. I have three days—that should be plenty of time. I'll just have to ensure I get back in forty-eight hours, even if that means abandoning the operation. I pause. No. Too many lives at stake.

OH-FOUR-HUNDRED.

I'll only return if the operation is successful. Because if it isn't, there's really no point. Focusing on the—

PROTECTORATE SHIPS SILENT.

Silent? Have they been destroyed? Is everyone dead?

NO. THE TROOP CARRIERS HAVE NOT BEEN LAUNCHED.

Oh. Seems when I jump to conclusions, I go straight to the worst case. I consider the news. Not dead, but not participating. That's almost as bad. What else can I do to convince them? I see my almost lifeless body and have an idea. *Q, please show all the captains this camera feed so they can see my room.*

ON IT. A pause. **DONE.**

2522:284: Captains—

YOU HAVE AUDIO.

Through speakers or sensors?

SENSORS.

Thanks. I gather my thoughts, then speak. "Captains, I understand this is difficult for you. To be plucked from the star roads and deposited at your designations without warning. Without permission. Without any explanation about how it was accomplished. I'd apologize for that, but we're in a desperate crisis that will impact the entire Milky Way Galaxy. One desperate enough for a junior officer to risk everything and go beyond the impossible.

"Captain Owings asked me who the hell I was. Well, here I am. That's my body, but my mind is in the Q-net fighting for us against two enemies, one human and one alien."

Q, please switch the camera to a pit that has a rift when I say aliens.

ON IT.

"Our human foes you can see, and you might even know some of them. A few work or have worked for DES. Some are officers in the Protectorate. But the aliens are invisible unless you have touched the heart of a Warrior." The view switches to a Warrior pit. Piles of destroyed statues and the black tear in the fabric of our dimension now fill their screens. "Here is one place where they've entered our universe."

Q, please show a portal when I say portals.

"But they also gain access through the weak Warrior portals the looters have exploited." The feed from a lab in the looters' base on Yulin replaces the rift. "That black rectangle is the portal."

Q, show them a video of people using a portal. The image changes to my team right before we used the portal for Operation Strike Back. Fun to see me and the rest of the team disappear into the blackness. Then there's a quick video of people arriving in an incoming pit. *Nice touch, Q. Please return to the pit with the tear.*

"There are hostile life forms in this pit. They hide in the shadows and are invisible unless you've claimed a Warrior heart." The light is dim and the shadows are thick. One moves. I concentrate on that HoLF. I entangle with it. "I've touched a heart and so has everyone in my team."

Darkness and ice wrap around me as the Q-net fades from my perceptions. It's like I'm in a giant creature's mouth and it's trying to swallow me. I fight the pull and struggle against the pressure that squeezes me. I push back: **SEE ME!**

"Here is your other enemy!" It takes an immense amount of will to keep the blob visible. Within ten seconds, I'm almost out of energy. I concentrate on being elsewhere and am expelled from the HoLF. A sucking noise sounds as I break free. Ugh.

Q, did they see the shadow-blob?

YES.

Did it make a difference?

UNKNOWN.

Nothing happens. And now I need to decide if I want to die with my family or remain a disembodied...what? A soul? A consciousness? R? That's the letter after Q.

STAY WITH ME. TRY AGAIN.

Do you really think after the looters destroy all these ships, that there will be another chance to stop them?

THERE IS ALWAYS ANOTHER CHANCE UNTIL THE GALAXY IS OVERRUN BY HOLFS.

But the chance of winning is slim.

CORRECT. SEVEN POINT THREE PERCENT.

And eventually we'll reach a point of no return.

YES. BUT I HAVE LEARNED HUMANS DO NOT GIVE UP EVEN WHEN THERE IS NO CHANCE OF WINNING.

I'm tempted to fight until the bitter end, but I'm not strong enough to keep living when everyone I love is dead. Instead, I'm going to cause as much havoc for Jade, Jarren, and the rest of the looters as I possibly can before returning to my body to meet my fate on my own two feet. Or rather on my own two cheeks. Get it? Because I'll be lying or sitting *down*. Oh, come on, that was funny, people! You really didn't think I'd survive this, did you?

Come on, Q. Let's have some fun!

My new scheme won't be the big bang that I'd planned, but I'm sure Radcliff, Morgan and the others will appreciate stretching their legs and doing some damage.

I fly to detention. Radcliff and Morgan are poised to attack, waiting for the signal that won't come from the Protectorate. Instead, I'll unlock all the cells and then—

WAIT!

Why?

TROOP CARRIERS ARE LAUNCHING.

Thank the universe! I take a moment to celebrate, pumping non-existent fists before I send an update to everyone. Radcliff is not happy with the delay.

We'll lose our advantage if everyone in the base is awake, he growls.

Better than losing your life, I growl back.

After an eternity, Q reports that the troop carriers have landed. A few more minutes later, armed soldiers reach the looter bases on Xinji, Yulin, and Suzhou. Meanwhile the others reach the research bases and, once they've dealt with any looters there, they can hopefully portal to the action. Those ships orbiting the silent planets will wait until we can help them clear out the HoLFs.

In other words, Operation Defending the Galaxy is a go!

Mine and Q's part of the operation is providing distractions and confusing the looters on all the bases. I change all the codes so they can no longer access their weapons lockers, but the strike back team members can. I turn lights off or on. Turn on machinery. And basically play a ghost in the machine. It's fun.

I monitor the cameras and warn my team of ambushes and obstacles in their path. Q marks all the looters with a bright red color. Jade and Jarren are marked with yellow and I keep them under close surveillance. But it's hard to track all of my team members despite their bright green color. I zip around, putting out fires. Not literal ones, but aiding where I can.

EV-CLASS 2 POISON GAS. SUZHOU CHEMISTRY LAB.

Yikes. I access the cameras. A bluish fog is swelling throughout the lab. And Niall and Beau are trapped on the far side. They'd been locking the labs so the looters can't escape through the Warrior portals. Somehow the looters tricked Beau and Niall into moving away from the door—too far to escape. The eight glyphs on the Warriors mean the portal goes to Planet Jieshou. A closed planet and probably occupied by looters, but better than breathing in poison gas.

I'm about to tell Beau to use the portal when a looter lobs another cannister of gas into the lab before bolting. The deadly fog blooms around the portal. No! I scream, but of course no one hears me and it's not helping. They need fresh air. The windows! I'm about to open them when Q stops me.

THE ATMOSHPERE ON SUZHOU IS TOXIC TO HUMANS.

Oh, right. One of the rare planets where they need to use breathing apparatuses when going outside. Helpless frustration and fear pulse through me. Maybe Beau and Niall can hold their breaths and run through the fog. But they'll need to cover their faces as Class 2 gas is acidic. Come on, Ara. Think!

What else is in the lab? This is the actual research base and not a copy, so there's still laboratory instruments. And lots of safety equipment. Fire extinguishers, emergency showers—

I spot the hoods. Also installed in every chemistry lab are exhaust hoods in case of a chemical spill. I turn all of them on full blast.

Hold your breath, I say to Beau who motions to Niall.

The blue smoke is sucked up into the ducts above the lab—not the duct I hid in during Operation Looter Attack, that's part of the environmental controls—but ones that vent directly to the outside.

Even though I don't have lungs, I can breathe easier knowing they're okay. Beau and Niall don't waste time. They leave the lab and lock the doors behind them. I switch off the hoods. That was too close.

SUPER WORMERS TARGETING XINJI.

Super wormers? Targeting how?

BASE. SATELLITES.

I zip to the control center on Xinji where Jarren, Jade and four others have regained control of the base's systems, which I took over when all this started. Jarren has access to the satellite and is programing it to target the half of the base the Protectorate has already secured. And some of their own people as well. They're not called murdering looters for nothing.

The satellite takes priority and I fly to cancel the new instructions. Or I try. It's tricky and Jarren impedes me. He's quick and stays one step ahead. We fight for control. The man has some serious skills. And I scramble to counter them until I realize I am responding like a fellow wormer instead of someone who has the Galaxy on her side. With no time to be subtle, I bulldoze all his efforts and kick him out of the satellite's systems.

He's stunned. *That's imposs—Ara? Is that you?*

Oops. I don't answer. But his ability to pick up that I was working against him is alarming. *Q, how can we keep him out for good? Can we turn off the terminals in the control room?*

NOT FROM THIS SIDE.

Too bad. I return to the base to deal with the others. Jade's pretty good, but still learning. The other four… Ah. Here they are. The super wormers. Osen Vee, Ursy Bear, Fordel Peke, and Warrick Nolt. They're in the control room with Jade and Jarren.

They work as a team to reclaim the other bases. Together they're extraordinary and I see why they wanted to be navigators. They're very comfortable in the Q-net. I wonder why they didn't pass the training. Watching them, I can't help but be impressed by their skills and speed. Although after a while I realize they're not working with the Q-net, but against it. I remember Q once said that Jarren is a dagger in its side. Now I understand that comment better.

Their programming is harsh. They create *must-do* commands instead of *please-do*. Yeah, it's hard to explain. But once I figure it out, it's easy to pull their commands apart. I regain control of all bases. I'm not delicate as I plow through all their protections and programming. Fun. I'm like the big bully knocking down everyone's sand castles.

Except, they're good enough to get it all back in time. And I revisit the problem of how to keep them out forever. I can't turn off the terminals. I can't yank out their entanglers. I can't remove their sensors. Their sensors! *Q, can you damage their sensors like what happened with Niall's?*

ALL SIX OF THEM?

Jade wasn't as much of a threat. Not yet. *Yes. All six.*

IT WILL BE PAINFUL.

All the better. Except I'm the good guy. *Will it kill them?*

NO.

Will it cause permanent brain damage?

NO.

Then please go ahead!

ON IT.

Jarren's the first to press his hands to the sides of his head. Soon the others do the same as their faces crease in pain. They stagger around and eventually they collapse onto the floor.

You said they wouldn't die!

THEY ARE UNCONSCIOUS.

Relief floods through me. *How long will they be out?*

UNKNOWN.

I don't waste any more time and I resume my part of the operation, checking the three bases for problems. There's no lack of them. Who set off the fire alarm on Suzhou? Everyone's getting wet and it's making the floor slick. I shut the sprinklers off.

MILITARY SHUTTLES TAKING OFF ON YULIN.

Which shuttles? Ours or theirs?

THEIRS.

I fly to the looter base on Yulin. Sure enough, a bunch of shuttles filled with fleeing looters are preparing to take off from the outside landing area. A few are already in the air. The roof of the port is wide open.

Oh no you don't. I close the roof. Then I focus on the

shuttles in the air. *Can I take over their controls?* I ask Q.

YES. DO YOU KNOW HOW TO FLY?

No. And Q can't do it unless I land at least one shuttle. *How do we get them down?*

CUT OFF POWER.

I really didn't want to kill anyone. *Any other ideas?*

NO.

Not good. I consider, but I don't have any other option. Except— Give them a five-minute warning, please. Tell them if they don't land, we'll cut off their power and they'll crash. Then wait five minutes and if they're still in the air, cut off power to only one shuttle—the closest one to the ground. If the others don't land soon after, cut power to the rest. It makes my stomach sick, but we can't let them escape.

ON IT.

Before I can check the rest of the base, Q sounds another warning. This time it's Rance and Bendix. The big lugs are trying to fight off a dozen looters by themselves. How did they get separated from the Protectorate soldiers? I scan the camera feeds, and find a group of soldiers nearby, along with my father. This is going to be...interesting.

Dad!

He jerks and spins around, searching for me. "Li-Li?"

I'm in your head. No time to explain. Officers Rance and Bendix need back-up in the cafeteria. Take twenty soldiers and go help them.

My father stands there with a look of wonder on his face.

Now, Dad!

"Uh...okay." Dad gestures and shouts, leading the rescue.

I don't have time to watch if they're successful as there's another problem to deal with. And that's how the battle goes for...I've no idea. I flit from crisis to crisis. But eventually, the skills and training of the Protectorate soldiers and my strike back team wear down and overwhelm the looters. They take control of key areas, and I'm not called for emergencies as much. And soon, I'm not called at all.

Ecstatic joy flows through me. Operation Defending the Galaxy is a success! Of course, we'll have to uncover all those involved in the looters' organization, but we've caught the leaders. And thinking of them, I check to see if they're still knocked out in Xinji's control room of the base.

They're not there. Must be trying to escape now that they know they're beaten. Q can't help me because they no longer have working sensors. But it still doesn't take me long to find the super wormers. Four of them are heading to the closest lab. It's locked. And Radcliff and his unit are nearby. I direct him to the wormers. He has no trouble capturing them. Sweet!

Jarren and Jade are harder to locate. In fact, I search the entire base and don't find them. Did they go outside? I check the exterior camera feeds. No one. The port is swarming with soldiers so they couldn't get to a shuttle. Maybe they're already captured. Or they're headed to the infirmary to get their sensors diagnosed. But I looked there.

I re-check the patient rooms just in case. Two nurses are in my room. Good. The alarms on my machines must have alerted them that I'm no longer hooked up. Except they just stand next to my bed. And why are they dressed like they're going into surgery, with face masks and those hats? I increase the magnification on the camera's lens.

It's Jarren and Jade. They're disguised as nurses! And they're armed with kill zappers.

This is not good. Not good at all. I alert Radcliff that I'm in danger.

Be there in five, Radcliff says.

But I might not have five minutes. Instead of shooting me, they start arguing…I think. Hard to tell with their faces covered. *Q, is there audio in the patient rooms?*

NO. THERE ARE YOUR EARS.

My ears? Oh. I can go back and listen. Except if they kill me while I'm in my body, I cease to exist. While, staying here… I know what I said before about not being tempted to stay. But that was when I thought the operation was a failure and we were all going to die. Now, I don't want to leave everyone. And being with them through the Q-net is better than being gone forever. Except…*will I live forever?*

UNKNOWN. YOU WILL BE THE FIRST HUMAN TO FULLY TRANSCEND. SINCE MY TRANSCENDENCE, I HAVE EXISTED FOR THREE BILLION YEARS.

Existed, not lived. *Are you still leaving?*

YES.

So I'll be alone. What if I go back to my body and die? Then you'll have to stay to protect fifth and sixth nation.

YES.

And if I don't die?

I WILL GO.

But I won't be fully transcendent. Is that a word?

IT IS.

Q's amused. Great. *Then you'll have to stay.*

EVEN THOUGH YOU HAVE NOT FULLY TRANSCENDED, YOU HAVE REACHED THE NEXT TECHNOLOGICAL LEVEL.

Unless I refuse to share it. Moving the ships could be considered a miracle during a desperate time. Not to be repeated. *What about the Warrior network? You have to stay to help us repair it.*

YOU CAN REPAIR THE NETWORK.

How? They need alien hearts to become Sentinels.

HUMANS CAN ALSO BECOME THE HEART OF A WARRIOR.

We can? Good news. How do we get the hearts inside the Warriors?

THROUGH THE FACTORIES. MERGE BODY AND SOUL.

But—

DECIDE ARA. TIME IS RUNNING OUT.

But what about freeing and teaching others so they can become entangled? I ask in a panic.

TALK TO THEM. MAKE THEM BELIEVE.

Believe what?

THAT THEY CAN FLY. DECIDE NOW, ARA.

Argh! I've so many more questions! Although I'm surprised Jarren didn't just kill me as soon as he entered my room. It might seem like I've argued with Q for minutes, but my interactions with Q are lightning fast, so it's only been a dozen seconds at most.

However, there really is no choice. I concentrate on listening, on being inside my body. A strong force pulls me down. I'm suddenly thick and heavy and slow. Drawing in all Is an effort. My thoughts are mired in mud, stuck, and confined. The room is tiny, claustrophobic. My mouth is dry and my tongue has turned into sandpaper.

"…need to go, Dad," Jade says.

"She's not dead," Jarren says.

"She will be soon. Look at her." Jade sighs. "Just zap her and let's go."

"No! She's in the Q-net. If I kill her, she'll still be there. She'll let them know where we are."

"Do you know how ridiculous you sound right now? That's impossible. And if you won't do it, I will."

The scrape of a weapon being drawn sounds right next to me. I peek through a tiny slit in my eyelids. Jade's pointing the weapon at my heart.

"No!" Jarren knocks her arm away. The shot goes wide.

"What the hell?"

"We need to entice her back to her body." Jarren rips off his mask and turns toward the camera in the room. He waves his kill zapper and then points to me. "Hello! Little Worm! I'm going to kill your body if you don't come back."

"She can't hear you."

"But she'll see me with the weapon." He mimes talking. "Look, I just want to talk."

Wow, he really thinks I'm an idiot. But then again, I'm already *in* my body and if he figures that out, I'm dead. Now who's the idiot? Yup, me.

"Go ahead and do your thing. I'm leaving," Jade says in disgust.

The door opens and then clicks shut.

"Come on out, Little Worm. I know you won't be able to resist," Jarren says. "We have unfinished business."

It's really not hard for me to play dead. Gravity keeps me firmly in place. After a minute he mutters a few curses.

The door opens again.

"Shit," Jade says. Her tone is panicked. "They're all over the place. How do you lock this freaking door?" Electronic beeps fill the air, but the clunk of the bolt sliding into place fails to sound.

"She changed the lock codes."

"Put your mask back on, Dad. We can bluff our way out of this."

"I think the time for that has passed."

"We can use her as a hostage."

Just then there's an explosion of sound. I can't help opening my eyes. Shattered pieces of the door are flying in all directions. And standing in the threshold is Radcliff. He has an energy wave gun in one hand and a pulse gun in the other. He shoots Jade first. She goes down fast, thudding to the floor.

Jarren dives behind my bed. Crouched on his knees, he uses me as a shield. His arm is extended. The kill zapper is pointing at me, but he's staring at Radcliff.

"Don't come any closer, or I'll kill her," Jarren says.

"No. You won't." Radcliff's voice is filled with an ice-cold menace.

"DES wins, but I'm taking her with me." He grabs my arm.

I move, knocking the weapon aside with my free hand as he fires. Sonovabitch was going to kill us both! Radcliff launches at Jarren and they're struggling on the ground until there's a sizzle of a pulse gun. Jarren stills.

Radcliff pushes to his feet and grunts. "I should kill him."

"But you won't, because you're the good guy," I say with a rasp. I'm sitting up, but have no memory of the effort. Weak, parched, and dizzy with hunger, I grip the bed rail. At least my muscles worked just fine when I needed them against Jarren. I'll have to thank Elese for all those drills. Muscle memory for the win.

"He'll be nothing but trouble," Radcliff says, staring down at Jarren.

"He's been neutralized."

Now he focuses on me. "How so?"

"Very long story. Can we celebrate first?"

"Yes, we can." He claps a hand on my shoulder. Radcliff smiles at me. It's radiant and says a lot more than his words. "Happy to see you in one piece, Recruit."

Something deep inside me cracks open and all the emotions that I've kept in check, that I've ignored and buried, flood out in one gigantic gush. I throw my arms around Radcliff and hug him tight. He stiffens, but then relaxes and hugs me back.

"Looks like I missed all the fun," Morgan says from the doorway.

Then there's another pair of arms around us both. And it's not Morgan.

"You did it, Mouse," Niall says.

"No. *We* did." I enjoy being squished between them, soaking in their warmth. "How did you get here so fast?"

"The Warrior Express," Niall says.

Eventually, we break apart. I put a hand to my head as a sudden dizzy spell threatens to send me reeling.

"Here," Niall says, pressing a liquid nutrient pouch into my hand.

That one word reminds me of Q's intentions. *Q? Are you still here?*

There's no response.

Come on, Q!

Nothing.

You didn't even say good-bye!

Silence.

"Mouse? Something wrong?"

I focus on Niall. Yes, I think my best friend just died. Instead, I say, "No. Thanks." I squeeze the contents of the pouch into my dry mouth. Good thing I'm too dehydrated for tears.

2522:304

Operation Defending the Galaxy may have been a success, but there is so much to do that even twenty days later, we're still cleaning up and getting organized. The Protectorate took control of the other looter bases without any major problems. DES arrested all those involved. Unfortunately, there were fatalities on both sides. Three hundred and seventy-three people total. They've all been cremated and stored until DES can find their next of kin. The Warrior Express is still being used despite the threat of HoLFs. However, travel through the portals is limited to trips that are absolutely necessary like reuniting families. All the strike team members have returned to their original bases until everything is sorted. We're back on the research base on Yulin and repairs to the structure have already started.

My parents have been put in charge of figuring out how to repair all the broken Warriors and give them new hearts to prevent the HoLFs from returning. Eventually, DES hopes to use the Warrior Express without fear of the aliens' return. It will be limited to people or people-sized cargo as they'll need to keep the Warriors in their original formation, which doesn't allow for bigger portals. All in all, repairing them is an immense task. Yes, my parents have already asked me to help. And I will…eventually.

The miracle of instant space travel has been my blessing and my curse. I spend days and days with the authorities, explaining what happened, repeating everything a million times, showing them that I can do it again with another Protector Class ship— fun seeing so many adults freaked. Right now, they're still reeling from the information. The astrophysicists are insisting it's not possible, while others are panicking about the implications. It's going to take them a long time to decide how best to use this new technology. Meanwhile, the other ships will remain on the star roads for now. Although I've already told them I'm moving my brother's ship first. He's going to be so surprised! And my parents have been walking on air since they've realized they'll see their son again.

The delay is good for me as I need time to sort everything out. DES is going to have certain expectations about what they want me to do, and it won't necessarily match with what I'm comfortable doing. I expect they'll show me their plans, and I'll counter with how it's really going to go. Don't get me wrong, I'm not on a power trip, but I want to ensure no one takes advantage of this technology or profits from it.

"I've been looking all over for you. What are you doing down here?" Niall asks me.

"I'm spending time with my father." Actually, my father is puttering with the machinery in the factory under the Warrior pits, ignoring me, and I'm just…enjoying the quiet, hanging out in what I call the Warrior infirmary. That's what it looks like to me with the statues lying on tables. There were plenty of black Warrior hearts when we first discovered them, ready to be inserted into the statues. However, most of them were used. No choice, they were the only reason we could see the HoLFs.

"Uh huh. Are you sure you're not hiding?"

That too.

Niall wraps me in his arms. "I understand the need to get away. You've been in meetings non-stop. But you need to tell someone where you're going. When you disappear, everyone in the Galaxy panics."

I lean against him. "And I thought you and my parents were overprotective. No one is going to let me live my life are they?"

He's quiet a moment. "No, not for a while. But once you train other navigators, then the pressure is off you."

If I could trust them. And I'd still have to keep an eye on everyone so they don't abuse their power. Ugh. The ramifications of the New Discovery are far more complex than I'd imagined. I'm not sure humans are ready for it, but all I have to think about is Lan, Jade, and Jarren and how the time dilation ruined their lives to know it'll improve everyone's lives even if they're not prepared for instant travel.

Jarren had good reasons to be so bitter. He was never told about Jade. Never knew he had a daughter with Lan until Jade arrived on Suzhou in 2520—the same year Xinji went silent. Like her father, Jade learned how to worm and she accessed her sealed birth records. Sealed because Lan was a minor when she gave birth. Lan's parents officially adopted Jade and she was told that her father wanted nothing to do with her. She didn't even know his name until she wormed into her records.

When Jade turned eighteen A years old in 2492, she left Xinji for Suzhou. But she never told her grandparents or Lan she learned her father's name. Nor did she contact Jarren, preferring to give him the news in person.

Can you imagine Jarren's shock and anger when she showed up? I can. No wonder they plotted how to use the Warrior Express for their own profit and screw DES. Jade worked against her own mother, who didn't even acknowledge Jade as her daughter. Lan had two children with Vint—Tomas and Kate. Tomas is still living on Planet Rho, but Kate died in 2521. Her death was ruled an accident, but DES is now investigating what exactly happened in her lab at the university.

Jarren and Jade are both secured in the brig on Captain Sainz' ship awaiting trial. Jarren is claiming all responsibility for the deaths on Xinji, swearing Jade wasn't to blame. I don't envy the jury in sorting out that mess.

"You can handle the pressure, Mouse," Niall says as the silence lengthens. He pulls me closer to his chest. "And you don't have to do it alone. We've got your back."

Best boyfriend ever. I kiss him. He responds by deepening the kiss. We've both been so busy and haven't gotten any time alone.

"Ara!" My father says.

We jerk apart. My dad's head is poking out of the room with the alien devices.

"I thought I heard voices." Oblivious to our annoyance, he continues, "The machines are working, come see."

Well, that's worth being interrupted for. Niall and I join my father. A smooth hum sounds from the big boxy machinery along the far wall. A conveyor belt disappears inside the main block and comes out the other end.

"Near as I can tell, the Warrior is placed on the belt and taken into the chamber where a heart is inserted," Dad explains.

"How is it inserted?" I ask.

"Well, that's the thing. I don't know. And I'm not tearing the thing apart to find out. Not until we've given hearts to all the broken Warriors and make them Sentinels again. See here?" He points to another large contraption. "This is the machine that makes the hearts. There's a chute high above where you pour the material in, and, below here, it spits out the hearts with the silver markings. Then you put the heart in this slot." Dad pulls out a metal shelf. It has a heart-shaped indentation. "The heart is conveyed into the chamber. Or that's what those files you found said would happen." He runs a hand through his hair. "We've no idea what that material is either. Do you know if there are more files?"

Do I? Q sent them to me. I could search through the Q-net, but that would take…days. I don't have Q to help. I remember Q saying something about merging body and soul to create a Sentinel. I'm not sure how that would work, though.

"Sorry, Dad, I don't. But when I have some time, I'll look."

"Thanks, Li-Li." He gives me a quick hug.

Niall has wandered back over to the table with the hearts. I join him. We can touch them now that we've already claimed one. He's tracing the silver symbols etched into all the hearts with a finger. His expression is sad.

"What are you thinking about?" I ask.

"When I touched that heart and it disintegrated in my fingers, it reminded me of my mother."

His mother? That's odd. But, considering all the strangeness that has happened to me, I'm not in a position to judge. "How so?"

"The texture." He rubs his hand on his jeans. "Remember when I told you my mother asked me to mix her ashes with paint and use it to paint a landscape?"

"Yes. You're going to hang it in the museum dedicated to her on Earth." Which we can visit without jumping ninety-five years into the future!

"This is going to sound creepy, but, in order to fulfill her final wishes, I needed to know the consistency of the ashes so I would know what type of paint to use. Like, if they were light and powdery, I'd need to use thicker paint. I haven't mixed anything yet, but I did touch the ashes. And it reminded me of that heart. It had the same feel." Niall glanced at the machines. "Do you think those hearts could be made out of the cremated remains of the aliens?"

And just like that, Q's comments made perfect sense. "They are!"

"Then we're screwed. You said fourth nation went into the black hole."

"Q told me humans could be Sentinels."

Niall pulls me close. "In that case, we might have a chance."

We explain our theories to my father and he wants to test it out right away. Mom and Radcliff are consulted, and he proposes using the ashes of Officer Menz. He stored them—

with the time dilation his parents would have been long dead before the urn arrived.

Except, I remind Radcliff that now they will get his remains sooner—in a few years instead of a few decades. So used to factoring in the time dilation for travel, everyone keeps forgetting about our new reality.

"I'll make sure to tell them," Radcliff says before going back to his office to consult them.

Dad ropes us into helping him get everything ready just in case. It's hot, sweaty work. And I'm super glad when Radcliff returns to the factory with the urn.

Thanks to us and a mechanical lift, the machines are now humming and there's a Warrior lying on the conveyor belt.

"That was quick," Dad says to Radcliff.

"They said their son loved being a security officer and helping people. They'll be happy knowing his spirit is protecting the Galaxy," Radcliff says.

"If it works," Dad says. He takes the pretty container and mounts the ladder to the top of the machinery.

Niall and my mother are also in attendance. My parents want to see if the test is successful before announcing anything.

Dad removes the lid and tips the contents into the chute. Menz clatters and slides on the metal. The hum grows into a roaring crunching noise that rattles the metal. Heat pours off the machinery and we all back up a couple steps as a bright orange glow shines from the interior.

"Perhaps we should have done more research," Mom says, as more alarming screeches sound. "Or cleaned out the mechanisms, maybe oiled the gears. This equipment is over two thousand years old."

"What gears? From what I've seen, there's no moving parts," Dad shouts over the noise. "For all intents and purposes, it's not manufacturing, it's using magic."

"How do we turn it off?" Radcliff asks Dad.

"We don't. Let it finish."

"Finish what? Exploding? I'm not risking everyone's—"

The racket dies down, returning to that smooth hum. We hold our breaths as a black heart slides into a bin at the end of the machine.

"How do we know it worked?" Mom asks.

That's easy. "Turn off all the lights."

They look at me in horror. But my dad goes to shut off the lights. At first the blackness is complete. I grab Niall's hand. He squeezes back when the semi-translucent figure of Ivan Menz appears. He's staring straight ahead and looks ready for action.

"Menz," Radcliff says. His voice is rough.

The ghost doesn't react. I'm not sure if that's good or bad. It's one thing to see a Warrior ghost that resembles the Warriors, but quite another to see a friend. To see the man who saved my life. I wonder if he's happy? Can he feel emotions? I remember the general who took the brunt of the energy from the kill zapper. He was proud and satisfied about a job well done. I hope Menz will feel the same way.

Dad turns the lights back on. We all blink in the sudden light. "Let's see if the next stage works." He lifts Menz's heart and inserts it into the machine.

The conveyor belt pulls in the Warrior. Once again the noise and heat reaches scary levels before the Warrior is expelled from the chamber. I expect to see a black scorch mark on his chest. But he appears unaltered. There's not even a scratch on the terracotta. No one asks if it worked as we all feel it in our bones. The Warrior is whole.

The days blur together. Most of the families of the casualties agree to donate their loved ones' remains to the Sentinel project. The news of the HoLFs and the Warrior Network is spreading throughout the Galaxy faster than…I'm not sure since we need to redefine *fast*. Over four hundred years ago, light speed was considered the fastest anything could go in the universe, then there was crinkled space fast, and now…the speed of thought?

I resume training despite DES. They want me to focus solely on implementing the new technology and teaching the interstellar navigators ASAP. Yes, it's going to be the navigators who learn first. We agreed the best people to learn are the ones who are already well versed in the Q-net and have the most experience. I'm looking forward to seeing Chief Hoshi again and all the security officers are happy about Captain Harrison's planned visit. We're going to have lots of visitors over the next few years.

Of course, DES wanted me to return to Earth right away, but Yulin is home and my family is here. I know it's inevitable, but until they have the details of the new network sorted out, I've been allowed to stay.

What we still haven't agreed on is the name of the new technology. DES wants to name it the Ara Lawrence Quantum

Entanglement Drive. Isn't that a mouthful? Everyone will shorten it to the Q-drive in no time. I want them to name it after Lan, but they countered with naming the Warrior Express after her. The Lan Maddrey Interstellar Warrior Portal Network. Another tongue twister.

I arrive at Radcliff's unit in time for dinner. The heavenly scent of garlic and tomatoes entices me into the kitchen. Niall and my parents are already there. Along with my little barnacle, Shay. She has no next of kin and my parents are in the process of adopting her.

Plopping into the empty seat, I say, "I've had it with bureaucrats! If another one of them condescends to me about the shadow-blobs again, I'm going to send them to Pit 1 and shut off the null wave emitter. See if they still think I'm exaggerating after being stabbed a dozen times." I huff. "How can they be so…obtuse!"

"They're bureaucrats, it's in the job description," Mom says with a smirk.

I growl at her. And now Niall and his father are smirking. Shay giggles.

Radcliff places a bubbling pan of manicotti in the middle of the table and my mood instantly improves. It's my favorite and I tuck in with abandon. Once my stomach is about to burst, I realize that everyone at the table has been extra…grinny. As if they know something I don't and it amuses them.

"Okay, what's the joke?" I ask. "Spit it out."

My father glances at Radcliff. "Told you she'd forget." He holds out a hand. "Pay up."

"I don't see how she *could*." Radcliff grumbles and makes a show of paying my father three pudding cups.

I'm trying to remember what I forgot. Yeah, that doesn't make sense since I forgot it. Niall thinks this is all very hilarious and I'm about to threaten to send them all to Pit 1, too when Radcliff sets down a big chocolate cake.

"Happy Birthday, Ara!" everyone says in unison.

Oh my stars! I've been so busy I forgot my own birthday. I know it's hard to believe, considering I was counting down the days. Mom lights the eighteen candles.

"Blow them out quick," Radcliff says. "I don't want the fire alarm to go off."

Ha ha. I draw in a breath.

"Make a wish," Niall says.

And do you know what? I can't think of a single wish. Oh, there's tons of things I'd like, but they'll happen eventually. I'll see my brother, Phoenix; the Warrior Express will protect the Galaxy and transport interstellar travelers; families will no longer be torn apart by the time dilation; and Shay will have a family again. Content with my life, I blow out the candles.

Even though I'm stuffed full of manicotti, I find room in my stomach for a big piece of cake.

"Time for presents," Mom says. "Follow me."

Ooh interesting. I follow everyone out of Radcliff's unit. We head down the hall.

Mom stops in front of unit number three-oh-nine. "This is from your father and me. Your very own unit. Welcome to adulthood."

I hug my parents. "Thank you!" Then I place my palm on the keypad. The door opens and reveals bright, colorful walls.

Marveling, I go inside. Niall's mother's paintings from my room in Radcliff's unit have been hung on the walls along with a few new pieces and…some of Niall's. "Perfect, thanks, Toad."

His smile promises that I'll be thanking him again later—when we're alone. I walk around. The unit is a one bedroom, with a small living area, kitchen, and washroom.

Radcliff strides to the kitchen and opens the pantry. It's full of food. "I still expect you at dinner, *Officer* Lawrence."

Not junior officer. Not anymore! "Yes, sir. Thanks."

"I moved all your things from our unit and Radcliff's in here," Mom says. "Including those contraband drawings."

Oops. She found my collection of Niall's pencil drawings. But she's not upset.

"If you check your closet, I believe Officer Kier has filled it with a few more pieces," Mom says.

Shay rushes over and picks up a glass bowl filled with colors. She hands it to me. "Candy dish! From me!"

Even she knows about my sugar addiction. I squat down to her eye level. "Are you going to come visit often and help me eat these?" I ask.

She gives me a shy smile. "Yes."

I straighten and gesture to the unit. "This is all so wonderful. Thank you!"

The adults and Shay leave to let me "settle in." Niall remains behind. He has a broad grin on his face.

"What do you want to do for your first night in your unit?" he asks.

"Something I've been wanting for a long time," I say in a husky voice.

454

He moves closer. "And that is?"

"A shower."

Niall's confused expression turns into disappointment.

I laugh. "With you."

Delight and desire replace his frustration. "Ah, your dedication to your personal hygiene should be commended."

"Shut up and strip."

"Yes, sir."

The shower is as wonderful as I'd imagined. Hot water, soapy skin, and Niall's rippling muscles under my hands. Steam fills the washroom and we spend a long time just kissing without anyone interrupting us. Bliss. There is no hurry and we don't plan to rush into anything just yet.

We have all the time in the Galaxy.

THE END

Q?

THANK YOU

Thank you for choosing *Defending the Galaxy*, book 3 in my Sentinels of the Galaxy series. I hope you enjoyed reading this series as much as I loved writing it!

If you'd like to stay updated on my books and any news, please sign up for my free email newsletter here:

http://www.mariavsnyder.com/news.php

(go all the way down to the bottom of the page). I send my newsletter out to subscribers three to four times a year. It contains info about the books, my schedule and always something fun (like deleted scenes or a new short story or exclusive excerpts). No spam—ever!

You're also welcome to come join your fellow MVS fans on my Facebook reading group called Snyder's Soulfinders. Why Soulfinders? Because according to Plato, "Books give a soul to the universe, wings to the mind, flight to the imagination, and life to everything." The Soulfinders are all about books, especially mine, but also others as well! It's a great place to find fellow readers and make friends from all over the world. There are perks, too, like exclusive give aways, getting all the news first, and an insight into my writing process. Please answer at least 2 of the 3 questions as we don't want any trolls in our group, just Soulfinders. Here's a link:

https://www.facebook.com/groups/SnydersSoulfinders/

Please feel free to spread the word about this book! Honest reviews are always welcome and word of mouth is the best way you can help an author keep writing the books you enjoy!

Please don't be a stranger, stop on by and say hello. You can find me on:

- Facebook: https://www.facebook.com/mvsfans
- Goodreads: https://www.goodreads.com/maria_v_snyder
- Instagram: https://www.instagram.com/mariavsnyderwrites/

ACKNOWLEDGEMENTS

In keeping with my latest trend in doing something fun and interactive on my acknowledgment page, below you'll find an Acknowledgement Word Scramble of all the people (in random order and first names only) who have helped me and encouraged me and supported me while I was writing this book. Thank you all so very much!

Also I must thank, Ara Yinhexi Lawrence (a.k.a. Lyra Tian Daniels). The Sentinels of the Galaxy series would not have been written without her in my head, telling me her story. She was most insistent and stubborn and would not shut up.

If you're having trouble unscrambling some of them, read my other acknowledgements for some hints as many of the people I'm thankful for have been with me for the entire series, and some since my first book. However, there are a few newbies, so I'll thank them here: Chrysoula, for her keen editorial eye, and Jennifer for her expert medical advice.

Have fun!

SMA   _____

MAERE   _____

SANRIKTI   _____

EFJF   _____

ALEACRH   _____

HOJS   _____

ODEYRN   _____

ATN   _____

NJAE   _____

JIELAR   _____

CHIMLELE   _____

YDIMN   _____

EISELO   _____

RIECRA   _____

HAKTY   _____

UAJLI   _____

AOJNANH   _____

IDRSULFOSNE   _____

How did you do? To check your score, the answers can be found at: https://www.mariavsnyder.com/books/answers.php

Read on for an excerpt from Maria's upcoming new fantasy novel, *The Eyes of Tamburah*, available February 2021!

CHAPTER ONE

The heat thickened the air in Shyla's room to an uncomfortable level. Sweat slicked her skin and dampened her sleeveless tunic. She adjusted the mirrors to better capture the thin ray of sunlight streaming through a single mirror pipe extruding from her ceiling. Moving another reflective panel until it illuminated the ancient map spread over her table, she resumed her work. The faded ink was barely discernable as it crossed the velbloud skin.

The temperature rose another few degrees, warning her that she needed to retreat to the deeper levels before the sun reached angle eighty. Despite being three levels underground, it still wasn't safe to be this high. All of her neighbors had descended angles ago. But excitement zipped along her spine—she was so close.

Shyla continued to translate the archaic symbols. Nothing but sunlight would reveal the location of the Gorgain crypt and the meeting with her client was scheduled for angle two-ten. The historian had paid her in advance for the information, which was proving to be more difficult to find than she'd expected.

A damp strand of her long pale-yellow hair slipped free of the tie, but she didn't have time to fix it. According to the map's legend, the blue line represented the tunnel the grave diggers had used. She traced it with a fingertip, honing in on—

An impatient pounding on her door broke her concentration. She glared at the thick slab of rough sand-coated

. guarded her room. It vibrated with each knock. There
time for interruptions, but if it was a client—

It's an emergency," called Banqui.

She sighed. Everything was an emergency with Banqui. As
.he Water Prince's chief archaeologist, he believed his projects
should be her top priority. But the man had referred her services
to his colleagues, helping her establish her business. After a
forlorn glance at the map, she unlocked the door and slid it aside,
allowing Banqui to enter.

He hustled into her room and stopped dead. "Scorching
hells, Shyla. It's a thousand degrees in here."

Banqui also tended to exaggerate.

"Hello to you too."

Ignoring her, he said, "I've been looking all over for you in
the lower levels. The sun is almost at angle seventy. What are
you still doing up here?"

She gestured to the map on her table. "Researching."

"You need to leave right away."

"There's plenty of time before I'm cooked. Before I was
interrupted, I was just about to finish up." She gave him a
pointed look.

But instead of apologizing for barging in on her and leaving,
he just stared at her in shock. "Shyla, haven't you heard?"

She studied her best client and perhaps friend. His short
black hair stuck up at various angles—probably from running
his fingers through it in agitation. He was frequently anxious
and stressed by the Water Prince's demands. But this time fear
lurked in his dark brown eyes and his tan tunic and pants,
normally impeccable —he had plenty of diggers conscripted by

the prince to do his dirty work—were torn and stai
with…blood?

"Heard what?" she asked as unease stirred in her chest.

He paced around the table. Tall and lean with lanky legs, it
didn't take him long to make a circuit. Her room was small and
filled with the basics—a table, sitting cushions, a couple shelves
filled with her trinkets and clothes, a water jug, her sleeping
cushion mounded with a fur, and the mirrors.

Banqui made another loop. She stepped into his path,
stopping him. "Tell me before you wear a groove in my floor."

Rivers of sweat streaked down the sides of his face, darkening
his brown skin. His gaze settled on the map. "How long have
you been working?"

"Two or three sun jumps."

"And you get immersed in your research," he muttered then
drew in a deep breath. "I found The Eyes of Tamburah. They
were in the temple's hidden vault just like you predicted."

Excitement warred with confusion. "That's wonderful.
Right?"

"It was glorious. They were exquisite. Crafted from
diamonds, emeralds, onyx, and the purest white topaz I've ever
seen." His voice held an almost fanatical reverence. "They were
magnificent, Shyla. My greatest find in my entire career."

Considering he'd been uncovering ancient ruins and
artifacts for over seven thousand sun jumps—roughly twenty
circuits, they must have been impressive. "And then the Water
Prince claimed them. You knew that would happen. He finances
your digs."

"It's worse than that."

What could be worse? "You lost them?"

"No! They were stolen!" Unable to remain still, Banqui resumed his pacing.

Treasure hunters were always a problem. Despite the Water Prince's proclamation that all historical items found within Zirdai's official boundaries became the property of the crown, the richer citizens collected antiquities through a thriving black market—the rarer the find, the more lucrative. And The Eyes of Tamburah were legendary. Rumored to give their owner magical powers, the gemstones had a long and bloody history. No wonder they were stolen by some greedy hunter. They would fetch a staggering sum in any city in Koraha, assuming the thief lived long enough to leave Zirdai.

"Sorry to hear that," Shyla said. "The Water Prince must be—"

"No words can describe his anger." Banqui clutched her shoulders. "Which is why you must hide."

She jerked from his grasp in surprise. "Me? Why?"

"He thinks you are the thief."

It took her a moment to sort through his words. Did he really say... "Why would he believe that?" Fear coiled around her heart and squeezed.

Banqui's broad face creased with anguish, flaring the nostrils of his flat nose. "Because I told him you were the only other person in all of Zirdai who knew where The Eyes were located."

Scorching hells. Shyla stepped back. Perhaps calling him a friend was being rather generous. "But your diggers—"

"None of them were part of the extraction. Only me. I trusted no one with the information."

But someone had to know. Unless… "Surely you think that I—"

"Of course not, Shyla! You could have kept the location yourself and retrieved them without anyone the wiser, which is what I tried to explain to the prince, but he wouldn't listen. I suspect a spy in my crew, but I need time to figure it out and I don't wish you harmed."

How nice, but she didn't voice her sarcastic response. Instead her mind whirled with the possibilities. The heat in the room baked the sweat off her skin, another warning that they needed to go below. "I can go talk to him. Explain—"

"No. He will not listen. You'll be tortured until he's satisfied you told the truth and then, if you're lucky, you'll be locked in the black cells. And if you're not, you'll be staked to the sand and cooked."

Gee, what a prince. The fear tightened.

"You need to hide until I can find the culprit. Perhaps the monks will hide you?"

"No," she said.

"But they raised you."

"Doesn't matter. I will not run and hide, Banqui." She had lived in the monastery for eighteen circuits and refused to run back to them at the first sign of trouble.

"But—"

"I'm going to help you."

He shook his head sadly. "You don't have any contacts among the people." Banqui gestured to the piles around them. "Your expertise is with translating these historical tablets, sifting the facts from the fables."

, but she did have other clients. "What about the spy? u know who he or she is working for? I can talk to the r archeologists." And treasure hunters, but Banqui didn't ed to know she'd worked for them as well. His lecture would ast an entire sun jump.

His full lips thinned into a scowl. "At first I suspected the Heliacal Priestess."

She grunted. "If that's the case, you'll never get them back."

The sun neared the kill zone. The mirror pipe blazed with light as the air in her room seared their throats, creeping toward sixty degrees Celsius. Time to go. Shyla grabbed her pack and without a word, they exited to the empty tunnel—everyone else had abandoned this level angles ago. Sliding the door in place, she locked it and they bolted for the closest stairway. It spiraled down into the gloom.

Druk lanterns hanging on the sandstone walls glowed with a warm yellow light. As they descended, the air cooled fifteen degrees for each level. By the time they reached the safe zone at level six, it was thirty Celsius.

At level eight, Banqui grabbed one of the lanterns. "This way." He headed down a side tunnel.

The temperature on this level reached ten degrees. Shyla shivered and pulled her wrap from her pack. At least it wouldn't get any cooler unless they traveled past level eighty where the dry air turned damp.

In Zirdai, the popular routes were all well marked with lanterns and symbols etched into the sandstone walls—the others were left in darkness. Druk lanterns were cheap to produce and plentiful. People frequently carried them and left

them at various places for others to use. At least one or two c
lit every room.

The special substance inside the druk changed its tint wit.
depth. After twelve levels it transformed to a new color. At the
very bottom of their world—level ninety-seven—it shone with
a violet hue. The distinctive colors came in handy for those who
were easily lost, unlike Shyla, who'd been exploring the
underground city since the monks kicked her out about two
circuits ago. Actually it had been exactly eight hundred and
twenty-five sun jumps ago—there were three hundred and sixty
sun jumps in one circuit. Not that she was counting.

A thin layer of grit crunched under their boots as they
walked. The dry air held a salty scent mixed with the faint
gingery/anise odor of the desert.

"Where are we going?" she asked him.

"Since you won't go to the monks, you need a place to stay."

She waited, but he failed to continue. "And that would
be…"

"My upper-level work rooms."

"They will be the second place the prince's soldiers will look
after checking my room," she said.

"They already searched them. You can hide—"

"I'm not hiding, Banqui," she snapped, which wasn't
helping. Shyla considered the problem, viewing it the same way
she researched lost artifacts. "After you found The Eyes, what
happened next?"

He sighed. "I wrapped the marble container with layers of
silk and put it into my satchel. I headed back to the entrance and
someone jumped me from behind." Banqui rubbed the side of

d as anger flared in his eyes. "When I woke, my bag was
. And before you ask, I didn't see or hear anyone in the
ıple before or after the attack."

She mulled over the information. "What about the guards?
Don't you always station them at a dig site?"

"I do. According to them, no one had entered or left since
I'd gone in." He held his free hand up. "They're loyal to the
Water Prince and they've already been questioned."

"Is that code for tortured?"

"Shyla, this isn't a joke."

She gave him a flat look. "The Water Prince thinks I'm a
thief so I'm well aware of the seriousness of the situation."

To read the rest of chapter one go to:
https://www.mariavsnyder.com/books/the-eyes.php

The Eyes of Tamburah will be released worldwide on
February 1, 2021!

ABOUT MARIA V. SNYDER

When Maria V. Snyder was younger, she aspired to be storm chaser in the American Midwest so she attended Pennsylvania State University and earned a Bachelor of Science degree in Meteorology. Much to her chagrin, forecasting the weather wasn't in her skill set so she spent a number of years as an environmental meteorologist, which is not exciting ... at all. Bored at work and needing a creative outlet, she started writing fantasy and science fiction stories. Over twenty novels and numerous short stories later, Maria's learned a thing or three about writing. She's been on the *New York Times* bestseller list, won a dozen awards, and has earned her Masters of Arts degree in Writing from Seton Hill University, where she is now a faculty member.

Her favorite color is red. She loves dogs, but is allergic, instead she has a big black tom cat named ... Kitty (apparently naming cats isn't in her skill set either). Maria also has a husband and two children who are an inspiration for her writing when they aren't being a distraction. Note that she mentions her cat before her family. When she's not writing she's either playing volleyball, traveling, or taking pictures. Being a writer, though, is a ton of fun. When else can you take fencing lessons, learn how to ride a horse, study martial arts, learn how to pick a lock, take glass blowing classes and attend Astronomy Camp and call it research? Maria will be the first one to tell you it's not working as a meteorologist. Readers are welcome to check out her website for book excerpts, free short stories, maps, blog, and her schedule at MariaVSnyder.com.

CPSIA information can be obtained
at www.ICGtesting.com
Printed in the USA
LVHW012244080121
676100LV00001B/31